I0780996

HE WHO IGNITES THE FLAME

LUNA LAURIER

He Who Ignites The Flame
Book 2.5 of the Shadow and Moonlight Series
Book 1 in the BarrettxThalia Duology

Story and Art Copyright © 2024 Luna Laurier
Cover Design by TrifBookDesign
Case Design by Luna Laurier
Editing by Natalie Cammaratta & The Fiction Fix
Illustrations by Huangja

IDENTIFIERS
ASIN B0DNK1H5TF (ebook) | ISBN 9781962409087 (Paperback)
ISBN 9781962409070 (Hardcover) | ISBN 9798308813002 (Amazon Paperback)

Represented by Beck Literary Agency contact Josi at
josi@beckliterary.com

2025 Edition

CONTENT WARNING

While these are not all the focus, please be aware that this series contains scenes of the following

Abuse	Mention Of Self-Harm
Alcohol	Mention of Rape
Alcoholism	Misogyny
Anxiety	Needles
Assault	Physical Violence
Blood	Panic Attacks
Chronic Illness	Profanity
Child Abuse (Implied)	Pregnancy
Death	Poisoning
Depression	PTSD
Death Of A Child	Reincarnation
Discussion Of Child Loss	Rape (Implied)
Domestic Violence	Sexual Assault
Death In Childbirth	Sexually Explicit Scenes
Drugs	Smoking
Drug Use	Snakes
Emotional Violence	Suicidal Ideation (Implied)
Fire	Terminal Illness
Hospitalization	Torture
Kidnapping	Violence
Loss of a Spouse	Verbal Abuse
Murder	War
Medical Content	

If you or anyone you know is contemplating suicide, please call the National Suicide Prevention Lifeline at 1-800-273-TALK (8255). Please do not struggle in silence. Your friends and family care. I care.

For the most up to date list visit lunalaurier.com

Glossary and Elythian Translations in the back of
the book, read with caution to avoid spoilers

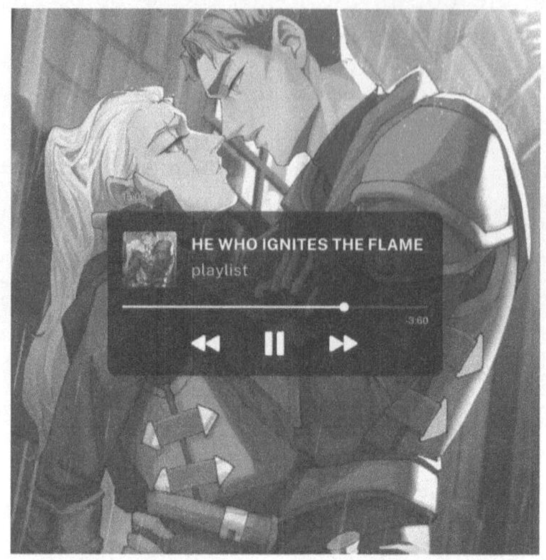

Listen to the official Spotify Playlist

https://tinyurl.com/barrettxthalia

Chat with other OSAM readers while you read. Check out the
official discord server with over 400 readers! General chat (both
spoiler and non-spoiler), chapter checkpoint discussions, end of
book discussions, unhinged theories, quizzes, and more!
https://discord.gg/xszrmWVEkC

To those who never truly healed.

PROLOGUE

THE BOY WITH A FLAME SOUL

1409

"Cali, stop pulling on me," I grumbled as my little sister tugged me eagerly through the streets of Moonhaven. We wandered past the few homes and shops still barely standing, avoiding those that were now rubble.

Calliope's disheveled blonde braid flew over her shoulder as she whipped around to face me only to whine and tug harder on my hand, causing me to trip. Despite being a few years younger than me, the five-year-old housed enough strength to force my step. "I wanna see the south district."

I planted my feet into the dirt, halting her advances. "You know better. Mother and Father said we aren't to go there. The Order's still searching the rubble for survivors. I overheard Mama say one of the houses fell on top of them. It's too dangerous right now."

More than half of our village had been destroyed in the darkling attack. The only places left standing were a few shops turned into shelters and places for refugees to receive rations, the north district where we lived, and the king's keep. The air had smelled of ash, burnt flesh, and something sickeningly sweet and acrid for days as they cleaned up what remained of the south side of Moonhaven.

Mother said things would return to normal, but I wasn't stupid. The adults' worries filled Moonhaven like a plague as they quietly discussed the possibility of giving up on repairs. Rumors about our people relocating and building elsewhere for fear of the darklings attacking again had spread on whispered voices.

Calliope's soft green eyes grew bigger, her lower lip jutting out. "But I wanna see if Serah is all right, and—"

"You should mind your big brother, *mikros*," an injured female muttered from where she sat huddled against a wall—once someone's home, now barely recognizable beyond scorched wood and stone. She was wrapped in a blanket as she ate a bowl of porridge. I'd watched many like her line up to receive rations from the members of The Order.

My nose wrinkled at the scent of ash and blood clinging to her.

Calliope inched behind me, clinging to my arm as she eyed the stranger as if she might eat us like the crones from Mother's stories who wandered the shadow steppes, seeking to devour any who trespassed on cursed soil. I grimaced at the throbbing pain radiating from the bruise Father had left the night before as her grip tightened, and I resisted the urge to pull free of her. I dipped my head in respect, unable to imagine the horrors she'd seen when the darklings attacked Moonhaven a few nights ago. The dark shadows under her eyes were evident, the tormented darkness seeming to stem from her eyes. So many souls had passed to Elysium. Everyone mourned the fallen queen, and I'd overheard Mother telling Father of her worries for the king who'd secluded himself in his keep.

"Sorry to disturb you," I murmured, and we hurried past the female.

"Don't stay out too late, now," she called after us, and I could almost hear a teasing smile in her tone. "The fae like to take little ones across the veil—especially those left unattended."

I shook my head, ignoring the female's story meant to scare children. Mother told us stories of the fae in the Godsrealm all the time; I didn't believe them. They were just stories to make children listen to their parents and follow the rules. She didn't need to tell me scary stories for me to do that; Father was scary enough. Calliope tracked the female as we continued down the pathway to the small forest in the center of Moonhaven where the creek ran.

Birds sang as I eased onto a boulder in a clearing, and Calliope ran forward to pick flowers along the creek. She turned to flash a wide grin as she held out one of the tiny pink and purple blossoms that littered the grass. I smiled; they had always been her favorite. I didn't know what they were called, but she had decided they were twilight flowers, as they gave the appearance of little stars scattered across the ground. I wouldn't correct her, though Father might have found it foolish.

"Are you picking some for Mother?" I asked.

She nodded before continuing. "I'm gonna make her a flower crown."

Movement caught my eye, and I shot up, my heart plummeting for fear it might be a monster before I realized it was a girl observing us quietly from behind a nearby oak. Calliope squeaked and ran to hide behind me. The girl ducked her head back behind the tree, and for a moment, I caught the sight of her hands trembling against the bark.

"Cali, that's rude," I muttered and gave the girl an apologetic look. "Sorry, my sister didn't mean to scare you. You wanna play with us?"

The girl tilted her head, seeming to assess us. Her cornsilk hair spilled over her shoulder. The rays leaking through the trees lit the strands like a burst of sunlight with each movement, and her eyes were the prettiest gray, like churning clouds before a powerful storm.

She hesitated but stepped out, her clothes in tatters, hair a mess, face covered in ash, dirt, and blood. A tiny carved Pegasus was clutched tightly in her hands, the wood singed and blackened, one of the wings broken.

Something tugged in my chest, something I couldn't quite place.

Had she been among those attacked by the darklings? She looked to be around my age.

I lifted my satchel over my head and set it down on the grass. "Are you hungry?"

She looked down at the fresh bread as I pulled it from the bag, and her lips parted, as if the sight of it made her mouth water. How long had it been since she'd last eaten? Had she been hiding here since the attack?

"Take it," I said, holding it out. Her stormy eyes lifted to me briefly, and she took a cautious step toward us. That tugging feeling in my chest grew stronger with each step, winding around something deep within me.

Where were her parents? Was she among the orphans now wandering the streets with no one to care for them? I hoped she wasn't, but by the looks of her, I feared my suspicions to be true.

She finally drew close enough to take the bread and spared me a glance before she devoured it, wincing each time she swallowed. After she downed the last bite, she licked her dirty fingers and palms for any crumbs she might have left behind. Calliope gained the courage to leave the safety of my back and approached the girl on hesitant steps. Their gazes met, and Calliope's lips curved into a bright grin before she took the girl's hand.

"There's twilight flowers over here. Wanna help me make a flower crown?" Calliope asked, her presence lighting up the forest. It was a gift. She always had a way of brightening the space wherever she was.

The girl looked at me from the corner of her eye before nodding at Calliope, and they trotted off to the patch of flowers.

She never spoke, never said a word, and I feared the smoke from the fires might have severely hurt her. She needed to see a healer, but I didn't know how to get her to one.

Calliope eventually coaxed me into making crowns with them, which I could never get quite right. When I handed my poorly made flower crown to the girl, it fell apart, and my shoulders sagged in defeat. Calliope trotted to my back and dropped her own perfectly woven crown of tiny blossoms atop my head. I didn't fight it, no matter how goofy I felt wearing one. I'd always humored my sister and her delights at dressing me up every chance she got, even when Father scolded me for it, saying it wasn't right for males to be seen with flowers in their hair. I didn't care what anyone thought of me. I'd do anything for her, do anything to see her smile.

The girl looked at me as the crown, which was a bit too big for my head, slid down over my eye and landed on the bridge of my nose. She smiled, and something warm filled my chest.

I wanted to make her smile more, hear her laugh.

We played together for hours—on and on until the sun began its descent behind the mountains surrounding the valley. My chest hollowed at the sight of the changing colors of the sky as sunset neared. "Come on, Cali. It's time to go."

Calliope let out an exaggerated moan of protest. "I don't wanna go!"

"Cali," I said sternly. Her cheeks puffed out, but she didn't argue further.

"You'll be here tomorrow?" Calliope asked, tugging on the girl's hand.

The girl looked at her before lifting those stormy eyes to me and nodded. I looked across the woods; the only thing she seemed to have was the damaged Pegasus carving. I set my satchel down, slid my coat off, and held it out to her.

Her pale brows furrowed, and I smiled.

"It's cold at night. Take it. Use it to stay warm, and I'll bring you a blanket tomorrow."

She hesitated, and I scoffed, walking around to place it over her shoulders. She stiffened, but then she pulled it tighter around herself, her shoulders rising as she seemed to burrow into it.

"I'll bring you some more food tomorrow too," I said with a smile.

"I can bring my brush and we can braid your hair," Calliope said. "Mother taught me how to do it."

The girl smiled, and my heart leaped.

"Come on Cali." I took her hand. "Father's gonna be mad if we're late for dinner."

I smiled the entire way home, excited to return to the park to play more the following day. There was no chance Father would let us bring her home—I was afraid to even ask him—but that didn't mean *we* couldn't help her.

Father's shouting persisted later that night than usual, but it wasn't what kept me up. A storm hit Moonhaven in the dark, moonless hours, and I'd been unable to sleep, worrying about the girl as the winds and rains raged against our home. Every time I'd closed my eyes all I could see was her, alone, scared.

The following day, we returned to the creek, but as we made our way through the trees and to the clearing, the girl was nowhere to be found. Dead branches and leaves littered the grass from the terrifying storm that had ravaged the valley.

Had she taken shelter somewhere?

Calliope grabbed my forearm, pointing to the tree where we'd first seen the girl. I winced as she unintentionally gripped the fresh bruises left by Father when he'd learned I'd 'lost' my coat. I'd been too cowardly to tell him the truth, to tell him of the girl we'd found. What if he went looking for her? What if he hurt her? I could barely protect Calliope from his anger.

My gaze landed on the tree; a massive branch had snapped and was now lying in the dirt where we'd first seen her, but she wasn't there.

I neared the oak, kneeling to see if I might find any sign of her, but all that remained was the subtle hint of black spruce and pine. The scent had been faint beneath the cloak of ashes and blood, but it was hers.

Was this where she'd slept?

My heart twisted as I stood, scanning the clearing for any sign of where she might have gone, but there was nothing. We spent the next few days searching every inch of the small patch of woods, even wandered what streets we could with the relief efforts still underway, but there was no sign of her anywhere. I didn't even know her name to ask the adults around Moonhaven. We searched and searched, and yet no matter what we did to look for her, she seemed to have just...vanished.

And I would never get the chance to play with her again.

PART I

1469

(60 YEARS LATER)

CHAPTER 1

BARRETT

"Eyes on me," I said through gritted teeth as I wrapped my fingers around the throat of a female—one whose name I hadn't cared to learn. She rode my cock in a steady rhythm, her skirts bunched around her hips and *fuck* did it feel good to be inside a female again.

Her eyes fell to me; they were a flat gray, glazed over in her drunkenness and barely catching the light of the single candle resting on the nearby shelf.

What the hell was I searching for in them?

She moaned as I tightened my grip, restricting her flow of oxygen as my other hand grabbed her hip, and I lifted mine to meet her in a thrust. Her back arched as she tightened around me. I pulled her off before she could come and rolled her onto her stomach as I rose to my knees and grabbed her hips. In one, smooth motion, I plunged into her from behind, slamming into her without hesitation or care. Her back arched as she gasped, and I worked my hips, sinking myself deeper and deeper until I was fully seated.

I shouldn't have cared if she finished, shouldn't have cared if she enjoyed it, but perhaps there was still something good in me, something that...cared? Fuck. What was I thinking? Why did I care? Why *should* I care? I didn't owe this female anything; not my name, my thoughts, my—

She's using you just as much as you're using her. They only want you for what you can give them. It's all they ever want. She'll use you and throw you away.

My fangs lengthened as the hunger crawled up my throat, and I couldn't remember the last time I'd fed. No, I wouldn't take from her, didn't want to feel her in my system after we were done. I ground my teeth together and ignored the hunger as I slammed into her, her body jerking against me. "You like it rough, don't you? Want me to ruin this little cunt?"

"Yes... *please.*" I planted my hand on her shoulder and pushed her chest into the stone floor as I thrusted deeper, harder. "Mark me as yours."

The flames raged within me at the command, the claim, and I pulled myself from her as I shoved her forward onto the dirty floor.

She collapsed in a panting mess before she pushed herself up on unstable arms. "What are you—"

"I'm not yours, and I won't be claiming you," I said through clenched teeth as I rose to my feet and pulled my trousers on.

She pushed herself up, her hair disheveled, her dress bunched and wrinkled, her sleeve sliding off her shoulder. "W-what?"

I didn't respond as I checked my chest, ensuring she hadn't left any marks when she'd kissed me earlier before going down on me.

None.

Good.

She seemed to realize the best orgasm of her life was about to walk out the door, and I honestly didn't give two shits that I was still hard. I turned from her as I pulled my shirt on, eager to find someone else to finish what we'd started.

"Wait, you can't—" She reached for me, her fingers catching on the delicate gold chain on my wrist.

I stiffened as she tugged on the bracelet in an attempt to draw me back to her. My heart plummeted at the thought of the bracelet breaking. Something snapped, and heat flared beneath my skin, the candle's flame growing larger on the shelf, the wax melting at an alarming rate.

Before I could think, my hand wrapped around her throat and I slammed her up against the nearby wall. She gasped, and her eyes popped wide as I pinned her in place, lowering my face to hers.

"I am not *yours*," I growled, enunciating every word, my fangs bared. "You are nothing but a quick fuck."

My fingers trembled against her skin, the flame pressing against the cage of my body, eager to devour her. "Put your hands on me again, and I'll snap your fucking neck."

Tears welled in her eyes, her hands fumbling at my arms. The last words I'd heard from the bracelet's owner rang out through my mind, and the flames raging within me shuddered and diminished, something pulling me away.

Please... Stop... I can't brea—

I released her as I stepped back, my hands shaking. The female collapsed to the floor, her hand shooting up to her throat where a red outline of my hand marked her skin.

No... I'm not him.

I hesitated, guilt dousing the flames as she shook on the floor before me. I should comfort her, apologize. *Fuck.*

"Stay the fuck away from me," I growled and turned, leaving her in the storage closet of the pub.

A sharp knock at my door jolted me from sleep, and the room spun as I sat up with a groan. I blinked; my head was pounding, my mouth bone dry. Gods, how much had I drank last night? I'd managed to find another female; she'd been a decent fuck, but based on the lingering burning in my throat and stomach, I'd neglected to feed. Beyond that, I couldn't remember much else.

The sun leaked through the window of the small room, burning my eyes, and I rubbed my hands over my face. I didn't remember finding my way back from the pub last night, nor what time I'd collapsed in my bed. My jaw ached, my muscles tight and sore, knuckles red. Had I gotten into a fight?

The knock came again, followed by a familiar female voice. "Barrett? Are you awake?"

Fuck, what time was it? Was I late to training? She was going to kill me.

"I'm up," I croaked, rubbing my hands over my face again, as if they could wipe every bit of what happened the night before from existence. "It's unlocked. Come in."

The door creaked open, revealing the female I was still unsure of yet owed everything to. Her long, curly black hair was already tied into a braid that tumbled over her shoulder. Her pale silver eyes roamed the room she'd set me up in, which was now a mess of the few objects I possessed and little else. She donned the black training attire of The Order, her loose black top tucked into her black trousers that hugged her legs until they were swallowed by her tall black boots.

I'd once worn that uniform, before...

"Lucia," I muttered in acknowledgment, but it came out a bit more annoyed than I intended.

"Good morning, Barrett," she said, her voice soft, patient, a little cheerful. She tossed a sack onto the foot of my bed. "I brought your training uniforms. You never came by to get them yesterday. I figured you might have been a bit preoccupied exploring the town."

"Shit," I groaned, pushing myself up, but I froze as the blanket slipped down to my hips and the cold air kissed my naked skin. I pulled the blanket back over myself. "Fuck—sorry."

She huffed a laugh and seemed to pay me no mind as she turned to the nearby window. "It's nothing I haven't seen before."

Sunlight flooded the small room as she drew back the curtains. I grimaced, shielding my eyes. What part of the underworld did morning people crawl out of, and why was their first instinct at sunrise to fucking blind themselves?

"Sounded like you enjoyed your first night of freedom," she said, and I could hear the smile in her tone. Why was she so fucking cheerful? "Glad you didn't take off on me."

I cringed. What had Semele told her? Had the female run her mouth? Something twisted in my chest, and irritation at the thought of the pub owner turned to guilt. Lucia approached the bed and leaned down to my level. Before I could pull away, she lifted my chin to examine my face, and her other hand rose. Every instinct went on high alert, my body tensing of its own accord, as if preparing to be struck.

But she didn't hit me.

Her fingers brushed my brow tenderly, and I winced.

"Get into a fight last night?"

I didn't answer—not because I didn't want to, but because I couldn't remember. Semele stocked ambrosia liquor in her pub. The shit hit hard if you didn't have a tolerance for it, and it had been decades since my last drink. I hadn't even realized how drunk I was until I found myself in a storage closet with that female. Something icy crawled over my skin as I wondered if I'd left a mark on her throat.

She reached into a pouch affixed to her belt, retrieving a small, amber glass bottle. "I don't care if you have a good time, but please try to stay out of trouble—for my sake." She removed the lid and ran her fingers through the creamy contents before reaching out to my forehead. I flinched, my hand shooting up to grab her wrist. She didn't react, didn't draw back, and that stupid warm expression remained on her face. "It's all right. It's a healing salve I made."

I eyed her wearily but eased my grip, and she spread the solution over the wound. It almost immediately soothed the sting, and my shoulders eased.

A soft smile curved the corner of her lips, as if she was enjoying tending to me, and her gaze drifted over my face, likely checking for other wounds. "I may have gotten you out of the dungeons once, but that doesn't mean I will be able to keep you out if you do something stupid."

My eyes dropped from her, the truth of her words leaving smoldering irritation in my chest like a wyvern who'd held back their flame. I wanted to argue, but for the first time in my life...I couldn't. Shit, I should be grateful for what she'd done. I owed her everything. By every right, I should be rotting in a cell right now—for the rest of my life—after what I did.

"Here," she said, replacing the lid on the container before handing it to me. "In case you find yourself with any more of these *mysterious* injuries. Promise me next time that you make sure it's someone who deserves it."

I eyed her wearily but took the glass jar she offered before looking down at it. The light caught on the delicate gold chain on my wrist, the one that had nearly broken the night before. It was the only thing I had left of her, and I'd thought it lost when I was locked away. Fuck, I couldn't believe I'd snapped on that female the way I had last night.

"You all right?" Lucia asked, the inner corners of her black brows curving upward.

"Yeah, I'll be fine," I lied, grabbing the clothes.

Her silver gaze lingered on me a moment, as if assessing whether I was telling the truth or not, but then she drew a deep breath and turned for the door. "Get dressed and meet me in the hall. We have some things to do before you start training tomorrow."

CHAPTER 2

BARRETT

24 hours earlier

The groan of the old wood door bounced off the stone walls of the dungeon chambers, and I winced as sunlight leaked in from the narrow passage. It was the first glimpse of light I'd seen in weeks.

"Get up, boy," the guard commanded, and I sighed as I pushed myself up from the straw and rough fabric I'd slept on every night since I'd been locked up. I didn't even know how many years it had been at this point. Thirty? Forty? Perhaps I should be thankful there was enough room for me in this cell to at least get some exercise.

"Is this him?" I stiffened at the sound of the female's voice, and my eyes shot up.

She was dressed in the black, Elythian leather armor of The Order, a half cape hanging from her right shoulder. Her pale silver eyes were gentle yet piercing. I hadn't seen such pale eyes as hers—eyes that were revered among our kind, who believed favor was bestowed by our Goddess, Selene, on those who possessed them. Black hair framed her porcelain face, hanging in loose waves down to her waist. Her frame was small, and she carried a sword at her hip, her gloved hand resting atop the hilt. I recognized it immediately—a sword of legend. The hilt was gold instead of the standard issue silver, intricate details and enchantments carved into the Elythian steel, and I didn't need to see the blade to know it was black and gold instead of black and silver.

Fuck.

Moira's reincarnation... The queen and the demigoddess of the immortal race.

Rumors had made it to the dungeons some time ago, cellmates muttering about the queen reincarnating again. I'd been skeptical, to be honest. I remembered when Queen Elena had fallen, remembered the sorrow I'd felt as a child for a person I'd never met. I had seen the kindness she'd shared with our people—the sacrifices she'd made to protect us.

"This is him, Your Majesty," the guard said in confirmation. When she approached the cell door, his hand shot up. "Don't get too close to the bars. They're warded, but he's a nasty bastard. He's caused more fights in the last few decades than I've dealt with my entire career, even without his magic."

I huffed a laugh as I pushed myself to my feet, my bones sore from lying against stone, muscles stiff. "Awe, and here I thought we were finally getting close, Stephan."

The male eyed me as I lifted my arm to rest against the bars, the dwindling, subdued flame in my chest recoiling at the contact with the warded iron. I leaned in, looking down at him. "It *is* Stephan, right? I mean, that's what the female cried out the other night down the hall." The guard bristled, his cheeks going red. "I knew you had it in you."

"You should have heard it," I said, unable to hide my smile.

She didn't react or respond. Her expression remained soft, but it didn't hint as to what she thought or felt. The guard seemed to vibrate at her side, his anger lighting the air. I liked the scent, like smoldering oak in my nose. I wondered how far I could push him this time. Maybe I could get him in this cell, work out some of this pent-up tension and frustration that had been building for the last couple of weeks since I'd been put in confinement after smashing another prisoner's face in.

I lowered myself to the female—the queen, if that was truly what she was—and whispered, "Between you and me, though, it didn't last long. I think he finished before she did. Poor girl."

His hand shot through the bars, grabbing the frayed collar of my shirt. He jerked me against the iron, the bite of the warded metal forcing the flames within me to retreat further, and I internally winced. "Shut it, boy!"

"Stephan," the female said in a calm command.

A grin tugged at my lips as he ground his teeth but released me. "Good boy, Stephan."

"Barrett Stratos," she said, and my eyes shifted to her, narrowing.

I humored the female. "That would be me."

She opened a scroll. "You murdered your family."

The flames stirred beneath my skin at the mention. "What of it?"

"Why?" she asked.

I froze, blinking. "What?"

"*Why*?" she reiterated.

My brows furrowed. Pent-up magic stirred within me, eager to be used, to be unleashed, like a leathery beast leashed too short for too long. "Because I wanted to."

Her silver eyes met mine, warm and kind, and a soft smile curved her lips. The sight of it irritated me.

"Lie," she said, her tone hopeful and with such clarity, such solid confidence, that I didn't know how to respond.

I drew back. "What do you mean, *lie*?"

"Your sister," she started, disregarding my words.

My hands balled into fists, the flames pressing against my skin, the room warming despite the wards that should prevent them from surfacing. "Don't you dare say her na—"

"Calliope?" she confirmed, lifting her gaze from the scroll. "Did you kill her too?"

The flames were doused beneath my skin, my blood running cold, and my heart stuttered at the name I hadn't heard spoken in decades.

"No," I muttered under my breath, barely loud enough to hear.

"Lies," the guard grumbled under his breath. "Fuckin' kinslayer."

That warm smile returned to her face, and she shifted her weight as she returned her attention to the paper. "That's not what the details of your charges say. Barrett Stratos, charged with the murder of his family. Mother: Cassia Stratos; father and Kyrios of House Stoicheion: Elias Stratos; and sister: Calliope Stratos."

My fingers trembled, and I tightened them around the bars. What was the point in all this? I'd accepted the charges for my parent's deaths and whatever punishment came with them, but when I fought the claim that I'd killed Calliope, when I tried to tell them the truth of what had happened that night…

I'd been silenced and left to rot in this dungeon.

"If you didn't do it, who did?" she asked, something changing in her demeanor, in the air around her.

I didn't answer, didn't want to think of him, didn't want to hear his name. He didn't deserve to be remembered—*neither* of them deserved to be remembered. If it were up to me their very memory would have been burned from both realms.

"I have a theory, but I need your help," the female said, resting a hand against mine. My eyes fell to where she touched me before shifting back to her, finding warmth still in her gaze.

My thoughts warred, winding and overlapping one another like a den of snakes.

She'll use you. She'll betray you just as the others did. They always do. You're only good for how you can benefit them. They're all the same. Don't trust her. She wants something.

"Why?" I asked.

"Because I have a feeling I know what truly happened, and I don't think you deserve to be imprisoned for the actions of others."

"Why help me? What's in it for you?" I asked, and the guard grumbled. "If you've got a problem, Quickie, speak up."

"Qui—" he huffed, chest puffing out as he stormed toward me.

Yes, just a little closer. I'd wanted to lay this bastard out numerous times. He'd learn real fast how weak he is, even with these warded iron bars separating us. The mere proximity of the specially concentrated metal left my skin tingling, but it was worth it just to get to him.

"Stephan," the female said, her voice commanding, and he halted. "I would like to speak with Barrett in private."

The guard's eyes flew to her. "B-but—"

"I will be fine," she said, as if she didn't have a care in the fucking world. "Oh, and leave the keys, please."

I blinked.

"Your Majesty, it's not safe."

She smiled. "I can handle him."

The flames bristled within me. Who did she think she was? *Handle me?* I'd like to see her try.

The guard let out a sigh but handed her the ring of keys. "As you command." He dipped his head to her and turned for the only exit from the dungeons.

I lowered myself to her level, my forearms resting against the bars as I leaned in. My eyes roamed down her body. She was pretty, I'd give her that. A bit small, but she might be able handle what I could dish out. It had been far too long since I'd gotten inside a female; she looked like she'd feel good...taste good. I may even make it good for her as a reward. "You want to go a few rounds with me..." I frowned. "What's your name?"

"Lucia," she said, smiling as if she was chatting with a friend. It irritated me how this female spoke like she knew me.

"*Lucia,*" I started and glanced back at the bed of straw. "There's not much to offer as far as bedding, but I can promise you a good time." I nodded toward the guard as he opened the door to leave. "Far better than Quickie ever could."

He froze, his hand gripping the doorknob tightly, but he didn't answer before jerking it open and slamming it shut behind him. The keys jingled, and my attention snapped back to Lucia as she unlocked my cell. Shit, was really going to let me out of the cell? Was she out of her fucking mind?

The iron door groaned as she opened it.

Magic swelled within me. "You shouldn't have done that."

Flames surged to life on my skin, the wards on the cell broken by the opening of the gate, no shackles binding my wrists to weaken my magic. Gods, it felt so fucking good to set the flames loose again. I grabbed her by the throat, slamming her up against the bars of the cell opposite mine. "You should have listened to Stephan."

She smiled, and my blood boiled at the sight. My fingers tightened around her throat—

I frowned as my grip loosened instead.

What the fuck?

The flames spread over my skin, but when they reached her—as they crawled up her arm—she didn't flinch away, didn't react as the fire licked at her body. Her soft eyes remained fixated on me as the flames swept over her, but they didn't burn her, didn't so much as blister her leather armor. They died without my command, and I looked over myself. I tried to call the fire back, but it only further curled within me until it fell completely dormant, like a dog happy to come to heel.

What the fuck was happening to me? Something swelled in my chest as those pale silver orbs pierced me, as if she could see every bit of me that had been snuffed out since that night. There was no anger, no hatred, within that gaze.

It's fake. She's fake. She's lying.

"Why do you fight me?" she asked. "I just want to help you."

"Why, though?" I ground out, my hand shaking as I released her throat and lowered it against my command. "Why help me?"

She took my hand, the one that had just threatened to choke the life out of her. I took a step back as something warm and soothing seeped into my skin where she touched me, her presence overwhelming.

It's a lie... It's—

She didn't falter, her scent void of any fear or anger, and any words I might say were tangled and lodged in my throat.

She...she was the real thing. She was Moira's reincarnation, the queen our people had missed more than anything. Her hand fell to the satchel strapped to her belt. A glint of gold caught my attention as she pulled something from the pouch.

My heart stopped.

A bracelet...*Her* bracelet... The one I'd gifted her on her eighteenth birthday, before everything went to shit.

"Because..." she started, her warm smile resonating in her eyes as she clasped the delicate gold chain around my wrist.

Could I trust that smile? Could I trust her?

She spoke again, and for a moment, I almost felt I could forget every fake, manipulative smile that had led me to this cell, almost felt I could trust her. "You're innocent, and I'm going to clear your name."

CHAPTER 3
THALIA

Potential warriors congregated before me in the training yard, all untested. Thirty sets of eyes watched me as I paced, assessing each and every male and female. I wondered how many would make it through training, how many would fall on their first hunt before they took their vows as fully fledged warriors—how many of them would only serve as flesh to satiate the darklings' endless hunger.

Dust kicked up from those training nearby, the dirt dry from the hot summer months and little rain we'd had recently. The heat that had set in early in the day left sweat beading on my skin, stray strands of hair that had loosened from my braid clinging to the back of my neck. It was going to be a joyous day of training if the warmth persisted, and I expected it would.

"My name is Thalia," I said, folding my arms over my chest as I stepped in front of the lineup. "I have served Lady Lucia and Lord Damien for ten years now, hunting darklings and assisting in training recruits to serve The Order."

The recruits stood at attention, their arms tucked behind their backs as they stared forward. This group seemed better prepared than the previous year's. We would see how long that lasted. Training wasn't going to be easy, and they would learn this wasn't some fast track to glory and honor for their families. They would sweat and bleed every step of the way, and even after all that hard work, they may end as nothing more than ashes in Moira's Rest.

If we even managed to recover their bodies.

"Breakfast is served at six sharp every morning, and you will be in lineup at seven to begin warmups. You will not leave this training yard until I say so, am I clear?"

"Transparently," they said in unison.

"Good."

My gaze snagged on Micah beyond the lineup, training with other warriors across the yard. His lips kicked up into a brief half-smile before he blocked a downward strike of his opponent's blade. His shaggy brown hair was already drenched in sweat from the heat of the day, the curls defined with the moisture.

I pulled myself away at the sight of him, of the coiled muscles peeking from beneath his black tunic as the images of the things we'd done the night before resurfaced. I returned my attention to the recruits before I let on what had crossed my mind. A pair of males muttered to each other, and one of them snickered. I ignored it for now, continuing down the line.

"Apologies, but you said you've been serving for ten years. Aren't you a recruit yourself?" a female asked, her tone genuinely curious. "How have you been serving for ten years? I thought training only lasted for three."

She wasn't the first to question it, and though the irritation coiled in my chest, I bit it back.

"I am a third-year recruit, yes, and I will be taking my vows with our Goddess in six months, during the *Belariôs Retala*. My situation is unique, as my services began *before* I joined The Order. I did not require the training you all do, but there are still steps that must be met to take Selene's vows." I looked over their faces. "You all will undergo the same length of training, working up the ranks of recruitment. There are three tiers of recruits, one for each year you spend in service proving yourself."

"When will we start hunting darklings?" another asked.

"At the end of your second year." I continued down the line, taking in each face but none too deeply. Few would likely remain to take their vows, and I knew better than to get too attached. "Your first year will be spent building your strength and learning defense tact—"

"What makes you qualified to train us if you're only a recruit?" a male asked, and I stopped mid-step. "You've got that fancy scar, but did you really get it fighting?"

I froze at the mention of the scar running down my face, its presence an ever-lingering reminder. The beast within me bristled, teeth bared in the dark recesses of my soul. No matter how much I tried, nothing hid the mark. Makeup came off with sweat; by noon, it no longer concealed the hideous reminder.

The pompous male continued, his tone impatient and cocky, and I fought the urge to sweep his feet out from under him. "Shouldn't a warrior who's completed their training be teaching us?"

How amusing that the male recruit I'd caught whispering earlier was once again interrupting my lesson. He elbowed his friend, who glanced nervously at him. A growl snaked its way up my throat, but I swallowed it back down before the beast lingering in the core of my being could make him submit. There were times when it was necessary, but I didn't need to resort to that. I didn't have to be that monster anymore.

Though sometimes, I wanted to be...

No. There were other ways I could break him. I lifted my chin, forcing a smile across my face that was all teeth. "My apologies for the misunderstanding. What is your name, recruit?"

He ran his fingers through his short dark hair. I internally rolled my eyes at the recruit fresh out of his *settling* before me. Absolute male arrogance exuded from every pore of his very being as he spoke. "Lucas."

"Lucas," I echoed and turned to step over to the rack of weapons. "I assume you are practiced with a blade. Am I correct?"

"I've had a little training." His voice was laced with confidence, but my nose told me otherwise, and my lips twitched as I fought a smirk.

"Good." I bypassed the wooden training weapons their level would start with to grab a short sword from the rack. "Then you can give us a demonstration. We shall see which of us is more qualified to train your group."

I tossed the sword to him, and he caught it, albeit hesitantly. Perhaps he did have some skill, but I would test that for myself. He glanced at me nervously, and I grinned as his scent turned acidic.

The beast's thoughts echoed through my mind as it watched. *You are wise to be afraid.*

He and his friend exchanged nervous looks before he stepped forward.

"I want all of you to pay attention," I said, my voice harsh and unyielding, reaching each and every ear as I locked eyes on the male. "My training came long before I joined The Order, fighting creatures you would never encounter on this side of the veil."

Dread coiled in my gut at the thought of that place, but it was clear they weren't taking me seriously, so perhaps it would do well to instill a little fear.

I turned to Lucas as he widened his stance. "Darklings do not fight fair."

My gaze swept over him, assessing his form to find that his left foot wasn't fully stable. A weakness, but the rest of him seemed solid.

I glanced back to the group watching us. "When you face a darkling, it will be nothing like facing an immortal. The darklings are vicious, relentless, instinctual, and if you don't stab them between the eyes or in the heart—" I leveled my gaze on the male before me, and my lips twitched at the sight of unease on his face—"they will rise again."

The group of recruits tracked every movement I made, the weight of their stares burning into my back as I watched Lucas.

He gripped the hilt of the sword and glanced at my empty hands. His brows furrowed as I widened my stance. "What about your sword?"

"Oh, I don't need one." I had never needed one, had fought with my fangs and claws alone for decades—and I wouldn't even need those. "I'll give you the first swing. Let me see how much bite you have."

He didn't hesitate and lunged forward with a downstroke of his blade, of which I easily slid out of the way. I slipped my foot out to trip him, a grunt bursting from him as he hit the dirt before he pushed himself to his feet and whipped around to face me. A hushed snicker reached my ear, and his attention slipped from me briefly to look at those watching us.

I rushed for him. "Eyes on me. A darkling won't wait for you to pay attention. They will go for the easy kill."

He stepped back, eyes widening as he hesitated. Big mistake. He swung at me, and I slid around him, avoiding his attack before I came to a stop at his back.

"You'll have to be faster than that. You'd be dead twice now," I whispered. His shoulders were already rising and falling in heavy rhythm. Poor thing. He was untested, had likely only worked with a wooden training sword, had probably never held real Elythian steel in his life.

"Little bitch," he muttered under his breath, and the beast within me growled.

He twisted around and swept his sword in an arch, blade aimed for my ribs. I grabbed his arm before he could land a blow and guided his movements into a spin. He cursed as he missed before stumbling onto his knees.

"That's three times you've died," I taunted, looking down my nose at him. "If you can take me down, I'll buy you a drink tonight, *mikros*."

The term seemed to rile him, his irritation smoldering the air in my nose like a forest catching fire, and my lips curved into a grin. He bared his fangs as he pushed himself up from the dirt and growled before charging.

"Do not let your pride cloud your instinct." I ducked to the side as he swung downward, his sword plowing into the dirt. I slammed my boot atop the tip of his blade and anchored him in place before I swung my other leg out, my boot connecting with his jaw.

He hit the ground, and dust kicked up around him. The recruits all gasped, and some of them brought their hands to their mouths. I glanced at Lucas' friend, whose eyes were locked on the downed recruit.

I stepped over to him, and I couldn't deny the bit of satisfaction at the sight of his heaving chest, his furious glare.

"You have potential." I held my hand out to him. He ground his teeth together but took it, and I pulled him up. I leaned in to whisper in his ear, to instill one bit of advice before I allowed him to return to the lineup.

"Next time you decide to run that tongue, be careful you don't accidentally bite it off."

"I almost ended your class early," Micah whispered from behind me, barely loud enough to register over the sound of the crickets and cicadas chirping in the late-night air. A smile curved my lips as I ran a damp towel across my face. The was an edge to his tone that bordered on possessive.

"Oh?" I said, my heart fluttering at his proximity, at the way he had snuck up on me without my knowing—and the knowledge that we were the only souls remaining in the armory now that training had ended for the day. All other recruits and warriors had returned to their rooms in the barracks or were paying a visit to Semele's pub to unwind and relax.

"Watching you lay that arrogant prick on his ass..." Micah's fingers traced down my shoulders, along the length of my biceps, farther down until they slipped from my arms to land on my hips. "It never ceases to turn me on when you do that."

My breath hitched in my throat as his fingers slid up my shirt, the delicate touch sending ripples of ecstasy over my skin. His erection pressed against my ass as he settled against me, and Gods, I wished there weren't clothes separating us.

"What if it was *you* I was laying out?" I said with a grin, as one of his hands gripped my hip and ground me against him while his other traveled higher. I braced myself on the nearby wall as I shuddered. He lowered to graze the top of my shoulder with his lips. My head fell back, and I melted into him as he pulled me closer. Our skin was slick with sweat from the summer heat, but I didn't care. I couldn't get enough of him touching me.

He hummed against my skin. "I'd be honored to have a female such as you kick my ass. I'd love even more when I sank my cock between those pretty thighs after I'd taken the beating."

Heat pooled in my core, and a soft laugh bubbled in my throat. I bit my lip as his thumb brushed the underside of my breast and he dragged his fangs along the side of my throat. His hand slid into my trousers, the other cupping my breast, and I gasped as his fingers found my center. A growl of satisfaction rippled from his throat as he slid his fingers through the wetness pooling between my thighs.

"Mmm... So responsive to my touch," he breathed into my ear.

"Are the—" I moaned as he dipped two fingers inside me—"guards still stationed outside?"

"They are," he said, his sinful smile lacing his voice. "What of it?"

They could walk in on us, could catch me pressed between him and the wall, yet...

I was impatient enough to not care.

I'd been craving him all day, had craved him since we'd gone our separate ways for training that morning. It didn't matter that we had been tangled up in each other most of the night before. I didn't think I could ever get enough of him.

My knees trembled, and I panted as he ran his thumb over my clit with each thrust of his fingers. His other hand massaged my breast as his tongue worked along my throat.

"They know not to enter," he growled. "I bet they could scent my need the moment I approached the door. They would be fools to come in."

He bit down on my throat, and I gasped, my back arching as he continued to pump his fingers in and out of me. The feel of his fangs surged through me, sending an electric sensation skittering across my skin, my senses out of control beneath the heady waves of pleasure. I moaned his name as my release neared.

Micah pulled his fangs free long enough to breathe, "Come for me, Thalia. Let me taste your release,"

He bit down again, and it was all I needed to tip over the edge, my orgasm shattering me. His groan spilled over my neck as he drank it down. By the time he pulled his fangs free, I was panting, body a mess of shakes, and his weight sagged at my back as we melted against the wall together in a sweaty mess.

His hand slid free of my trousers, and he lowered his face over my shoulder as he lifted his fingers to his lips. A low growl rumbled from his throat as he drew them into his mouth, tasting me.

I shuddered as I turned enough to meet his gaze, to see the heat in those soft, sky-blue eyes.

"It's late. We should get home." He brushed a kiss to my shoulder, leaving my skin burning. "I can't wait to tie you down and pick up where we left off this morning."

I hummed a laugh as I turned toward him, settling against the cool stone wall as our bodies pressed flush against one another. He hesitated a moment, lifting his hand to run it along my cheek.

"I heard what that recruit said earlier," he said, the heat softening into something else. "About your scar."

My smile faded.

"I know you hate it, that it's a constant reminder, but..." He leaned in and pressed a kiss to my cheek, his lips brushing over the base of the scar that *was* a constant reminder.

I forced a weak smile and cupped his cheek. "I'll be fine. I'm tough."

He eyed me as I grabbed his hand and tugged him toward the exit. "I didn't say you weren't tough."

"I know, I know. It's just..." I didn't know what to say. "I don't think he'll be making any more comments like that in the near future after that embarrassing display today."

He gave a pained smile, and I hated it. I hated the pity.

"He'd be a fool," he said, and his words brushed over my skin like the touch of wild grasses, leaving goosebumps in their wake. "Because if he so much as breaths wrong in your direction again, he'll have to deal with me."

LUNA LAURIER

"He'd be a fool," he said, and his words brushed over my skin like the touch of wild grasses, leaving goosebumps in their wake. "Because if he so much as breaths wrong in your direction again, he'll have to deal with me."

CHAPTER 4
THE GIRL WITH STORMY EYES

60 years prior

I was cold. So cold…and alone.

Icy wind snaked over my skin, and I curled into myself, hugging Arion to my chest. The little wooden Pegasus gave me some comfort in the smooth edges defining its wings and powerful form. Papa had carved it for my birthday last year—his stories of the mightiest stallion who fought alongside our goddess, Selene, were always my favorite. He recited them to me almost every night at bedtime, and I rarely asked to hear any other story.

Tears welled in my eyes, and I sniffed, blinking them back. Arion smelled heavily of smoke now and little of Papa, of Mama, of home. I wanted so badly to hear Papa tell me a story. I didn't care if it was about Arion, or the siren and the *Oneiroi*. He could even tell me the scary stories of The Fates and their threads, or the ghastly creatures of The Shadow Steppes he used to share at supper. I only wanted to hear his voice, hear Mama's voice.

I clung to the little Pegasus, the only thing I had left of our home, praying Arion might bless me with his courage. Wind whipped through the trees and the scent of rain filled the air. My body quivered, but I tried to steel myself.

Be brave.

It could be worse. Tonight wasn't as cold as the last few nights had been, and I had a jacket this time. I smiled as I curled into it, pulling the fabric around me tighter.

The boy promised a blanket tomorrow. I wanted to see him again, play with him. I hadn't gotten his name, only his sister's: Cali. What were they doing now? Probably curled up with their mama, warm and safe.

Loneliness sank into the pit of my stomach, and I wrapped my arms around my knees. I whimpered as my thoughts drifted to Mama and Papa. Where were they? Why hadn't they found me yet? I'd searched and searched for them, but I hadn't found them anywhere.

I flinched as a branch snapped above me, and I screamed as the small limb crashed to the ground at my feet. Panic shot through my body as I pressed against the base of the tree, and the tears came harder. I wanted to go home, wanted to be held by Mama, hear her tell me it was going to be all right.

Mikros?

I stiffened at the soft voice echoing through the forest. The sound of the winds died out, but the branches continued to sway just as violently. A soft hum sank into my bones, warm and comforting.

Over here.

A warm lull settled over every inch of my body, as if the very air was wrapping me in its embrace, tugging me forward. I gripped Arion tightly, my fingers trembling.

The voice. It was Mama's…right?

I scanned the dark woods. Where was she? My lips parted to call out for her, but the rawness of my throat was too painful to speak, the fire and ash from the attack a few nights ago leaving my throat so raw and sore, it hurt to even drink or eat.

Warmth filled my chest, the world swaying as I quietly begged Mama to find me. The forest went deathly quiet—the whisper of the branches disappeared, and the rustle of the leaves, the chitter of the night creatures that had kept me company in the recent nights, vanished.

I reached out for the voice again, praying to hear Mama respond.

Where are you?

It was soft, barely a whisper, but I heard her again, and my heart swelled.

I'm here, mikros.

I winced as pain lanced across the underside of my foot, and I blinked.

Unfamiliar forests surrounded me. When had I stood? When had I left the tree or the creekside?

I lifted my foot to find blood rolling down the underside before dripping to the stone I'd sliced it on. A branch snapped in the darkness, and my heart lurched in my throat as I looked around.

"Ma—" I grimaced, clutching my throat as pain shot through me, erupting into a coughing fit.

Mama?

Hands grabbed me from the darkness, muffling the scream that tore from my throat.

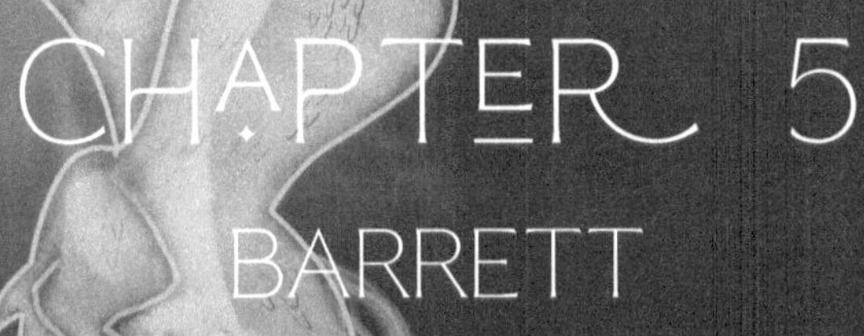

CHAPTER 5

BARRETT

I braced myself against the edge of the basin, water rolling down my face to drip into the pool. Drip. Drip. Drip.

The sting of the cut above my brow had nearly vanished with the help of Lucia's salve, but the dull headache from the hangover still lingered, pulsing behind my eyes. I desperately needed to feed.

I looked at my reflection in the mirror, and it was the first time in Gods knew how long that I'd looked upon myself, upon the eyes I hated so much. *His* eyes.

A spark ignited within me at the sight of them, of the painful reminder. The flame pressed against its confinement in my body, and I tightened my grip on the basin to keep from smashing my fist into the glass.

I ran my fingers through my wet blond hair, far too long for my liking after my imprisonment. Daily baths weren't exactly a privilege where I had been kept, and I might have spent a bit longer than I should have in the baths of the barracks. Grabbing a freshly sharpened blade, I began cutting away at the unwanted growth. It wasn't perfect when I finished, the sides and back shaved close with the top longer and swept back, but for the first time in decades, I almost felt like myself. I ran my hand over my freshly shaven jaw, finally clear of the faint beard that had grown back from the last time I'd burned the hairs away, when I'd had a chance to expel some magic during my imprisonment.

The gold chain bracelet clinked against the porcelain water basin, and I lifted my hand to see it better. A message in the old language was engraved in fine handwriting on the thin gold pendant. The mere sight of it brought forth memories of her. It had been far too long since I'd last heard her voice. I missed the sound of it, of her laughter.

"Cali..." I whispered, running my fingers over the delicate chain.

"Sneaking off again?" I called from where I sat on the window seat as she tiptoed down the stairs.

She stiffened and turned toward me hesitantly. A guilty smile crawled across her face, and she fiddled with one of her blonde curls, something she always did when she was up to no good. "Not at all. I was going for a walk through the gardens."

"At night?" I said, arching a brow as I set my book to the side.

She sidestepped, and the way she chewed her lip was all I needed to know she was full of it. "The jasmine should be blooming. I wanted to see them."

"Uh huh. It didn't seem that was where you snuck off to last night." I rose from the bench, my book forgotten. "That aside, I have something for you. I wanted to give it to you, but I got in late from training and didn't want to wake you up. Since you're awake, though..."

Her blonde brows rose as I pulled a box from my pocket. "My birthday isn't until tomorrow."

"Yeah, and we both know Mother has plans to whisk you away to be presented to the aristocracy. I'm afraid I won't get to see you."

Something akin to uncertainty flitted across her face, and I didn't blame her for it. We weren't their beloved children, weren't prized for the reasons we should be. We were tools, objects for our parents' benefit, our sole purpose being to strengthen their influence and power.

"You're probably right. It's all she's talked about for months," she said, her voice smaller than it should ever be, not like the child I once watched run through flower fields, singing at the top of her lungs. "Uncle Atticus and Aunt Jissena have helped with the planning as well. I don't like how Jissena fawns over me like some pet."

Atticus. I had never liked him. He was entirely too involved in Father's dealings, and I feared he knew the truth of what happened behind closed doors—feared he didn't care.

"I wanted to gift you this," I said, extending the box to her again. "Because there's no telling if we'll get any alone time tomorrow."

A soft smile tugged at her lips. "You've never been fond of audiences." She took the box and lifted the lid to reveal a delicate gold chain bracelet.

"Oh my goodness, it's beautiful," she whispered and lifted it from the satin bedding to inspect it closer. Etched into a delicate gold plate was a message written in the old language.

Tears welled in her eyes as she read it. "I love it."

"Here," I said, taking it from her. She held up her wrist for me, and I clasped the bracelet in place, the chain a touch too loose.

I frowned. "We can get it adjusted."

"No. I love it as it is." She lifted her wrist, and her smile widened as she read the message again.

"I love you so much," she said as she stretched onto her toes to wrap her arms around me and press a kiss to my cheek.

"I love you more."

"I love you most," she said with a snicker.

I arched a brow. "What are you really up to?"

She stiffened before glancing nervously to the entrance. "I, um…"

I gave her a knowing smile, and she slumped.

"I met someone."

My stomach dipped, and I hated that it was my first reaction to something that should be special. "Who?"

"A… Just someone from the market. We bumped into each other, and we started talking, and—"

"Cali, do you know what would happen if Father caught you sneaking out?" I said, a cold sense of dread winding in my chest. "And to be seeing someone?"

She put her hands on her hips, lifting her chin to meet my gaze, but she didn't have Father's steel eyes as I did. Hers were softer, an almost greenish gray— like wild sage. It was a trait she'd inherited from Mother. Some of the aristocracy frowned upon the color of Mother's eyes when she and Father were bonded. The presence of green in the silver was a sign that, somewhere in her bloodline there had been a mixing—whether with human or fae, we didn't know.

They were the eyes I wished I'd been given. Sadly, I'd inherited Father's, cold and hard as steel, and it was one of many traits that left me subjected to Father's talks of how I would be like him—how I would carry on the family name, become a warrior of The Order, and one day take over his position as Kyrios of House Stoicheion.

I'd have rather died than follow in his footsteps, continuing the farce of perfection he displayed to the outside world.

"He won't find out if you keep quiet," she whispered loudly, and I let out a sigh.

"It's not safe for you to go out this late," I said, glancing toward the main room where Mother and Father were likely relaxing for the evening. "What if a darkling finds its way into the village, or you bump into the wrong person? Did you stop to think about that?"

She crossed her arms over her chest, a cocky smile curving her lips, and I braced myself for the snide remarks to follow. "Two weeks into recruitment training and already, you know everything about the darklings and their activities?"

I rolled my eyes. "Don't start that. You know I'm—"

"He's arranged my bonding…" she admitted, and my heart lurched.

"He what?" He hadn't mentioned anything like that to me. "When did this happen?"

"He told me a few days ago."

Something fractured inside me at the way she hugged herself, at the way she averted her eyes.

"Did he tell you who?" When she didn't answer, I grabbed her arms, forcing her to look at me. "Cali, who is it?"

Her eyes finally met mine, and my stomach plummeted at the sight of the tears welling within them. "Jude."

"Jude Galanis?" I confirmed, and she reluctantly nodded.

I felt the blood drain from my face. He was the son of the Kyrios of House Leukós and had been bonded once before. Rumors arose shortly after his bonded suddenly passed away, but they had been quickly silenced. I'd seen him once or twice while accompanying Father to meet with the other council members. He was a smug bastard, cocky and entitled, and I'd personally interrupted him getting overly familiar with a female servant who was clearly uninterested in his advances—intervened when he wouldn't take no for an answer.

Would she end up like his first bonded? Or worse?

"Cali, he can't—"

"It's already been decided," she said numbly, as if she'd just accepted it without a fight.

"But…but you haven't even gone through your settling yet. You're only eighteen."

"The ceremony is to be held in two weeks."

I frowned. "Why so soon?"

She shrugged. "Does it matter? Nothing I do or say will change his mind."

What would he get out of this? Favor with House Leukós? Favor with Jude's father? The flames within me coiled tighter with each second, but I shoved them back. I couldn't lose my temper, not here. I'd lost it during the first week of training and had injured someone. I couldn't risk injuring her.

"I'll talk to him," I said.

She paled. "Don't—"

"Talk to me about what?" Father said, and we both stiffened, my heart launching into my throat as I turned to find him standing in the hallway. By the subtle slur of his words I knew he was already drunk—not like there was ever a night when he wasn't. His steel eyes narrowed on us, and Mother came to a stop beside him, running her hand over his back.

"Shouldn't you be in bed, Calliope?" Mother asked, offering her a soft smile.

"Why aren't you?" Father asked, turning to Calliope, and she drew a sharp breath, her mouth opening but failing to produce words.

"I was taking her to see if the jasmines were blooming in the garden," I said, stepping in front of her and taking her hand.

Father's steel gaze snapped to me, and I hated how with that single look, I was a helpless child again—an easy outlet for his drunken rage.

"Do you think me a fool, boy?" he spat, his lips peeling back.

Mother curled her hand around his arm, drawing close to him. "My lov—"

"Don't try to distract me, Cassia!" he barked, his flushed face reddening further.

Calliope's grip on my sleeve tightened and she winced as Father swung his arm from Mother's hold, knocking her back against the wall.

My hands balled into fists at my sides, the flames surging beneath the surface of my skin, begging to be released. I was no match for him, the head of House Stoicheion. He was a powerful flame wielder, possibly the strongest in the village. It was the only reason I willingly joined The Order, in hopes that the training might help me one day become strong enough to face him. To destroy him.

"You've always coddled them too much," he grumbled to Mother before turning his sights back on us. *"It's why he's so soft."*

I drew a deep breath, holding my ground under the weight of his glare.

"Answer me, boy, and you had better be honest. Why is she out of bed?" he demanded, stalking toward us, each massive step building a new layer of fear within me that only left me angrier at how weak I was.

I stood firm, my chin tipped up as Calliope tensed at my back, her hands trembling. "Night-blooming jasmines. They should be blooming right now."

His fist connected with my jaw, and Calliope cried out as I crashed onto the stone floor. I groaned, pushing myself up before running the back of my hand across my busted lip, the taste of copper coating my tongue. Fuck.

Father turned to Calliope before he stormed toward her and grabbed a fistful of her hair. She cried out as he jerked her toward him. "If I see you sneaking about again, it'll be the last thing you do."

A knock at the door pulled me back. My hands recoiled at the sight of the water within the basin boiling and bubbling, and my eyes shot up to the mirror fogged with steam and cracked from the heat.

"You'll be late for your first day of training," Lucia said from the other side of the door.

I cursed under my breath and grabbed my shirt before pulling it over my head and heading for the door.

Over forty-five years later, the bastard still had his claws in me.

"You entered the recruitment program once before, correct?" Lucia asked as I followed her through the training yard, the morning sun already hard at work, beating down on us. The flames within me seemed to preen in its presence, like a lizard basking in the rays.

"I did once," I said, humoring her despite the throbbing headache that hadn't fully let up.

I eyed the recruits as we passed, each one quietly assessing me. Did they know who I was? That I'd been in the dungeons since before most of them were born? I cracked a grin at a male as he looked over me, curious if he had the balls to approach, to act on that judgmental stare. None of them came forward.

I huffed a laugh. Pitiful.

"What happened?" she asked, looking over her shoulder at me.

"I got thrown in the dungeons," I deadpanned. "Did my file not say that?"

"Yes, it did, but I was hoping you could tell me more."

"Look, Lucia." I drew in a deep breath, irritation boiling in my chest, like a flame ready to be unleashed. She was so focused on digging up information on what happened. Why? It wasn't any of her business, and it wasn't as if it would change anything. "I appreciate everything you're doing, but I don't see the point. I killed my parents. The files didn't lie about that."

"I understand their deaths; that isn't the issue. What I want to know is what led to that, what truly transpired that night," she said, turning to me.

I didn't respond, wondering if she would throw me back in the cell if I didn't answer, or if she would throw me back in the cell if I *did*—if all this was just some elaborate ruse to further drag out the misery of my sentence.

"You don't have to tell me now. It's difficult to talk about the past, I know." Her eyes dipped briefly, and I couldn't help but feel like something lingered in them, as if she was reliving something in her own past. "We have all the time in the world, though. In the meantime..." She turned away from me, beckoning to a male who trained with another nearby. "Micah!"

His brown brows rose, and he halted mid-swing before dismissing his sparring partner. He was shorter than me by a few inches but well-built. His brown hair was a mess of sweaty curls, and as he approached us I could faintly smell juniper and sage. A dendron wielder, perhaps? They always tended to smell like plants or flowers.

He dipped his head briefly to Lucia, his breath heavy as he spoke. "Your Majesty?"

She crossed her arms, and one corner of her lips tipped up. "Micah, you know better."

He smiled guiltily. "Sorry, Lucia. What can I do for you?"

"I have a new recruit I'd like you to meet," she said, lifting her hand to me.

He looked me over briefly. I was so fucking tired of the assessments. "Thalia already started with the new recruits yesterday—"

"He won't be following their training schedule. He has some experience, and I'd like you to see where he falls," Lucia explained, as she glanced back at me. "I want to know what he's made of."

Micah gave a nod. "I can do that." He turned to look at me. "Any former training?"

I crossed my arms across my chest. "I killed a guard once."

Lucia let out a sigh and rubbed her hand over her face.

"Wait." Micah's eyes flitted from me to her. "Is he the one you spoke of last night?"

Lucia placed her hand on her hip. "Yes, this is Barrett Stratos."

"*Shit*," Micah said, and I prepared myself for the insults, for the judgment to be dished out. He cracked a smile. "Heard you took out three guards unarmed."

I frowned, unsure how to take the... Was he complimenting me?

"Yeah," I said. "I wanted some peace and quiet, and they wouldn't shut their mouths, so I shut em' for them."

He huffed a laugh. "How'd you get out early?"

"Good behavior," I said dryly.

Micah cocked an eyebrow at Lucia. "Why do I have a hard time believing that?"

Lucia smiled. "*I* pulled him out. He was up for execution in a month." My heart stalled. Execution? They hadn't told me that. When I had been sentenced, it was for life. "I stumbled across a record of his hearing the other day, and something didn't feel right."

I forced my expression into one of indifference. "She thinks I'm some sort of saint. Perhaps I'm a messenger sent by Celestia herself, come to deliver us from the darklings."

Lucia shook her head and looked at Micah. "Can you get him started for me? I have to meet with Damien to discuss some news from the Godsrealm. I fear someone is reorganizing The Pits in Tenebria."

Micah's skin paled a bit.

Lucia's voice dipped, and she leaned in closer to him. "Don't mention it to her. No need to stress her out."

My gaze snagged on Lucia. Who were they talking about?

"Are you going to send a team to look into it?" he asked.

Lucia nodded. "She won't be on the team, though. I promised I would never ask her to return to the Godsrealm, and I stand by my word. Damien and I will oversee it."

He offered her a smile. "Thank you, Lucia."

She patted his shoulder before pinning me with a knowing look. "I'll see you tomorrow. I'm sure you can find your way to your room without winding up in a bar fight?"

I sighed, and Micah looked between us before his gaze locked on me. "You didn't..."

"Oh, yes, he did. On his first night out no less," Lucia said with a knowing smile before brushing past me.

I glanced over my shoulder to see her wave a dismissive hand without looking my way. "Try not to burn my training yard down, hothead."

I groaned. I couldn't quite figure her out. What exactly did she want with me? The training yard was filled with countless warriors and recruits, and it was clear she had more than enough bodies serving The Order. Why go to the trouble to pull me out of the dungeons?

"You can trust her, ya know," Micah said, as if my thoughts were plastered across my face.

"What is this supposed to be? You talk her up, and I suddenly fall to her feet, willing to serve at her beck and call?"

Micah huffed a laugh and shook his head as he walked toward the training ring. "Man, they really did a number on you in there."

I rolled my eyes but followed him. "I hate to break it to you, golden boy, but getting thrown in a cell for over forty-five years doesn't exactly inspire trust in others."

Micah didn't seem to have a response, and I shouldn't have been as satisfied as I was that he'd finally shut up.

After a moment of silence, he spoke up as he rerolled the sleeves of his black tunic. "I'm not saying it lightly, so you know. You *can* trust Lucia." His eyes shifted to her as she made her way through the training yard, stopping periodically to speak with recruits. "She looks out for us. I'm proud to serve under her."

"I'll be sure to tell her mate how much you love *serving under her.*"

Micah huffed a laugh. "You'll figure it out in time for yourself, but be careful talking like that about her around Damien. He's rather protective of her, especially when it comes to males cracking jokes."

Damien. The King of the Immortals. I'd heard stories of him, the sole living heir to House Skiá, the only surviving member of those who wielded shadow magic. I wondered what he was like.

"So, the king is a possessive male, then?"

Micah shook his head. "It's not like that."

"Why are you so confident she can be trusted?" I asked, crossing my arms. "What's so special about her?"

He smiled as he grabbed a waterskin and took a quick swig before saying, "She knows each of us by name, takes the time to listen to us—*truly listen.* She fights at our side instead of barking orders at us from a safe distance while we fight for our lives, hunting the darklings."

I didn't speak, didn't have a response, because the words he spoke... I could somehow see them in her, but I'd been too afraid of taking a closer look, of opening myself up to her. The last time I'd done that, I'd been thrown in a cell to rot for the rest of my unending life—or perhaps not, as clearly someone had other plans for me, if an execution had been scheduled so suddenly.

"What's this pit she was talking about?" I asked.

Micah blinked, seemingly caught off guard by the question, and he seemed to search for words. "Um... Ten years ago, Lucia and Damien caught wind of an illegal fighting operation in Erebus' domain. I don't even know how long they'd been running it when Lucia learned they had been taking not only human children, but they had two of our kind fighting for them.

The fae running it had been taking children across the veil for decades—possibly even centuries. We learned they had several immortals at one point, but sadly, only one made it out alive in the end."

Something twisted in my chest, and I couldn't help but feel a sense of nostalgia. Children being taken across the veil...

Don't stay out too late, now. The fae like to take little ones across the veil.

Who had said that to me? Mother had told me scary stories of the fae...but the voice that clung to a lost part of my memory wasn't Mother's. It felt slippery in my memory, like poison, and I couldn't understand why.

"Who was Lucia not going to send with the team to look into it?" I asked, unable to contain my curiosity.

"I—" Micah hesitated. "That's not something I can talk about. Sorry."

For once, I didn't argue. The look in his eyes as they slid away from me carried enough sadness to make me bite my tongue. I tracked his gaze to a female watching us from afar, her hair pale in the sunlight. She averted her eyes from mine the moment ours met, and she yelled something at the recruits sparring before her.

Something stirred deep within my chest, something familiar, and I frowned.

"So," he started, dragging me back, and I couldn't miss how eager he was to change the subject as he widened his stance, clenching and unclenching his fists. "Show me exactly how you laid out three guards unarmed."

My lips twitched at the tone in his voice, at the hint of curiosity and amusement, as if the thought of it entertained him. I rolled my neck and cracked my knuckles as I stepped toward him, and I couldn't help but feel like I might grow to like this male more than I'd cared to admit.

CHAPTER 6

THALIA

"Who's Micah training with today? I've never seen him before," Zephyr asked, and my brows furrowed, my attention drawn from the group of trainees whose sparring I oversaw.

I'd tried to avoid looking at the male since he'd met my gaze earlier, but it had been difficult to keep my eyes from wandering. He was tall, his blond hair swept back from his face, save for the few strands that had slipped free during their training. Where had he come from? He hadn't been at the morning's roll call.

"He looks a bit out of shape," I said, noting how he panted in the brief moment before they exchanged blows again.

Zephyr huffed a laugh, his massive arms crossed over his chest as he tilted his head. "Definitely new to fighting."

"I wouldn't quite say that," I said as my eyes narrowed in assessment. He was still standing, and I wasn't sure if Micah was going easy on him or if he was truly holding up.

Wait—was I defending this male?

I shook the thought away, but as I tried to focus on our own recruits, I couldn't seem to keep my attention from them. Not from Micah, whose brow was coated in sweat from training, veins popping on his forearms, and not from the strange male whose throat bobbed as he swallowed, his eyes locked on my bonded.

Gods, why was I staring?

"Did we get a batch of new recruits?" Zephyr asked, and I blinked, praying I didn't look as obvious as I felt.

"Recruitment happened three days ago, and he was not among the thirty who made it through the preliminary testing," I said, tilting my head as I assessed his movements. It was something I had to do as a trainer. I couldn't improve any weaknesses if I didn't pay close attention to their flaws. It was strictly professional.

There was an unorthodox way with which he fought, as if he learned to fight more through necessity than training. Yet, at the same time, I could see similar steps the recruits used.

Something tugged in the back of my mind, something familiar and strange.

The beast deep in my chest seemed to purr, and my cheeks heated at the implication.

What the fuck?

I grumbled internally. *In case you hadn't noticed, that's our bonded he's fighting.*

The beast seemed to huff at that statement. *Then tell me why your heart races, little one.*

I internally rolled my eyes at the name. I hadn't been a *little one* for over fifty years.

As my attention returned to them, I couldn't help but let my mind wander, letting my eyes do the same. Gods, they were beautiful, bodies powerful as they held each other off at every step.

"His name is Barrett."

I stiffened at Lucia's voice, even more so at the knowing smile on her face.

"Where'd he come from?" Zephyr asked. "I don't recognize him."

"That's above your rank," she said with a tilt of her head before leaving us in silence.

I frowned, glancing at Zephyr, who looked just as confused. He was third in command. if it was above his rank, then... That meant only she and Damien knew. Who the hell was he?

I had a shift to assist Damien with his work in a couple of days. Perhaps I could learn more then. Surely there was information on his file for The Order. Did I really want to know, though? I couldn't help but feel a sense of guilt for the way my heart fluttered at the sight of him. It was stupid. He was just a pretty male, with his fancy blond hair and hardened steel eyes that shined in the sunlight.

The beast within me seemed to huff a laugh. *That's an awfully detailed description of his eyes.*

I growled and shot back at the beast. *Shut up!*

"Thalia?" Zephyr said, and I cleared my throat before turning my attention from the two males who had somehow sent my heart racing.

I blinked, internally scolding myself when the beast's amusement flitted through my mind. "Sorry?"

"You good?" Zephyr asked, and I lifted my gaze to find him staring at me hesitantly.

"I'm wonderful," I said far too fast before I turned to walk away. "I have a lot of work to do, so I'll see you later."

I couldn't let myself get distracted. There was work to do, debts to be repaid.

I sat atop the roof that night, taking in the night sky. Even ten years later, it still felt strange to stare up at a single moon instead of two.

"I was wondering where you were," Micah said, and I smiled at the warmth of his voice. His magic caressed mine, our bond humming within the markings of our binding tattoo between my breasts. I lifted my hand to it, feeling the warmth beneath the fabric of my shirt.

He sat down behind me, his arms coming around to pull me between his legs. I eased back against him, the feel of his arms around me the only thing I could ever need, could ever want.

A whisper of his magic flitted between us, and my eyes fell to a bud developing and unfolding into a brilliant blossom in his hand.

"I thought you were above wooing me with flowers," I said with a smile as he held the delicate bloom out for me. I took it, and leaned closer against him, twisting to feel him press his lips to my temple.

"I'm above nothing when it comes to making you smile," he said. "What's bothering you?"

"Why do you think something is bothering me?" I asked, looking back up at the stars.

"You don't usually hide away on the rooftop unless something is bothering you."

"Perhaps I wanted you to hunt me down," I said in challenge.

A satisfied hum rippled from his throat, deep and low, and his hands slipped over my stomach. "Is that what you wanted?"

I smiled, but my breath caught in my throat as his hand found my breast.

"To be hunted?" he added.

My head fell back as his lips brushed against my throat before he dragged his fangs over my skin.

"Is that what you are, flower boy?" I teased. "A hunter?"

He huffed a laugh at the nickname I'd given him when we had first met all those years ago. "I'm *yours*."

"Then be mine," I said. "And I'll be yours."

He bit down on my throat then, and a moan slipped from my lips as he drank. One of his hands roamed down my stomach to undo my pants while the other palmed my breast.

"Gods," I moaned.

My body shivered as he released my throat and whispered in my ear, his voice thick and heavy. "It's been a while since I've taken you under the stars."

His hand slid beneath the waist of my trousers, and he growled as his fingers found the slick heat waiting for him.

"Always so wet for me," he whispered into my ear.

My head fell back against his shoulder as he slipped two fingers inside me, and I could feel his eyes burning into me as he watched me unravel for him.

As the need climbed higher and higher, until I felt I might explode, he slid his hand from my pants and pulled me around to face him. Our lips crashed together, and I reached for his shirt, desperate to get it off him, to feel his skin, to feel him inside me.

His lips curved into a wicked grin against mine. He huffed a laugh as we broke apart to peel each other out of our clothes, and then he was pulling me down onto him, his cock sinking so deep inside me that I cried out.

The binding tattoo between my breasts tingled as we fell into a rhythm, my hips rolling as he lifted his to meet me in heavy thrusts. I grasped his shoulder and rested my forehead against his as I rode him.

"Gods, you feel like heaven," he groaned, and I gasped as his fingers closed around my throat. He tilted my head back, forcing my gaze to his as his other hand gripped my waist. Pure hunger and need lit his pale, blue-gray eyes as he watched me, and he pulled my hips tighter against him on the next thrust, reaching deep enough to drag a moan from me.

"Fuck, you're beautiful riding my cock," he growled, and a smile curved my lips.

Gods, I loved how he watched me, how I could make him feel, the sounds I could drag from him. His fingers loosened as I leaned into him, my fangs lengthening, hunger driving me to the edge. My lips parted, and he tilted his head to the side as he released my throat.

I bit down into his own shoulder, our moans blending in the most delicious way as I tasted his pleasure. His senses heightened, the ecstasy erupting between us. His blood was powerful, sweet and heady, and I drank deeply, feeling his magic—his power—coat my throat with each gulp.

He moaned, his pace quickening, and I rolled my hips, meeting each deep, desperate thrust. I released his throat, panting as my body cried out for release.

A smile curved my lips as I felt the familiar snaking of vines crawling over my thighs, my hands—his vines.

They wrapped around my wrists, farther up my arms, and then my neck, pulling my arms to my sides, forcing my back to arch as he watched me come undone. His heated eyes met mine as he used both his free hands to grab my hips, pulling me down as he slammed into me harder, exactly as I wanted. Right as I felt myself tipping over the edge, I felt a brush of his thumb over my clit.

My mouth fell open on a silent moan, the vines tightening their hold as he claimed me. So close. So fucking close.

I cried out his name, my body tightening around him.

"That's right, fucking come for me," he growled, pulling me down on him again.

I shattered, my orgasm crashing through me in unrelenting waves, but he didn't let up. He never did, and I didn't want him to. He would draw me over the edge, far beyond it, to a place I never wanted to return from.

Tears dotted my lashes as he fucked me harder, drawing it out, intensifying it beyond belief, and on the next thrust, his body shuddered, a moan spilling from his lips as he pumped his release into me. The vines quivered around me before they slackened their hold.

I collapsed against him as the vines receded, my body quivering, my skin sensitive as he caught me. He shifted and turned to ease me onto my back, twisting around to hover over me, his smile warm.

"So perfect," he whispered, gazing down at me. "My bonded. My Thalia."

I smiled despite the sadness winding its way through me at the sound of the name on his lips.

His eyes flitted between mine, the same sadness dulling them. He brushed his thumb over my cheek, and it was only then I realized an errant tear had slipped free without my permission. "What is it, love?"

"I wish you knew my true name," I admitted.

"I don't need to know your true name to know the true you," he said, his eyes burning into mine. "To know you are the greatest thing to ever happen to me."

CHAPTER 7

THE GIRL WITH STORMY EYES

60 years prior

What is your name, mikros?

The warm, familiar voice slipped through the darkness, slithering and curling into my thoughts, a voice that sounded like home—like warm meals and tender embraces.

My name?

Yes, your name. Can you give it to us?

My name is Ly—

My mouth clamped shut at how the air was pulled from my lungs, my voice muffled—as if my name had been swallowed up and swept away into nothingness as it passed through my lips, leaving me hollow and lost, as if a part of me had been taken. The voice didn't respond, leaving me in a sea of silence.

Mama?

The air was cold and damp as it filled my lungs, and a strange sensation crawled over my skin, something unnatural and dreadful. I was moving… No. I was being carried.

My eyes cracked open, lids heavy and fighting to slip closed again. I was cradled in someone's arms, my body swaying with each echoing step of boots against stone. I couldn't make out who carried me, their face shadowed under their hood as the dark slabs of rock surrounding us.

I groaned, my body weak, as if my muscles and bones had been lulled into a deep rest.

Sleep.

My eyes threatened to close again.

Rest.

Yes. Rest. Rest sounded nice.

My lids slowly slid shut, but with the next shift of the person's step, the little wooden pegasus tucked against my chest threatened to fall, and I stiffened. I clung to it before it could slip from my grasp, and the woody, smoky scent of the boy with steel eyes that lingered in his coat I still wore reached my nose, nearly drowned out by the musty, damp smell of the cave. He promised he would come back for me, but I had wandered from our spot by the creek. Where was I?

A hiss echoed through the cave as we passed the mouth of another tunnel, and for a moment I thought I saw eyes watching from the dark depths—six enormous eyes, but they vanished almost as quickly as they'd appeared, leaving me wondering if I'd dreamt them up.

"I see you're awake," the male carrying me said, the old language leaving his tongue fluidly, but still, I understood them. There was something dark in his amber eyes, shadowed in the darkness of his hood, something that flared every instinct within me to get away. I gasped and jerked back, pushing out of his arms. He grunted, and I spilled from his grasp before crashing onto the stone below. The rock bit into my side, and I twisted onto my hands and knees.

He cursed under his breath, reaching for me as I scrambled away. The cut on my foot stung as it reopened, leaving a broken trail of blood along the stone behind me. I crashed into the rocky wall, and my chest heaved as I frantically looked around the narrow cave. My pulse thrummed in my ears as I searched for any means of escape, but we were deep under the mountain, only the dim light of...

I scrunched my eyes as I watched the little floating orbs of light fluttering and flickering around us, *with* us. They were like fireflies, only they weren't. They were something else, something that didn't belong here.

"You won't get far. Just come quietly, and you won't get hurt," the male said, approaching me cautiously. He didn't sound at all like he meant the words he spoke. He held his hands out as if showing he was unarmed, not dangerous, but instinct told me not to trust him. Mama's voice danced across my thoughts, drawing back to the present.

Always trust your instincts, mikros. The beast protects us.

I shrank away from his hands. His fingers were decorated with rings, the near-gray skin of his knuckles peeking from his fingerless gloves marked with black ink. As I took him in, I noticed more ink marking the skin along the side of his throat before disappearing beneath the collar of his shirt. They were intricate inscriptions like those written in the books Papa read to me in the Archivallia—the old language of the gods. Movement caught my eye from behind him. There were others like him, unconscious children in their arms as well. They had all stopped, watching and waiting.

He grabbed hold of my arm, and I screamed despite the pain lancing up my throat. "Come here, girl!"

I kicked his chest, fighting to free myself from his grip with everything I had. The unnatural feeling coiled around me once more. He dragged me farther into the cave. "No!"

"Stop fighting me. There's no escaping now," he grunted.

I realized my hands were empty, and my eyes darted to the tiny wooden pegasus lying on the stone behind us, the distance growing with each step.

"No!" I reached for it, my voice hoarse and cracking as I cried out, my vision blurring. "Arion!"

"Rhyas," a male ahead of us called, and my captor stiffened. "Don't fall behind. She blessed our passage, but Scylla may mistake you for an intruder if you're not with the group."

"Understood," Rhyas said stiffly, a hint of panic painting his tone for a moment as he tightened his grip on me.

"You've got your hands full with that one," one of the others said, but I didn't see who, too busy pulling against his hold to get back to Arion. I couldn't leave him behind; he was the only thing I had left of home.

Rhyas didn't ease up his grip. He scooped me up, his arm looping around my stomach as he hoisted me against his side. He didn't seem even remotely fazed as I kicked and hit him. "She's got fight, that's for sure."

I froze as the one he spoke with fell into step at our side.

The male lowered his hood, his shadowed green eyes dragging over me, assessing me, and my heart stuttered when I saw the short, curved horns protruding from his forehead, the delicately pointed ears peeking from beneath his tawny hair, and the thin tail swaying behind him with each step. "Good. He'll be pleased with this one. She'll be perfect for The Pits."

The Pits? Dread crawled over my skin as we continued deeper and deeper into the cave. My body cried out, instinct screaming within me.

Don't go there, little one! Stay away!

I tried to listen to my instincts, tried to get free, but it was no use. No matter how much I kicked and fought, his grip on me only tightened.

The air was unsettling, laced with something sickeningly acrid and slimy. The feeling intensified as we grew closer and closer to something… it was something invisible and so alive, it breathed with energy, with power, its presence leaving the hairs on the back of my neck on end, my heart pounding.

A strange sensation washed over me, instinct shuddering and recoiling—as if the beast within me was cowering—as we slipped through whatever it was. The sensation was weighted, icy, and I flinched as it clung to me, as if the intangible presence was feeling out every inch of my body, down to the furthest depths until I could have sworn it brushed against my very soul.

And then, it vanished.

"Welcome to your new home," Rhyas whispered, and I opened my eyes, the air halting in my lungs. We emerged from the mouth of the cave, the expanse of the world before me almost too much to process. A soft blue glow emanated from the woods surrounding us. I couldn't quite pinpoint the source of it, as if the forest itself was alive with the glowing haze. The colors were brighter, more intense than they were back home. The air was warm against my skin, soft, humming with something I couldn't place. Life? Energy?

Magic?

Most of the little orbs of light scattered from us, fanning out across the forest. My eyes widened as I found orbs of purple light floating down from the bows of the towering trees, and the tiny lights that had traveled with us shifted in color, dancing around one another, as if being welcomed home.

Mama had told me stories of little spirits living in the forests of the Godsrealm.

Fates spare me. The Godsrealm. We were in the Godsrealm.

No. I couldn't be here. My heart quickened, fear winding around me. I needed to get back. If I was here, Mama and Papa couldn't find me.

My captor's hold tightened on me before he grumbled, "Better stop fighting me, little beasty. We've still got another day before we reach Tenebria, and if you keep making this difficult, you won't have a good time of it."

I ground my teeth together, and the beast in my soul—though unable to emerge until my *settling*—bristled, its anger slipping deep into my chest.

The male carrying me halted without warning, his heartbeat leaping into an intense pace as he sucked in a breath and dipped his head. I twisted in his arms, and my heart launched into my throat as a hoof, large enough to crush us, settled into the cushiony moss before our group. Rhyas eased me down cautiously, his free hand held out to the beast.

"Silvash," the green-eyed fae male with horns said in acknowledgment, dipping his head as well. "I see you as guardian of your domain and respect it. We only wish for safe passage."

The creature's eyes passed over him in quiet assessment before it lowered its head, moss and vines hanging from its enormous antlers swaying with each movement. Its fur—which was no single color but a rainbow of greens, blues, browns, and oranges—was covered in moss. Its nostrils flared as it drew in a powerful breath, the strands of my cornsilk hair fluttering toward it as it scented us.

"Stay still," Rhyas whispered, his head held low as he pulled his hood down, baring himself to the beast. I caught sight of his pointed fae ears. "Don't panic. You're safe."

Don't panic? How could I not panic? I ignored the thoughts and stilled, stifling the fear drowning out my own thoughts, and I swallowed at the feel of Rhyas' trembling hands. The beast remained standing for a moment, but finally, it gave a light bow of its head and rose before continuing its path through the forest.

Rhyas let out a breath, his body relaxing. "If you would have screamed, he might have seen us as a threat and thrashed us with his antlers."

"Or crushed us with his hooves," said a female with blue and green dragonfly-like wings that looked as if they had been battered and broken. She huffed a laugh and continued along the path.

I didn't respond as I watched the creature, admiring its beauty and power.

"Santor! Rhyas! Get a move on!" another male captor called out. "No more delays. It took us long enough to collect them. He'll be impatiently waiting."

"Aye, sir," the fae male with horns, Santor, said, and nodded his head to Rhyas before following him, his own captured child tucked over his shoulder, still unconscious.

The light was fading, the sun dipping behind mountains in the distance.

"We'll be making camp soon; don't want to travel through these woods at night," Rhyas muttered as he scanned the forest around us. "If you behave yourself, I'll let you walk. I'm sure you'd like to stretch your legs, and I'd rather not have to carry you all the way. We can make this a bit more pleasant for both of us."

I glanced back to the cave not far behind us. If I could remember how to get back to it, maybe I could escape and make it home. I only needed to pretend I would obey and stay with him. It wouldn't be long before dark; maybe I could slip away as soon as he fell asleep.

His amber eyes fell to me, and he arched a dark brow. "Well, little beasty? Will you behave?"

I nodded.

"I know you can talk," he said and turned before releasing me. I looked down in awe at the moss beneath my feet, so moist and soft that I couldn't help but stretch my toes out and curl them in to feel it squish against my skin.

Rhyas cleared his throat, and my eyes shot to him. I parted my lips but hesitated to speak, my hand rising to my sore throat.

"Did you do something to your throat?" he asked, and I nodded, my mind revisiting the sight of the fires, of our home burning around us as Mama shoved me out of the building before it collapsed.

Tears welled in my eyes. Mama and Papa must have gotten out another way. They had to have been looking for me.

"Here," he said, reaching for his belt to retrieve a pale gourd with a cork stopper. He pulled the cork out and offered it to me. "Water from the Latrias Springs. It has healing properties. It won't heal deep wounds, but it should soothe your throat."

I hesitated, but I was so thirsty, my mouth like cotton. My gaze flitted to him briefly, assessing him, but I took the gourd of water and drank deeply. The water hit my mouth, my throat—bright, cold, and refreshing— and I found myself drinking more and more, unable to get enough.

He pulled the gourd from me too soon. "Easy now. We've still got a day of walking. We have to make it last."

I panted, the water soothing the pain in my throat, and I blinked at the subtle, numbing tingle left in its wake.

"Better?" he asked, tying the gourd back to his belt.

I nodded, my voice a near whisper as I spoke. "Yes. Thank you."

"Stay close to me and don't run off."

I glanced back at the cave behind us, but I nodded and followed after him as he followed after the group.

CHAPTER 8

BARRETT

"Did that bracelet belong to your sister?" Lucia's words dragged me from my thoughts of the female who watched Micah and me train the day before.

I forced myself to remain focused on the stretch of hall before us as we walked through the barracks. "It did." Lucia didn't speak again for a moment, and I arched a brow at her. "Is that the only question you'll be bombarding me with today?"

A smug smile tugged at her lips. "I knew you weren't lying when we first met. It wouldn't make sense for a murderer to cling so tightly to an object owned by his victim."

I let out a sigh at her persistence and muttered, "You never know when to quit."

"Correction, I know when not to give up," she said, her head held high, as if she had claimed some sort of victory.

I rolled my eyes. Clearly that was the difference between us, because I had given up long ago. No matter how much I had tried to fight, it hadn't mattered in the end, so why bother?

"Ungrateful child!" I froze at the sound of Father's angry voice followed by the shattering of glass as I passed the closed door to his study.

My blood chilled, and I stepped closer to listen.

"Have you heard from Jude and his father?" I stilled at the sound of Atticus' voice. Of course, the bastard knew of Calliope's betrothal. "Do they realize she's run off yet?"

Air rushed from my lungs.

"I haven't heard anything," Father growled. "But if she doesn't show up to the binding ceremony in the next half hour…"

Half hour? Her binding wasn't supposed to take place for another week. When had he moved it up?

"I took care of her useless attendant, so you won't have to worry about her," Atticus said. "Not worth anything if she couldn't keep track of a single girl."

"I should've seen her there myself," Father grumbled, and there was a brief pause. I imagined he was downing another glass of Ambrosia liquor. "We'll find her. I have my men turning over the entire village searching for her now. She has to turn up somewhere. Selfish girl. I should have known she would pull something like this."

"It's shameful," Atticus said with disgust. "She should be grateful to be given such an opportunity. Bonded to the future Kyrios of House Leukos, she would have brought her family hon…"

I turned, my feet moving on their own as I ran up the stairs, unable to listen further. It couldn't be true. Servants stumbled out of the way as I ran down the hall, muttering to themselves, but I didn't pay them any mind.

"Lord Barrett, have you seen Trista? She was supposed to return an hour ago," one of the servants asked as I brushed past her, and my heart shuddered. Trista. Calliope's attendant. I didn't waste time answering her, my boots pounding into the carpet as I neared her room.

This couldn't be happening. She wouldn't run. She couldn't. He would kill her.

I shoved Calliope's bedroom door open and froze at the sight of the empty, dark room. Wind whistled through her open window, the outside night sky cast in pitch blackness without the light of the new moon.

No. Please, Gods.

I hurried to her bed, ripping back the blankets, praying to find her sleeping, that I had imagined the entire conversation. Empty. I turned and ran for the closet to find it also empty.

"Godsdammit, no," I muttered, stumbling back, my hands shaking. Where could she have gone? There were no other immortal settlements she could have taken shelter in. What if she left the safety of the village to get away from him? What if a darkling found her?

The sound of wind rustling paper caught my attention, and I turned to find a folded piece of parchment sitting atop her nightstand. Dread constricted my chest as I stepped toward the parchment, anchored against the breeze by a delicate gold bracelet.

The room spun as I took them both in my hand. The carved message in Elythian burned my skin where I held the gift I'd given her only a week earlier. I opened the note.

'I love you most.'

I couldn't breathe, my hands trembling as I read her message over and over again. My grip on the bracelet tightened, and I ran for the door, the note falling from my hand.

There was no telling what Father would do to her if he found her. I couldn't let him. I had to find her first, get her to safety.

Fuck, even if I found her, what the hell was I going to do? We couldn't return home. Where would she even go? The laws of the aristocracy placed unbound females under the care of the heads of their households. Mother wouldn't defend Calliope against Father's rage—she never did, and he would be furious, embarrassed that she stood Jude up at their binding ceremony. They could burn for all I cared. There would be no binding ceremony. I had spent the past week brainstorming how to get her out of it, and while I hadn't come up with a solution...

There wasn't time to dwell on the thought as I snuck past Father's study and slipped out the front door onto the dark street. None of it mattered if I couldn't find her—if he got to her first.

People passed by as I ran down the streets, every alley, giving me odd looks as I scanned every face in search of hers.

"Where are you, Cali?" I muttered as I turned down a narrow path to avoid a group of males stalking through the crowds. I recognized some of them from Father's personal guard. Had Atticus brought some of his own hired thugs?

I continued farther down the alley onto another conjoined street, my feet barely meeting the ground as I ran, searching. Where would she go? Where would she hide? Was she with this person she spoke of? Was it a male or female? Fuck, I hated that I hadn't gotten that information out of her when I had the chance.

Half an hour later, I had searched half the town and still hadn't found her. My chest heaved as I paused, struggling to think past the terror. She was smart. She would hide somewhere Father wouldn't know to look. Somewhere familiar. Safe.

The creekside.

My heart raced as I turned, lifting my gaze to the mountains lining the valley. Would she really brave leaving the safety of the city at night? Of course, she would. Father wouldn't give up until he found her, we both knew it, and Father would never think of looking near the ruins of Moonhaven.

I glanced back before hurrying out of the alley and through the city toward the main gates, wishing I had my sword. There was no time to return home to grab it. I pressed my back to the wall at the mouth of the street, searching for signs of any guards. The gates were closed for the night, but the door beside them was unmanned, the guards likely making their rounds along the wall in the dark hours. They weren't meant to keep us contained, but to keep darklings out. Immortals knew not to leave the safety of the walls. Those foolish enough to leave took their fate into their own hands.

The forest was quiet as I hurried for the ruins of Moonhaven, praying I was right—that Calliope had taken refuge at our old play spot. I couldn't risk calling out for her. Darklings could be nearby, and I didn't have a weapon to defend myself, my magic still too unpredictable to rely on as anything more than a last resort in my early training.

The trees thinned, and relief flooded my chest as I found Calliope sitting at the edge of the creek, her back turned to me. She wasn't alone, sitting next to a figure cloaked in black, their hood up. The figure glanced over their shoulder, revealing tanned skin and shoulder-length copper hair. The moment she caught sight of me, she shot to her feet, her fangs bared as she ripped her dagger from her sheath.

"Vesa, stop!" Calliope shouted as she jumped to her feet to step between us. "It's Barrett."

"Thank the Fates," I panted as I rested my hand against the tree, struggling to catch my breath.

"What are you doing here?" Calliope asked as she ran to me.

"Father knows. He has his men searching for you all over town." I looked her over. "Are you all right? What the hell happened? I overheard Atticus and Father say something about your binding ceremony happening tonight. I thought it was a week from now."

"The bastard moved the date up," the female said as she sheathed her dagger and tugged her hood down to scan our surroundings. By the look of the black leather armor, and the black and silver dagger, she was a warrior of The Order. My eyes widened as I took in the faint points of her ears, the soft purple of her eyes. She was half fae.

"I couldn't do it." Calliope's voice cracked, her hands trembling in mine, and I looked back down at her.

I pulled her into a hug. "I won't let them do that to you. You won't end up like Jude's previous bonded. I don't care what I have to do."

I lifted my gaze to the female and released Calliope. "Is this..."

Calliope fidgeted with her skirt and stepped back a few paces. "This is Vesa, the one I told you of."

"I wish we could have met under better circumstances," Vesa said as she stopped at Calliope's side. "She's told me wonderful things about you."

"I wish I could say the same of you," I said, my heart twisting at the fact I was only now meeting her, that we couldn't feel joy in something that should be nothing short of celebrated. I turned to Calliope. "We have to find somewhere to hide. It's not safe to go back tonight."

"When things calm down, I plan to seek an audience with Lord Damien," Vesa said. "He is an honorable male; he wouldn't turn a blind eye to this."

"What do you plan to do until then?" I asked. "You can't just hide out here. It's only a matter of time before you run into a darkling."

"We—" An arrow slammed into Vesa's shoulder, and she cried out as she stumbled back, clutching the shaft.

"Vesa!" Calliope cried, catching her before she hit her knees.

I twisted around to find a group of males surrounding us, two standing back a safe distance with bows drawn.

"I knew you'd lead us right to her." My heart stilled at the sound of Atticus' voice, and the flames flared beneath my skin as he stepped from the shadows of the trees, greeting me with a sickening smile. Realization dawned on me. They would have spent all their time searching the village, would never have thought to search elsewhere. Calliope and Vesa had been hidden, had been out of Father's reach...

And I'd fucking lead Atticus and his men right to them.

"You two get out of here!" I yelled, placing myself in front of Calliope and Vesa.

"I can't leave you!" Calliope sobbed, and I spared a moment to look back, finding Vesa pushing Calliope behind her.

"Get her to safety!" I hadn't met the king, but if Vesa trusted him, I had no option but to trust her word. I turned to the guards stalking toward me, weapons drawn. "Get her to Lord Damien!"

"Come on," Vesa said, her voice pained.

"No, please," Calliope begged. "We can't leave. They'll kill him!"

Vesa grunted, and I looked over my shoulder to find her falling back to her knees, sweat beading on her brow. Her skin had turned sickly, and she panted, clutching the arrow in her shoulder.

"Vesa?" Calliope crouched next to her, eyes full of worry. "What's wrong? Look at me."

"She won't be getting far," the bowman said with a cocky grin, "Not with Aethersbane in her system."

My heart shuddered. Fuck. Aethersbane was a toxic plant native to the Godsrealm, the toxin harvested and used as a poison to render fae and other magical beings of Elythias powerless. I didn't even think it was legal to harvest and use. She would be cut off from her magic, weak, unable to fight back.

"Fucking bastard!" I yelled and charged at the bowman.

Atticus stepped back as more guards swarmed us, cutting off my path to the male nocking another arrow. "Take them."

I slammed my fist into one guard's face before another crashed into me, arms wrapped around my waist. We hit the ground, and I grunted before fighting to get out from under him. We rolled, grappling with one another until I managed to wedge him beneath me. I punched him again and again until his blood splattered my fist, my face. Hands grabbed my arms, halting my assault.

I fought their hold as they hoisted me off the bloodied male on the ground. "Let me go!"

Calliope's scream drew my attention to them as guards tore Calliope and Vesa apart.

"Lord Damien won't stand for this!" Vesa shouted weakly as she fought the hold of her captors. The guard twisted the shaft of the arrow protruding from her shoulder, and she cried out.

"Lord Damien will know nothing of tonight," Atticus said lowly as he stalked toward her, and he nodded to the guard at her back.

The guard drew a dagger and ran it across her throat, crimson spilling down the front of her armor, and my heart plummeted.

"No!" Calliope screamed. "No! Please, Gods, no!"

My knees gave out as the guards forced me to the ground, the world going silent as Calliope tried to get to Vesa who grabbed at her throat, blood bubbling from the wound as she gasped for air. Then her arms fell slack at her sides, the light dying out in her pale violet eyes.

The guard tossed her lifeless body to the ground, her mouth moving but no sound coming forth before she went still.

Calliope screamed Vesa's name, tears coating her cheeks.

"Leave her for the darklings," Atticus said, turning to walk toward the tree line once more. "No one will search for a deserter."

A deserter? Would that be the story they'd fucking spin when they realized Vesa was missing? It wasn't enough that they would fucking murder her for defending someone she loved, they'd dishonor her memory by naming her a deserter?

"You fucking bastards!" I shouted. "I'll kill you!"

Calliope crumbled, her cries filling the clearing as she was dragged off back toward town, toward Father and whatever awaited us.

"Get your hands off her!" I shouted, and Atticus stepped in front of me, blocking my view as they dragged Calliope away. "You fucking bastard! I'll rip your throat out!"

Atticus smiled cruelly at me before leaning down to pat my cheek. "Oh, I don't think you will."

"Barrett?" Lucia said, and I looked to find her face full of worry. Something deep in my chest twisted at the concern. I hated that I felt anything, that, despite everything I'd endured, despite everyone who had betrayed me, I still wanted to believe there might be good in her.

"Sometimes, no matter how much you fight it, the Fates have other plans," I said, my voice eerily calm despite my clenched fists. "You may be important, but the Fates deemed me disposable. That's all I'll ever be: a means to someone's end." Her lips parted, but I didn't give her the room to argue. "We don't all have the blessings of a goddess, *Your Majesty*."

"What did you do now?" Micah's voice reached my ears over the sea of voices in the pub. It was a busy night, full of warriors and trainees winding down from the day's training.

"Why do you think I did anything?" I grumbled and took a swig of the Ambrosia liquor in my glass. I grimaced at the way it burned a path down my throat, but I relished in the pain.

Pain drowned everything else out.

"What'll it be tonight, Micah?" the pub owner, Semele, asked as she grabbed a glass, the torchlight dancing off her dark skin.

"Make it strong, Semele," he said.

"You got it!" she called back and got to work preparing him a drink.

"Lucia looked a little defeated when I saw her earlier," he said without looking at me. "You wouldn't happen to know anything about that, would you?"

Another sigh crawled out of my lungs, and I looked down at my half-empty glass. No matter how much I tried to ignore the guilt that had nagged at me, I couldn't. I had avoided her ever since our conversation, hiding out here all evening.

"She doesn't know what she's getting involved in," I said, knocking back the last of my drink and setting the glass down. "It's better if she stays out of it."

Micah huffed a laugh. "Clearly, you haven't learned how hard-headed that female is."

Semele slid a glass of something in front of Micah before taking my empty one.

"She doesn't know how to give up," he said, his voice softening. "And she won't if she sees your worth."

I rose from my stool, setting down a heavier than necessary amount of coin to make up for the troubles I'd caused Semele my first night out. Lucia might not have liked how I was spending the money she'd given me, but I didn't care. She should have thought of that before she pulled me out of that cell and given me the means of getting into trouble on her watch.

Semele's brows rose at the money before she looked at me. I dipped my head, hoping she got the message, and turned toward the doorway. "Well she can give up. I'm not some fucking charity case."

"Oh, no, you don't," Micah said, downing his drink and jumping up from his stool. He coughed harshly. "Fuck, that shit's strong."

"That's what you asked for!" Semele said with a chuckle.

I stormed out of the pub and onto the street, unable to stand the mass of conversations overtaking the pub any longer—or perhaps I was simply running away again.

Irritation swelled in my chest as Micah stumbled out behind me. "Where do you think you're going?"

"Getting away from you," I grumbled, walking blindly down the street with no clear destination. It was too early to head for the barracks, and I wasn't ready to face Lucia again, not with the way I'd shut her out earlier. Not with the pained look she'd given me before I had left her alone in that hallway.

Micah followed after me, and I was about ready to slug the stubborn bastard. "Look, I know she put you in charge of me. I *promise* I won't get into a fight, so you can scurry off to wherever you'd like and enjoy your evening."

"Nope, we're gonna get to the bottom of this," he said with a smile, and I rolled my eyes.

I rounded the corner of an alley, not caring where we ended up. "What is with you fucking people?"

"We don't give up on our family," he said, meeting my long strides.

"Oh, and I'm family? You don't even know me."

"The moment you joined The Order, you became part of our family," he said. "Lucia sees it, and I do too. You're a good guy, Barrett, no matter how much you deny it."

I was so over this optimistic bullshit. "*Shit*. You've opened my eyes. Why don't you get Lucia? Get the other members of The Order while you're at it. Let's have a bonfire and celebrate my rehabilitation from dungeon scum to upstanding citizen."

Micah arched a brow. "You're not fooling anyone with the attitude."

I didn't stop, didn't slow my pace as we continued aimlessly through the streets. "Then what will it take to get you guys off my back?"

"Just let us in." Micah placed his hand on my shoulder. "Let us help you."

"What makes you think you *can* help me? It won't change anything." I hated how his words tore at me, how a part of me wanted to give in. "It's too late for help."

His voice softened. "It's never too late."

Tell that to her.

"What happened to you?" he pressed. "You are so hellbent on shutting all of us out. Why?"

I don't know why I bothered responding, but the words came without my permission.

"Because when someone puts their trust in me…" My words fell short as my feet came to a halt. I hadn't realized exactly where they had led me, and something fractured in my chest at the painful reminder of the truth, of why I could never allow anyone inside again.

Burned remains stood before us. Even the stone hadn't been spared from the flame's wrath. I hadn't come to this place since I'd been released, hadn't wanted to see it. It was as if time had stopped that night, what little remained of our home abandoned, nearly untouched.

"…I fail them."

CHAPTER 9

THALIA

Barrett Stratos.

My eyes passed over the paperwork for his enlistment into The Order's recruitment program. Something had nagged in the back of my mind from the moment I first saw him training with Micah two days prior. I had never seen the male before…

So why did I feel as if I had?

There was no mention of his background, his family, his history—just his name, and his description.

I knew the family name—the current head of House Stoicheion was a Stratos—but I had no knowledge of him having a relative named Barrett.

"Who are you?" I mumbled under my breath.

"Thank you for helping me get these done," Damien said from where he sat at his desk. I looked to find him bent over a stack of parchment, quill tipping back and forth furiously as he wrote.

Marcus huffed a laugh. "You'd never be on time with anything if it wasn't for us."

"Our impeccably organized king would *never* be late submitting his work," I said with a knowing look.

"All right, you two," he chided. "I'm not behind, I just need to get this done before I head to the Godsrealm for a few days." Damien's voice seemed to tip off at the end, as if he had said something he hadn't intended to.

"You're leaving for the Godsrealm?" I asked, arching a brow as I set a stack of completed paperwork on his desk for him to sign.

Marcus and Damien glanced at each other nervously, and I frowned. He rarely went to the Godsrealm. There were those of us who did, either for diplomatic missions with The Twelve or for importing goods the way Semele did, but rarely did he join.

"Speaking of the Godsrealm," Marcus said, seeming to shift the direction of the conversation. "Vivienne should be back tomorrow."

Damien's brows rose. "I received word Tobias' mate welcomed a baby girl a few months ago in the Godsrealm."

"I didn't even know she was pregnant," Marcus said, his lips pressing together. "I guess I shouldn't be surprised. Tobias doesn't exactly like me. I don't expect him to say anything, but I thought Vivienne might've at least mentioned it to me."

"That is odd," I said. I hadn't seen Vivienne since she suddenly up and left for the Godsrealm nearly a year prior. I hadn't realized she and Tobias were close. They were siblings, yes, but Vivienne had faced backlash when she and Marcus were bonded without her family's blessing. Perhaps things had been resolved.

"I haven't really spoken with Tobias. I only heard the news through Xavier," Damien said. "I wish I could give you more insight."

"Why did they go to the Godsrealm to begin with?" I asked.

"I'm not entirely sure," Marcus said, his brows furrowing. "Vivienne seems to avoid my questions in her letters."

"Why didn't you tell me?" Damien said, lifting his attention from the paper on his desk.

"You've had enough on your plate," Marcus said. "Besides, I'm sure she's all right. I'm probably overthinking things."

"It isn't a diplomatic mission?" I asked, glancing at Damien, who seemed to contemplate that thought.

"I honestly don't know what they're there for," he explained. "I don't think they have family there, but I might be wrong. I'm not always involved in the actions of The Council. It could very well be a visit with one of the courts."

It could very well have been. The Kyrios did act as emissaries if they chose, but usually, they sent someone in their stead. It wasn't normal for them to bring their families.

"Perhaps it's just a family vacation to repair things," I suggested.

Marcus let out a low breath. "I'm eager to see her. The last letter I received from her, she sounded… I don't know, off."

I tilted my head. "What do you mean?"

He shrugged. "I can't quite place it, but something about how she's spoken to me in her letters since she left has just been…off. She left so suddenly to begin with, and there were a few times where the gaps between her responses to my letters went a bit longer than I'd like."

"I wish I didn't need you here as much as I do," Damien said in a near apology.

Marcus shook his head. "I'm sure she's all right."

"Mated males *can* be a little overprotective at times," I said in a teasing tone as I returned my attention to my work.

"Yeah," Marcus said, narrowing his eyes on me, but he shook his head. "It's been a little over a month since I received her last letter. I'm sure she's been busy helping Tobias and Jesta with the new babe."

"A new baby is a huge deal," Damien said.

"I'm probably just being an overprotective mated male," Marcus said, his voice full of sarcasm as he slid me a teasing grin.

I snickered.

"Thalia, can you take this to Salwa for her to log in the Archivallia?" Damien asked, gathering the mess of parchment papers before tapping them into a clean stack.

"Sure," I said, rising from my seat and hurrying to his desk to take them.

"Try not to worry your little head, Marcus," I said, nudging him. "I'm sure Vivienne is well and just as eager to see you as you are her."

He gave me a half smile. "I'll try not to."

I left them to their work and hurried down the hall toward the small study, the one where Salwa worked when she wasn't tending to the Archivallia. Muffled conversation reached my ears as I neared the door to Salwa's office. I stepped closer and stiffened when I heard Lucia's voice.

"…the complete file on Barrett's case yet?"

Salwa's voice was muffled and more distant, likely sitting at her desk at the far end of the room. "I finally found it. It was oddly misfiled."

"That's unlike you to be disorganized," Lucia said, confusion lacing her voice.

"I haven't handled this file since I cataloged it in"—the faint sound of flipping pages reached my ear—"1422. After his trial."

I stiffened. Trial?

"So someone else took it?" Lucia asked.

Gods, I shouldn't be listening in on this, but I couldn't bring myself to knock, couldn't pull away.

"It's been modified," Salwa said after a brief silence.

Footsteps, ones I assumed were Lucia's, echoed off the wood. "Modified? By who?"

"I'm not sure. Take a look."

My heart hammered. If Salwa, the Tabularius, was unaware of a change, it was an unauthorized modification.

Lucia let out a breath. "I thought it odd for a prisoner of forty-seven years to suddenly be in the lineup for execution with no explanation."

My heart launched into my throat.

"Something doesn't feel right, Salwa. He's had past incidents during his imprisonment, but nothing warranting execution. When I spoke with Damien, he informed me it wasn't run by him or approved by The Council."

"His original sentence was for life in the dungeons." There was a moment of silence, and I pressed my ear closer to the door. "The records of the trial state there were some who opposed the decision, given it was a Kyrios who he murdered."

My hand rose to my mouth, muffling a gasp. How was he not put to death for murdering a Kyrios? Why would Lucia bring him into The Order? Oh, Gods. Micah was working with him. What if he did something to him? He needed to know.

"Were there any witnesses?" Lucia asked.

Pages flipped. "There was one."

"Who?"

"His uncle, Atticus Stratos," Salwa said.

There was a moment of silence.

"I believe the circumstances of Elias Stratos' death were not as they were presented," Lucia said, pulling me back.

The world stilled. *Oh, Gods.*

He wasn't the son of Atticus, but the son of a past Kyrios of House Stoicheion.

"What do you mean?" Salwa asked.

Her voice softened, and I tried to listen. "I have reason to suspect that Atticus may have given false testimony. I believe Elias' death was not malicious but in self-defense, or something of that nature."

"Why would Barrett defending himself result in not only the death of his father, but of his mother and sister as well?"

I stopped breathing.

"I don't believe he murdered his sister," Lucia said. She paused for a moment. "I think—"

I stiffened at the sound of footsteps approaching down the hall and straightened before knocking and cracking the door open.

Lucia and Salwa both looked at me, brows raised.

"Hi—Oh, Lucia!" I said, feigning surprise in the hopes they hadn't realized I had listened in on their conversation. "I hope I'm not interrupting anything."

Lucia's eyes softened and she smiled warmly, which left guilt curdling in my stomach. "Not at all, Thalia."

I turned to Salwa and extended the papers to her. "Damien asked me to bring these to you to catalog in the Archivallia."

"Oh, perfect. I'll see it done," she said as she took them.

I headed for the door, eager to get away, fearful they might realize what I had done.

"I hope to see you around, Thalia," Lucia said as I took hold of the doorknob.

I looked back at her, her silver eyes near glowing as she smiled at me, and I didn't miss the smug, knowing look in them.

She knew.

I sat at the dinner table later that night, rolling a small potato along my plate with my fork, my mind reeling with what I had overheard only a few hours earlier.

If what Lucia said was true, did that mean Barrett had been wrongfully tried? Wrongfully imprisoned? Was he framed?

Atticus Stratos. He was the Kyrios of House Stoicheion. I didn't know how he came to be Kyrios, hadn't been involved in the matters of The Council for as long as I'd been part of The Order. To think he had testified against Barrett... Had he truly lied? Why would he do such a thing? Lucia was no fool; she saw through more than any of us did, and I trusted her judgment. She even seemed to know I had been listening.

How long had she known? Had she continued to speak, knowing I was eavesdropping? If so, why?

I couldn't wrap my mind around it.

Micah was equally quiet across the table—unusually quiet.

"I saw you training a new recruit the other day," I said absentmindedly as I speared some green beans and took a bite.

He cleared his throat. "Uh, yeah. Lucia sort of dropped him in my lap."

"I saw his file when I was working with Damien."

"What did it say?" he asked, scooping some food onto his fork.

"That's what's strange. There was no history on him. No family, nothing," I said, watching him. "When Zephyr asked about him, Lucia basically said it was classified."

He blinked, seemingly surprised by that statement, and I narrowed my eyes.

"Did she tell you anything?"

He hesitated, his lips parting then closing.

I lowered my fork. "You know something, don't you?"

"Not much," he admitted. "Only that he was imprisoned. When she told me about him, it was in typical Lucia fashion. Vague as shit."

I couldn't help but smile at that. She definitely worked in mysterious ways, always behind the scenes, guiding us like chess pieces. It wasn't in the way of pawns; no, it was more of nudging us into a place that fit us perfectly, or as fate would have us.

"Um…speaking of Lucia," Micah said, and my brows rose.

He swallowed, and I frowned. Something was wrong.

"I'm leaving next week for a few days on a mission."

I blinked, resting my fork on the plate. "Where are you going?"

He scratched the back of his neck. "It's classified."

I frowned, and Damien's words flew across my thoughts. He was also leaving for a few days…for business in the Godsrealm.

I rose. "Are you going with Damien to the Godsrealm?"

He blinked. "He told you?"

"Told me what?" I asked, laying my hands on the table. "Why are you going to the Godsrealm?"

He swallowed, eyes darting around as if searching for something. "It's…it's nothing you need to worry about."

"You're going to the Godsrealm. Damien is going to the Godsrealm, something he rarely does. I feel that it *is* something I need to worry about." I paused for a moment and pinned Micah with a look. "Is Lucia going as well?"

He couldn't hide the confirming look in his eyes.

"What is the mission for, Micah?"

His shoulders sagged, and he let out a sigh. "Someone's reorganizing The Pits."

CHAPTER 10

THE GIRL WITH STORMY EYES

60 years prior

The forest had darkened by the time we stopped to make camp, a soft blue glow from the night sky slipping through the thick canopy of towering trees. As I looked skyward, I could almost make out the two massive moons amidst the stars through breaks in the branches high above us. They were magnificent. The trees here were gigantic compared to the ones in the Mortalrealm, so high that I wondered if the branches danced with the glittering constellations. Or perhaps I was just so small.

I wasn't sure how much time had passed as we trekked through the wood, and I tried my best to remember the direction the cave was in, clinging to the hope I could find my way home to Mama and Papa, to the boy whose coat was the only piece of home I had left. Rhyas was settled up against the trunk of a large tree as he surveyed the camp. A few other fae settled in around the fire, the other children they had carried still unconscious on the ground at their sides.

"Why won't they wake up?" I asked.

"They've been put under a spell," Rhyas said, his face unreadable as he pulled something from his pouch. "They won't wake until we make it to Nastra."

My brows furrowed. "Why did *I* wake up?"

"You're unlike the other children," he said. "The beast within you does not tame easily."

I eyed him wearily. How did he know I was a shifter of House Thiríon?

"I can smell it on you, sense the beast slumbering," Rhyas explained, as if seeing the unspoken question in my eyes, and held out a piece of dried meat. "Hungry?"

My stomach was hollowed out from the days of near starvation after the darkling attack, and my mouth watered at the sight of the meat. I took it without question, shoving it into my mouth, and groaned at the salty taste.

He chuckled and continued eating. "How old are you?"

I swallowed the last bite and was nearly ready to beg him for more. "Eight."

Sadness flitted across his face. "I'm sorry."

My body stiffened, and I lifted my gaze to him. Sorry?

"Try to get some sleep. We leave at first light," he said as he settled against the trunk, tugging his hood over his eyes before folding his arms across his chest. "And don't think of wandering off unless you want to get eaten."

I swallowed and took in the forest surrounding us, the darkness too thick, the animals too quiet. What creatures lived in these woods? I leaned into the trunk next to him, pulling the boy's coat tighter around me as I closed my eyes just enough to look like I was trying to sleep. It didn't matter that there might be creatures out there; I only needed to sneak past them. I just needed to wait until Rhyas and the others fell asleep.

Then I could slip away.

It was a couple of hours before his breathing settled into a slow, even pace, and the rest of the camp had quieted. One of the fae had stayed awake, watching the camp. I pretended to sleep, lids cracked just enough to watch him. He would rise periodically to walk the campsite, and the next time he did so—his back turning to me—I glanced to Rhyas, whose eyes remained shut. My pulse thrummed in my ears as I quietly eased away from the trunk, gaze locked on the fae male as he stepped away from us. Then, I slipped into the dark of the forest.

I could barely see around me, the silence of the forest unnatural and unnerving. My feet were light as I stepped carefully through the darkness, my heart pounding as my ears narrowed in on every nearby sound. The moss cushioned each step as I wandered, returning in the direction we'd come, and I nearly tripped over countless roots and stones in the dark.

A branch snapped nearby, and I froze, my heart stuttering as a low growl rippled from the darkness.

Oh Gods... Oh Gods, oh Gods!

The instinct flitted across my thoughts, senses heightening as the beast bristled deep within me.

Run.

"Girl?" Rhyas called from the darkness.

I glanced over my shoulder, unsure if I should run toward or away from him. No. He was no protector. I wouldn't be safe with him. Before I could linger longer, before I could see what hunted me, I took off, feet barely meeting the mossy ground as I ran for the cave.

A snarl reached my ears as I gasped, pushing myself forward.

"Where are you, girl?" Rhyas shouted, his voice growing closer, almost concerned.

Light stretched into the forest at my back as their torches painted the forest in a warm glow. Whatever pursued me shrieked, but I didn't look back, didn't risk falling or being captured. The trees parted before me, and the cave came into view. My heart soared.

Home!

Run faster, little one!

Moss turned to stone as I entered the cave, that terrible magic reaching for me as I neared what I could only assume was the veil—the border between the Mortalrealm and the Godsrealm.

"Stop!" Rhyas' voice echoed through the cave.

Would he follow me this far, or would he give up? Would he chase me into the Mortalrealm? I couldn't be far from the veil. Its presence danced over my skin like a whisper of wind. As I began to feel hope that I might escape, icy dread washed over my skin, instinct flaring so hard and fast, my body nearly collapsed on the cave floor.

A hiss echoed from the dark depths of the cavern, and I stopped breathing as something slid into view through the tunnel, blocking my path. I couldn't move, my body frozen.

The pounding of Rhyas' feet was nearly drowned out by my pulse pounding in my ears as the massive creature met my gaze. Its body was a mass of scales and shadow, its tongue slipping from its lips as it sized me up, its six slitted eyes—the eyes that had watched us as we'd passed through earlier that day—promised death.

The creature's head rose, lips parting to reveal fangs as it hissed at me, ready to strike.

Rhyas slid to a stop in front of me, his hand rising as the creature's head shot forward. "I have Eris' blessings, Scylla!" he shouted, his voice echoing to every corner of the cavern, fear painting each word as it left his tongue. "Eris' blessings!"

The creature halted before it could crash into us, stretched jaws inches from devouring us both. Its six glowing eyes roamed over him, as if assessing him, before it lowered its head, coming so close that I stopped breathing as I gripped Rhyas' shirt with trembling hands.

Scylla's tongue slipped from its lips briefly, flicking against Rhyas' extended hand, which I noticed was inked with something. His body was tense, chest heaving as he stared down the beast. A hiss slipped from its throat before it turned and slithered back into the dark depths of the cave.

I couldn't move, couldn't breathe as I stood frozen behind him.

Rhyas whirled and grasped both my arms. "You fucking idiot. What were you thinking? Do you have a death wish?"

My vision blurred, my knees threatening to give out beneath me.

"I told you to stay with me! You're safest with me!" When I didn't answer, he groaned, his head falling forward as he let out an exasperated sigh. "Come on, we need to get back to the others."

He took my hand, and I couldn't bring myself to fight him as he led me out of the cave and back toward the camp. Tears rolled down my cheeks as I stumbled at his side, my attention latched onto the cave as it slowly vanished from sight.

"I'm sorry," he whispered. "I'd let you go back if I could."

His pace seemed to slow, as if he was considering something, and he glanced down at me before kneeling to my level. "Do you remember your name?"

I frowned. Why would I not remember my n—

All thoughts eddied out of my mind as I tried to recall my name. The name my parents had given me was...gone, as if it had never been mine to begin with. My hand slipped from his as I clutched my head, racking my brain, scrambling for the name.

L—

Ly—

Oh Gods. How could I not remember my name? Rhyas winced at the look of terror on my face.

"They took your name," His pity-filled eyes lingered on me, as if he understood my fear. "There's no going home for you. You belong to Arden now."

Dread crawled over my skin at the thought of what awaited me.

CHAPTER II

BARRETT

"You don't have to remain silent, you know," Lucia said as she worked to sharpen one of her throwing knives. "You *can* talk."

I inspected my dagger, turning the blade over. It had been two days since I'd left her in the hallway; she hadn't stayed away for long. "What exactly do you want with me?"

She didn't react to my question, her attention fixed on her blade held against the grindstone, her foot pumping the peddle, turning the stone as she sharpened it.

"There is nothing I want from you," she said finally, lifting the blade to inspect it.

She's lying. Micah's lying. They always want something.

"I knew your father, Elias."

I winced inwardly, my grip tightening on the hilt of my dagger.

She continued to focus on her blade. "I didn't like him."

The admission cut through me, nearly shattering the mask of indifference I had donned for decades. An odd quiet followed and I realized I had stopped working on my dagger, as had she. She sat up, the stone wheel rolling to a slow stop.

"He always made decisions that benefited him instead of our people," she said, sitting back and wiping the sweat from her brow with the back of her forearm. "We fought during The Council meetings often over the most trivial of matters."

"In your past life?" The words slipped from my lips without my permission.

Her eyes softened as she turned to me and nodded. "If you could tell me what truly happened that night, I might be able to help you."

Something inside me recoiled the moment she pried, fear and anger flooding my system. There was a part of me that wanted to trust her, wanted to believe I could trust *someone* after all these decades. Another part of me couldn't. The last time I'd opened up to someone about what happened...

She was dead.

She was dead, and I...

The wooden door leading out of the prison chambers groaned as it opened, spilling light into the dark cell, and I flinched away from it. It was the first light I'd seen in Gods knew how many days.

How long had it been since she'd taken her last breath? How long had it been since I'd heard her voice?

I love you most.

I didn't even have her last letter, didn't even have a portrait of her. It had all been lost, every scrap, all proof of her existence wiped from the face of this realm in a matter of moments.

"Barrett Stratos," the guard said, his voice sharp. I didn't spare him a look, my eyes held captive by the delicate gold chain hanging from my wrist. It was all I had left in the hollow, numb wake of what had happened.

How had it gone so badly so quickly?

"You have a visitor," the guard said, kicking the bars before me.

"Gods, you smell terrible." The voice was familiar and full of pity. I lifted my gaze to find Jissena, Atticus' bonded, standing from the other side of the bars, her face full of a kind of sorrow.

I couldn't even feel the flames surge within me at the sight of her, my magic brought to heel by the warded iron shackles on my wrists and the bars caging me in. It felt wrong, like a violation, to be cut off from my magic. It had always been there, even if I couldn't use it. It was as if they had taken away a part of me.

As if I hadn't lost enough.

My chest swelled with fury so hot, the room should be set ablaze as I remembered all the things her bonded had done.

"What do you want?" I growled.

She nodded to the guard, taking the lantern from him before he stepped out and shut the door behind him, cutting off the light of day I'd craved for too many endless nights. Her knees met the stone floor. I stiffened, watching her movements, but she lifted the strap of a satchel over her head and pulled a small loaf of bread and a waterskin from within it. I swallowed at the sight of it, my stomach hollowed out from lack of food. They'd withheld food and water, only giving me the bare minimum needed to keep me alive until my trial.

"I want to help," she said, her voice soft, sympathetic as she held the bread and waterskin out to me.

I stumbled toward her and grabbed the waterskin before downing the water, coughing as it hit my parched throat. She settled back, resting her hands on her lap as she watched me tear into the bread and drink the water desperately.

"Why would you want to help me? Atticus is your bonded," I said, peering at her as I bit into the bread. The lingering warmth from the oven hit my tongue, and I groaned at the taste.

"I know what your father was truly like," she said, her voice softening. I couldn't even bring myself to react. "I know what happened that night. Poor Calliope. She didn't deserve that."

"No, she didn't."

"I'm disgusted by what Atticus did," she said, her voice cracking, her eyes glistening. "I overheard him speaking with one of his guards about it. If he knew I was here, I don't want to think what he would do to me, but I can't sit back and watch what he's doing."

"What's he doing?" I asked.

"He somehow convinced The Council of a terrible lie." My blood iced over as she spoke, her voice shaking, tears dotting her eyelashes. "He's going to testify against you, paint you as the one responsible for your family's deaths to clear his name of his involvement."

My hands balled into fists. I didn't care about Father and Mother. I'd take the responsibility for what happened to them. They deserved it...but Calliope...

Every bit of truth, every bit of what Father had done to us behind closed doors, how he had wronged so many... It would be covered up; Atticus would see to that. I had no doubts about it, and I would take the fall for him.

It should be him in this cell, rotting away, up for execution for aiding in Father's corruption, for his abuse of power, for the abuse he had inflicted on us our entire lives.

"They won't let you speak at the trial," she said, and the air halted in my lungs. "Your father had too many friends in influential positions. Many have called for your immediate execution, but the laws require a trial be held with evidence presented."

Evidence that Atticus had likely tainted.

"Atticus is a witness, but so are you," she explained.

And yet, I would be left without a voice, without a way to defend myself, to tell them the truth of what had happened. What was the point? Atticus had far more connections than I did. I was nobody compared to him, a murderer in the eyes of many.

"If you allow me, I will speak on your behalf," she said, her voice near pleading.

I stiffened. "Why would you do that? You said so yourself: you're terrified of what Atticus would do to you if he learned you were even here. In speaking out in my defense, you would be placing a target on your back."

Guilt and sadness dulled her eyes. "And if I sat back and watched you die for doing what should've been done a long time ago, I would deserve infinite torment in the depths of Tartarus."

"You know what truly happened that night?" I asked, leaning against the bars.

She swallowed and nodded. "I only need you to sign this so I may testify on your behalf. I can share your side."

"Why would they allow you to testify for me if they won't allow me to speak? You weren't there."

"Because I overheard Atticus," she said, glancing back and forth down the hall through the dungeons before pulling a folded piece of parchment from her pocket. "I can testify not what you shared, but what Atticus did in his own words. Then, I can share your side of the story. This gives me the ability to speak on your behalf, to represent you."

I narrowed my eyes on her before looking down at it. Fuck, was this my only option? If what she said was true, I would be walking into a death sentence, stripped of any ability to defend myself. It would be Atticus' word and his word alone. Fucking bastard. I wished he had burned with the rest of them, wished I had watched him turn to ashes for what he had done.

Jissena remained silent as I contemplated my options.

I had none.

"I did murder them," I admitted. "My father and mother, their guards. They burned."

"I know," she said, her voice wavering. "And they deserve to burn a thousand times more for how much they made you suffer."

I looked down at the piece of parchment. There wasn't much to read. It essentially stated that I gave Jissena the ability to testify on my behalf, to speak for me, as she said it would.

"Together we could put Atticus in this cell," I said, glancing at her, and I caught a hint of hesitation. "What would you do if he gets thrown in here and you're left alone to deal with the fallout?"

She lifted her chin, her eyes lighting with a sort of determination. "I would sleep with a clear conscience."

"You were given an unfair trial," Lucia said, her silver eyes dulling as they slid from mine. "The system was manipulated, and our laws failed you."

To say they had failed me was an understatement. They hadn't failed me, but they had failed Calliope. They failed Vesa, who, for all I knew, had been left to rot in the forest, her memory dishonored.

"What do you know of it?" I asked, arching a brow.

She shook her head. "Not enough. Your file had an unauthorized modification, and the more I look into it, the more things don't add up. Portions of the file are missing."

My grip tightened on my dagger. Of course, someone had tampered with it. I stared down at the blade in my hands, my skin heating. "You told Micah I was up for execution."

She nodded. "When the Tabularius, Salwa, looked into it further, it wasn't part of your original sentencing. It was added recently without authorization. Damien didn't authorize it. He had no knowledge of it, and neither did The Council."

When I didn't speak, she leaned in, reaching out to rest a hand atop mine. "Who wants you dead, Barrett?"

Voices echoed through the grand hall, the attendees shouting over each other. I barely made out curses thrown my way, the demands for my death. The guards at my back stood at attention, their hands resting atop the hilts of their swords. I lifted my gaze to The Council, eight heads sitting side by side in their chairs. One chair—the one Father would have taken— was left empty. The king stared down at me from where he sat, donning the immortal crown made of shadow-stained dimós branches, adorned with starlight imprisoned in gemstones. Damien Archonis, a living legend for what he had done for our kingdom in the near four hundred years since he'd been crowned after his parent's assassination. His eyes were cold, unreadable... tired. I'd seen him a few times before but had never been introduced.

"The witness may step forth," a voice called, and I flexed my hands, hating the icy touch of the warded iron shackling my wrists—how it snuffed out my magic that wanted nothing more than to watch him burn.

Atticus stepped forward, avoiding my glare.

Jude's father and Kyrios of House Leukós, Hestis, spoke from where he sat at the end, his short silver hair swept back from his face. I watched, unable to speak against him, to share of his personal ties to Elias and whatever deal they had formed over the binding of Calliope to his son.

"Atticus Stratos," Hestis said, his cold gaze sliding to my uncle, "you are here to testify as to what occurred the night Elias and his family were murdered. Do you swear to speak true?"

"I do," Atticus said.

Hestis dipped his head to him briefly. "Share your knowledge."

"Your Majesty, Kyrios of The Council," Atticus said, his head swiveling as he looked to each and every one of them. "I stand before you to beg justice be swiftly dealt for the murder of my brother, Elias Stratos, his bonded, Cassia Stratos, and their daughter, Calliope Stratos."

I stiffened.

"I implore you to share what happened three nights ago with the rest of the congregation," the Kyrios of House Latros said, her head held high as her hands lay folded against her cream healer robes.

My stomach turned as I imagined all the different ways Atticus could spin this to his benefit, the lies he would weave.

"I was summoned by Elias that night when Calliope disappeared before her binding. She had agreed to be bound to Jude Galanis to form a union between our houses."

My skin heated despite the wards, anger flaring deep in my chest, and I ground my teeth together. I wanted to protest, wanted to correct the lies he was already laying out, but Jissena's warning flitted across my mind.

You must be calm. Don't let your anger get the better of you. If you're calm and show them you aren't the dangerous person he will paint you out to be, you will stand a better chance.

"He worried for her safety, as did I," he said, and I bristled as I remembered how cruelly he had smiled as he set his men on us, when he watched as they slit Vesa's throat in front of Calliope. Her screams haunted my thoughts in every moment since, and I feared they would forever.

"We searched for her, only to find she had abandoned the village, fleeing her oath," Atticus said, his face solemn, as if he was saddened, and my gut twisted.

Gods, he was twisting the truth far worse than I could have imagined, painting her as a deserter, an oath breaker. She had never agreed to be bound, instead forced by Father. She hadn't been given a choice.

He continued. "We encountered a warrior of the order, Vesa Lanis."

For a moment, I almost wondered if I had imagined Lord Damien stiffen, a flicker of something passing across his face as his brows pinched together.

"We only wanted to talk, to bring her back to safety," Atticus said. "She was crazed, and it wasn't until she attacked one of my men that we realized she was using Aethersbane to render them powerless."

White hot fury shattered my thoughts like blistering wyvern's breath. My chest heaved as I wrestled down the urge to strangle him, forcing myself to listen to this monster tell one lie after another, allowing it to stoke the slumbering flame until I could unleash it in a full untethered blaze to burn him alive in the most agonizing way. I could still hear Vesa's cry of pain as the arrow—laced with the Aethersbane **he** *had used—pierced her shoulder, rendering her powerless.*

No. They couldn't believe this.

"A warrior of The Order attacked a member of the aristocracy?" the Kyrios of House Aíma said, his brows furrowing.

Atticus nodded. "We tried to reason with her, but the moment she took out one of my men, we knew she wouldn't listen to reason."

"Where is Vesa?" Lord Damien asked, leaning forward to rest his elbows atop his knees, lacing his fingers together.

"She wouldn't come quietly, tried to kill more of my men when we approached her. Unfortunately, she was killed in the process." He pressed his hand

to his chest. "I wouldn't force my men to allow her to kill them. They defended themselves."

Lies. Fucking lies!

Vesa's face flashed in my mind, her eyes wide, lips parted as she tried and failed to breathe as he'd slit her throat, the scent of her blood filling my nose, as fresh as it had been that night.

"We brought Calliope back," Atticus continued. "She was hysterical, not herself."

"And how did all of this lead to Barrett's involvement?" the Kyrios of House Dendron asked.

"He has always had anger issues—constantly fought with Elias, causing problems for him, getting into trouble during his training for The Order," Atticus explained, and my vision went red.

"Elias voiced his concerns to me regularly. How could someone with such a short temper and dangerous tendencies take his position as Kyrios of House Stoicheion? Barrett would be a terrible fit as Kyrios, so he placed his faith in Calliope's union with Jude. Though Calliope was not born with the gifts of the elements, he hoped she might produce a wielder who could lead as Kyrios in his stead."

My fists shook in the shackles.

"When Barrett learned of this, he went into a rage, accusing Elias, Cassia, and Calliope of plotting to steal his inheritance behind his back," Atticus said. "Elias tried to reason with him, but Barrett attacked him before he could defend himself, and that was when his fire magic spun out of control. He killed not only Cassia and Calliope, but several of my guards as well."

Hestis, the Kyrios of House Leukós, rested his chin against his hand, his assessing gaze passing over me. I held his stare, silently calling him out on his bullshit, for he likely knew the truth of that night. He averted his eyes nervously before looking at Atticus. "The flame of the Stratos family is powerful. It's a miracle you escaped."

"I barely made it out with my life; suffered severe burns," Atticus said, feigning a look of fear. "Thankfully, I was able to reach a healer."

"He's too dangerous!" a voice shouted, and I twisted to look at the crowd of onlookers occupying the rows of seats that curved around the room high above us.

"Someone who could kill their own family can't be trusted!"

"Kinslayer!"

I struggled to breathe as the entire room turned on me. No. They had been turned against me before I even set foot in this place.

"Is there anything more you have to share?" Lord Damien asked.

"There is nothing more, Your Majesty," Atticus said, bowing his head. "Only the request that you serve him with a punishment suited for a murder such as this."

The Kyrios all turned to me, I looked into each of their eyes, finding nothing but pure contempt. Damien rubbed his hand over his jaw.

"Were any remains recovered from the Stratos house?" Damien asked, looking to the other Kyrioses.

The Kyrios of House Leukos shook his head. "The power of the flames was too great. Not even bones remained."

Damien's gaze returned to Atticus, his brows pinched together. "And Vesa's remains?"

Atticus shook his head, feigning a look of regret that boiled my blood. "I did not have the manpower to bring her back with us. And sadly, I don't remember where in the forest we had found them."

Damien let out a sigh and slouched back in his chair. "Vesa was a powerful warrior. I never took her for a deserter."

"I was just as surprised," Atticus said, his voice pained. "It's a shame to lose any warrior, let alone one with such promise. I was in disbelief when I learned they had fled the village."

Hestis looked at Damien. "I sent guards to search for Vesa's remains, but they couldn't locate her. Darklings likely dragged her body off to devour her."

"Shall we continue?" the Kyrios of House Nous asked, and Damien's attention flickered to me briefly before he nodded.

"The accused has relinquished his right to speak to a representative," the Kyrios of House Leukós announced, and my heart faltered.

Relinquished? No. Jissena had told me I wouldn't be allowed to...

Jissena emerged from the doorway behind me, her eyes downcast, hands folded in front of her. The crowd fell into a sea of murmurs and whispers.

"Jissena Stratos," Hestis said, looking down at her. She lifted her chin to meet his gaze. "You stand before us to speak on Barrett's behalf?"

"I do," she said, and something chilled in my bones at the expression on Atticus' face. There was no hint of surprise, none of the anger or fear I expected.

Damien lifted his hand, and the room went quiet. "As the bonded of Atticus, what qualifies you to speak on Barrett's behalf? Is there not a conflict of interest on your part?"

"Cassia was my best friend. I've known Barrett and his sister since they were young. I knew Barrett couldn't have done what he did maliciously," she said, raising her hand to her heart before she reached into her pocket and pulled forth the piece of parchment I had signed.

"He asked for me to speak on his behalf for fear he would not be able to say the right things."

Damien narrowed his eyes as he rested back in his seat. "You may speak."

Jissena nodded. "I visited Barrett yesterday to speak with him. He confided in me his testimony, confessing to his crimes."

I stopped breathing. "What?"

She took a step forward. "He admitted to what occurred, that he had lost his temper and had lost control of his magic. It was an accident that they died."

"You expect us to believe it merely an accident?" someone shouted from the seats high above.

Atticus turned to her, his brows furrowing.

Jissena looked around. "He is young, his magic still new. He was barely a month into his training and has been struggling to maintain control of his magic. The flame Stoicheion is notoriously difficult to control when one's emotions are so out of balance."

No. This wasn't happening.

"Liar..." I muttered, taking a step toward her.

"He admits to his guilt, asking that The Council grant him mercy," she said.

"You liar," I said, stepping forward, "Fucking lia—"

My words cut short, my lips clamping shut. I fought to speak, but something was stopping me. The guards grabbed hold of me, pulling me back.

The room erupted, shouts echoing off the walls, some of the Kyrios rising to their feet as the guards forced me to the ground, the stone bruising my chin.

I growled, my muffled words unable to breach my lips as I fought their hold.

"You relinquished your right to speak," the guard said, and I stiffened at the familiar voice. I twisted to look at the guard over my shoulder. The lower half of his face was masked, darkened gray eyes peering down at me with a horrifying delight, but I recognized his voice immediately.

She won't be getting far—not with Aethersbane in her system.

It was him. The bowman who had fired the poisoned arrow. He had been there that night.

No! This couldn't be fucking happening.

I wrestled against their hold, but my body rose against my will, all control taken by the Nous user at my back. Jissena stumbled away from me, fear flashing across her face as she met my furious gaze.

I'd fucking gut her for this, for tainting Calliope and Vesa's memory, for twisting the truth and lying to me.

"His actions were his own," Atticus argued, and Jissena turned to him.

"You understand fully how difficult it is to master the flame," she said, placing her hand over her heart.

He seemed to consider it a moment, the phony bastard.

The Kyrios of House Latros shifted in her seat. "We cannot expect someone who is so prone to losing control of their magic to just wander the streets, endangering our people."

"I do not ask that he go free, but that we grant him mercy for a grave accident."

Atticus rubbed his jaw. "It would be a shame to lose such talent. Perhaps some mercy would be kind. Maybe he can be rehabilitated and be of use to The Order one day."

The Kyrios of House Aíma arched a brow at her. "Truly, you would beg mercy for a male who could do such a thing to his own flesh and blood?"

"I beg mercy for a young male who has lost everything in a moment of misplaced anger," she said, and I couldn't fathom what their plan could possibly be. "Enough life has been lost."

The Kyrios looked amongst each other, some leaning in to whisper with one another.

"You have a kind heart," Hestis said, rising from his seat, and the room went silent. "We have come to an agreement, then?" He looked between the Kyrios, who all nodded their heads. "Barrett Stratos. As you have been cooperative to this point and admitted to your crimes, you shall not be sentenced to death but shall live out the remainder of your life in the dungeons."

I screamed against my sealed lips. This couldn't be happening.

Hestis looked down at me with disgust. "May you contemplate the lives you took."

Lucia's eyes searched mine, something more real than I had seen in so long lingering within them.

I wasn't sure why, but I finally allowed the wall to crack. "Jissena tricked me."

CHAPTER 12

BARRETT

"Jissena was the one who testified on your behalf," Lucia said, her eyes drifting from mine, as if recounting the records of my trial.

"On my behalf," I scoffed. "The bitch lied to me, tricked me into signing away my right to speak during my trial, and then she threw me to the fucking wolves."

Lucia's lips parted, but she didn't speak.

Good. Maybe that'll shut you up. I rolled my neck before returning to cleaning my freshly sharpened blade, working the oil into the metal.

"Forgive me for not falling at your feet," I said bitterly, hating how quickly I wanted to rebuild the wall to shut her out once again. "Jissena was the last person I trusted to tell my side, and it cost me everything."

"I'm so sorry," Lucia muttered, and I couldn't stomach the pity.

It didn't matter; there was nothing she could do, nothing any of them could do. "If someone wants me dead, it would be Atticus and Jissena. I'm the only one alive who knows of their involvement. Wouldn't make sense that they would wait this long when they had the chance to have me executed during the trial."

Lucia's brows furrowed. "They were involved?"

I nodded, pain slicing through my chest as Vesa's and Calliope's faces flashed across my thoughts. "He…"

She waited for me to speak, but I couldn't bring myself to, couldn't dive deeper into the memory. Every time the thoughts of that night resurfaced, the pain was too much to bear. I wanted to find the fucker, to burn him from the inside out. "I don't know how he'd get clearance to access the Archivallia to modify files, though. Aren't Kyrios the only ones allowed access?"

"He would have access," she said, eyes widening a fraction, as if everything suddenly made sense. "As Kyrios of House Stoicheion, he would have access to the entirety of the Archivallia, even the restricted sections."

The world stilled, and metal clinked against rock as my dagger fell from my hand. "What?"

"You didn't know?" she asked.

"How the fuck would I know?" I growled, shooting to my feet. "As soon as the trial was finished, I was locked up in the dungeons."

"He was named Kyrios a few months after your trial. Surely you got news."

I stormed closer to her. "Have you ever been locked up in the dungeons, *Your Majesty*?"

She flinched at the words but stood her ground, lifting her chin to meet my gaze, and I hated how the act made me respect her more. "No, but—"

"We don't exactly get news in the dungeons," I said, lowering my face to hers, the flame writhing within me. "We get whispers of rumors from time to time if we're lucky, but other than that we are closed off from the world. We don't exist to those enjoying their freedom in the sunshine. We are left to rot, to be forgotten."

"*I* didn't forget you," she said, her voice barely more than a whisper.

The flame dousing at her words, I stilled. Calliope had been the only one who had ever cared, and I'd failed her. She didn't forget? She wasn't even there, hadn't known me.

I turned from her, trying not to give into the sickening hope rising in my chest, shoving it back down to the forgotten place where it had slumbered all these decades. "The fucker got me out of the way so he could take my father's position. Probably used the act he put on during my trial to worm his way into The Council's favor to do so. He likely wants me dead, to ensure no one discovers the truth."

A hand landed on my shoulder, and warmth seeped into my skin.

"Don't think for a moment that he will get away with what he has done," she said, her voice soft yet laced with a powerful promise. "I failed you in my absence, and while Damien tried to seek insight as to whether you were truly responsible for their deaths during your trial, his hands were tied by our laws. Atticus had covered his tracks, hidden evidence that could have proven your innocence. Jissena never should have had access to you before the trial, but the moment she convinced you to sign that paper, Damien was bound. She represented you. There was nothing he could do."

I swallowed back the simmering anger.

"If you can tell me anything at all, it would help me bring them to justice. I understand if it's too difficult to speak about what happened that night. You don't have to talk, but anything you can give me... Names, places, any guards you could identify; it could help me in building the case against him."

"Atticus killed Vesa Lanis," I said, my stomach turning as I remembered her final moments, her blood as it painted her skin in crimson and seeped into her Elythian leathers, Calliope screaming her name.

"Vesa..." A wrinkle formed between Lucia's brows. "She was mentioned. Atticus had labeled her a desert—"

"She wasn't a deserter," I bit out, my hands balling into fists. "She loved Calliope, was helping her escape my father and Hestis Galanis."

"The Kyrios of House Leukos?"

"Calliope was promised to his son Jude. It was never her choice. She had never agreed to anything, and Atticus painted her as an oath breaker, stating she fled her promise. It was all bullshit, every last word. He accused Vesa of using Aethersbane on his guards, but it was *his* guard who used an Aethersbane-tipped arrow to render her powerless before they slit her throat." I couldn't stop the words, the chaos of thoughts spinning out of control like a wildfire as I remembered the day they had brought me before The Council. "One of my guards during the trial was on Atticus' payroll—the fucker who shot her. When Jissena started lying before The Council and I tried to speak out, he silenced me with his *Nous* abilities. He knew, and he watched as I—"

My hands began to shake, anger surging within me, and I drew a deep breath as I felt the flames burn through my control, felt them rage and rise up like a fiery beast ready to burst from its cage, spread its wings, and lay waste to everything in its path.

"Gods, just how deep have his connections reached?" she whispered.

"Pretty fucking deep," I muttered. "I wouldn't be surprised if Hestis knew the truth and was in on it as much as Atticus and Jissena."

Lucia dipped to grab my dagger before brushing dust off the black and silver blade.

"He will pay," she said. "I swear on all I am that he will pay. They all will."

I looked down at the blade, the inscriptions inlaid in the metal. The price of their actions was too steep for them to repay with their lives. No, I wanted them to burn for what they had done. Slowly. "What do you want from me in return?"

She blinked, as if surprised I'd even asked. Then, she smiled, and it was soft, softer than any I'd been gifted in what felt like a lifetime. "Your friendship."

My brows furrowed, my mind warring with the desire to shut her out and the need to give in. I'd been alone for so long, left with no one I could trust, no one I could rely on.

And for a moment, as she stood there, smiling up at me, I saw Calliope, her radiance—a soul far too pure for this world. Neither this realm nor the realm of our creators deserved to bask in her light.

"I can work with what you've given me for now, continue gathering what evidence I can," she said.

Surely, it couldn't be that easy. "Who will believe you? Who will believe me?"

"You have not lied to me once," she said, her eyes softening.

My brows furrowed, but then realization flooded my mind. She was Moira's reincarnation. A demi-goddess. She could use each and every ability the immortals possessed at a level far stronger than any of us could. She could read my thoughts, feel my emotions.

"Did you—"

"I have not once read your thoughts, Barrett Stratos," she assured me. "Though it would have been far easier than dragging it out of you, I refuse to cross that boundary. I can, however, feel if you are being truthful with me."

Part of me eased at that notion, though I didn't want to. It made sense, though. Why would she continue to pester me with questions if she'd read my thoughts, my memories? She could very easily have plucked all the answers from my head without my knowledge. "Why would you do all this for me and not want anything in return?"

"Because," she said, as if it was the silliest question, "you were innocent, and it was terrible what happened."

Her smile faded, and something darkened her silver eyes. "Every child should be cherished by their parents. They should never be treated as objects for their benefit. And those who do so deserve to burn for it."

Something stirred deep within me at the look on her face. Fuck, how did she do it? How could this little goddess wear down every wall I'd built to shut everyone out? For the first time in a long time…I wanted to believe she meant well, that someone could truly do something for unselfish reasons.

And a part of me—regardless of whether she wanted it—wanted to return the favor, help her in some way.

"You need assistance in the Godsrealm?"

She seemed to blink out of whatever thoughts had pulled her under. "What?"

"Micah told me you're building a team to go to the Godsrealm. Something about fighting pits."

She seemed hesitant. "We are. It's a covert mission, though."

"I want in," I said. "Let me help."

"I can't guarantee your safety," she said, and I huffed a laugh.

"That's all the more reason to back you up," I said. "If you can't guarantee my safety, then you can't guarantee yours either."

She gave me a knowing smile. "Does that mean you care, Barrett?"

I shrugged. "Can't exactly clear my name if you're dead."

She snickered and grabbed her dagger before turning from me. "Good attempt at hiding the truth from me, hothead."

And as she walked away, I couldn't stifle the smile curving my lips.

CHAPTER 13

THALIA

Micah was to leave for the Godsrealm in less than a day. He had asked me to stay behind, nearly begged me not to mention it to Lucia or Damien.

How could I, though?

Recruits paced around in the training rings before me, the sun's heat beating down on my skin. My mind had been lost in a haze all morning, unable to stay on task. What if it was true? Could they have really brought The Pits back? If so, who was responsible? How long had they been operating? How many more children had they stolen? How many more souls had they broken?

The beast bristled within my soul, feeding off my emotions like a pack of wolves devouring their prey.

Micah let out a grunt, and I lifted my eyes in time to see him hit the ground, the new recruit staring down at him, his chest heaving with each labored breath.

Barrett Stratos.

I hadn't unearthed any new information on him, hadn't wanted to dig any further than what I'd overheard last week for fear of what I might find. Something deep in my chest left me wondering whether learning anything more would leave me further tangled up in the thoughts winding their way through my mind since I'd first laid eyes on him.

He was no better than a hunter's trap.

Micah pushed himself up, brows shooting skyward as he blinked up at Barrett, who had just thrown him during their sparring match.

Barrett huffed a laugh and stuck his hand out for Micah to take before pulling him up from the dirt. Micah hadn't spoken of Barrett much, but from what I'd seen, they seemed to have kindled some sort of friendship.

I frowned, my eyes lingering on Barrett for a moment too long and I froze the moment his gaze shifted to mine. Before I could give myself away further, I turned to the recruits, crossing my arms.

For a moment it almost felt as if the beast was laughing at me before its thoughts flitted across mine once more. *So flustered.*

You're annoying.

The beast seemed to settle at the sight of them, and I tried to focus on the recruits before me instead of them.

You've always liked Micah, but I've never felt you fawn over him.

It huffed in response. *The steel-eyed warrior has bite.*

I rolled my eyes, and it seemed to tug at my attention, wanting me to watch them, when it spoke again. *Perhaps you should take some of that bite out on him.*

I glanced sidelong at Micah and Barrett as they paused for a break, ladling water from buckets to take a drink and splash over their heads. The water soaked into Micah's shaggy brown hair, dripping down his neck and rolling down the tightly wound cords of muscle in his back, his arms.

Gods…

I could almost feel the humor in the beast's thoughts. *I think you're drooling.*

I stiffened, running a hand across my lips to find it had lied. *Annoying creature.*

Irritation swelled in my chest as it seemed to curl up, content to leave me flustered. Despite the urge to turn and ignore them, I couldn't deny the way they looked together, how they somehow complimented one another.

I let out a sigh and stalked toward them.

Micah's brows rose when he caught sight of me, and he turned in time to press a kiss to my cheek.

"Come to watch me get my ass handed to me?" he teased, his hands grasping my hips as he brushed his nose against mine, dragging a smile out of me.

"I thought I'd step in and see what the newest recruit has to dish out," I said, glancing at Barrett.

Barrett peered over his shoulder before taking one last drink and facing me fully. His blond brows furrowed for a moment as he seemed to really look at me, steel eyes flitting between mine, as if searching for something.

"Does he know how to talk?" I asked, arching a brow.

Micah huffed a laugh, and Barrett seemed to blink out of whatever trance he had fallen into. "Barrett doesn't usually have any issue speaking. More often than not he only manages to shove his foot in his mouth when he does."

"This your bonded?" Barrett asked, gesturing to me.

He nodded. "This is Thalia. Thalia, this is Barrett."

"Pleasure," I said, giving him a smile that was all teeth.

Barrett huffed a laugh and pointed to himself. "You're wanting to spar with me?"

"Too afraid to accept?" I asked, tilting my head as I crossed my arms over my chest.

Micah bit back his grin.

"Never backed down from a challenge," he said, arching a brow. "I hope you offer more of a fight than your bonded."

Micah stuttered, gaping as he held his hands out in clear offense. "Low blow! You got a lucky shot at me."

"Keep telling yourself that, pretty boy," Barrett said with a cocky grin as he turned his back on him to get one more drink and—Fates spare me—pour some over his hair. He shook it out, the water droplets rolling down his sweat-slicked skin.

I held my hand out to the ring, trying to regain any sort of control over myself as the beast seemed to chuckle in the depths of my soul. "After you."

Barrett tossed the ladle back into the bucket of water and stalked past me.

As I turned to follow him, Micah's arm snaked around my waist, pulling me back against him, his lips brushing against my ear as he whispered, "Show him who's in charge around here."

The corner of my lips twitched. "Enjoy the show."

Barrett came to a stop in the center of the ring, rolling his neck as he stretched his arms out and cracked his wrists. "I've been watching you with these recruits."

"Really now?" I asked as I stopped before him. "Didn't realize I'd attracted the attention of our newest. I hope you've enjoyed the view."

That cocky grin curved his lips again, and irritation swelled in my chest at the way it left my heart fluttering, at the way the beast preened within me that he had been watching us.

Our bonded is watching, you traitorous creature.

It huffed. *You say that as if our kind doesn't share.*

I chewed the inside of my lip, unable to respond. It wasn't wrong, but still, I couldn't shake the feeling of guilt at the way the beast responded to Barrett. It was reminiscent of the way it felt around Micah. It had taken a liking to him from the beginning, but this... There was something different about it.

"You sure like to stare," Barrett whispered, and I stiffened at the coy smile spreading across his face. "Don't think I didn't see you watching us train the last week."

Had I been so obvious?

The beast nuzzled against my consciousness. *You weren't exactly secretive in your observation.*

Shut up!

"Shall I have my likeness painted for you to admire whenever you like?" Barrett whispered, and I ground my teeth.

"I shall have your likeness ground into the dirt beneath my boot," I growled, running forward.

Barrett huffed a laugh, seeming triumphant as I charged for him. What he didn't realize, though, was that while others might become flustered when angered...

I thrived.

Barrett narrowly evaded my first strike, and I smiled at the grunt that burst from his lips as my other fist connected with his kidney a second later.

Micah broke into laughter as Barrett stumbled back. "Just remember, you asked for this!"

I didn't give Barrett the chance to respond, swinging my leg through the air. His arms shot up, blocking my kick before he reached out to grasp my leg. He wasn't fast enough as I snatched it out of his reach and paced back, flexing my fingers as the beast prowled within me, just as eager to fight as I was. Shouts broke out, and I realized the recruits had stopped their training to encircle us, watching our match.

This was freedom. This was where I belonged: feeling the rush of the fight, the energy of those watching, feeling the blood race through my veins as I put everything I had into bringing my opponent down.

Barrett stepped forward, and I met him in the middle. I punched, he blocked. He kicked, I evaded. We fell into step, our bodies moving in a rhythm that flowed like the rivers and streams, like the birdsong through the maple leaves.

The beast relished in the feel of our bodies colliding. *I told you he had bite.*

Air rushed from my lungs as his fist connected with my gut. Our movements paused a moment as we stared at each other, panting.

He cracked a cocky smile. "Not tapping out on me, are you?"

I met his smile with one of my own, and he blinked, as if surprised. "Don't get full of yourself."

I slammed my face forward, our foreheads connecting, and he cursed as he stumbled back.

A collected groan echoed from the crowd surrounding us, and I stalked around Barrett as he clutched his face, blood already rolling down his chin from his busted nose.

"*Not tapping out on me, are you?*" I mused, taunting him with his own words.

His steel eyes lifted to me, lit with something I couldn't place, and my heart danced in my chest. Was he…enjoying this? Who exactly was this male?

He cracked his neck and balled his hands into fists. "Not at all."

My thoughts scattered at the sight of the smile still lingering on his face. He seemed to relish in the fight when I had expected him to lose his temper. I shouldn't have liked that as much as I did. I bit back the irrational anger, the irritation bristling through my bond with the beast. I shouldn't feel this, shouldn't find delight in sparring with this strange male.

The beast prowled within me, bristling at the display of confidence. *Show him we are better. Make him submit.*

I launched forward, and Barrett took a step as well, but when he reached for me, I ducked out of his grasp, slipping past him around to his back. He tried to turn to me, but I kicked his knee out from under him. He went down and I leaped up, winding my arm around his throat, my other over his head to trap him in a headlock. We hit the dirt, and he fought against my hold.

The recruits went silent as we struggled, Barrett's movements kicking up dust. He grunted, body wound tightly as he failed to break free.

"She's got you!" Micah called. "Tap out!"

Barrett's chest heaved, and at first, I thought he might choose unconsciousness to submission.

"You've lost," I said through gritted teeth, my arms quivering as he tried to pry himself free.

He let out a groan and finally tapped my arm.

I released him and stumbled back.

The recruits erupted in cheers around us, but I didn't pay them any attention as I walked around to extend a hand to Barrett. "I like the way you fight. Reminds me of myself."

His eyes lingered on my outstretched hand for a moment before he looked up at me and took it. I helped him to his feet.

I dusted off my pants and straightened my tunic. "Could use some shaping, but I think you might last longer than others here."

His eyes flickered between mine again, something akin to confusion within them.

"Shit, I thought you were gonna pass out!" Micah said as he hurried toward us. "Stubborn bastard."

Barrett blinked as Micah patted him on the shoulder. "You weren't kidding. She packs a punch."

"Maybe we'll make a warrior out of you yet," I said and turned to the recruits around us. "Aren't you supposed to be sparring? Or have you found yourselves so bored by my instruction that I should give you something more entertaining?"

They all stiffened before quickly dispersing, and I snickered at how quickly they busied themselves.

"I'll let you get back to what you're doing," I said, turning to head toward my trainees, but I paused, glancing back. "Oh, and Barrett?"

His blond brows rose.

I gestured to my nose and mouth. "You've got a little something here. Might want to get it checked out."

Micah stifled a laugh as Barrett ran the back of his hand across his mouth, smearing the blood from his busted nose.

The beast nuzzled against my consciousness as I stalked out of the training yard, feeling something I couldn't quite explain, couldn't quite place. It left me no less irritated than I had been moments earlier. *The steel-eyed warrior has potential. He is worthy.*

I shook my head. *His name is Barrett, and stop talking about him. He's simply another recruit.*

Keep telling yourself that, little one.

I growled. *Stop calling me that.*

Would you prefer I call you little beasty?

My steps halted. I hadn't heard that name in what felt like ages, and it brought about a painful longing.

CHAPTER 14

THE GIRL WITH STORMY EYES

60 years prior

"Stay quiet," Rhyas muttered as we emerged from the edge of Silvash's Forest, the warm, fresh air of the wood fading into something that reminded me of the attack, a familiar dread twisting my gut. His grip on my arm tightened as I looked over the short stretch of land dividing us from whatever The Fates had sentenced me to.

No matter how much I tried, my body quivered as I took in what could only be described as a stone fortress carved into the mountainside. Male and female fae garbed in leather armor paced along the top of the wall on either side of the enormous wooden gate, and my stomach twisted at the sight of the swords strapped to their hips. They almost reminded me of the warriors of The Order. Still, where the warriors had always been sweet and protective, there was something about the way the fae's eyes passed over us as we approached in cold assessment—as if I wasn't a person, but something else entirely.

With each step, new details came into focus. The grass seemed to die out the closer we got, as if the magic in the land couldn't reach us in this place. I wasn't sure what stained the stone walls, the dark marks and unrecognizable chunks of...something, hanging from ropes. It left a touch of ancient terror that needed no explanation, and the beast recoiled into a deeper part of me at the sight and the terrible smell.

"What is this place?" I whispered, my voice barely breaching my lips.

"The Pits," Rhyas said, a hint of disgust slipping through his mask of indifference, as if he couldn't stomach the words. "Your new home."

Air grew thicker in my lungs with each step, and my body began to lock up.

"Be mindful of your surroundings," Rhyas warned. He didn't look at me, a strange coldness touching the features of his face, but his voice didn't reflect his expression. "Be careful who you trust."

I swallowed, turning to the monstrous wooden gates as they parted, the groan of chains rattling my bones as they wound round the wheel opening the mountain as if a beast eager to devour us whole. Rhyas guided me forward until my feet stopped inches from the threshold. I fought against him, my bare feet sliding against the stone, gravel biting into my flesh.

No. No, no, no, no.

"Don't die on me, little beasty," he breathed, and I twisted around to him. Hands grabbed me from behind, and I gasped.

"No! Please! Don't let them take me!" I cried, pulling against their hold as I grasped onto the sleeve of his dusty tunic before I was ripped free of him.

A flicker of something passed over his eyes before they hardened, and his posture straightened as a male approached us. It wasn't his golden eyes passing over me that drew my attention, but his emerald hair that framed his face in short, loose waves. Never before had I seen hair like his.

"She's awake?" he asked, arching an emerald brow as he turned to Rhyas.

"A shifter, sir," Rhyas said—as if that was explanation enough—as he tucked his arms behind his back, avoiding my pleading stare.

"A shifter?" the male echoed before he approached me. My skin prickled with a strange energy the closer he came, something familiar caressing my mind. The sensation was wrong, just as it had been when we'd crossed the veil. The hands holding me adjusted their grip, and I found myself held in place by two guards. They anchored me steadfastly as I tried to pull back from the strange male crouching before me.

"Immortal?" he asked as he ran a hand over the short emerald beard lining his jaw.

Rhyas nodded. "We have six immortals, as you requested. Adresta's team brought three humans, and Cyros' managed four fae from the bordering villages of Pelagonia."

My breath quickened. We hadn't been the only ones to be taken. There were other children who had been stolen from their homes. But why?

"She will be pleased to learn we captured so many immortals. Let's see how many survive the first night. They will be her warriors once they've proven themselves in The Pits," the male said, reaching out. I flinched away from his touch and froze when his fingers combed through my hair. "Nearly as silver as hers was..."

The beast growled, and I bared my teeth, my hands balling into fists.

His golden eyes almost lit up, and a smile curved his lips, showing a hint of his slightly elongated canines. He muttered under his breath, "You have bite. That's good."

Another guard ran toward us. "Arden, sir!"

I stiffened at the name, Rhyas' words flitting across my mind. *You belong to Arden now.*

Arden groaned as he pushed himself to his feet. "What is it?"

"We're ready for The Proving," the guard said.

A shiver ran up my spine as Arden turned to look back down at me, one corner of his lips kicking up into a half grin. "Excellent."

There was something cruel in his expression, an unknown promise that left a cold sweat breaking out over my skin. "Let's see if you can make it through the night. Prove your worth to me."

Metal ground against metal, rattling my bones as I turned to find the gates closing, sealing me inside this horrible place, trapping me within the belly of this wretched beast. No! I needed to get out, needed to get home. I parted my lips to protest, but the two males grasping my arms shoved me forward, and I twisted, trying to see Rhyas over my shoulder as they dragged me off.

"Rhyas! Please!" I cried, our gazes briefly meeting, but he looked away from me, something akin to guilt dulling his amber eyes.

They pulled me through a doorway, and Rhyas vanished from view. "No!"

A scream reached my ears from down the hall, and my voice lodged in my throat. The coppery scent of blood filled my nose, the acidic scent of fear tainting the air.

We can't go there. Fight them.

Another scream echoed through the tunnels as we descended a stairway lined with torches, but it was sharply silenced, leaving an eerie quiet in its wake, and I stopped breathing. Where were they taking me? What were they going to do to me when we got there?

Torchlight spilled into the opening before us as we reached the foot of the stairs.

"How many have we lost?" a male's voice barely echoed from inside the room, the faint sound of sobs growing stronger with each step.

"One," another responded. "Two have survived so far."

"Arden will be pleased to hear that. We need some fresh meat to replace the losses we suffered last season," the male said, and the near-pleasure in his voice launched the beast within me into an uproar, as if it could already feel their sickening intentions closing in on us.

Quiet whimpers caught my attention, and I turned to find a number of children huddled in a cell at the far side of the cavern, their clothes and faces dusted with dirt. Some looked like me, but some were unlike anything I'd seen, with skin various shades of the softest tans, grays, blues, greens, and purples. Some looked as if they were wrapped in bark, like the aspen trees in the meadows back home. Delicately pointed ears pierced through their tangled hair, the tips a deeper shade of the color of their skin, while some had tails, some tufts of fur or feathers decorating parts of their bodies. They were fae.

Oh, Gods.

The guards guided me toward the barred gate at the far end of the chambers, and fear skittered over my skin like chips of ice. I couldn't see what lingered past them for the darkness beyond. One of the guards grabbed the handle and jerked it open, the old metal groaning as it swung wide, and he shoved me inside.

I cried out as I hit the stone, rocks scraping my palms and bruising my knees. My heart lurched as the bars groaned once more, and I shot up, running back as they closed me in.

"Please! Let me out!" I reached my arms through the bars, my body barely big enough to leave me trapped.

A growl echoed from the darkness behind me, and I spun around, my chest heaving as I pressed my back against the icy bars. I searched the void-like cavern, my eyes adjusting before I felt the blood drain from my face at the faintest sight of movement in its depths.

"Good luck," one of the guards whispered, and I looked to see his violet eyes turn cruel—his lips curving into a wicked smile. "She's hungry."

Arden's words flitted across my thoughts.

Let's see if you can make it through the night. Prove your worth.

How exactly did he want me to prove my worth?

"What do I do?" I muttered, my hands trembling, my knees quivering beneath me as the sound of padded steps reached my ears. A veritable pat...pat...pat...

Another growl rippled in the darkness, and the beast within me bristled, teeth bared.

Torchlight reflected in silver orbs, and I sucked in a breath as it emerged from the dark depths of the cavern. Its body was cloaked in feathers and fur, its features like that of the panther shifter who served under the king. Its gray, feather-tipped tail flicked as it prowled closer, and I could faintly see the feathers fanning out from the base of its legs. My back pressed tighter against the bars. A snarl slipped from its throat as its bloodied lips peeled back to reveal rows of sharp teeth that dripped with the same crimson liquid.

Rhyas' words echoed through my thoughts.

Don't die on me, little beasty.

It launched at me with a roar, talon-tipped paws stretching out toward me. I dove out of the way, and it crashed into the bars, the guards cursing as they stumbled back before laughing.

Stone cut into my feet as I scrambled to get away, the cavern coming into view despite the shadows cloaking them as I ran. I dared a second to look around, searching for any means of escaping. The cave was large, with tunnels carved into the surrounding stone, but I saw no signs of an exit. A whimper reached my ears, and I twisted around to see the creature stumble away from the bars before running its paw over its face repeatedly, as if to wipe the pain away.

The guards laughed on the other side as it shook its head and continued to rub its eyes.

There was no time to worry about the poor creature, who was likely as much a prisoner as I was. I had to get away, had to find a way to outsmart it and survive. The creature cried out, the sound rattling me to the bones, and I didn't waste time looking back before I ran, eyes darting to each tunnel. Would they be dead ends? Or would they lead me to safety? Perhaps I could get out of its reach if I climbed.

The pads of the creature's paws slammed into the stone floor behind me, and I gasped. I ran for the stone wall and leaped to grab hold of a rock jutting from the wall.

Faster!

I cried out as I pulled myself up, my heart racing as I climbed higher and higher. My eyes dropped to the creature as it leaped and swatted at me. Its strike connected with my ankle, and I screamed as my foot slipped from the stone ledge.

The beast within me roared as I hit the ground.

Get up!

The creature stumbled back as if startled, and I shot to my feet to run. I didn't get far, my feet slamming into something hard on the ground, and I crashed onto the floor. Air flooded my lungs in short bursts as I twisted around before it left me entirely, the distant torchlight reflecting in the unseeing eyes of a child staring back at me. I recognized him. He had been one of the children who'd been taken, had been carried in the arms of one of Rhyas' companions, Santor.

Fates spare me.

Was this what my fate would be? Would I die here?

No, little one. You will not die. You will survive.

The creature ran for me, and I scrambled back as it hissed, teeth bared. It struck, its claws slashing down in a smooth arch, and searing pain carved a path over my right eye. I cried out, my hand rising to my face as I rolled away and ducked into the nearest tunnel.

The sound that peeled from the monster's throat could only be described as pure, frustrated fury, and it left me all the more desperate to get away. I couldn't let it catch me, couldn't let it do to me what it did to the child who hadn't stood a chance. My hands clambered over the stone as I crawled into the tunnel in a blind path to wherever it led.

Don't look back!

Sounds of scraping claws reached my ears, and I twisted back despite the beast's warning. I gasped as the creature forced its way into the tunnel, its body crammed too tightly, its claws tearing into the rock as it fought to get to me.

My vision blurred, my right eye burning as blood pooled within it. Sobs broke from my lips as I crawled, farther and farther, the tunnel growing tighter until I barely fit before I stuck my head through the exit. I struggled, my body going nowhere. *No.* It was too tight, and my heart skipped a beat as the creature grew closer. The stone cut into my shoulders as I forced my way through the tiny opening, biting back a cry as my skin was cut and split. I spilled onto the stone floor as the creature's paw shot through the opening, claws grazing my ankle before I could scramble away.

Its cries and hisses echoed through the chamber as it swatted at the air before me, unable to get through, unable to get to me.

"Excellent work," Arden's voice startled me, and I twisted around to find him standing with several guards. Hands grabbed me before I could do anything, and I fought against their hold as they hauled me to my feet and guided me toward him.

His golden eyes trailed over me, and my skin crawled at the odd look of pride within them. It was nothing like the pride Father showed when I did good, though—it was more like greed, a hunger for something of value. He reached out and I pulled back, but the guards held me in place as his hand grasped my left shoulder.

"You will serve me well," he whispered before blinding pain shot out from where our skin met, agony like a wildfire snaking down my left arm. The beast cried out within me, my voice somehow drowned out by the sound of its own pain as what felt like chains encircled it, tethering it—me— to Arden. My body recoiled on its own, fighting to escape the pain, and just when I thought I couldn't take anymore, he released me.

I slumped in their hold, head lolling forward, saliva dripping from my lips to pool on the stone below. The guards dropped me, and I collapsed, my body too weak to support itself. Tears rolled down my cheeks, and my eyes trailed over my arm, covered by the now-shredded coat the boy had gifted me, to the exposed skin of my wrist, where inscriptions in the old language inked my skin...the same as those that marked Rhyas'.

Arden stared down at me, a sickening smile spreading across his face. "You are mine."

CHAPTER 15

BARRETT

Eyes like storm clouds, churning with the promise of destruction. Something familiar tugged in the back of my mind.

Where had I seen them before? Or…had I ever?

"We'll go in in teams of four," Damien said, and I blinked, drawn from the thoughts that had overshadowed all else since I'd sparred with Micah's bonded the day before.

Thalia.

I'd never heard that name before, couldn't place any possible connection to my past. I wondered what family she came from, if they might have known mine. Her scent of black spruce and wintergreen had hit me so hard, it left me fucking speechless.

And the way she fought… It wasn't like the warriors of the Order. It was raw, more instinctive than training.

Damien continued, and I watched him, still weary, his face lingering in my mind from when he had watched on high as I was thrown to the wolves. "Ansel, Jasper, and Eunice's teams will man the perimeter. Focus on bringing down any guards before they can alert anyone of our approach and keep watch while we're inside."

"We have limited knowledge of what's happening within Nastra's walls," Lucia started, and every set of eyes shifted to where she stood at the wood table in the center of the room. A map was laid out, detailing the location of the fortress we were to infiltrate. "There is no telling how many guards are present, who is in charge, or whether they have successfully revived The Pits. The team we sent to observe noted some activity a week ago. We take no chances; everyone comes home. If there are captives, we get them out."

I raised my hand, and Lucia's brows rose. "Yes, Barrett?"

"Given I'm a bit new to the mission, can you explain exactly what The Pits are?" I asked.

Some turned to her, brows rising in curiosity, but some dropped their gazes, and I wondered if they knew.

"Some of you were with us the last time we brought them down, but for those of you who weren't, The Pits were an illegal underground fighting ring operated by a group of criminals in Erebus' territory, Tenebria. They focus their efforts on kidnapping children from both realms, binding the children to the Pit Master's will and forcing them to fight in The Pits."

Micah's body tensed next to me, his arms crossed over his chest, his eyes the coldest I'd ever seen. He'd been in a foul mood all morning, and for some reason, Lucia's words seemed to feed his anger.

Lucia continued, "It's a den where cruel souls go to gamble, bet on fighters, and purchase warrior slaves. The Pits are no normal fighting ring; they not only force captives to fight against each other but against terrible creatures."

I couldn't imagine a child being forced into something so terrible.

"When we found The Pits ten years ago, we discovered they had taken some of our own," she said, and I blinked. How had our own children been taken?

"Sadly, many of them died during their captivity, but we were able to save one, along with countless other fae and even a few humans who now live among us," Damien explained. "The Pit Master was brought down, and the survivors who served under him scattered. Most of the victims were reunited with their families. Our mission is to ensure that this organization is destroyed once and for all."

Another hand rose. "Will Erebus be assisting us in this mission, as it's within his territory?"

Lucia glanced at Damien before he answered. "Erebus cooperated with us in the past, allowing us passage. He sent some of his warriors to assist us last time, but he will not be involved in this mission."

"Does anyone have any questions beyond what we've gone over?" Lucia asked.

The room remained silent.

Lucia lifted her head, her voice solid as stone. "You were provided with maps of the surrounding area and what we have on the interior, as well as any additional details you may need to prepare. Everything you have is everything we know. We leave this evening at sundown for Selene's Temple, where we will pass to Tenebria."

I looked down at the piece of parchment clutched in my hand, fearing what exactly we were going to find in this place.

"You're dismissed," Damien said, and everyone began to file out of the room.

"You good?" I asked, glancing at Micah as he lingered, leaning against the wall.

"Just ready to destroy this place," he said, his voice ice cold.

"Lucia!" We both froze at the sound of Thalia's voice, Micah's eyes darting to her as she forced her way through the departing warriors.

Lucia and Damien stiffened as they looked at one another before turning to her.

"What's wrong?" Lucia asked.

"I'm going with you," Thalia said, and Micah's body tensed.

He stormed forward. "You said you would stay behind."

She shook her head. "I can't do that."

Lucia lifted her hand. "I swore I would never ask you go back there and—"

"You aren't asking," Thalia said. "I'm volunteering."

They didn't speak, and Damien drew in a heavy breath.

Thalia continued. "Don't ask me to stay behind. I'm the only one who knows how that shithole works, how to navigate the tunnels."

I frowned before realization dawned on me, my chest constricting.

We were able to save one.

Micah looked pained. "Thalia—"

"Let me help you destroy that place, Lucia," she said. "Don't make me stay when I can help."

The room went silent.

"I want to see that place burn as much as you do, Thalia," Lucia said hesitantly. "Are you sure?"

The promise of death danced within Thalia's stormy eyes. "I will do whatever it takes to destroy anything that remains of that vile place."

CHAPTER 16
THE GIRL WITH STORMY EYES

60 years prior

A groan of metal forced me awake, and then I was being tossed onto a cold stone floor before the door was slammed shut behind me. I tried to push myself up, but everything ached, my skin still burning where Arden had marked me. What did the inscriptions mean? What had he meant when he told me I was his?

"Try not to push yourself," a soft voice cut through the silence, and I stiffened, pushing through the pain to rise to my knees, scanning the darkness of the new chamber.

"Easy," she whispered. "I won't hurt you."

Rhyas' warning darted across my thoughts, sparking fresh terror. *Be careful who you trust.*

I slid along the floor, wincing each time my scraped palms met gravel, until my back met the bars. The beast didn't respond, its silence putting every part of me on high alert. It had never been silent, had never left me alone before.

"You're new," she said, and I turned back to find a woman lingering just out of reach, her hands held out in quiet assurance that she meant me no harm. But was that true? Could I trust her? Could I trust anyone in this horrible place? Rhyas seemed to be the only one whose words might ring true, but he was the very reason I was here. Could I even trust him?

She lowered herself to the floor, her brown hair brushing the top of her shoulders, her silver eyes soft. I looked down at her extended hand as she reached out for me, moving to the iron shackles secured around her wrists, inscriptions carved into the metal. Something within me recoiled at their presence, at the subtle hum ringing from them.

"Looks like Yressia left you with quite the wound." She stood before hurrying to the far end of the chamber. I tracked her steps to where she stopped before a shelf-lined wall littered with items that she began riffling through.

"Yressia?" I asked as she returned with a small bowl of water and a rag.

"The Featherclaw," she said as she knelt before me. Water dripping echoed off the stone walls as she wrung the wet cloth over the bowl. "She's Arden's pet. I heard he had her smuggled in from somewhere long ago. She tests each of his fighters before he marks them."

I couldn't form a response.

"He keeps her caged and underfed so she's always ready to hunt," she said as she lifted the cloth to my face.

I pulled away from her reach, and hurt flitted across her face. "I promise I won't hurt you."

"How do I know can I trust you?" I asked, my voice quivering despite my attempts to be brave. I couldn't feel the beast's presence, hear its voice, its guidance. Its instinct.

I had never felt more alone.

She let out a low breath. "There is nothing I could do to prove you can. It's smart of you to be reserved." She looked past me to the hallway beyond our cell door. "There are some here who would sell you out for a bite of bread."

I resisted the urge to follow her gaze, too afraid to turn my back.

A somber smile curved her lips as her gaze returned to me. "You're an immortal."

I frowned. "I am."

"That must be why they put you in my cell," she said. "They took me from Moonhaven when I was a child."

My heart shuddered, and I pushed myself up, a strange hope rising in my chest. "You..."

She nodded, her smile fading. "I don't even know how many years it's been."

I winced as she carefully dabbed the rag against my injured eye, but I held still, allowing her to clean it.

"You're still so young," she said, as if it broke her heart to say it. "If you were past your *settling*, you would have healed without issue, but this… I fear it will leave a scar."

"I can still see," I said.

She smiled. "That is wonderful news, *mikros*."

My heart swelled at the word. It sounded like home.

"How is Moonhaven?" she asked as she continued to clean the wound.

Hope died in my chest. "I don't know."

She frowned. "What do you mean?"

"The darklings attacked a few days before I was taken." My voice began to quiver, my vision blurring. "I got separated from Mama and Papa. There was so much fire."

Her eyes widened, her breath picking up, but then she she drew a deep inhale. She didn't speak again for a long while as she dabbed and cleaned my wound.

"Do you have a name?" she asked. The question was hesitant, fearful.

A name… Did I? I couldn't remember. Had I ever had a name?

I did. It had been taken from me. Stolen.

"I don't remember it…" I muttered, tears blurring my vision, and I winced at the sting in my right eye.

"I hoped you might've somehow kept it, but it was foolish of me."

"Do you?" I asked. "Have a name?"

"It is not the name gifted to me by my parents, but you can call me Kish," she said as she pulled back. "I guess you'll need one."

She tapped her chin as she looked me over. "What to call you…"

Silence stretched on, and a strange anticipation swelled in my chest before a smile stretched across her face. "Thalia."

"Thalia?" I echoed, brows furrowing.

"It's a special name, one I hope will have great meaning for you," she explained as she cupped my cheek. "It's a name of prosperous destiny, one that I gift you in the hopes you will thrive and flourish."

"I think that's a lovely name, Kish."

I gasped at the sound of Rhyas' voice and twisted to find him leaning against the stone outside our cell.

His soft amber eyes welled with pain the moment he saw my face, and he knelt. "Is that the only wound Yressia gave you?"

"It's the only one I've found so far," Kish explained.

"That's a relief," he said and checked both ways down the hall before reaching into one of the satchels tied to his belt. "Here."

He held out a small container, and Kish reached out to take it, her eyes narrowing to make out what it was before her body tensed. "If they find out you gave us somethi—"

"Better not let them find out," he whispered, and for a moment, something passed between them as he held her hand through the bars. "Take it. Make sure she's well and tended to."

"Why do you care?" I asked. "You took me."

"He didn't have a choice," Kish said, her sadness filling the room with the scent of freshly fallen rain. "He was like us once."

"Once." Rhyas scoffed. "I still am."

"But you're not caged," I said.

"Don't mistake the lack of bars on my cage for freedom," he said, and pulled the sleeve of his shirt up, revealing the same inscriptions that now marked my skin. "He marked you too, right?"

I looked down at my hands, at where the ink peeked from beneath the hem of my sleeve. I pulled the coat off, and my heart plummeted at the sight of the inscriptions decorating my entire left arm, from my wrist all the way past my shoulder.

Rhyas' and Kish's eyes lingered on the tattoo, something akin to pity dulling their expressions.

"As long as that mark remains, he will have power over you," Rhyas explained. "Over you, your magic, everything."

"How can I get rid of it?" I asked, my heart hammering. I needed to get back home, needed to find Mama and Papa.

"You can't," Kish muttered. "Unless he dies or releases you, you are trapped here."

"What will he do to me?" I asked, my words flying from my lips. "What does he want with us?"

Rhyas rested his head against the bars in defeat. "You are to fight."

Fight what? The creature that had attacked me?

"I'm sure you heard them speak of The Pits," Kish said.

I nodded, glancing between the two of them.

"You will be trained, conditioned, and you will learn how to spill blood in the most brutal of ways," Rhyas said, his eyes hardening as they burned into the stone floor. "Then, when you come of age, you will fight for their entertainment. You will kill or you will be killed."

"No," I muttered, tears blurring my vision. "I don't—"

"You must," he said, his amber gaze capturing mine.

He reached out and took my hand through the bars. "I've watched as countless children have been taken, conditioned, and killed, all so his pockets could be lined with coin. I've resisted, tried to find loopholes where I could." He let out a sigh of defeat. "I tried to let you return home, give you a chance to be free, but he had already taken your name."

His words from when I had nearly escaped resurfaced in my mind. *Do you remember your name?*

"Arden did?" I asked.

Rhyas nodded. "It's one of the ways he traps his fighters. If you would have reached the veil, you would have found you couldn't have passed through."

My breath quickened, fear flooding my system. I wanted so badly to feel the beast's comforting presence in my soul. Rhyas' hand landed on my shoulder, and I looked up at him.

"Promise you won't die on me, little beasty," he pleaded. "Promise me I won't have to watch another child die from my actions."

I shook, fear clawing at me, but I nodded.

"I promise."

CHAPTER 17

BARRETT

Thalia was once a captive of The Pits, had been taken as a child.

Something felt so profoundly wrong in that knowledge, as if a part of me couldn't bear the thought of it. I couldn't…but why? I barely knew the female.

Leather hissed as I slid my dagger into a sheath before buckling the holster of my short sword around my hips. The flame smoldered in my veins in quiet anticipation, as if it too was eager to get into this place, to destroy it.

She wanted it burned to the ground. I could see to that.

I shook my head, pulling myself from the strange thought. She was bonded and clearly didn't like me, so why did I care? It wasn't like I felt any affection for her. It wasn't as if we were friends.

Forcing the thought down, I checked the clasp of Cali's bracelet to ensure it was secured. I couldn't bring myself to leave it behind, couldn't bear the thought of ever being separated from it again.

"Just wait a little bit longer, Cali. As soon as I take care of this, I promise, I'll make Atticus and Jissena pay," I whispered, running my fingers against the delicate gold before tucking it under the sleeve of my Elythian leathers.

The sun was disappearing behind the tops of the mountains surrounding the valley as I stepped into the keep, finding myself amidst a several other warriors all geared up, as ready for a fight as I was. I hadn't seen Micah or Thalia since the briefing. He hadn't looked too thrilled about her coming, but given what I knew now, I couldn't say I blamed him for never wanting her to have to set foot in that place again.

I shook my head. It wasn't my business whether she came along or stayed behind.

Whether she got the retribution she deserved.

Fuck, I'd spent far too much time with Lucia, was starting to care too much.

"Barrett!" Lucia called, gesturing me to her side. "You're on my team."

Damien approached from behind her, and the flames within me recoiled.

"Damien," he said by way of introduction, holding out his hand. I eyed him before taking his hand to shake, and his voice lowered. "I apologize for everything that happened to you. I swear, if I could've, I would have done something that day. Atticus was smart in his approach."

I didn't respond.

"We're working hard getting everything we need to bring Atticus and Jissena to justice," he added, glancing at Lucia, who offered him a warm smile.

"We'll see," I said, still unsure how we could when Atticus had exploited the laws so skillfully as to climb the ranks to Kyrios in only a few months. Regardless, they would either be put in chains or I would put them in the ground myself.

Damien grasped my arm, forcing my attention back to him. His tone shifted, his voice dipping lower. "I'm trusting you to look out for her in there."

Lucia rolled her eyes. "We'll be all right, *mea sol.*"

"I want to know someone has your back when I'm not there," he said without taking his eyes off me. "If she trusts you, I trust you."

"I've got her."

He nodded, giving me an appreciative smile before turning to the others, lost conversation.

"There you are," Micah said, and I glanced over my shoulder to find him and Thalia slipping through the crowd toward us.

The sight of Thalia was like a punch to the gut, her cornsilk hair pulled back in a braid, her body clad in black leather, armed to the teeth with daggers.

"No short sword?" I asked, arching a brow, trying not to focus on every dip and curve of her body.

She's your friend's fucking bonded. Friend… Fuck. Was that what Micah was becoming? Gods, I was getting soft.

Thalia crossed her arms, responding with a deadpan look.

"Can't believe you're making me stay behind for this." I turned to find a male come to a stop at Lucia's side. I'd seen him around the training yard. He was big—not tall, but strong and, from the scent of sage and pine, I assumed he was a shifter.

"Who else could I trust to hold this place together while we're gone?" Lucia said, turning to him.

His pale green eyes flitted to me briefly, something like distrust flickering within them before he muttered to Lucia, "You're seriously going to trust this guy to be on your team? Why not someone else? Put him on anoth—"

"Zephyr," Lucia said, her voice soft and even. "We'll be all right. Barrett is a good person. I trust him to do what I need him to. He will come through for me when things go south."

Something stirred deep within me at her words, something I'd been shoving down since she'd dragged me out of that cell.

"So you say, but how can you be sure?" he retorted.

Lucia planted a hand on her hip. "Have I been wrong about a person before?"

Zephyr let out a sigh and grabbed the back of Lucia's neck to pull her closer to him, pressing his forehead to hers. "Gods, there's never any talking to you once you've made up your mind. Just come back to me in one piece. Don't make me lose you a second time."

"Calm down, *big brother*. We've all got her back," Thalia assured him.

"I'll kick your ass if she comes back hurt," Zephyr said, pinning me with a glare that burned with promise. A part of me relished the threat.

I crossed my arms over my chest. "Care to test that theory now, *big bro*?"

"All right, that's enough, you two," Lucia said, shoving at Zephyr's big frame. "This isn't about me or you. It's about the prisoners."

He seemed to soften in response, and he pressed his finger to her forehead. "And I know you'll get them out. Stop making that face, or you'll get permanent wrinkles."

Lucia's shoulders sagged, and she rolled her eyes as he left us to stand at Damien's side at the head of the room.

"Thalia, you and Micah are with Damien," Lucia said before she turned to me, gesturing to a male standing next to her, his pale blond hair cut short along his skull, his pewter eyes lifting to mine. "Barrett, this is Marcus. He's with us."

"Pleasure," he said, holding his hand out.

"Delighted," I said flatly, shaking his hand. Fuck all these pleasantries.

"Attention!" Damien called out, and the room quieted, warriors straightening, their arms folding behind their backs.

I crossed my arms as Zephyr checked roll to ensure everyone had arrived, followed closely by Damien calling out orders and finalizing assignments.

"Is your brother always this pleasant?" I whispered to Lucia.

The corner of her lips kicked up into a half smile. "He'll warm up to you."

I huffed a laugh. "I doubt that."

"Have you ever been to Selene's temple?" Micah whispered, cutting into our conversation.

"Nope," I said, popping the 'P.' "I'm sure she'll be thrilled to meet me, though."

Micah stifled a laugh, and I glanced over my shoulder to find Thalia's attention solely focused on Damien, on every word he spoke as he gave the latest update from the team scouting The Pits. Guards had been spotted on the wall, more than before, but they still had no knowledge of any captives.

Thalia's eyes hardened and her hands tightened into fists. Micah took her hand and whispered something into her ear. She nodded, her expression softening before she looked up at him, and I drew my attention away as he brushed a soft kiss against her lips.

Magic hummed through the air around us, and I turned toward the head of the room where Damien stood near an altar. I'd seen it before—it was the Propylaea, the gateway to Selene's Temple within the Godsrealm. Father had one in his study to gain access to the Council chambers, where they held their meetings.

"Everyone with me!" Damien called as wind whipped around us, caressing my skin with a featherlight touch, the magic within me rising to meet the magic within it like an old friend.

I drew a deep breath and let my eyes fall closed as the gateway opened, drawing us in.

The ground disappeared beneath my boots, ice clawing over my skin. I hated the feeling, the world flipping around me as if there was no up or down. My feet slammed into marble, and I gasped as I stumbled forward. Lucia grabbed my arm, stabilizing me.

"It's tough your first time," she said softly, and I opened my eyes.

I stilled at the sight of the glowing trees surrounding us, of the stone so ancient, the very fabric of time seemed to be etched into the cracks. Tiny creatures chittered as they scurried about, heads turning to us, glowing eyes lit with curiosity. Their bodies were made of pure night and starlight, long ears and tails swaying with each step.

"The astral sprites are busy, as always," Lucia whispered, as if the question was plastered across my face. She smiled as some of the tiny creatures trotted up to her to brush their tiny, clawed hands against hers. "I promise we won't make a mess of your temple. We're only passing through."

"Goddess," Damien said, and my thoughts scattered as everyone lowered to one knee.

My heart lurched at the sight before us, her skin glowing as brightly as the moon, her hair falling in silken silver waves to pool on the floor around her. Lucia tugged me down to her side, and I followed her lead, lowering to my knee.

"You may rise, *mea bellarios*," she said, her voice carrying across the marble hall like the rush of a tidal wave, the cadence beautiful yet lethal.

We all rose as she descended the dais, each step fluid and graceful. I couldn't form words even if I wanted to, the sheer power of her presence overpowering, overwhelming me.

Damien stood at the head of the group, his head held high as she came to a stop before him. Her opalescent eyes passed over us, and I avoided meeting them, couldn't bring myself to.

"Is your company prepared?" she asked, her voice delicate despite its power.

"We are," Damien said in response.

She extended her hand to him, dropping something into his palm. "Use this to call me when you are ready to return."

He dipped his head to her. "Understood."

She looked to the rest of us. "May Celestia bless your endeavor."

"And may she bless you, Goddess," the others said in unison, and I stiffened, looking around.

Lucia cracked a slight smile as she snickered, and I rolled my eyes. "Sorry. I don't often find myself in the presence of a Goddess."

"You are forgiven, poor, sinful male," she said, her tone teasing.

I shrugged her off before my attention was dragged toward Selene as she lifted her hands.

"Prepare yourself," Lucia warned.

"For what?" I whispered.

"She's sending us to Elythias."

I nodded as the glow of the trees around us grew brighter, the blue flames in the sconces growing. I'd never been to the Godsrealm—er...I guessed I was there now if we were in Selene's Temple. It was strange to think of the other realm, of an entire world that nearly mirrored ours in the Mortalrealm. Stories had been shared with us our entire lives of the different continents, each unique—the land so rich with magic, you could feel it in the air, taste it in the water.

The light of the trees winked out, the blue flames dousing as darkness swallowed us. We plummeted, descending into an abyss I feared may never release us. My boots met mossy soil, and the darkness receded, revealing lush forest, the green of the moss and leaves so vibrant, that the plants of the Mortalrealm paled in comparison despite the cover of night.

Gods, it was beautiful.

The forest was so…alive. Enormous vines and ferns littered the trees that stretched toward the sky. Tiny, glowing orbs in purples, blues, and greens darted and danced through the trees, some huddling in the crooks of the branches as if hiding from us. Their lights illuminated the canopy above us, revealing tiny creatures watching with hesitant curiosity, and, for a moment, I could have sworn I could hear the faint sound of distant laughter.

I took a step forward, unable to take my eyes off the creatures watching us from up high, and I stumbled before Micah grabbed my arm to stabilize me. My eyes fell to the moss-covered soil to find I'd stepped in…

Holy Gods.

It was a hoof print, so massive, I could have laid down within it with room to spare.

"What the fuck made this?" I asked.

"Silvash," Thalia muttered, her arms crossed over her chest, her gaze lingering on the forest, as if watching for something. "He must have passed through here not long ago. It still smells of him."

There was no wonder in her eyes, nothing save for cold recognition and calculation. Thalia stepped forward and lowered to her knees before running her hand over the mossy dirt. Darkness crawled over her skin, swallowing her whole before falling away to reveal a large gray wolf, the scar overlapping her right eye stark against her gray fur as she lowered her muzzle to the ground.

Gods, she was stunning, her fur near silver.

"A pack of Kalruks came through here recently," she said, turning south. "I'd say three to four of them, possibly a few hours ago. Headed south."

"What's a Kalruk?" I whispered to Micah.

"Nasty creatures," he responded. "They stalk anything that wanders the forest at night, hunt them down and tear them apart. One isn't too bad, but you don't want to be taken by surprise by a pack of them."

"Xander," Lucia said, attention still drawn to the south.

A male approached, his bronze skin cast in the blue light leaking from the canopy of the trees. He glanced at me briefly before focusing his attention on Lucia, widening his stance and folding his arms behind his back. "Yes, Lucia?"

"You and your team will keep an eye on the forest, make sure the teams on the wall aren't taken by surprise by those creatures.

"Understood," he said before turning to call forth his team to get into position.

"Amaris, Keir."

"Yes?" they said in unison.

"You have your orders; see the wall is cleared for us to get this mission underway," she said before looking across the group. "The rest of you with us. We'll split off once inside."

"Thalia?" Micah's voice drew my attention, and I found Thalia shifting back to her immortal form.

He grasped her arms before whispering something to her. She nodded, and something tugged deep in my chest at the hint of sorrow marking her face.

What exactly had they done to her in this place?

I pulled my attention away from them, walking at Lucia's side toward the edge of the forest. It wasn't my place to offer her any comfort, and I couldn't understand why I cared enough to want to.

My brows furrowed as the green moss turned a shade of mottled brown beneath our feet as we walked before dying out entirely to be replaced with dark gravel.

"We're here," Lucia muttered, and we all lowered ourselves behind dying brush and trees. The flames at the center of my being curled within itself at the sight of what could only be described as a fortress carved out of the mountainside, the flame bristling and desperate to be unleashed on everything it represented. My stomach turned at the sight of severed heads spiked atop the walls, entrails staining the stone below. Crow-like creatures littered the grounds to peck and feast on the remains, their caws echoing across the sparse expanse of land between us.

"Coronis," Lucia muttered under her breath as she watched the birds scavenge for meaty scraps.

"Gods," I whispered, my nose wrinkling at the stench. "They kept her here?"

Lucia nodded. "You can't imagine what we found the first time."

My skin crawled at the thought as Lucia drew a deep breath. In the distance, I caught sight of a large bird flying over the battlement before it shifted into one of our warriors and crashed into an unsuspecting guard, silencing him before he could alert others.

Damien lowered to his knee at Lucia's other side, taking her hand and gently squeezing it. They nodded to each other before Lucia returned her sights to the warriors currently overtaking the wall. "I only pray it isn't as bad."

CHAPTER 18

THALIA

Nothing had changed.

My fingers grazed over the rusty mechanism that controlled the main gates, and the beast within me recoiled as I remembered the terrible sound it made when it had first trapped me in this hell, remembered how that same sound brought hope when I'd finally been freed.

Damien came to a stop at my side and rested a hand on my shoulder, drawing me back from the memories burned into my mind. "We'll get them all out."

I nodded, looking forward to where Micah was checking the tunnel that led to the prisoner's block. We started toward him, two other teams following closely behind us. Before I turned into the tunnel, I glanced at Lucia, at Barrett standing amidst Marcus and other warriors as she discussed the plan with them. Barrett's steel eyes lifted briefly to me, something akin to worry flitting across them before he averted his gaze.

Something twisted in my chest, and I pulled myself away to lead the others into the tunnel. Barrett and Lucia would be all right.

The beast nuzzled against my consciousness. *Surely you're not starting to care about the steel-eyed warrior.*

I let out a sigh as I took each stony step with care, watching for any sign of guards or fighters...or creatures. *You should be focused on what we might find down here.*

It isn't anything we haven't faced before.

I couldn't argue with the beast's logic, but it had been ten years since this place had fallen. There was no telling what manner of foul creature had taken shelter here, what terrible atrocities the fae might be committing deep within this hellscape.

The tunnels broke into three directions before us, and I came to a stop.

"We split here," Damien said, turning back to the teams. "Each tunnel leads to one of three cell blocks. There is no telling what we will find there. You have twenty minutes to scout each location before we regroup here. If you're not back, we will assume you were attacked. If the area is clear and you find captives without the presence of aggressors, send two members of your team back to report."

The others nodded before they headed down their tunnels and I turned down ours, the walls far more familiar than I wished they were. Each step grew heavier, voices echoing in the back of my mind, voices that had been snuffed out by the cruelty of Arden's actions, of every fae's actions in this Godsforsaken place.

The tunnel opened into a larger hall of carved stone, walls lined with barred rooms extending as far as I could see.

Micah's hand took mine as I stood at the entrance, near frozen as I assessed everything I'd ever known growing up. Every memory was covered in a thick layer of dust and cobwebs.

I lowered to a knee, carefully inspecting the floor where the dust had been disturbed, whether by some creature or fae guard, I wasn't sure.

"Stay alert," I muttered, and the warriors drew their weapons as they stepped around Micah and me to search for any captives that might be held here.

The hall was silent, but I continued, drawn in by the horrible familiarity of it all. I'd sworn I would never set foot in this place again, and yet, here I was.

The beast curled within me as if wrapping me in an embrace. *It is not without reason.*

It wasn't, but this would be the last time anyone would set foot in this place. I would make sure of that, no matter what it took.

My feet moved of their own accord, leading me to a familiar cell. I lifted my fingers to touch the bars. The warding on the iron was weak but still present enough to leave my skin tingling, my magic recoiling. The rusted metal resisted as I tried to open the door, but it eventually gave way with a heavy groan that left the hairs on the back of my neck rise, and I stepped into the cell. I took in the deteriorating wooden table and shelves littered with cracked pots and bowls, the twin cots side by side in the corner.

I drew closer to the bed, finding familiar lines carved into the stone above it. My heart quickened at the sight of them, and I lifted my hand to run my fingers along the grooves, the weight and meaning of every etching leaving my heart heavy—so many lines, marking an immeasurable passage of time.

Micah's presence brushed against me as he lingered in the doorway to the cell.

My cell.

"I didn't know when my birthday was," I muttered, and Micah stopped at my side, looking around, and something within me hated him seeing it all. "None of us did, so we always celebrated together. Few of us were ever allowed to go outside, so many lived their lives never to see the sun or moons. We used the fighting seasons to measure time."

Micah's hands balled into fists, his fury burning in our bond inked between my breasts.

"I guess it was pointless to try," I muttered, feeling each groove, remembering each mark I'd left in a desperate attempt to not let this place swallow me whole.

CHAPTER 19
THE GIRL WITH STORMY EYES

10 years prior

Stone rasped as I carved out another mark above my bed.

Exhaustion clung to my bones, the deep aches and healing wounds from yesterday's match sapping every bit of energy I had left. My fangs throbbed, bringing forth a dull headache, and my throat was parched, desperate for a soothing rush of blood. I'd downed gulp after gulp of water, but it did nothing to quench this thirst.

I dragged my fingers over the lines carved into the stone. There had been thirty-six yesterday, and yesterday marked the start of the thirty-seventh. I would have marked it yesterday had I not collapsed with exhaustion the moment they'd thrown me back into my cell after my match. A victory hard-earned only to be rewarded with being thrown back behind bars with the promise of no rest and another match to come.

We always celebrated our birthdays on the first day of the fighting season. It gave everyone a chance to celebrate, as they weren't guaranteed to survive to the end of it. So many fell to the beasts in The Pits—to each other.

The record wasn't accurate; I'd missed a lot of time when I was young, thrown into training as soon as I'd been able to stand after Arden had marked me. It hadn't been long after my training began that Arden had thrown all the children into The Pit, forcing them to fight for their lives against lesser creatures for entertainment, allowing patrons the chance to assess us and start planning favorites or prospective warriors to acquire.

I couldn't even remember how old I had been when I'd been taken, could no longer remember my parents' faces, their names. The only thing that remained of what life I had, was in the tattered remains of the coat the sweet boy had gifted to me, which remained on my cot. Every night was spent curled up with it, trying and failing to remember what he looked like, the only thing remaining his kindness, his warmth, his scent, which had been all but snuffed out from the coat years ago. I slipped the scrap of fabric in my pocket, praying his lingering presence might bring me good luck when they dragged me back to The Pit for my next fight.

"She had the most enchanting silver hair and became Arden's favored for her beauty and power."

I glanced over my shoulder to find one of the cell mothers telling stories to the children. I'd been told the same story as a child.

"Who was she?" one of the children asked.

"She was Niassa, a princess of the wyverns, taken from her home on Hesperian's Reach as a child."

"A wyvern?" one of them asked in awe.

The cell mother nodded, her smile warm in a way that seemed near impossible. How could someone hold onto such warmth amidst the cold of this place?

"Arden kept her here, vowing she would serve him forever, for the wyverns do not die. Their flame souls burn for eternity, and only when wyverns relinquish their flame and forsake their leathery form can they die and pass into Elysium."

I couldn't help but listen to the story, clinging to the only thing that had given me hope as a child.

"She gave up on ever finding the freedom she craved, to be able to take her true form and spread her wings, to take to the skies. But there was another who was held captive, one who loved Niassa. A lost love—who'd once been held captive just as she was—broke into the cells one night. He had been believed to be dead, cast out after losing a fight in The Pits when they were younger."

The children listened in bated silence, their eyes bright with wonder and excitement.

"He found her in her cell, and he vowed to get her out. Together, they fled, fighting their way out of Nastra, but in their struggle, he was gravely wounded."

The children gasped and broke into a mix of questions, asking what happened—if he survived.

Gruff voices echoing through the cavern cut through the story, and the cell mother and children instantly quieted as guards stormed down the walkway. My heart launched into my throat at the sight of Kish slumped in their grasp. The smell of blood reached my nose, and I shot to my feet as they tossed her limp body into our cell.

I fell to my knees at her side. "Kish!"

A soft groan of pain was her only response, and I quickly turned her over to find her covered in deep wounds and quickly-forming bruises.

"Gods, what did they do to you?" I asked, quickly biting into my wrist, desperate to give her blood to help her heal.

"No," she gasped, shoving away my hand as I lowered the wound toward her lips, blood rolling down my skin to drip onto her already blood-stained clothes. "You need…"

"You're up!" the guard yelled, grabbing hold of my arm.

"No! We can't leave her like this!" I shouted as they dragged me away from her, leaving her on the floor, chest heaving. "You bastards!"

I fought to get to her, and the Kobalos guard jerked me against him, a putrid stench wafting from his too-big leather armor. He forced my attention to his grotesque, goblin-like face, his ashen, bulbous nose reddened from what I assumed was an indulgence of fairy wine he'd likely stolen from one of The Pit's spectators.

"If you won't come, we'll throw her into the pit in your place," he growled, his milky eyes narrowing on me, sharp-toothed grin spreading with the promise of violence against those who wouldn't stand a chance.

I froze, my pulse roaring in my ears.

"Go…" Kish gasped, and I twisted around to look at her. She couldn't even push herself up.

"I'll be back," I promised, and the guards guided me out of the cell. "I'll be back!"

The beast within me bristled, growling lowly at the guards as they escorted me down the tunnels and to the entrance of one of the fighting pits. How bad were her wounds? Would she make it to the end of my match so I could tend to her?

We passed Rhyas in the tunnel, and I pulled against the guards. Rhyas stiffened when he caught sight of me but didn't speak, didn't react, *couldn't* react, lest he give away how much he aided me and the other captives.

"Kish!" I cried out, hoping and praying he understood.

The faintest hint of panic and terror flashed across his face as we passed, and I twisted to see him rushing toward the cells once he was out of view of the guards. I turned forward, fury burning in my chest, the beast within me pacing back and forth in quiet anticipation of what we stood to face.

A familiar face stood next to the gates, arms crossed over his leather-clad chest. The memories resurfaced as if they were yesterday, of him carrying an unconscious child through the tunnels, how he had watched from the other side of the bars as I ran for my life from the Featherclaw who had shredded nearly half of the children he'd helped kidnap to pieces.

He had spent every moment since that terrible day ensuring my life was as difficult as he could make it.

"Well, hello there, Thalia. Ready to put on a show for us?" Santor said, his green eyes lighting up as he leaned against the wall. I didn't give him the satisfaction of a response as I caught sight of a new signet affixed to his breast. He'd been promoted again, and I wondered just what he'd done to curry favor with Arden more than he already had.

He huffed a laugh. "So cold. I wonder if you'll be that cold when we bring you in for Arden's enjoyment again."

The wooden gate groaned as it rose, and I flinched at the bright light of the pit as it flooded the tunnel, the roar of the crowd flooding my ears in deafening waves.

"Good luck," he whispered and shoved me forward.

I grunted as I hit the dirt and resisted the urge to look back at the wooden door as it closed behind me, locking me within these terrible walls. No, I couldn't let myself get distracted, not from what I stood to face.

My hands tightened into fists as I looked up at the massive creature crawling along the cage ceiling encapsulating the pit. Its long, armored body, lined with countless legs, wound and twisted as it turned its attention on me. Its head was a mass of countless beady red eyes and a razor-lined mouth armed with two monstrous pincers.

The beast growled within me, teeth bared, relishing in the fight to come—in all the ways we could bring this creature down.

Its blood will stain these walls just as the others did.

Blood soaked into my fur—my dappled gray coat painted in the crimson of my own blood mixed with the foul green of my prey—before pooling in the dirt beneath my paws. I panted, barely able to keep myself upright as I stood over the body of the creature who had put up far more of a fight than I cared for. The deafening sound of the crowd's applause was unbearable. Most of the patrons cheered while some seemed displeased that I'd survived, clearly hoping for a more gruesome show. My legs quivered with exhaustion as I stumbled off the body.

I lifted my gaze to them, barely able to make out their faces in the darkness of the seats beyond the blinding lights of the pit. If only I could get up there, tear every one of them apart for what they subjected us to.

Something crawled over my skin as my attention was drawn to one spectator in particular, her eyes as black as the souls of those around her, her skin gray. Her smile was wicked, and there was power in her stare, the sort of power that promised violence and cruelty. She wasn't like the other fae, and I wondered if she was even fae at all.

The beast within me recoiled under her gaze, but I didn't allow myself to buckle. These monsters would never break me. They deserved to be trapped in these pits, to be beaten and bloodied, torn apart by these terrible creatures. I wasn't sure what came over me, but I launched into a run, teeth bared as I charged toward the crowd. Their cheers quieted as I leaped at the cage, biting the metal, desperate to tear through it and get to them.

I was tired of being their entertainment, tired of fighting for their pleasure. It was their turn to entertain me, to bleed for *me*.

The patrons broke out into laughter, but as the metal started to bend under my jaws, they quieted, their laughs quickly fading to worried murmurs, then screams as the cage cracked. Guards rushed into the pit below, shouting at me as I continued to tear and fight to get through.

Pain shot up my spine, my skin burning where Arden's mark inked my skin, and I whimpered as I released the cage and fell. Guards rushed me as I hit the ground, pain racking my entire body, Arden's mark on fire as he brought me under his control.

"Fuck you!" I shouted as my magic dissipated, the beast falling into the darkness of my soul, our connection severed under Arden's magic. "You'll all bleed as we have!"

Hands grabbed me, yanking me to my feet before dragging me into the tunnels and out of view of the patrons. Arden stood at the mouth of the cavernous tunnel, waiting for us, arms crossed over his chest, his golden eyes lit with fury as he watched me. I panted as I hung from the guards' holds, my strength giving out, my magic abandoning me under his command.

"What the fuck were you thinking?" he demanded.

I met his glare, eyes burning with every ounce of hatred I held for him, but I gave him no answer.

"You won. All you had to do was return to the gate, and I would have tended to your wounds," he said, letting out a sigh.

"How merciful of you," I said flatly. "Tending to me while the others suffer."

I flinched as he lifted his hand to brush a callused thumb over my cheek.

"You are not like them," he said, his voice softening. "You are my most prized fighter." He leaned closer to me to whisper, "My most beautiful."

My skin crawled at the way he looked over my body, as if I wasn't a person but a possession.

"You're disgusting," I said through my teeth.

"Perhaps I'll have the guards bring you to my chambers tonight," he said, something unnerving in his expression as his eyes hardened. "Then I can show you just how *disgusting* I can be."

I bared my teeth at him, desperate to tear him to shreds and leave him for the Coronis to pick and tear into pieces while he still breathed.

"Take her to her cell. Her wounds don't seem too severe," he said and lowered his cold gaze on me. "Maybe next time, you'll be more receptive to my offer of care."

"Don't hold your breath," I growled.

His lips twitched into a half smile before he grabbed the collar of my shirt and jerked me closer to him. His breath poured over my face as he spoke, stinking of ambrosia liquor. "You will bend to my will, Thalia, or I will break you."

He roughly released my chin and stepped to the side, nodding for the guards to continue. No strength remained for me to fight, Arden's magic sapping me dry, and I found myself unable to stay on my own two feet. I slumped against them as they dragged me into the tunnels and back to my cell, the shouts of The Pit's patrons rising into a roar as the next match began. It was a distraction to the outburst I'd caused, and it annoyed me how quickly the terror I'd made them suffer had been swept under the rug.

Fighters and other captives rushed to hide in their cells, murmuring to each other as they avoided the guards' attention. I could barely make out their dirt-stained faces as they watched us from the darkness of their dwellings. Bars groaned as they opened the door to my chamber, and I cursed as the guards threw me onto the cold stone floor before slamming it shut and storming back down the hall.

"Thalia," Kish groaned from her cot as she tried to push herself up.

"Stop, Kish!" Rhyas said, slipping into view from where he had hidden himself. He rushed to my side as I pushed myself onto my hands and knees, Arden's magic finally releasing me from its hold.

"You actually beat that thing?" Rhyas asked, searching me for wounds.

"Before I went for the patrons," I groaned.

He stiffened. "Are you fucking insane? You know what, you don't have to answer that."

I winced as he forced my head back and poured water over the gash across my forehead to flush the creature's blood from the wound.

I hissed as the liquid burned into my flesh. "That's not fucking water!"

"No, it's alcohol to kill any infection. Now shut up before you attract the guards," Rhyas retorted. "What did you think you'd accomplish going for the patrons?"

I huffed a laugh. "You should have seen the terror on their faces when the cage cracked."

"You cracked the cage?" Kish asked from her cot as she struggled to push herself onto her elbows.

Rhyas twisted around to pin her with a glare. "Kish, for the love of the gods, don't get out of that fucking bed. Your leg is broken."

He disappeared from my side, hurrying to Kish and forcing her to lay back down. I grunted as I pushed myself to my feet.

"I'm all right," she said, and relief flooded me to see her fully conscious. "You gave me your blood; this will be healed in a day or two."

I stumbled over to the cot before easing down, wincing as each movement tore at my injuries. "Is it only your leg?"

She shrugged, and I knew she was downplaying it. "That and some cuts and bruises."

As I looked over her though, I could see she was just as drained as I was, just as worn. Rhyas took a while to tend to my wounds, ensuring everything was cleaned as best as he could, leaving no room for me to speak as he chastised me.

"We're going to get out of here," I muttered, looking at Kish, who sat beside me on the cot as Rhyas headed for the shelves lining the wall nearby.

She blinked for a moment, seeming shocked, but then doubt passed over her face like a looming cloud. "I don't know how that's possible."

"I don't care what I have to do. I *will* kill Arden," I said, my hands balling into fists at the memory of how he touched my face, of how he'd shown his *favor* over the years. "Whatever the cost."

She huffed a laugh, but I grabbed her hand. "Promise me."

A weak smile curved her lips. "Whatever the cost."

"Fuck," Rhyas breathed.

"What is it?" Kish asked.

"The guards are going to start their rounds to distribute food and water for the day," he said, stashing the salve back in its place. "I'll return. Just stay put."

He disappeared out of our cell and hurried down the hall.

"Mealtime!" someone shouted, and the captives and fighters all crowded the entrance of their cell across from us, desperate for the only meal we got each day.

"Get back! You know the rules!" one guard shouted, shoving some of the captives back before dropping a bucket of water and another with whatever food they'd decided to grace us with for the day. The moment the guard moved away from the cell, the cellmates rushed for the food, fishing out bits of bread and scraps before devouring it.

Those who had been here for a long time knew to ration their food, to be careful of making it last, but there were some who hadn't learned, who had fallen into an endless cycle of feast or famine.

"Enjoy," a guard said as he dropped a bucket of water and two trays of food. Fighters were afforded more food than others on fighting days. As soon as the guard stepped away, I rose and slipped my arm under the handle of the water bucket before grabbing the food trays.

"Wow, we have meat today," I grumbled, staring down at the filet of fish that looked like it was already missing a bite. I set the food down on the bed beside her and hurried to the shelves to grab two wooden cups before returning to Kish's side to get her a drink. "Here."

She took the cup and downed the water in swift gulps before gasping for air. "Thanks."

I drank some water down, relishing in the temporary cool relief it gave me, but still, I remained thirsty.

"You need to feed," Kish said, holding out her wrist.

My fangs lengthened at the thought of it, but I shook my head and pushed her hand away. "You eat and focus on recovering. I'll feed once that leg is healed."

She let out a sigh and sniffed at her food. "Ugh, I think they fished these out of the sewers."

"Probably," I grumbled, pinching off a piece and popping it into my mouth. "Yum, not even salted today."

Kish's brows drew together as she blinked, swaying.

"Kish?"

"I'm…" she started, but she slumped against me, her body going limp.

"Kish? What's—" The room began to spin, my body weakening. "Fuck."

I stood but immediately fell to my knees. Figures appeared in the entrance to our cell. I tried to stand but couldn't, and I was hoisted up, my strength quickly fading, darkness touching at the edges of my vision.

A familiar figure appeared before me, his emerald hair the only distinguishable feature in the blur.

"Arden," I growled, my words slurring. "What did you—"

He captured my chin, lifting my face to look up at him as he split into two, three.

"I think it's time for another lesson in manners." He released my chin and gestured to his guards. "To my bed chambers."

CHAPTER 20

BARRETT

The flames pressed against the cage of my body, pulling me back in the direction we'd come from as we descended the stairs into deeper caverns. I drew a deep breath, running my hand over my face as I tried to focus on anything but the thought of her, of how she had looked from the moment we'd set foot in Elythias and how fucking stupid I felt for even caring.

"How is Vivienne settling in?" Lucia asked, glancing at Marcus as he held the torch up to light her path. A few warriors separated us as I took up the rear, watching for any signs of an ambush or creatures that might follow, but I could still hear them clearly.

"She's doing all right," he said, a hint of hesitation lacing his words, as if he himself didn't believe them. "She spoke with Salwa yesterday, seemed a bit disoriented when she got home. When I asked her about her trip, she couldn't seem to remember parts of her visit. That, or she was confused as to when things happened."

"Did something happen?" Lucia asked.

"Tobias said she started acting strange in the last couple of days before their return. I'm a little worried about her."

I tried not to focus on their conversation, instead checking the stairwell at our backs as I extended my hand, flames dancing within my palm to the stairs behind us. It proved near impossible, though, in the tight confines of the stairwell.

"If there's anyone who can help her, it's Salwa," she said.

"Thanks," he said and slid her a teasing grin. "Maybe our resident songbird will grace her with a visit. She always enjoyed listening to you sing."

She swatted at him. "You catch me singing to myself in the Archivallia once, and now you won't shut up about it."

My nose wrinkled as the air grew fouler with each step, the stench becoming near unbearable as we reached the base of the stairs. "Fuck, it smells foul down here."

"They once held a creature in captivity here," Lucia explained as we stepped into a large, dark cavern. It was empty, void of any signs of activity, but as I stepped forward, Marcus lifting his torch and I my hand, I could faintly make out bars built into the stone wall on the far side.

It wasn't only animal waste I smelled or the damp, moldy scent of stagnant moisture—it was death, fear. Not just fear, but pure terror, the sort that shredded your insides and left you unable to sleep. I searched the dark corners of the room, listening for signs of anything that might be here with us, every inch of my body keenly aware of how wrong the air felt against my skin.

What had happened here that would leave this space tainted with the scent of terror so many years after it had been cleared?

"Thalia said this was where the Pit Master tested the children they took," Lucia explained, and something crawled over my skin.

"Tested?" I asked, frowning.

She lifted her hand, and flames sparked to life in her palm as she stepped forward. Her hands swept through the air in front of her, more torches lighting along the walls.

"Marcus, Alec!" Lucia called, and Marcus and another male swiftly approached. "Guard the stairwell. Make sure we aren't taken by surprise."

"Understood," they said in unison and hurried to the stairs.

I lowered my hand, dousing the flame as I took in our surroundings. An old wooden table stood nearby, broken down the center and covered in dust and cobwebs. Dread curled in my gut as I neared it to find small shackles littering the ground amidst the bits of wood and debris.

"How exactly did they test them?" I dared to ask, my stomach twisting.

"The creature hunted them," she said as she paced toward the bars. "They either escaped or died."

She came to a stop at the bars, reaching out to the cell door that lay ajar, the bars twisted and marred. "Looks like the creature finally got free."

"Please tell me the fucker got what he deserved," I said through gritted teeth as I came to a stop at her side. The cavern beyond the bars smelled far fouler than I thought imaginable, and I found myself stifling the urge to let the flames consume everything that remained.

"Not the death I would have preferred for what he'd done," she said, something darkening her silver eyes, and the flames around us flickered.

"We continue the search," she said, turning to the others as we gathered in the center of the room. "These tunnels go farther, and there's no telling—"

Her steps halted, and I stiffened at the presence skittering over my skin and the sound of a low growl at our backs. I twisted around and looked skyward to meet the gaze of something in the darkness.

A shrill cry pierced the air as a creature launched at us from the dark ceiling above the bars, the monstrous, cat-like beast stretching out clawed paws for us.

I crashed into Lucia, knocking her out of its path, and it collided with another warrior. They both fell to the stone before it bit down on his throat, tearing and shredding at flesh and bone as the other warriors drew their weapons. Shouts erupted around us as Lucia and I jumped to our feet, drawing our own weapons.

"Lucia!" Marcus called.

"Stay your ground!" she shouted, and he and Alec halted.

The dark creature lifted its bloody maw from the fallen warrior's throat, its feather-tipped ears pinned back as it growled at us. It was cloaked in fur and feathers, its tail tipped with long plumage that reflected the light of the torches in hues of green and blue.

"This the creature you spoke of?" I asked, flames snaking from my hand down the blade of my short sword.

She widened her stance. "It is."

The few warriors stepped in, shouting, trying to get a hit on the creature, just for it to twist and swat their weapons away. I steeled myself and launched forward. It twisted around, yellow eyes latched onto me before it shrank from the flames I wielded.

It leaped away, plowing through the few warriors and barreling for the stairwell where Marcus and Alec steadied themselves. Marcus drew his sword, and Alec bristled before shadows consumed him and fell away to reveal a bear.

The warriors followed it, but as the creature reached the entrance, it seemed to hit something, as if an invisible door barred its exit. It clawed at the air—tore and ripped in desperation to get free, and something like unease pooled in my gut as carved text around the entrance began to glow.

I blinked, my brows furrowing as what appeared to be a collar of light glimmered faintly beneath its fur in response.

My pulse roared in my ears as I stepped closer to Lucia. "Lucia…"

She gasped as the creature started to break through, the text glowing brighter, and a sense of dread wound around my stomach. "It's warded! Get ba—"

Light erupted, and the stone beneath our feet shuddered as a strange energy tore through the air, the magic knocking us back. I groaned as I pushed myself up, and cracks crawled and wound through the stone above us, debris and dust falling on us before it began to collapse in massive chunks at the entrance.

"Lucia!" Marcus shouted before rocks blocked the entrance, cutting off his voice and separating us from them.

Pain splintered across my head, and I twisted around to Lucia as she stepped back.

"Get down!" I shouted and shoved her under me as the ceiling collapsed, casting everything in darkness.

CHAPTER 21

THALIA

"It's going to be all right," I said, keeping my voice low and calm as I held my hand out toward a fae child curled up beneath a table. "We won't hurt you."

Her violet eyes darted between me and my outstretched hand and, finally, she reached out a trembling one. Her porcelain skin was dusted in shades of green and blue, and her teal hair was matted, cloaking her feather-dusted shoulders.

"You're one of the feather folk, right?" I said with a gentle smile as I took her hand, helping her to her feet. It was difficult to mask the fury I felt seeing a child in this wretched place again. I'd hoped we wouldn't find any, but after an hour or two of searching, we found her, and I knew it was only the beginning. We would find more, and I only prayed they were alive and unharmed.

Feather-tipped ears rose from beneath her hair, twitching at what I assumed was the first acknowledgment of her kind in gods knew how long, and she nodded before sniffling.

"Do you have a name?" I asked, dreading the thought that someone might be binding these poor children again. "Did they take it from you?"

She shook her head. "My name's Aesos."

A sense of relief washed over me; perhaps whoever was responsible for all this wasn't using Arden's same cruel methods or at least weren't skilled enough to. It would make getting them all out far easier.

"Aesos, this is Damien and Micah," I said, gesturing to them as they stood nearby, watching quietly so as not to startle her any further. "We're all here to help get you out. Are there others?"

She looked from me to Damien, Micah, and the few warriors at the entrance before turning back to me and nodding hesitantly.

"Do you know how many?" I asked.

She shook her head.

Unease coiled in the pit of my stomach, but I continued to smile. "That's all right. Can you take us to them?"

She glanced at Damien and the others nervously. "But the guards..."

"They're no longer here," I said, and her eyes widened. "You're free. We're getting you all out."

"Truly?"

"Truly," I said, my heart twisting at the first glimmer of hope in her expression. "You can trust us."

I guided her toward the others, hating how filthy she was, how her beautiful skin was marked with scrapes and bruises. How many others like her had never seen the light of day again?

Damien lowered to his knee. "Just a little longer, and you'll be able to see the sky again. We'll get you home to the floating islands quickly."

Tears welled in her eyes, her lips curving into the first smile of what I hoped would be many more.

The ground shuddered beneath our feet, the walls shaking, and my heart lurched as I braced myself against the table, instinctively shielding Aesos with my body. She cried out, curling up into me as she looked to the ceiling, dust raining over us.

"What was that?" Micah asked, looking around nervously.

The beast within me paced and my heart raced. "Someone tripped a ward."

Damien stilled, and our gazes briefly met, dread crawling over me like ice.

"Damien?" Micah said, glancing at him.

"Thalia, I need you with me. I need to make sure Lucia is all right," Damien said, his skin paling. "You'll be able to track her down the fastest."

I nodded before lowering myself to Aesos' level while Damien barked orders to the others, grabbing an earth magic wielder to join us. "Listen to me. I need you to be strong. This is Micah, my bonded. I want you to go with him and show him where the others are to get them out. Can you do that for me?"

She drew a deep breath and nodded.

"You get them out, Micah," I said, turning to him. "No matter the cost."

He drew closer to me, his voice dipping low. "I've seen what those wards can do, lost friends to them when we pulled you out of this hell. I'm not leaving your side. If there are more wards—"

"Promise me," I said, my voice far harsher than I intended as I grasped his hand. "Promise me."

Fear painted his face. "I promise."

"I'll be all right. I'll meet you at the gates," I assured him before pressing a kiss to his lips.

He held me close, resting his forehead against mine. "I love you."

"I love you, too," I said, before pulling away to lead Damien into the tunnels, leaving the other warriors to aid Micah in searching for the remaining prisoners.

We couldn't leave anyone behind. Not Lucia, not the captives, no one... Not again.

CHAPTER 22

THE GIRL WITH STORMY EYES

10 years prior

White hot pain shot up my spine, carving a burning path down my arm.

Hands grabbed my face, pulling me back against a solid body, and hot breath poured over my skin, the scent foully sweet with lingering hints of ambrosia liquor, of fae wine and gods knew what else.

A deep voice poured into my ear, guttural and low. It clawed its way into my brain, searing into the ink staining my skin. "How many times do I have to teach you this lesson before you learn?"

I couldn't respond, biting down another scream as agony tore into my shoulder, my face smashed sideways against stone as he held me in place. Rock cut into my bare skin, tearing into the wounds that still lingered. My lashes lifted, the room spinning too fast, surroundings blurred. I tried to move, tried to fight, but my body wouldn't respond, my limbs leaden, legs useless.

"You. Are. Mine," he growled in my ear, his body pressed against me. "You will always be mine, and you *will* submit to me."

Never.

My fingers twitched, failing to follow my command to ball into a fist as he slammed me against the stone again and again. Then, he stilled.

The stone beneath me shuddered, and the weight at my back vanished, air flooding my lungs as I was allowed to breathe. Every breath burned, every attempt to move sending electric shocks through my body.

"What's going on?" he shouted.

Rushed footsteps filled the chamber, but I couldn't find the strength to lift my head, to turn to see who had entered the room.

"We're under attack, sire."

"By who?" he shouted, his voice drifting farther away, the hiss of fabric reaching my ears, followed by the sound of a zipper.

"We aren't entirely sure," the guard admitted, barely able to meet his gaze. "They've breached the main gate."

"You're all fucking useless! Call the fighters. They will defend The Pits or they will die. I want..." The door slammed shut, and I was left on the floor, weak, unable to move, to speak.

The pain in my tattoo faded in his absence, but my magic didn't return, the beast still cut off from me. How long had I been here? How much had he drugged me this time? In the past, he would drug me enough to make me weak, wanting me to be fully conscious for every second of his punishments. Did he plan to keep me here longer than usual?

Was Kish all right? Had she been taken as well?

My heart stilled at the subtle sound of steps, and boots appeared in my line of sight. Fingers laced into my hair, and my head was pulled up. I grimaced at the bite of pain but could do little more than that.

"You're lucky he's claimed you," Santor said as he forced me to look at him.

Words bubbled up my throat, but I couldn't work my lips, my tongue.

He leaned in closer, his whispered voice like poison. "That's all right. We know what Rhyas has been doing for you and your immortal friend."

No...

"Just wait until you see what Arden has in store for you once we've dealt with this inconvenience," he said as he dropped me back onto the cold stone floor. My bones rattled as I grunted at the impact. The door opened and closed once more, and I prayed I was finally alone.

Every inch of my body ached, throbbing pain splintering across my head. I drew a shaky breath, trying to find my way through the haze to regain control of my body before he returned.

No matter the cost.

Silence stretched on, and the room shook as a distant boom echoed through the tunnels. Was someone breaking through wards? Were the tunnel systems collapsing?

"Fuck," I rasped, trying to push through and move.

Arden would eventually return, and I refused to be here waiting for him like this—waiting to be used again. Kish needed me, the others needed me, and if Arden and Santor had plans, they needed to be warned of them. If Nastra was under attack, this could be our chance.

A growl slipped from my throat as I barely managed to lift my head from the ground, but no amount of blinking could clear the fog. No matter how much I reached out to it, the beast remained silent. Had he drugged me with Aethersbane?

The door slammed open, and I stilled.

"Gods."

Air rushed from my lungs in relief at the sound of Rhyas' voice, his heavy footfalls echoing through the chamber as he raced for me.

"Thalia!" He turned me over, averting his eyes from my naked, shivering body. "I've got you."

He eased me onto my back before pulling his cloak off and draping it over me. He looked a mess, his gray skin coated in sweat, his hair disheveled, and his armor... Gods, his armor was covered in blood.

"What's going on outside?" I rasped, fighting to sit up.

"A group of warriors in black leather are attacking The Pits," he said, rising to rush to Arden's dresser for clothes.

"Do you know who they are? Where they came from?" I asked as he returned, dropping the clothes at my side before unsheathing a dagger.

"I don't know anything yet," he hissed as he ran his blade across his wrist. "It won't be enough to clear the Aethersbane from your system entirely, but it should help clear the sedative enough for you to move."

He pressed his wrist to my lips, and my fangs elongated immediately at the taste of his blood, at the deluge of fae magic. It was potent enough that I couldn't stop myself from latching on and drinking deep. It had been too long since I'd last fed, and the rush of it was like a punch to the gut.

Before I could give wholly into it and take too much, I pulled away, though every part of me screamed for more. I bit back the hunger, panting on air that was too thin. "Where's Kish?"

He began dressing me, my limbs still unresponsive.

"Rhyas," I demanded when he didn't answer.

"She's evacuating the survivors," he said through gritted teeth.

My blood chilled. "Survivors?"

"It's a shit show out there right now. Guards are using the chaos to drag females off, prisoners are trying to escape, one of the beasts got loose. Their binding triggered one of the wards and collapsed the lower tunnel cells."

"Oh, gods." I forced the fear back, balling my hands into fists. The effects of the drug were starting to fade as his blood soaked into my system. "Why the fuck are you here and not with her?"

"I couldn't leave you to face Arden alone," he said and then looked at me guiltily. "And she told me either I came for you, or she would."

Gods, anything but that. If she had come when Arden had still been here…

"You can understand why I told her to evacuate while I broke you out," he said.

I drew a deep breath and pushed myself up to sit, my fingers still numb, my body still aching but useable.

"What the hell are you doing?"

We twisted around to the open doorway to find two guards staring at us. One of them turned to look over their shoulder. "Get Arden!"

The two guards charged for us, and Rhyas leaped to his feet, drawing his sword before he blocked one of the guards' blades.

"Get up!" Rhyas growled without looking back at me.

I groaned through the pain, muscles protesting my commands.

Get up, get up, get up!

The feeling returned to my hands as I pushed myself onto my hands and knees, desperate to get out, to help him as blades clashed and grunts of pain filled my ears. A guard crashed into the dresser before he fell to the ground in a heap. I crawled toward him, elbows buckling under my weight, my sweaty palms slipping against the stone.

Rhyas slammed into the wall, barely bracing the guard's sword as he tried and failed to hold his ground. Fuck, I needed more time, just a little more. I could feel the drug's effects wearing off, but not fast enough. Rhyas grimaced as the guard overpowered him, the blades shaking as they inched closer to his throat.

I grabbed the sword from the unconscious guard and steadied myself against the dresser. Rhyas' amber eyes flashed to me as I forced myself to move, running the sword into the guard's side. He cried out before we collided, falling to the ground in a mess of limbs. His sword clattered onto the ground, and Rhyas quickly kicked it aside before pulling me off him.

"Come on! We've got to get out of here!" he shouted, shoving me toward the door before slamming his dagger into the guard's throat, silencing him for good. I hesitated, my eyes falling on the pile of clothes on the ground nearby, *my* clothes.

"The fuck are you doing?" Rhyas shouted.

"I can't leave it," I said, feeling stupid in my inability to leave it behind as I dropped to my knees and fished the small scrap of remaining fabric from the boy's coat out of my pocket. I rose, rushing after him and stumbled into the tunnel, my legs and arms strengthening.

Rhyas stopped at my side, looking up and down the tunnel, blood rolling down his face from a cut above his brow. The ground heaved, and we stumbled against the wall for support.

"Sounds like another creature broke loose and brought down another ward," Rhyas growled, pushing off and grabbing my arm to help me down the tunnel. "We've got to get back to Kish and the others."

We hurried through the tunnels, ducking out of sight when we crossed paths with guards, running once they'd passed. As we reached the mouth of a tunnel that opened up into a cavern, Rhyas grabbed my arm, pulling me back behind cover. I gasped at the sight of an enormous creature gorging itself on the entrails of one of the guards, bodies littering the ground from its rampage.

"Looks like the ward didn't take this one out," Rhyas muttered, looking around for any way to get past it.

I hated how I couldn't shift, how I could still barely sustain my own weight. Useless. Fucking useless...

The creature's head shot up, and we stilled, air halting in my lungs. It was hideous, patches of fur missing from its wrinkly skin, face sunken in, eyes a ghostly white. Blood coated its maw, chunks of flesh dangling from its serrated teeth. It twisted around, attention drawn to movement on the far side of the cavern as a woman stepped from the darkness, her silver eyes cold, her black hair dancing around her as fire erupted at her feet. Her hand shot out, and the flames surged as the creature launched for her. It went up in a pyre, its shriek lasting only seconds before it crumbled into dust.

She moved with graceful steps as she scanned the area.

"They're the ones who attacked the front gates," Rhyas whispered, holding me in place.

Others dressed in black leather poured out of the tunnel after her, weapons drawn as they searched the cavern. She looked in our direction, and Rhyas and I ducked deeper into the tunnel.

"Go back. We don't know what they're here for," Rhyas whispered.

"Please stay." Her voice was soft—powerful, but soft.

Rhyas cursed under his breath. "I'll hold them off. Take another route to the cells and regroup with Kish near the gates."

"There's no need for you to hold us off," she said, her voice growing closer as we twisted around. "We're here to end this wretched place and free the"—her eyes found mine, and her steps slowed—"prisoners."

She held out her hands as if to show she was unarmed, the light returning to her silver eyes. She'd seemed so cold moments before, so detached from the weight of taking a life.

"You're immortal," she muttered, shock painting her face.

My brows furrowed, and another of the warriors rushed to her side, his long, dark hair pulled back out of his face, his olive skin coated in a sheen of sweat. She held her hand up, and he stopped before following her gaze to us.

I shrugged off Rhyas' hand when he tried to pull me back. "Why do you ask?"

She offered me a smile. "We are as well. My name is Lucia." She gestured to the male at her side. "This is my mate, Damien. We're here to bring you home, to free the other prisoners."

I carefully assessed her before glancing at Rhyas. "This is Rhyas, and I'm Thalia."

"Is he your friend?" she asked.

I nodded, watching her wearily as we stepped toward them before taking in each warrior who entered the cavern behind them. I faintly caught sight of some with pointed ears. "You're working with fae?"

"Erebus' warriors," she clarified.

Damien turned to her. "I just heard from Zephyr's team. They're gathering the other prisoners near the gates to start the evacuation once we arrive."

I stiffened. "You can't!"

They simultaneously looked at me.

"Every one of us is bound to Arden," I explained, pulling back my sleeve to reveal the ink on my skin. "We cannot set foot out of this place without his permission. If we do, we'll trip the wards, and our only escape will collapse on us."

Lucia and Damien exchanged looks briefly. "Then we kill Arden."

Hope blossomed in my chest. I'd forgotten how hope felt, how it fluttered and danced like the forest sprites I'd seen as a child. Was this really happening? Would we truly be free?

Rhyas stepped forward as Damien eyed him wearily, his hand going to the hilt of his sword. Rhyas seemed to notice and pulled back his sleeve. "I'm just like her. I was a guard, but I'm a prisoner as well, forced to serve. I don't serve him willingly and will gladly slice his throat if given the chance."

Lucia lifted her hand to Damien, and he eased, releasing his sword. "He speaks true."

"My mate is on the lower levels," Rhyas said, his words a near plea. "She's evacuating the other prisoners to a safer place."

"The lower levels are crawling with guards," Lucia said, and my blood went cold. "Our teams are working to break through them now."

Rhyas took a step forward. "Please, we have to go to them!"

Lucia and Damien nodded, and she looked at me. "Can you fight?"

"Arden poisoned me with Aethersbane," I said, hating how weak I still felt with it in my system. "I can't shift, but that won't stop me from tearing them apart."

CHAPTER 23

THE GIRL WITH STORMY EYES

10 years prior

It was a bloodbath, bodies wedged together tightly as they fought in the cavernous tunnels. Blades narrowly collided against one another, guards and warriors crying out as blows were delivered.

And Kish was nowhere in sight.

Rhyas growled as he pulled his sword from the gut of a fae guard, the blue tint of his skin turning a sickly gray before he collapsed. I watched from the corner of my eye as Lucia held her hand out toward a group of guards charging at her. They stumbled to a stop, grasping their throats as their bodies seemed to crumpled in on themselves before disintegrating into piles of dust. Water collected around her hands before she sent a wave of droplets tearing into the crowd.

Her warriors were skilled, cutting down Arden's men left and right, but there were too many of them, too many pit fighters forced to fight and too afraid to stop. Even Lucia looked as if she was beginning to tire.

"Kish!" Rhyas shouted but received no response. Had they gotten out? Had they been captured by Arden's men?

"Looking for your friend?" I twisted at the sound of Santor's voice, narrowly catching his blade before he could slice me down my back.

"What did you do?" I growled, shoving him back before slicing the head off another guard charging for me.

"Wouldn't you like to know?" he said, his smile curling my stomach as he stepped back, allowing other guards to rush us.

"You bastard!" I shouted, slicing through the guards. "Cowardly bastard!"

"Thalia!" Rhyas yelled, and I turned to him as I took down another guard.

He came to a stop, his gray skin pale, his breath ragged.

"Santor's here," I said wearily.

"Where?" he asked, searching the crowd.

"I just lost him in the crowd," I said, panic clawing its way into my chest. "He knows you've been helping us."

His eyes flashed to me, the same panic I felt reflecting in them.

"He said Arden knew and had plans."

Rhyas turned, yelling as he grabbed the shoulder of a guard who was fighting another before running his sword through the guard's stomach. I rushed to his side, cutting down guards, fighters, I didn't care. If Santor had Kish or was trying to capture her, I didn't care who stood in my way. I would get to her, and I would skin him alive.

Whatever the cost.

Her voice echoed across my thoughts. That couldn't have been the last time we would speak, the last time I'd hear her voice. I'd lost my parents all those years ago. I couldn't remember them—their faces, their names. Kish had become something of a mother to me, had cared for me, taught me everything she knew. I couldn't lose her too.

Terror flooded my system with each second as I took down one guard after another, blood painting my skin in streaks of crimson, onyx, emerald. So many I'd once shared cells with, so many who didn't deserve to die.

Air whistled sharply in my ear, and I flinched away from it. I scanned the crowd, finding Santor across the sea of fighters at the mouth of a tunnel. He lowered a bow before handing it off to one of the guards despite having missed me. He tipped his head to me with a smug grin and disappeared from view once more. Rhyas grunted at my side, and I turned to him, freezing at the sight of the arrow protruding from his neck. His lips parted, his body locking up as he gasped for air, his hand rising to the shaft.

"No!" I caught Rhyas before he could hit the ground. "No, no, no!"

He grabbed onto me, pulling and tugging on my tunic as he gasped and choked, blood bubbling from his lips before pouring out onto his armor.

"Shh, shh," I whispered, tears blurring my vision.

His lips parted and closed, his bloodied teeth clamping together as he tried to speak, each movement only causing him to bleed out faster.

"Don't talk," I begged, looking around for anyone who might be able to help as Lucia's warriors pushed the guards back, leaving us in the sea of lifeless bodies.

"Ki—" He choked before he could fully form her name, blood splattering across my face.

"It's gonna be all right," I said, my voice breaking. "We'll make it to her. We'll make it out together."

"Ki..." His grip on my tunic slackened, his struggles slowing, his body easing in my arms.

"Rhyas?" I whispered, tears rolling down my cheeks.

He didn't respond, didn't move, his amber eyes no longer that bright shade I'd grown to know, to love.

"No," I muttered, my vision blurring. "No, please. Don't—"

I pulled him closer to me, the sound of his heartbeat gone.

"Don't leave me," I sobbed. "I need you."

My cries turned into screams as I called out to him, rocking his body amidst the chaos.

"Thalia!" Lucia grabbed my shoulder and her eyes widened at the sight of Rhyas, of his blood coating my body. "I'm so sorry."

"Help him!" I begged.

Sorrow clouded her expression. "I can't."

"He has to... He can't be—" My voice broke, sobs clawing their way up my throat.

"We can't stay here," she said, but I couldn't look at her, couldn't take my eyes off his face. "You're the only one who may know where the prisoners are, and I need you now more than ever to be our guide."

Our promise to one another echoed in the recesses of my mind.

No matter the cost.

Was this the cost of our freedom? How many more lives would we lose? Would Kish...

I didn't allow myself to finish the thought as I eased Rhyas onto the ground.

"I'll get her out for you," I promised him, my voice breaking. Tears threatened to fall once more as I slid my hand over his eyes, closing them, hating how they would never brighten my day again. His deepest regrets resurfaced, and I hated that he wouldn't be able to see the end, to all this, wouldn't be free of the guilt he felt all these years. "I swear, I'll kill Santor, and we'll bring Arden down so we can all finally be free."

I'd killed so many guards—so many of my fellow fighters. I knew some of them, tried to reason with them to stop fighting us and to help, but Arden had them too terrified.

And so, I continued to kill.

I wasn't sure who exactly Lucia was, but the power she had at her disposal was too much to comprehend. She wielded every magic, just as the gods did...but she was immortal. With her leading the attack, the guards had become desperate before we'd broken through, coating their blades and arrows in Aethersbane. Lucia had been hit, leaving her powerless and us at a disadvantage.

"We're through!" one of Lucia's warriors shouted as they broke through the line, forcing guards to back into another tunnel, opening the path to where I knew Kish and the other prisoners were likely hiding.

I kicked a guard off my blade before sprinting toward the head of the fight, leading them into the tunnels toward the lower level.

Fates spare them. Let them be safe.

My heart dropped into the pit of my stomach as we drew closer to the cavern, bodies of prisoners littering the ground. I searched every face, checked for pulses, but none were hers. None were alive.

I ran faster, leaving Lucia and her warriors to check for any survivors. "Kish!"

I stumbled into the mouth of the cavern to find a group of survivors huddled together, fighters at the forefront.

"Thalia!" Kish cried out, running for me. "Santor and his men nearly broke through to us, but they suddenly retreated and..." Her steps slowed as she drew closer, and her reddened eyes fell to my bloodied tunic.

She could smell him—his blood. They were mates... Had she felt it the moment he'd fallen? When he'd taken his final breath? Her cheeks were stained with tears, and my heart constricted. She blinked away more tears and looked back at the prisoners hiding behind her. "We need to get them out."

It was like a blow to the gut not to feel her pull me into a hug, to not acknowledge what I feared she already knew.

"We've cleared a path," I said, but I hesitated. "We have to hurry though; they likely have more reinforcements coming."

She nodded and looked back at the others. "Hurry!"

They hesitated, exchanging nervous glances, before rising to their feet.

Lucia emerged from the tunnel. "Come on!"

We ran, allowing Lucia and Damien to take the lead while her warriors, Kish, and I took up the rear to guard their backs. Kish hadn't said a word about Rhyas, and I couldn't find the strength to speak his name. I had to focus on getting her out, on getting them all out. Then, I would return for him. I wouldn't leave him in this place. He deserved to be laid to rest beneath the sky, beneath the shade of a tree.

Shouts echoed from the tunnel behind us, and I looked back to find more guards rushing for us. My blood chilled and boiled all at once at the sight of Arden leading them.

"Keep going!" I shouted as I slid to a stop. Kish ran to my side, along with several warriors. "We'll buy you time!"

We couldn't let them follow any farther. We had to barricade them in somehow, had to kill Arden if we truly hoped to escape.

"We can bring the tunnels down on them," Kish said.

"How?" I asked, glancing at her as they drew closer. "We don't have any wards to trip."

"I rarely used it," she said. "Was forbidden to."

My brows furrowed. "Use what?"

"Get them out," she muttered and ran toward them.

"Wait, Kish!" I cried out, running after her.

Her pace quickened while my strength waned, and the distance between us grew. She dragged her hand along the wall as she ran, and the ground beneath us heaved. I stumbled forward, crashing against the ground as the tunnel shook, rocks and debris falling from the ceiling.

"Kish!" I cried out, shoving to my feet, dodging boulders as they fell.

Arden and his men slid to a stop, scanning the ceiling, and his eyes flared as he looked at Kish. I immediately felt his influence in the tattoo, pain splintering across my skin. Whatever magic she was using, he would cut her off, and she would be defenseless. She pulled a dagger from her tunic and threw it through the air. It sank into his shoulder, and he stepped toward her before realization flashed across his face. He pulled the dagger free, inspecting it before throwing it aside. At that same moment, I felt his influence fade, the pain vanishing.

She'd somehow laced the dagger with Aethersbane.

A hand grabbed my arm, and I twisted around to find myself face-to-face with one of Lucia's warriors. His shaggy brown hair was covered in blood and dust, his soft blue eyes searching the collapsing tunnel before falling on me. "It's gonna cave in. We have to get out!"

"No!" I cried, turning to find Kish had slowed her pace, her hand firm against the wall. Arden and his men charged for her, and she turned around to look back at me.

She smiled, and tears flooded my eyes. "Kish! Stop!"

Her lips moved, all sound dying out as I narrowed in on what she tried to say but couldn't voice.

Whatever the cost.

And the tunnel collapsed on her—on Arden and his men.

Screams flooded the tunnel, ghastly, painful screams, and it wasn't until pain sliced into my throat that I realized it was me. I was screaming. I fell to my knees as Arden's magic died out from my arm, and from the corner of my eyes, I watched as the ink faded, inch by inch, dying out…

As he died.

He was dead.

As was Kish.

I pulled from the male's hold, crashing into the boulders keeping me from her. She couldn't be gone. She couldn't be… I sank to my knees, tears flooding my vision. Hands grabbed me, pulling me from the ground and up against a hard body, and I was carried out as the rest of the tunnel slowly collapsed.

CHAPTER 24

BARRETT

I blinked, agony lancing through every inch of my body, collecting and concentrating in my back.

"Barrett," Lucia whispered, and I looked down at her, at her wide eyes as she lay amidst the rubble beneath me. Blood dripped onto her cheek, rolling down onto the dirt.

"Don't move," I groaned, feeling the weight of stone pinning me down.

"You're bleeding," she said, seeming to take no notice of her own wounds.

"I'll be fine, just—" I winced as I pushed myself up, the rocks nearly too heavy. I managed to lift myself enough, muscles protesting as I shifted my weight onto one hand and shoved the sheet of rock off us.

I collapsed against it, chest heaving as I tried to pull in oxygen, the air too thin. "Fuck."

"No…" Lucia muttered, drawing my attention to her, to her wide, panicked eyes as she looked to where the entrance should be. She rose to her feet and stumbled toward it. "No. No. We can't…"

The scent of blood filled the air, and I grunted as I pushed myself to my feet. Crimson painted the stone, pooling on the ground and winding a path back to the pile of rubble that now barred our escape. The faintest glimpse of a leather-clad hand peeked out from beneath the massive pile of boulders and rocks.

"No," Lucia continued to chant, her hands passing over the stone as she searched for any means of escape. "We can't be trapped. Can't be—"

"Hey," I said, reaching out to touch her.

"No, I can't… Not again," she said, tears rolling down her cheeks as she clawed and scratched at the stone. "Let me out!"

It was faint, but a voice cut through the silence, muffled.

"We're here!" I called back, doubting they could understand. "I've got Lucia! She's all right!"

No distinguishable response came, and Lucia continued to pull at stones. Air caught in my lungs as the boulders shifted, groaning under the weight of what remained of the ceiling. It might collapse on her.

"Lucia. Hey, look at me," I said, grasping her arms to pull her away. Her wild, tear-filled eyes found me, her skin pale, her body trembling. "You're gonna be all right. We're gonna get out of this."

Her eyes wavered, drifting back to the stone, to the glimpses of crushed bodies. "I need to get out. I need—"

I forced her to look at me. "No, you look at me. I'm here with you. Focus on me."

She swallowed but nodded, her breaths shallow—too shallow. The air was already thinner.

"Breathe," I said firmly. "Slow. In through your nose, out through your mouth."

Her trembling hands tightened on my forearms.

"Close your eyes," I said, and she did, drawing deep, shaky breaths. Carefully, I guided her through the rubble, feeling our way to an alcove where she was well away from what remained of her warriors. She stumbled behind me, holding onto me tightly.

"Here," I whispered, turning to guide her down to sit.

"Please, don't—"

"I'm not going anywhere," I assured her as I lowered to my knees before her.

Her lids lifted a fraction, as if she was too afraid to look up. I'd never seen her this afraid. She was always in control, level, and calm.

How the hell were we going to get out of this? Were Marcus and Alec both alive on the other side of that wall of stone? Were they getting help? I feared if we tried to move any of the stone, the rest of the cavern could come crumbling down on us.

I scanned the darkness, unable to make out much of anything, couldn't even see the bars. Had every means of escape been cut off?

Lucia drew a shaky breath, and my heart twisted at how her hands trembled. I turned to settle in beside her, hating seeing her so shaken. I was supposed to watch her back, keep her safe. Now, she was trapped here, and I didn't know if I could get her out.

"I used to tell my sister stories about you," I whispered.

She didn't speak, but I felt her lean against my shoulder.

"She always hoped she'd get to see you reincarnated and meet you one day," I said. "She used to make these..." I huffed a laugh at the memory, my eyes burning as I remembered how small she was. "She used to make these flower crowns from the little blossoms that bloomed along the creekside of Moonhaven."

Lucia didn't speak, but her expression softened.

"She made them for years, practicing until they were near perfect," I said, my voice growing thick as I thought of how stupid it was that I was here and Calliope wasn't. She should be here, not me. "She always talked about how one day, when you returned, she would present you with one made of the jasmine blossoms that grow in Selene's temple."

"You were very close to her, weren't you?" she muttered, her voice a bit more even, though her hands still trembled.

"She was everything," I admitted. "You would have liked her. She was nothing like me. She was everything good in the world, deserved everything it had to offer."

"That same good lives within you," she said, and I couldn't bring myself to acknowledge her words.

"Your father was abusive," she said, not quite a question.

I drew a deep breath and nodded. "He was. Claimed he was molding me into the perfect future Kyrios of House Stoicheion, molding Cali into the perfect, submissive female to one day be mated to someone of importance."

There was a strange relief in saying her name out loud, to not hold her close but to share what remained of her existence with someone for the first time in decades.

"I..." She hesitated, and I tilted my head to get a better look at her. "I was furious when I learned of what your father had subjected you and Calliope to. So few of our kind are able to bear children, and for those who are able, for them to treat such a precious gift so cruelly..."

She drew a deep breath. "When I met you in that cell, saw how tightly you had locked yourself away from others...I almost saw myself. A child who'd been beaten down into submission too many times, forced to do whatever it took to survive, fearful of trusting anyone or anything because everyone had failed me."

Something curled in my gut at her words. She...saw herself in me?

"Did your..." I couldn't bring myself to finish the question.

"They don't get the privilege of being called my parents—they were never that," she said, unable to look at me. "They kept me hidden, locked away from the sunlight, from the moonlight, for most of my life. For so many years, I was a prisoner… sold and used."

The flames surged to life beneath my skin, white-hot anger flooding my system.

"Damien and Zephyr found me, pulled me out, helped me heal, but…"

"It's something you never fully heal from," I said when she couldn't finish.

She nodded slowly. "I swore I would do everything in my power to ensure no other child suffered that way. I hated when I found you, when I learned of what had happened in my absence, how I'd not looked into it sooner. I could have prevented it all."

"Don't put that on yourself," I said. "We were young when you were killed in Moonhaven, and he was really good at hiding what he truly was. He fooled a lot of people."

She drew a shaky breath but nodded. "Sorry you had to see that."

I shook my head. "Don't ever apologize for something like that. I'll tell you what," I said, releasing her to stand. "Since you shared your deepest fear, I'll share mine."

Her dark brows furrowed.

"I'm scared of spiders," I said.

She cocked a brow. "You don't have to lie to make me feel better."

I scoffed. "And here I thought you were the master of telling the truth from lies."

She blinked.

"Try again. I'm not lying."

Her lips twitched, revealing the faintest hint of a smile, and she stifled a laugh.

"No, it's all right. Get it out of your system," I said, relieved to see even the smallest hint of her cheerful self. "Can't stand the fuckers."

"Thank you. Your secret is safe with me," she said and rose to her feet, shaking her hands out as if she was shaking the remnants of her panic away. "I think I can focus now."

I tilted my head as she closed her eyes and drew in a deep breath.

CHAPTER 25

THALIA

My paws slammed against stone as I raced through the tunnels, Damien trying and failing to keep up.

She was trapped. She was *trapped*. I needed to get to her, to run faster.

It had been faint, and we feared she'd been injured, but Damien and I had heard her reach out to us, her voice flitting across our thoughts only moments ago.

A single word.

Help.

Marcus and Alec were at the base of the stairs, searching for a way to get past the rocks barring their entrance. They were both covered in dust and blood, but they didn't appear to be gravely injured.

"What the hell happened?" I demanded as I shifted back to my immortal form, rushing past them directly to the wall of boulders and rocks blocking the entrance.

"The damned beast tripped a ward."

"Yressia is still alive?" I muttered under my breath. "Lucia!"

I pressed my ear to the stone, listening for anything.

Silence.

I slammed my fist against the stone, suddenly finding myself facing the rocks that had crushed my dearest friend. No. No, this couldn't be happening again.

"Lucia!" I screamed and pressed my ear to the stone again.

Muffled voices echoed from the other side.

"Stay back! We've brought help!" I called, unable to discern anything they were saying. Was Lucia injured? Her thoughts had sounded weak, shaken, and Damien had feared she might not be able to concentrate on their connection if she was trapped in too tight of a space or injured.

"Step back," Damien said as he came to a stop beside me, followed closely by a female warrior. "Raina, can you feel them?"

She pressed her hand to the stone and closed her eyes in quiet concentration. "She's there. One other…"

Only one other? My heart leaped into my throat. Was it Barrett? What had happened to the others?

"All others are dead," Raina said. "The cavern is unstable; we'll get one shot to get them out."

Damien nodded as she stepped to the side and lowered to a knee, pressing both hands to the ground.

"You'll have seconds," she said, and Marcus and Alec jumped to their feet, ready to help.

"Just a little bit longer, *mea luna*!" Damien shouted. "Step back from the entrance!"

Raina nodded her head, and her lids slid closed. Stone groaned, the walls shaking before the boulders shifted, twitched, and then slowly rose. Raina ground her teeth together, her arms trembling as she forced them to move.

"Lucia!" Damien shouted, dropping to the ground to look under the stones as they lifted barely enough for us to get a glimpse of the cavern. They continued to rise slowly—too slowly.

"She's not gonna be able to hold them!" I yelled as I twisted to try to make out anything in the darkness. I was greeted with the sight of the crushed remains of fallen warriors and the Featherclaw who'd gifted me this scar.

Raina grunted and let out a desperate cry before the stones rose higher, leaving a clear path. Relief flooded me at the sight of Lucia, Barrett holding her steady as they stumbled toward us.

"Hurry!" Raina cried out, blood dripping from her nose.

Barrett dragged Lucia through the opening, their boots smearing a path of blood. The boulders fell the moment they were clear, sealing the entrance once more.

Raina fell back, gasping for air, and Alec caught her.

"Lucia!" Damien rushed to her. She smiled weakly up at him, and Barrett helped steady her, his eyes never leaving her.

Something tender reflected in his steel eyes. They had never seemed so soft, so full of worry and care.

"Thank you," Damien said, sparing Barrett a glance before scooping Lucia into his arms.

Barrett nodded, and my feet moved on their own, rushing to him at the sight of the blood painting the side of his face.

"Are you all right?" I asked before I could think better of it.

His eyes shifted to me, weary and exhausted.

"It's just a scratch," he said, but at the way his eyes wavered, the way his pupils expanded, I could see through the bluff.

"Thank you," I muttered, and he blinked, his brows rising, as if he had expected me to say something else.

He suddenly couldn't hold my gaze, and my heart squeezed as his lips parted and closed. His expression changed, hardening, and he shrugged past me. "I only did what was required."

Twenty-three.

We had managed to save twenty-three captives. Sixteen of them were children, the youngest only five. Had I been that young when I'd been brought here?

We had lost four warriors in the end, four souls who would never return to loved ones waiting for them. Several warriors stayed behind, earth Stoicheion dismantling the fortress, ensuring nothing and no one would ever set foot in that cursed place again.

Lucia knelt before a human child, probably nine or ten by the look of her. She was just as filthy as the others, her red hair a mess of knots and curls. A strange accent I had never heard before painted her tongue when she spoke.

"What's your name?" Lucia asked.

"Nora," she said timidly.

"Is that the name your parents gave you?" she asked, and I felt my breath tightening in my chest.

"It is."

I let out a sigh of relief. To hear a child made it out of that place and still had the ability to speak their true name brought me the most profound joy.

"Do you remember where you're from?" Lucia asked.

She shook her head. "They took meh from mah home when Ah was little. Ah donnae even remember me mummy and daddy's names."

"Sounds like she came from Scotland," Damien said, kneeling before the girl. "If you like, you're welcome to go back with us."

She glanced between them, and I could already see how she hesitated, how her body tensed.

Lucia offered her a smile. "You will never have to do anything they forced you to do here. You'll be free. We have plenty of food, we can get you fresh clothes—whatever you need, it will be yours."

I turned from them, walking through the makeshift camp we had set up to tend to the wounded before we made our way home. The sun crested the mountaintops, chasing the twin moons into their slumber. An envoy would be arriving from Erebus' kingdom soon to collect most of the prisoners. He would aid in reuniting them with their families—their domains. The feather folk child, Aesos, waved to me as I passed, and Micah, who was tending to one of her wounds, looked back to offer me a warm smile.

Warmth filled my chest at the sight of it, and I drew close enough to press a kiss to his cheek before continuing toward the forest.

The air was fresh, caressing my skin and rustling my hair. Sprites danced along the branches high above me, the tiny orbs seeming curious of my presence. Tiny, furry creatures scurried about, their long ears perking up as they paused to look back at me with big, beady eyes before running for cover.

I fell to my knees before one of the trees and reached down to brush moss away from the single stone anchored into the dirt at the base of it. It wasn't anything special, etched with simple words in the old language.

Rhyas and Kish. Beloved Mother and Father.

I reached out, running my fingertips over the rough surface, tears dotting my lashes.

"Sorry it's been a while," I muttered. "A lot's happened since we last spoke."

The sprites drifted down from the canopy, bouncing around the trunk and maintaining a careful distance from me, as if they couldn't resist their curiosity any longer. I didn't spare them a glance as I stared down at the stone.

"I'm doing well," I said, my voice growing thick. "I'm, um… I'm teaching others how to fight, and…we're making a difference in the Mortalrealm. I've found a family, I have friends."

The grass rustled as the tiny, long-eared creatures scurried closer to watch me.

"I'm bonded. He's wonderful to me. You would've liked him… Mom. Dad." Something built up in the back of my throat, my voice shaking. "I miss you so much."

Heavy yet quiet footsteps reached my ears, and the scent of moss and life filled my lungs. I didn't need to turn to know who stood at my back, his towering form casting me in shade.

Silvash lowered his head, the strands of moss hanging from his enormous antlers falling over me as he gently brushed his muzzle against my arm.

I turned to him, taking in his beautiful face, his fur as rich and colorful as it had been when we had first met.

"Hello, old friend," I said, wiping away the tears. He lowered his face, his eyes closing before I leaned against him, wrapping my arms around him in a warm embrace. "Thank you for watching over them."

I looked back at the stone, wishing they were here with me, wishing they could see what we did.

"We saved many lives today," I said, and I knew it would bring them as much joy as it did me when I said, "And no one will ever suffer in those pits again."

CHAPTER 26

BARRETT

I dropped a copper piece on the bar top the following night, and Semele eyed it as if it was some sort of creature ready to bite her.

"Not tonight," she said, and I frowned as she set a glass in front of me. "Lord Damien's covering the tab to celebrate."

I looked across the room to where Damien, Zephyr, and Lucia sat. Damien's eyes met mine, and a smug grin curved his lips before he tilted his head to me. I frowned at the lack of drink in his hand.

"Look at you," Micah said, nudging me as he took a seat at my side, drawing my attention from Damien to find Thalia following close behind him. "Survived your first trip to the Godsrealm."

I rolled my eyes before taking a swig of my drink, grimacing as it burned a path down my throat.

"Seriously, though. I'm glad you made it out of there all right," he said.

"Me too," I said. "This place is too fucking dull without me around."

Micah huffed a laugh and, for a moment, I thought I saw the corners of Thalia's lips tip up into a smile. Something blossomed in my chest as her eyes slid to mine. They were the softest of grays, like churning clouds before a storm. Something nagged in the back of my mind, a familiarity that scratched at the surface, but I shook it off before focusing on the amber liquid in my cup.

"How're you feeling?" Lucia asked as she took a seat on the other side of me. I couldn't have been more thankful for the distraction.

My brows rose, but I gestured to the newly healed skin on my forehead. "Good as new. The healers are ridiculously good at what they do."

She smiled before taking a drink.

My smile faded, and I lowered my voice. "How are *you* feeling?"

She smiled sheepishly. "I'm all right. Sorry you had to see me like that. It's been a while since I've lost it."

I shook my head. "Don't apologize."

"I had gotten better about being in tight places, but it all happened so fast, and I..."

"You don't have to explain," I said. "How's that kid settling in?"

Her brows rose. "Nora? She's adjusting all right. We set her up in a spare room in the keep so she isn't far from us. She's still unsure of everyone, but I think she'll warm up. She's the sweetest child. I can't wait to see her personality come out."

"Scotland," I said. "Do you think she has any surviving family?"

"There's no telling," she said with a shrug. "She doesn't even remember where she came from. No family name... It would be near impossible to find them. So, we're offering for her to live here with us." She cleared her throat. "Um... I need to talk to you, if you don't mind stepping out for a second."

"Pulling me away from my hard-earned drink?" I said as I arched a brow.

She elbowed me. "Oh, shut it. Come on."

I set my drink down and turned to Thalia and Micah. "Thalia, be a dear and watch my drink. Make sure Micah doesn't spike it with something and drag me to his bed."

Thalia spit out her drink, breaking into laughter, and Micah blinked at me as I slid out of the stool to follow Lucia.

"I may just be tempted to fucking do that!" he yelled across the pub.

As we stepped outside, I found Damien accompanied by a few warriors, and I frowned. "What's going on?"

"Sorry to pull you away from the celebration," Lucia explained, taking a roll of parchment from Damien, "but the paperwork was completed while we were gone."

My brows furrowed. "What paperwork?"

"The charges against Atticus Stratos and Jissena Stratos." She extended the scroll to me, and I took it, unable to form words, unable to believe what she was saying.

"I've been conducting the investigation since I pulled you out of that cell, as was Salwa," she said, her smile somber. "Zephyr completed everything while we were gone."

I unrolled the scroll, reading through the charges. The list was extensive.

"It isn't the justice Calliope or you deserve, but it's a start," Lucia added.

"I'm about to conduct the arrest personally," Damien said.

I hadn't seen Atticus in decades, wasn't even sure what to make of what they were saying. "This is really happening?"

She laid a hand on my shoulder. "It's really happening. The question is, do you want to be there when we bring him in?"

I looked down at the order, my pulse pounding in my ears. "Yes. I want to see that bastard's face when he finds out." I wanted him to see that I was out, that I was alive, that he had failed in silencing me, that he wouldn't win.

Damien nodded to the warriors at his back, and they took the lead. I fell into step with Lucia and Damien, unsure what to say. We walked in silence for a while before Damien cleared his throat.

"When you were being held in the cells," Damien started, and I cocked a brow, "did you make any friends?"

I eyed him wearily. "Depends on what you mean by friends."

The corner of Damien's lips kicked up into a half grin. "Did you play nice with any of the nasties with big connections?"

"I may have made some beneficial relationships," I admitted. "Why?"

"I need someone with your... *particular* connections," he said, his voice dropping to a near whisper. "Rumors have gotten around of an organization with ties to the Godsrealm; they could be a serious issue."

"Is this a formal job offer, *Your Majesty*?" I asked.

"If you're willing," he said. "It'll be dangerous. You'd be building relationships with the members of this organization, gain favor, keep tabs on them and report to me. If your covers is ever blown, they'd kill you."

I eyed him, but my lips curved into a smile. "Sounds like fun."

"Atticus and Jissena Stratos!" Damien yelled as he banged his fist against their door, and I stood at the back of the group of warriors who had accompanied him, curious to see how this all developed.

Lights came on in the window upstairs, and it wasn't long before Atticus appeared at the threshold, still in his night clothes.

"What is the meaning of this disturbance?" he shouted as he opened the door before he realized who stood before him. He stiffened at the sight of Damien and Lucia.

"Y-your Majesty," he said, dipping his head, and Jissena appeared behind him. "Is everything all right? You gave us a fright."

"Atticus Stratos," Damien said, unrolling the parchment and Atticus' brows furrowed. "You are hereby charged with use of Aethersbane, on a member of The Order, treason, tampering with evidence, obstruction of justice, conspiracy—"

"What is this?" he demanded. "These charges are preposterous!"

I stepped forward, folding my arms over my chest, the flames writhing beneath my skin, dying to devour him. "Shut your fucking mouth and listen."

He paled, his mouth falling open at the sight of me, and gods, if it wasn't the most satisfying sight.

Damien continued listing off the charges while Atticus stared at me. "You-you... What are you—"

"Jissena Stratos, you are charged with conspiracy, obstruction of justice, tampering with evidence..." Damien continued as they both stiffened, their attention turning to him as he listed the charges she faced.

Atticus stammered. "This is a lie! It's all a lie!"

"The only lies are the words falling from your tongue," Lucia said flatly, her face holding no kindness. "You would do well to shut your mouth and come quietly."

"I will do no such thing. I am a Kyrios of House Stoicheion! Females do not have any business speaking on matters of—"

Damien grabbed him by the throat and slammed him up against the wall. Atticus gasped for air, kicking as he fought to breathe. The air around us turned icy, the shadows twitching on the ground. "You would do well to remember who you speak to."

Jissena sobbed in the doorway, and one of the warriors stepped forward to put her in shackles.

Atticus gaped as Damien's grip tightened around his throat; the shadows around them converged until what appeared to be claws inched along the wall toward him. "That is your queen you are speaking to. You will show her the respect she deserves."

The shadows inched closer, darkness slithering along the ground at Damien's feet. "Or, we could forgo all this nonsense and I could feed you to the shadows now. They're eager to taste you."

Atticus shook his head, and I wrinkled my nose at the sour scent tainting the air. A dark stain appeared on the front of his trousers, and I huffed a laugh.

Damien released him, and he fell to the ground, coughing and sputtering.

"Put this bastard in shackles," Damien spat, leaving him on the ground. He looked to the guard holding Jissena. "And get her out of here."

Atticus rubbed his throat, growling before flames sparked to life. My feet moved on their own, shoving Damien out of the way as Atticus rose, fire erupting as he launched at him. My own flames rose to the surface, snaking through Atticus' fire as it engulfed me, and I drew my dagger before tackling him to the ground.

His skin grew hotter, his face turning red.

"I'll take you all with me!" he shouted, and my heart lurched at the molten veins crawling across his skin, his skin turning white hot. I slammed the dagger into his chest, and he stiffened, his eyes bulging, and the fire eased, his skin cooling and paling.

He choked on his blood, coughing before gritting his teeth together as he glared up at me. He clutched at the dagger, only for me to shove it deeper into his heart. "You were... a waste of good blood... It should've been you... that... night."

Air escaped his lips, and his hand fell away, his eyes drifting from me.

My hands as I clutched the hilt.

"Barrett," Lucia said softly, and I flinched, twisting around to look at her.

"I..." I looked over him, my heart racing. "I didn't... He went after him, was gonna use Telos Pyrai. He—"

She rested a hand on my shoulder, and warmth spread through my skin. "You're all right. He was a fool to attack Damien. You simply defended him, defended the innocent lives nearby who would have been killed in his attempt to stop this."

I looked down at my uncle, at his unseeing gaze.

"Come on," she said, and she helped me to my feet, my mind still racing, my heart pounding.

I settled onto the ground nearby, and she offered me a reassuring smile. "Just sit here for a moment. I'll be right back."

She hurried back to where the guards were now collecting Atticus' body. I blinked, my eyes falling to my hands.

I'd killed him...

Jissena would rot in prison for the rest of her unending life, but she wasn't the only soul who had wronged us. The corruption went deeper; the Kyrios of House Leukós and his son were still involved in some way.

"Foolish male," Lucia said as she sat down next to me, and I blinked, unsure of how much time had passed, how long I'd been lost in my thoughts. She watched as the guards and Damien took care of everything, locking down Atticus' house and searching it for any evidence of how far the corruption reached.

Despite my doubts, despite how much I'd resisted her help, Lucia had done as she promised. She had proven my innocence, had seen the people responsible punished for their crimes.

For a moment I felt a gentle nudge, as if Calliope stood at my back. And despite how much I had feared to trust her, to confide in her...

"My father killed Cali."

White dots danced across my vision as the side of my face slammed into the floor, my teeth smacking against one another as the taste of blood filled my mouth. Anger flared deep within me at the sound of Calliope's sobs, the salty scent of her tears filling my nose, and I fought against my captor's hold to glare up at where Father stood by his desk.

"Foolish girl," Father said, glass clinking against the wood as he set his drink down. The room stunk of ambrosia liquor, his eyes glazed over, his cheeks flushed. "Did you really think you could get away with this?"

"What were you thinking running away?" Mother demanded, her eyes reddened, more from tears than from drunkenness. Father had likely been taking his anger out on her the past few hours. It wasn't like I cared whether he had put his hands on her or not. She never cared to intervene when he beat us, never cared to stop his abuse.

I pushed myself up, but a boot slammed into my back, shoving me back onto the floor, and I growled. Father stalked across the room, and Calliope whimpered as one of Atticus' guards twisted her arm behind her back, forcing her to stand taller.

"Ungrateful child. You can't even fathom the opportunity laid out before you!" he shouted.

"You mean an opportunity for you," she retorted, and my heart stilled at the fire in her eyes. "I will never marry that bastard, and I will no longer bend to your will!"

A crack echoed through the room as his hand collided with her face, and she crashed to the floor, her cheek already red, her lip split and swollen. She twisted around to face him, the defiance burning in her eyes something I'd never seen.

He stormed toward her and grabbed a fistful of her hair to pull her from the ground. She winced, tears rolling down her cheeks, but she didn't cry out. The flames pressed against the surface of my skin, begging to be free. I couldn't risk losing control, couldn't risk burning Calliope. They wouldn't hurt Father anyway, not with his own magic.

I twisted around, knocking the guard off me before jumping to my feet. "Calliope!"

Father lowered himself to her level, his anger warming the room. "You will do as I comma—"

He jerked back as she spit in his face, and my heart launched into my throat. His chest heaved, the room growing unbearably hot as he slammed her up against the wall, wrapping his fingers around her throat.

"No!" I shouted, running forward, but hands grabbed my arms as Atticus' guards swarmed me.

Calliope's eyes popped open, her lips falling open as she grabbed at his hands.

"Stop!" I roared, fighting to get to her, to get to him.

"Elias," Mother started, hurrying to him, but he didn't stop, his grip tightening, his teeth grinding together.

"Please..." She gasped for air, her voice breaking as she kicked at the ground just out of reach. "Stop... I can't brea—"

A deafening crack reached my ears, chasing the sounds from the room, and her hands fell away from him, her soft green eyes staring into nothing. He dropped her to the floor, stumbling back, and Mother stared in silence, her hand clapped over her mouth.

"Cali?" I muttered.

She didn't respond, didn't move.

Flames exploded around me, and I couldn't contain them—didn't know if I wanted to. Perhaps if I let them run freely, they might consume me and take me out of this world entirely. What life was there to live without her?

Fire engulfed every guard holding me down in a pyre of screams. They released me, and Father turned to me, crazed and furious.

"What will you do, boy?" he demanded, his own flames rising to the surface, as if they relished the possible challenge.

The fire spread quickly, snaking around us, and Mother shrieked as she stumbled back. I couldn't think straight, my vision turning red as heat flooded my system, demanding to end him, to devour him, to burn every inch of this cursed place to the ground.

I grabbed one of the burning guards and reached into his coat, feeling a sickening satisfaction in the way he flailed, how his skin was already blackening, his screams melding with the others.

"I should've known you'd never amount to anything," Father bellowed, and I threw the guard to the ground before stalking toward him. "You've always been weak, just like your sister."

He swung at me, his flames winding around his arm, concentrating in his fist, and I dodged it before crashing into him. Air rushed from his lungs, his eyes bulging before falling to the dagger protruding from his gut, a dagger that one of Atticus' guards had carried—

The blade laced with Aethersbane.

The flames at his command flickered before dying out entirely, and he lifted his wide eyes to me as my own built and built.

I growled, my teeth grinding together as I let them grow. "Burn."

My flames wrapped around him, and he cried out as they crawled over his skin, burning every inch of him. Mother's screams filled my ears as she caught fire, and I let the flames do as they wished until nothing remained.

My eyes fell to her bracelet dangling from my wrist, the inscription engraved on the gold plate haunting me just as deeply as her face.

vôu hallôs apeirïsï.

Love you infinitely.

It was meant to be a joke, a way to one up her in the words we always shared, but now, it felt more like a promise—that I would always keep her with me, that her memory would haunt me until the day I died, that my failure would remain engraved in my mind the way my message was engraved in the metal.

"I hadn't meant to lose control like that, but I...I don't regret what I did." I admitted.

"He got what he deserved," she said, resting a hand against my shoulder. "And I hate that I let this happen when you were children, that I hadn't listened to my gut about him and launched an investigation."

I shook my head. "You made it right in the end."

"There's one more thing before it's fully right," she said, and my brows furrowed as she brought a slip of parchment into view.

"Barrett Stratos, you are hereby cleared of all charges." She tore the parchment in half before me. I couldn't speak, could only watch as she smiled and handed me the torn piece of parchment that had been my undoing.

"Enjoy your freedom, hothead."

LUNA LAURIER

PART 2

1889

(420 YEARS LATER)

CHAPTER 27

BARRETT

I was in hell.

There was no other way to describe it. Bodies littered the ground, making it near impossible to fight off the beasts coming for our throats without tripping. Exhaustion gnawed at my bones, clawing at every muscle in my body after countless hours of fighting, which seemed to get us nowhere. The foul, rotting stench of darkling blood had overtaken the scent of grass and life that once filled this field, and I longed for anything else.

Agonized cries of wounded warriors filled my ears as they bled out on the ground, their stomachs ripped to shreds, succumbing to the darklings' bites as they changed. I'd seen too many fall to the corruption, unable to end them before black veins crawled across their skin. The shadows swirled in their eyes as their mouths split into gaping smiles, their hands clawing at their necks as they writhed and rose again as creatures that hungered for death.

I was responsible for them, commanded a unit of fifty warriors, and yet, here I was…failing them. I always failed those who relied on me.

Nearly a third of my unit had fallen, and many of the other units had joined them. I'd lost track of how many of our own I'd killed before they could change into darklings—how many I'd failed to end before they'd changed.

How had we gotten to this point? How had the darklings gathered in such an overwhelming number in such a short time?

"Barrett!" Micah's voice was barely audible, and I shook myself away from the unseeing gaze of another warrior who'd passed before he could turn. It was a better fate for them than to be forced to fight and devour their own kin at the command of the darkling queen.

I turned to find Micah forcing his way toward me through the sea of bodies, his face ashen, his black Elythian Leather armor covered in blood and dirt. He was still alive, despite the weariness in his gaze, and relief soared through me.

"Have you seen Lucia or Damien?" I called back before slicing through a darkling as it launched for me, black blood spraying across my face. I looked over my shoulder as I braced for another creature to attack— whether it would be a darkling or one of the shadow beasts the darkling queen had summoned, I didn't know. We hadn't seen any of the shadow beasts yet, and while I was relieved, I knew it would only be a matter of time before they appeared.

"Damien and Lucia took up strengthening the pit when I saw them last!" Micah shouted, his voice difficult to hear over the cacophony of blades, shrieks, and cries.

I cursed under my breath. The pit was the center of the battlefield, where warriors intercepted every darkling that had broken through the front lines before they could reach the healers' tents at the rear. Fear tore through me at the thought of her, more than halfway through her pregnancy, risking her life in the center of all this.

"She shouldn't even be on this fucking battlefield," I growled, my grip tightening on the handle of my sword.

She should be resting. Damien had been the most resistant to her fighting, but there was nowhere she would be truly safe on this side of the veil, and with the chance of the darkling queen appearing…

Fuck, this was a disaster, and it almost felt as if the darkling queen had orchestrated it to be such. Had she known the only person who could meet her in battle on equal terms was not at her strongest?

"And Thalia?" I demanded as a darkling intercepted me, and for a moment, I nearly faltered as my attention snagged on how much blood covered Micah. Was any of it his?

He sliced through another darkling, his ungraceful strike ladened with fatigue before he continued. "I got separated from her not too long ago, but our binding remains intact."

Thank the gods she was still alive, somewhere in this hellscape.

As I looked out over the chaos, I feared none of us would live to see the other side. Nearly half our fallen warriors rose again as darklings, and the waves kept coming, overwhelming us until it seemed like there was no end in sight.

I prayed The Fates spared us when her shadow beasts made their presence known—prayed she didn't summon Lupa again. The mother of the

Lupai had been massive, and it had taken many of us to bring her down. Lucia had fought the hardest, suffered the worst at her death. It wasn't until after the fight that I learned of their past, of how they had once fought side by side as friends in the Godsrealm when she lived as Moira.

"Barrett! Micah!" Damien's voice cut across the chaos.

Micah and I twisted around as a pack of Lupai plowed through the darklings overwhelming the warriors around us. The Lupais' bodies were a mass of shadow and black mist, their forms that of nightmares, with their split jaws full of teeth and fangs, their eyes glowing a menacing blood red as they took the darklings to the ground before tearing their heads from their necks.

Damien emerged behind them, darkness licking at his skin as he turned his gaze to us. The king's power was terrifying, but gods, was it a relief to have those beasts on our side. His presence could very well be the key to pushing the darklings back, and we needed it more than ever with the crumbling hope of victory. At Lucia's side, he helped balance the playing field as the sole shadow wielder in our army. Still, I feared that balance may tip to a failing scale should we find ourselves face to face with the shadow beasts should they no longer answer his call.

I looked across the sea of warriors, expecting Lucia to be close on his heels, but she never appeared.

"Lucia received word that a separate horde of darklings launched an attack on the city," Damien said, his chest heaving as his eyes shifted toward the front lines. "Micah, I need you to split off your unit to defend the humans and remaining civilians."

I swallowed, briefly glancing at the city in the distance. We had tried to spare the city, taking a stand in a clearing in the mountains, far from the valley where humans and civilian immortals hid.

"What about the front lines?" I asked. "More darklings have breached their defensive wall, and we're struggling to keep up."

"I'm headed there now to aid them," he said, and I froze.

"You can't go to the front lines," Micah said, his skin paling. "We can't afford to lose you."

"You won't," he said with cold confidence. "We'll reinforce the defensive wall and reclaim this battlefield."

The Lupai panted, and one of them whimpered, ears folding down as if cowering from something, and I frowned at their odd behavior. They had always been vicious creatures, relishing in the hunt, their resolve stronger than any of us could maintain.

I approached Damien, but one of the Lupai snapped at me, their terrifying jaws splitting as they growled. Damien stiffened, his hands balling into fists, and for a moment, he looked as if he even feared his own wolves.

"Damien, what's wrong with them?" I asked hesitantly.

"We're running out of time. I believe she's attempting to influence them," Damien admitted before he looked between us. "Be aware of the shadow beasts if they come for you. They may not be under my command for much longer."

"All the more reason you shouldn't go to the front lines," Micah said, and Damien pinned him with a look that made him bite his tongue.

"You should dismiss them if they're not listening," I said in his stead, not afraid to make Damien reconsider himself.

"We can't afford to lose them right now," Damien said then turned to me. "Go to Lucia. She's conserving her magic in preparation for the darkling queen's appearance. Guard her back, as she's the only one who stands any chance of bringing that monster down."

I grabbed his arm as he brushed past me, knowing there was no way in hell she had willingly allowed him to leave her side to fight on the front lines alone. "Does she know where you're going?"

The Lupai seemed to bristle at my presence, and I let the flames flicker to life in my free palm, a gentle reminder that I wasn't as helpless against them as many of my brethren were. He didn't meet my gaze, didn't respond, and his silence was enough of an answer. She didn't know, or else she would be here, endangering herself to watch his back. When he glanced back at me, the plea in his eyes was explanation enough, and my grip slackened.

"You're buying her time," I said in acknowledgment. "A chance, by thinning out the darklings breaching the front lines."

He held my gaze, not gracing me with a verbal answer, and I turned to the wall of flame wielders, watching as fire erupted before dying out again. Time was running out, our warriors falling faster by the minute. If we didn't do anything to change it, she would be among those to fall.

I nodded. "Understood."

A weary smile curved his lips, and my hold on his arm tightened. "Be careful. She needs you."

"I don't intend to leave my mate and child behind," he assured me, placing his hand on my shoulder. "You be careful as well. She needs you too."

Something blossomed in my chest to hear those words, to hear someone I so deeply admired valued my presence as much as I did theirs. I didn't deserve it, not for all the problems I'd caused her from the beginning, but I would do my damnedest to live up to her expectations—would go to the ends of both realms to bring her enemies to their knees.

Damien nodded and continued forward, warriors and Lupai following him in a wave across the battlefield, cutting down darklings as they went. Micah dropped a hand on my shoulder and pressed his forehead to mine, our breaths ragged.

"We fucking make this out together," he said, and I nodded, bracing to part ways with him again.

"On the other side," I said, taking his hand in a tight hold, not wanting to let go.

"On the other side," he echoed, and he split off, calling to his unit as he ran toward the city to defend what remained of it. Fuck, there was no telling what he would find there, what he stood to face, how many humans and immortals had already been killed or converted by the darklings. We had lost enough warriors; we couldn't afford to be thinned further. I shook the thought away and shouted out commands to my own unit to regroup in the center of the battlefield.

I only prayed Lucia would be all right when we got to her.

CHAPTER 28

THALIA

The foul taste of darkling blood lingered in my mouth, and I spit more of it on the ground. Gray fur was swallowed by black mist as I shifted back to my immortal form and gestured toward a warrior who'd been skewered by a darkling before I'd torn its head from its body. "Get her to the healers!"

I turned my gaze to the front lines. Our defenses had been solid, flame wielders burning darklings to dust before they could reach us, but the first hour passed, then the second...then the third. The defensive wall was failing, the flame wielders' fire magic sputtering out before darklings surged to the break in the line and devoured them. I could hear the screams of agony as they were torn apart, and it was in those moments that I cursed our sensitive hearing.

He's not among them... It isn't him.

I paused for a breath, my own magic waning, my heart depleting of the hope I'd clung to over the countless hours we had fought. I might be able to shift once or twice more, but after that, I would be spent. We couldn't keep this up much longer.

My hand rose to the chest of my leather armor, feeling the hum of magic in my binding tattoo, the faint presence of Micah still lingering within the ink. He was all right, he was alive...but I didn't have the same comforting proof of Lucia's safety, nor Damien's... Barrett's.

The beast growled deep within me as a shriek pierced the hot air, and I swung my sword at a charging darkling, slicing through it before turning to cut down another.

Don't die on me, beasty.

Rhyas' words flitted across my thoughts, the request I held close to my heart, the one promise I refused to break. I would not fall here; I would not have survived everything I had to die by these creatures' claws. I would not let his and Kish's sacrifices be for nothing.

I *would* get through this, find my bonded, my friends, and I *would* live to enjoy the other side of this hell.

Familiar yips of the Lupai reached my ears and I turned to find Damien through the chaos, warriors cutting down darklings at his side, his Lupai tackling more of the creatures in quick succession.

"Damien!" I cried out in relief.

His eyes found mine, and he offered me a smile. "Glad to see you're still alive."

"The feeling is mutual."

"I want that defensive wall fortified!" Damien shouted to his warriors as they worked through the darklings. "Today is not the day we fall!"

I shoved down the desire to ask him if he had seen Barrett, of how Lucia was faring before they had separated. If he hadn't said anything, they had to be all right. Right?

The Lupai whimpered at his side, shaking their heads and blinking, and Damien looked down at them, his brows furrowing. One of them stumbled forward, their whimper shifting into a growl.

"Damien?" I said, taking a step back. Other warriors took notice, exchanging nervous looks.

"No," Damien muttered as, one by one, the Lupai started to growl, their heads dropping low as they stalked toward me, toward other warriors.

Damien cursed and threw his hand out, shadows converging beneath him before the Lupais' forms rippled. They didn't vanish, though, didn't disintegrate as they usually did when he dismissed them.

"What's going on?" I shouted as they turned on him, their red eyes glowing with malice.

"They're being influenced by her," he said through gritted teeth, sweat dotting his brow as he focused his attention on them. Two of them vanished, but that still left ten deadly creatures who could tear us apart.

I readied my sword as one of them turned their red gaze on me, but it was pointless. They could solidify and disintegrate their bodies at will, leaving our physical weapons powerless, and I couldn't wield the kind of magic they were vulnerable to.

One of the shadow wolves leapt for Damien. He cursed as he raised his arm to block it, the creature's fangs sinking into his flesh.

"Resist her!" he commanded, and the other Lupai whimpered, cowering back a few paces, as if his voice might've weakened her influence. The Lupai before him didn't back down, though, tearing into his arm as if he was its enemy.

No! This couldn't be happening. We couldn't afford to lose them, couldn't fight them too. I ran toward him, desperate to help him in any way, even if it meant facing one of the terrifying creatures.

Light enveloped Damien, and I slid to a stop as the Lupai released his arm, falling back before disintegrating. The other Lupai bristled as a light magic wielder emerged from the fighting, his silver hair tinged with blood.

Damien took the chance to throw his hand through the air, attempting to dismiss them once more, and they all vanished. His shoulders sagged and he dropped to his knees, panting, his arm falling limp at his side.

The torrent sounds of the battlefield rushed from my ears, a new wave of fear overcoming me at the thought of losing the Lupai to the darkling queen, of what little advantage against the darklings we had lost. Damien's eyes burned into the ground where he knelt, momentarily lost, and I rushed for him, as did the Leukós user. Damien waved us off, his arm bloodied but functioning.

"You should get that checked out, Lord Damien," the warrior said as he inspected his arm.

"There's no time," Damien said, sweat coating his brow as he pulled his arm away and forced himself to his feet.

His weary eyes rose to the front lines, and for a moment, I saw a dangerous look of terrified acceptance within them—the kind of look one held when facing death was their only means of escape. As one of the few powerful warriors standing between the dark death tearing down our front lines and his mate...I feared he very well could be contemplating something stupid. "If we fall back, we lose the front lines.

"We couldn't afford that, couldn't afford to lose any more ground than we already had. No more darklings could get through; we had to give the warriors a break, allow them to clear out what had already breached the wall of flame wielders.

Damien looked skyward, and I followed his gaze to the black cloud of winged creatures overtaking the sky. My heart plummeted.

"She's nearby. It's the only way she could have taken control of the Lupai," Damien muttered. "And now ,she's summoned the Coronis."

The Coronis—a mass of winged shadow beasts that promised one of the most painful deaths. They were fearsome creatures, their beaks sharp, their talons just as deadly, and my stomach twisted at the thought of them descending on us.

"I'll defend against them!" the Leukós user shouted before disappearing into the battle once more. Were there other Leukós users still standing?

"Thalia, with me!" Damien ordered, charging the short distance toward the front lines.

I shook the tremors from my hands, gripping the hilt of my sword tighter, and followed him.

"Let's clear these beasts out!" I shouted to my men as we charged through the battle, cutting down unsuspecting darklings as they attacked other warriors.

I searched the countless faces, leaving my warriors to focus on thinning out the darklings while I searched for Lucia. She could be anywhere in this mess.

We'd entered this battle with almost four hundred warriors; we had never imagined we'd face thousands of darklings. Needless to say, our resolve had been shaken when their army approached, and we had seen just how many creatures we stood to face.

A deadly chorus filled my ears, and my eyes shot skyward to the black mass above us, nearly casting the moonlit sky in darkness. I'd seen him summon the Coronis before, but something twisted in my stomach at the sight of the hoard of crow-like creatures as they flew not *toward* the front lines in aid at Damien's command, but *away*, toward The Pit and the rear, where the healers worked.

Be aware of the shadow beasts if they come for you. They may not be under my command for much longer.

They descended, and my heart lurched. Something deep in my bones demanded I run, take cover. Flames sparked to life at my fingertips.

"Above!" I shouted, and warriors looked skyward to the rain of death descending upon us.

A bloodied hand shot up from the sea of bodies, and light erupted from the palm, shooting up before exploding into a white mist that fanned out above us. The Coronis crashed into the shield of light, some of them disintegrating into nothing while others spread their wings and rose to fly elsewhere.

"Focus on the darklings! I'll keep the Coronis off as long as I can!" the light wielder shouted, and I stumble as I returned to my search.

My bones ached more with each muddy step. This battle had dragged out far longer than it should have, the darklings coming in endless waves, bound and determined to exhaust us, and now, with their attack on the city we were divided, our numbers already decimated.

"Lucia!" I shouted, carving my way through the crowd.

My warriors fanned out, aiding the equally worn and weary units who had held the last line of defense within the pit before the darklings could reach the rear where the healers worked. There had already been so few members of House Latros. We couldn't afford to lose a single healer.

The warriors standing their ground were worse off than I thought. Too many darklings had gotten past the front lines, spread their dark magic like a plague to bolster their ranks and tear us down from the inside.

As I broke free of the chaos, my blood iced over at the sight of Lucia on her knees, her hand clutching her swollen stomach. I ran for her, shoving past warriors before I fell to my knees before her.

"Lucia!" I called over the shouts and shrieks as I laid a hand on her shoulder.

Her head rose, face painted with exhaustion, and gods, she was covered in blood. Her lips curved into a weary smile, relief faintly lighting her silver eyes.

My gaze fell to her stomach, where her hand remained, and my heart stilled. "Are you hurt?"

Her brows rose, and she followed my gaze to her stomach. "Oh no, I'm fine. Just winded."

"Are you sure?" I pressed, unable to miss how heavy her breath was, how her fingers trembled as they clutched the hilt of her sword anchored in the ground to stabilize her. "I can take you to a healer."

She smiled, and fuck, if it didn't offer some comfort in this hell to see it. "I'm fine. Have you seen Damien?"

I bit down on my response and averted my gaze.

Her gaze hardened. "Tell me, or I won't ask nicely the next time, Barrett. *Where is he?*"

I let out a sigh. I couldn't lie to her—she'd know the second the deceptive words left my lips. "He went to the front lines." Her eyes flashed and briefly flitted to the chaos at my back. "They became overwhelmed when our forces were split to stop the darklings attacking the city and—"

A shriek pierced the air followed by a cry. Lucia gasped and shoved past me. I twisted around to see a warrior pinned on his back by two darklings. As I leapt to my feet, Lucia slammed into the darklings, their bodies hitting the ground with tremendous force, and I cursed as she rolled away from them before stabilizing on her feet, sword at the ready.

One of the creatures rose, turning on her with a hiss before I plunged my sword into the back of its head. She dropped to the ground, kicking the legs out from under the other darkling before she sank her sword through its heart.

They both crumbled into dust, and I paced back a few steps toward the warrior as Lucia ran to his side. I grimaced at the sight of his shredded stomach, blood already coating his armor and pooling onto the ground beneath him.

"Were you bitten?" Lucia asked, her voice somewhere between gentle and commanding. "Can you get up?"

He tried and failed to rise, letting out an agonized grunt, and it only aided in causing more blood to gush out of him.

"*Were you bitten?*" she demanded.

He shook his head and gasped as he clutched his stomach. "They nearly got me, though."

Lucia turned to me. "Get him to the healers."

No. I couldn't leave her here. "You should take him. I'll stay here and fight."

"He can't stand, let alone walk," she bit back, rising to her feet. "Does it look like I can carry him, Barrett?"

I couldn't argue with her there.

"Get him to the healers then find me again," she said.

"You're the only one who can stand up against the darkling queen!" I shouted. "Your wellbeing outweighs that of a single warrior who may not even make it to the healers!"

"That's an order!" she shouted, the gentleness gone from her voice.

I heaved a sigh and ran my fingers through my hair. There was no arguing with her, and I growled my frustrations. What could I do to convince her to stay at my side? "Come with me."

"I can't," she said, and I hated how quickly she turned me down. "I have to be ready if the daughter of Matthias appears."

She was right. There was no telling when that bitch would show her face or where. The pit was the centermost point of the battlefield, if the darkling queen made her appearance at either end of it, Lucia would be better placed to quickly intercept her.

A wall of fire exploded at the front lines, drawing our attention. I prayed Damien was holding up, that his presence was making a difference, and we could bring an end to this madness. Lucia's eyes welled with fear as she watched the front lines in the distance, and she took a hesitant step toward it, as if she might abandon her post to go to her mate. I feared she might very well do that if I left her.

I crouched and looped the injured warrior's arm over my shoulder before hauling him to his unsteady feet. He let out an agonized cry, unable to hold himself up as I supported his weight.

Lucia stood, her gaze shooting past me to the front lines where her mate fought. I stepped closer to her, and her gaze shifted to me, the fear residing within those silver pools breaking something in me.

He's strong. He'll come back to you. I wanted to give her all the comforting words but couldn't bring myself to, fearful I might give her false hope. "Be careful, spitfire."

A smile crept across her face. "You too, hothead."

I pulled myself away from her, cursing that I couldn't stay at her side as I started toward the healers. She was powerful, she could hold her own, and I'd be back to fight at her side.

A shriek at my back halted my steps, and my heart stuttered before I twisted around to find myself face to face with a darkling bound by vines, torn jaws snapping at the air. It fought to get free, to get to us, claws slicing through air but coming up short. Lucia grunted, her hands balled into fists as she willed the vines to tighten around her target before she jerked her hand back. Roots shot into the darkling's chest, through its heart. The darkling disintegrated, and the vines fell slack as Lucia sagged on her feet, her breaths coming in quick pants.

Could she truly do this alone? Would she stand a chance against the darkling queen in her condition? I took a tentative step toward her, ready to drop the warrior and stay at her side.

She ground her teeth, seeming to pull herself together, to mask just how exhausted she was. "Go!"

I cursed under my breath but dipped my head and turned to hurry through the crowd before I made the mistake of arguing with her. The sooner I dropped this warrior off with the healers, the sooner I could get back to her. With each step, the warrior grew heavier at my side, his grunts quieting, the scent of his blood growing thicker in the air, overwhelming the stench of darkling and death. I had to move faster.

"Hold on," I demanded. "Just a little farther."

The edge of the forest grew closer, the white tops of the healer tents peeking out from the view of colliding bodies until we reached the rear guard, where rows of warriors stood the final ground, defending the healers.

"Just a bit longer! We're here!" I yelled, jostling the warrior who was no longer responding.

The hairs on my arms stood on end as a strange energy surged over me, something unnatural and wrong halting my steps.

"Barrett?" one of the rearguards asked, brows furrowing as my pace slowed. Then, he seemed to feel it too, his eyes wandering.

"Something's..." I looked around. Something was wrong, very wrong. The shrieks of darklings quieted around us, and I looked over my shoulder to see their bottomless eyes lifted to the tall trees. They didn't seem to care that their distraction allowed our warriors to cut them down, as if they welcomed death willingly.

I turned, following their gazes, and my heart lurched as a figure leaped from the forest. Tendrils of darkness swept out from her body before she crashed into the ground, and a shockwave of power shattered across the field. It slammed into us, knocking us back, and shadows erupted like great beasts, swallowing everything. I hit the ground, air rushing from my lungs, pain slicing through me as the sky was swallowed by darkness.

My sword nearly slipped from my grip as it slammed into the dirt, fresh darkling blood painting the black blade. They kept coming, the waves of death seemingly endless. With each darkling I brought down, two or three replaced it. This couldn't be happening. It couldn't truly end like this.

"We have to fall back," I muttered as another flame Stoicheion fell, her screams echoing into my bones as darklings descended on her, tearing her apart. The scent of her blood filled my nose, and I flinched at the sound of bones crunching, of tendons and ligaments tearing as the darklings feasted on her before she had had a chance to take her last breath.

Damien carved his way through another darkling, his armor stained with black blood.

Something crawled over my skin, a sensation of something so very wrong clawing into me, and the beast seemed to recoil at the feeling. I stumbled back, my hand rising to my chest instinctively. The hum of our binding magic still remained—Micah was all right, but that wasn't what I felt. No, it was something else, something… deeper.

"Oh, gods! The healers!" someone shouted over the fighting.

I twisted around as screams filled the battlefield, other warriors tracking the sound of the voices, drawing everyone's attention to the rear. My heart sank at the sight of smoke and embers rising to the night sky, at the massive tendrils of darkness writhing at the back of the battlefield.

"Damien!" I shouted, and he stole a glance over his shoulder, his skin paling.

The darklings' attacks turned relentless, cutting down warriors faster than before, and we turned to focus on their assault.

"Is it her?" I asked, fear clawing its way into my chest.

"It must be. I'd expected her to attack the front lines, how the fuck did she get past us?" Damien growled, unable to take a single step to retreat without risking a darkling attacking his unguarded back. "Fuck! We have to get back there!"

Raw power surged over the killing field, knocking us forward a step, and the power of it shook me to my bones. That feeling returned to my chest, twisting and winding deep within my being, and the beast at the core of my soul winced, whimpering as if physically distressed.

What is it?

The beast whimpered. *He's hurt.*

"Micah?" I whispered, my heart stilling, but I didn't feel it through our binding, only the weight of exhaustion.

"Hold on, Lucia!" Damien shouted as he fought, unable to turn to search for his mate, unable to go to her aid, unable to do anything but fight the darklings trying to get past us.

This was going to take too long. We had to get to the rear, had to help them. The healers would be defenseless against her. Lucia... I couldn't let her face that creature alone, not being so far along. How had we made such a grave error in splitting up as we had? The darkling queen had succeeded in catching us off guard, dividing us so she might pick us off one by one.

"Bring them down!" Damien roared, and the warriors reformed the line, cutting down darklings with waning determination. "Hold fast!"

I swung for another darkling, but it evaded, stepping back and out of my reach. The darklings slowed their advance, and I frowned as they stopped all together. Our warriors turned the tides, advancing, their hope replenishing as we gained ground for the first time in hours.

What had happened? What had changed?

Warriors raced past me, forcing the darklings back, reclaiming and reforming the wall as I turned to the rear of the battlefield. There was no way to see what was happening beyond the warriors clashing with the remaining darklings. I glanced back at Damien to find him searching the distance, his chest heaving, his ashen skin coated in sweat.

Then, the darklings began to shriek, turning and running, and something akin to hope swelled in my chest.

I met Damien's gaze. "Did she..."

He rushed past me, shoving past warriors as they advanced to chase the fleeing darklings. I ran after him, my heart racing. Had the darkling queen somehow fallen? Lucia had been waiting, reserving her magic for when she appeared. It had happened so fast, but how?

"Lucia!" Damien shouted as his pace quickened, and I struggled to keep up.

Please be alive.

I looked across the massive field as the fighting thinned, darklings falling to blades at their backs. In the clear expanse of what remained, I searched the faces of those who passed: wounded warriors stumbling aimlessly in a daze, some helping to hold others on their feet, others searching the bodies for survivors. Lucia wasn't among them, but as my search progressed, something tugged deep within me, pulling me forward, and my eyes fell to the bodies littering the ground. Something shifted, and I wasn't sure when I stopped searching for Lucia, when I lost track of what was and wasn't important. The beast paced deep within me, alert to every scent, every sound. I searched, unsure of what I was searching for, yet knowing there was nothing else I *could* search for.

Blond hair.

I scanned the lifeless face of one of the bodies. Two. Three. Ten. Thirty. A hundred.

Gods, there were so many bodies, so many dead...and the smell...

Air halted in my lungs as I found a mess of blond hair peeking out from a pile of bodies, and I rushed toward it, falling to my knees and turning him over. Unseeing blue eyes stared through me to the sky beyond and air rushed from my lungs as I sagged to the ground.

It wasn't him.

I rose to my feet and found Lucia and Damien in the distance. Her fearful gaze locked on me, and the hope that should be swelling in my chest seemed to die out at the sight of her, at the fearful terror in her eyes.

He wasn't with her.

I scanned the endless sea of bodies, exhaustion weighing me down, but I pushed through it.

And I continued to search.

CHAPTER 31

BARRETT

I couldn't move—couldn't breathe.

Couldn't think past the numb haze holding me in its clutches.

Something heavy held me down, anchoring me in a way that prevented the slightest movement...or had I simply lost use of my body? As I opened my eyes I found I could not even see the sky. Or were my eyes actually still closed? I tried to move, only to be greeted by splintering pain, agony shattering through me, fracturing every inch of my body like chips of glass. My body went limp, bending to the pain.

What had happened?

Where was I?

The air was foul, stinking of blood and rot and...something else I couldn't place. Death? Voices called out inaudibly, speaking words I could not discern. No matter how much I tried, I remained where I was, limbs useless, body leaden. So, I let the creeping darkness win. It felt oddly relieving to give into it, to let it ultimately sweep me away to whatever awaited me in its depths.

"Barrett!"

My body grew heavier, a weightless sleep pulling me into its embrace, and fuck, I wanted to give in to it so badly. I'd fought for so long. Something tugged in my chest, though, something deep, deep down in the recesses of my soul begging me to stay. But the thread was thin, fraying...

Threatening to break.

"Barrett! Answer us!"

A different voice called me that time, one full of fear and something I couldn't place. It was a voice that lifted my soul and grounded it all at once, one I wanted to hear more of, let it fill my ears every waking moment of every day. I didn't deserve it, yet I craved it more than life itself.

I forced my eyes open, forced my body to move—to do anything. My voice was hoarse as I called back, searching for them as they were me. I wasn't sure if words actually left my lips or if I'd imagined them.

They didn't respond, and I began to wonder if I'd imagined them calling to me all together. Perhaps this was it; perhaps this was where it ended, my mind conjuring voices of those I cared for most, wishful thinking that they needed me as much as I needed them—to offer me comfort so I wasn't alone in my final moments.

If this was the end, so be it. I only hoped Lucia was all right, that Micah and Damien had made it through everything.

Thalia.

The weak flames within me flickered at the thought of her name before falling silent again, as if they were trying to reach up once more just for her. Fuck, I wanted to see her again, wanted to hear her yell and scold me for something stupid, wanted to make a shitty comment just to see her cheeks redden and hear her sharp tongue.

"Barrett!"

The weight was lifted off me and I managed to lift my lids just enough to see it was a body. No, not one. It had been multiple bodies pinning me down, their unseeing gazes staring into nothing, their skin pale and painted with blood—both black and red.

"Oh, gods. Damien! Lucia! He's over here!" she shouted, and my vision cleared barely enough to find her staring down at me with wide eyes. They were like storm clouds. I hadn't been able to get them out of my head since I'd first seen them.

"Barrett," she said as she leaned over me. There was something wrong with her eyes. They were red, swollen.

She shouldn't be crying, I never wanted to see her cry. I'd stayed away so she could be happy...with Micah. She was his, and I'd accepted it. Despite my acceptance, despite how much I had fought to keep her at a distance, I hadn't been able to shake her from my mind, every interaction only drawing me to her more, every spoken word, every look exchanged solidifying her presence in my chest. Regardless of whether it was the mating bond or not, she had *chosen* him—*loved* him—and I refused to take her from him, to cut into the joy she felt at his side. She was happy with him.

So why was she crying over me?

I tried to lift my hand to wipe away a stray tear as it rolled down her cheek, but I couldn't move.

"It's going to be all right," she said, and I couldn't understand why she said it. "I've got you."

Stop crying. I can't take it.

Lucia and Damien appeared at my side, and Lucia fell to her knees, her hands shooting out to my stomach. Darkness danced at the edges of my vision, and my eyes grew heavier by the second.

If I could just...let them rest...for a moment.

"Thalia, keep talking to him," Lucia instructed, her voice full of urgency. "Damien, I need you to pull it out. The second you do, he's going to bleed out, and I have to start healing him immediately."

Pull it out? Pull what out?"

"Barrett, keep your eyes on me," Thalia said, her voice a plea.

I blinked slowly, looking up at her, and my lips parted.

"I didn't...thin—" My voice cracked, and I inhaled, but the air wouldn't fill my lungs, they couldn't expand, and pain shot through me.

"Shhhh," she whispered. "Don't talk, just stay still."

"See you...again," I muttered, my voice barely loud enough for me to hear.

"I'm here," she assured me. "I'm right here."

"Make sure he doesn't move," Lucia said, and I frowned.

What was—

Pain sliced through my abdomen, and I cursed, my head falling back as I cried out.

"I'm so sorry!" Thalia muttered, her gaze darting to my stomach. "Hold still. Lucia's healing you."

Warmth crept across my stomach, chasing the pain away, and I tried to breathe through it.

"Lucia," Damien said in an almost warning.

"I'm just closing the wound so he doesn't bleed out," she said, and I looked at her, at the sweat painting her brow. She was pale, a strange weariness touching her features.

She let out a shuddering breath, the warmth vanishing, leaving in its wake a deep ache that made it difficult to move. I drew a deep breath, relieved to be able to do so again, and I blinked.

Lucia sagged against Damien, and he caught her.

"What..." I muttered.

"I thought we'd lost you," Lucia said with a weak smile, her words as ragged as her breathing.

I frowned.

"You were impaled on another's dagger," Thalia explained. "It must have happened in the blast."

The blast? My heart faltered as it all came back to me.

"Where is she?" I asked, shooting up and immediately regretting it as Thalia braced me.

"Stop. You can't move," Thalia said as she forced me back onto the ground. "You'll reopen your wound."

"But the darkling queen..." I groaned.

"She's gone."

My gaze snapped to Lucia as she spoke, but she wasn't looking at me. "Gone?"

Her gaze lingered on the barren expanse where the healers had been, and my heart plummeted at what remained. The only sign that anything had ever stood there was bits of splintered wood and shreds of white fabric. Where tents had once resided, where healers had practiced their craft and magic to heal warriors...was a gaping crater, the grass dead at the edges, the soil tainted with corrupted shadow magic.

There was nothing. Every healer, every injured warrior... They were gone.

I turned back to her. Something haunted lingered in her expression, something I'd never seen before.

"She's gone," she said once more, still unable to look at me. "It's done."

"How did you manage it?" I asked, hope soaring in my chest, but it faltered at the look of guilt in her eyes.

"We have to check on the city," Lucia said, ignoring my question, grunting as she pushed herself to her feet. She was weak, barely able to support herself as Damien helped her, and her hand fell to her swollen stomach. "Evacuate the survivors."

"Easy. We'll handle it," Damien said.

I turned to Thalia. "Where's Micah?"

Her gaze shifted to me, and her hand rose to her chest. Something akin to concern flitted across her face, and for a moment, I wondered why she was here and not looking for him. "He's still out there somewhere, but I—our bond remains."

I tried to get up. "I'll help you—"

"No, you stay here," Thalia said, rising to her feet. Black mist enveloped her before silver wings emerged from the shadowy depths, sending the shadows cascading around us as she ascended to the skies as a gyrfalcon.

Something fractured inside me to see her leave my side so quickly, but I shoved it down, forced it deep within me, where I hoped it would finally wither and die. Lucia and Damien stepped beside me, and I followed their gazes to the city, fire and smoke rising from the small buildings in the dark distance.

"Holy shit," I breathed, the blood draining from my face as I managed to get to my knees.

Neither of them spoke, but as I looked back at Lucia, something twisted in my chest at the sorrow on her face.

What had she done?

CHAPTER 32

THALIA

The wind couldn't carry me fast enough, and with each beat of my wings, my heart plummeted further. Guilt twisted my gut, churning into a pool of disgust. I'd been desperate to feel my paws against the ground in my wolf form, to seek out any hint of Micah's scent, but my gyrfalcon form was quicker.

Why had I gone in search of Barrett? I should have looked for Micah before anything.

"Stupid," I muttered under my breath. "So fucking stupid."

The beast nuzzled against the edges of my consciousness, as if to ease my guilt. *He is all right. The steel-eyed warrior was in danger.*

But how could it have known that?

My heart shuttered as my mind revisited the sight of him, relived the terror I felt when I found him buried under the bodies of those who hadn't survived the blast of energy the darkling queen had summoned—the dagger lodged in his gut, his blood pooled on the ground beneath him. The light had nearly faded from his steel eyes when I pulled him free, and something deep within me knew he had given up.

He had been prepared to fade...to die. To leave us.

To leave me.

Rhyas' bloodied face flashed in my mind, the feel of his blood on my hands and his struggles as he tried to breathe in his final moments still too fresh, even after so many decades. Kish's smile followed, her sacrifice to buy our freedom a cost I never wanted to pay again. I couldn't bear to lose anyone else.

Tears pricked my eyes, and I tightened my grip until my talons bit into my skin, pulling me back to what was important—my bonded.

I searched the city, looking across the expanse of countless buildings as they fell prey to devouring flames. Screams cut through the air as humans and civilians fought for their lives, and it was all I could do to listen for any sign of Micah and his warriors. Faintly, amidst the firelight below, a mass of beings moved through the city like a wave of darkness—emaciated, broken bodies crawling over each other in a desperate attempt to flee.

Were they retreating because the darkling queen had fallen? They had us outmatched, were close to bringing us down entirely. It made no sense for them to retreat when they could have continued the fight and destroyed us once and for all.

It was difficult to pick out anything over the screams and shrieks of victims and darklings below. I dove, tucking my wings in tightly until I was close enough to see every bit of destruction left in the darklings' wake. Bodies littered the streets, many broken and shredded beyond recognition in the aftermath of the darklings' feedings. The flames painted the sky a crimson red for miles before me, smoke reaching for the sky, embers fluttering around my feathers.

Gods, how would we recover from this? How would we rebuild?

It was Moonhaven all over, the destruction beyond belief. I barely remembered it, but pieces of it were still engraved in my mind, tiny flickers of horror—the smoke and embers burning my lungs, the crumbling buildings, the darklings tearing their victims to shreds. The death. I couldn't even remember the faces of my parents or how I'd lost them, yet I still remembered the feeling of terror.

I shook the fear away and searched, feeling the bond tattoo on my breast pulse in response to his stress. He was hurt... *Micah.*

The beast tried to soothe me. *It isn't serious.*

"How would you know? How would you know anything?" I bit out, descending further until I was weaving in and out of buildings, dodging the rush of heat expelled from the burning structures. "You led me away from him, sent me searching for someone else when I should have been at his side."

It didn't respond, and it irritated me to know I'd trusted in its instinct, let it guide me to Barrett instead of my bonded who needed me. The creature was right, though. Barrett had also needed me. Lucia and Damien wouldn't have found him in time if I hadn't been there. I shook the thought away as my mind pooled with the image of his steel eyes void of life.

The fires were spreading out of control, crawling across the ground to the neighboring houses with ravenous, insatiable energy, leaving the survivors screaming as they watched in horror or found themselves trapped inside. I couldn't stop to help them no matter how badly I wanted to, couldn't slow my search. Not until I found him, until I knew he was all right.

"Micah!" I called out, rounding a corner, and relief flooded me as I found him pulling survivors from the wreckage. I dropped out of the air, allowing the feathers to recede, the talons to retract as my boots slammed into the ash-covered ground. Hot air burned my lungs as I ran for him, my heart racing.

Hope lit his face, his arms reaching out to catch me as I crashed into him.

"Thank the gods," he breathed as he held me, his hand grasping the back of my head to pull me closer as he pressed his nose into my hair and drew deep breaths.

I pulled away, my hands shooting to his face as I searched him for any injuries. "Are you hurt?"

"Nothing serious," he assured me with a smile, and I grimaced at the cut lining his jaw. "What happened? I thought we were done for, and then the darklings suddenly fled."

"Lucia brought the queen down," I said, feeling hopeful for the first time since we'd charged into the swarm of creatures so many hours ago. "We won."

"We won?" he asked, eyes widening in disbelief.

I nodded, my chest swelling at the relief in his expression as he pressed his lips to my forehead. "We won."

"Micah!" a voice called from the distance.

Micah and I parted as one of his men ran for us, and I shook off the momentary celebration. We had won, but our work wasn't finished.

"We've managed to douse some of the fires, but the stone bridge is out of control, and its continuing to spread!" the warrior shouted. "We're evacuating everyone we can."

Micah glanced past him briefly. "Good. Do your best with the humans. Gather any *Nous* users you have to subdue them."

Thalia.

I sucked in a sharp breath at the sound of Lucia's voice in my thoughts, and I reached back out to her, unsure if she was still tapped into my thoughts. *You should be resting.*

I need you and Micah to withdraw with what warriors are still standing as well as any members of The Underworld still willing to help.

Why would she be calling us away from the city? There were too many humans scattered, and gods knew what remained of the immortal civilians.

I glanced sidelong at some of the approaching immortals, knowing them not as warriors but as the criminals who had agreed to a temporary ceasefire to help us through Barrett's connections. They couldn't be trusted, but we didn't have a choice. The city would have fallen if not for their aid.

"We managed to evacuate many of the civilians south—" Micah halted when he caught my gaze. "Everything all right?" he asked, and I blinked, unease settling in my gut at the sheer exhaustion in Lucia's voice.

I turned to him. "We need to get to Lucia and Damien."

Lucia and Damien were overseeing the search for survivors among the bodies strewn out across the killing field by the time we made it to them. A part of me crumbled at the sight of how few warriors searched the carnage for survivors.

How many had we lost?

"I'm relieved to know you're all right, Micah," Lucia said without looking, as if she didn't need to know we approached.

Micah looked over the battlefield. "How bad is it?"

"We won't know just how many we've lost until we've finished searching," Damien said, his eyes lowered on a bloodied dagger in his hands, and he shifted on his feet as he turned to us. "House Latros is gone."

"Gods," I muttered. The healers? Every single one?

Barrett wrapped Micah in a hug. I directed my attention away from them, guilt twisting my chest at how desperately I had searched for Barrett before I'd gone looking for my bonded.

If you hadn't, he would've been lost to us.

I ignored the beast's words, anger curdling in my gut at the creature and its foolish 'instincts.'

"Is this all that remains?" Lucia asked as she scanned the warriors at Micah's back.

He nodded. "It was a massacre. Hundreds of darklings flooded the city."

A member of The Underworld stepped forward, a scar etched diagonally across his face, splitting through his short brown hair. The way he carried himself, he appeared to be in charge. I watched him cautiously as he approached. "I expect you to keep up your end of the bargain. Lost a lot of my men defending those fucking humans."

The beast bristled within me at the way he spoke to Lucia and Damien.

Damien lifted his cold gaze to the male. "I didn't forget our agreement, Atlas."

He growled but turned, his gaze briefly meeting Barrett's, and they nodded to one another as he returned to his own fighters.

"How are we going to cover this up?" I asked no one in particular as I looked over what remained of the city. "The humans..."

"I will alter their memories," Lucia said, stepping away from Damien.

Damien grabbed her arm, drawing her back to him. "You've used enough magic."

"Do we have enough *Nous* users to manipulate the minds of tens of thousands of humans?" she asked calmly, avoiding his gaze. He didn't respond, because even I knew we damn well didn't. "I'm the only one who can alter the minds of so many people."

Barrett and Damien exchanged nervous looks.

She drew a deep breath. "I will force the survivors to leave their dead and evacuate the city..."

"That still leaves the bodies," Micah said.

Lucia looked over the city, the air a heavy silence. "The dam."

Barrett took a step toward her. "You want to flood the city?"

"It would cover up the lost lives *and* put out the fires." Her gaze didn't falter, her silver eyes near soulless. "I will alter the memories of the surviving humans so they believe the flood caused the destruction and loss of life."

Micah shook his head. "That would take forever to do, and we don't even know how many *Nous* users surviv—"

"I can do it in one pass," Lucia said, her voice unwavering, near cold.

Something twisted in my chest.

"You've used enough magic as it is," Damien said once more, stepping in front of her as he cupped her cheeks. "Surely, we can find another way to clean this up."

"Selene cannot aid us," she said, and thunder roared in the distance, the scent in the air shifting as the wind picked up. "The *Nous* users can only manipulate the minds of a few people at most." She looked toward the sky, where thick clouds had gathered, blocking out the setting moon. Lucia then offered Damien a smile, and it was too forced. "I will only guide them to leave the city and manipulate their memories until the plan has been completed. The other teams can handle sabotaging the dam."

Damien didn't respond, and he glanced at us nervously before looking back at her. "Lucia—"

"After this, I won't use any more magic," she promised, her hand rising to his chest. She then turned to me. "Can I entrust the dam to you?"

I stilled at the request but dipped my head. "I will see it done."

"Gather any surviving water wielders," Lucia said in a cold commanding tone as she turned back to the city, her hands rising before her as she closed her eyes. "Earth users may be beneficial as well, but you must ensure the dam failure appears accidental. Allow it to fail naturally if possible."

I stopped at Damien's side as Micah hurried through the field, calling for any water users to aid in falling the dam. "What happened to her?"

He didn't respond at first, but eventually, he shook his head. "She won't tell me."

CHAPTER 33

THALIA

"Do you know anything about dams?" Micah asked, shielding his eyes from the torrential downpour.

It had taken a day and a half for Lucia to manipulate the surviving humans out of the city and into the mountains where our warriors resided, and just a couple hours for us to trek the distance to the South Fork Dam once we were sure she had cleared as many as she could.

"Not much. We simply need to plug the drains and let it overflow."

Micah glanced at me nervously. "Sounds simple enough. I doubt it will be, though."

The stone wall was massive as I scanned it, searching for any weaknesses we could exploit through the rain pelting us with near blinding strength in the early-morning hours before the sun's rise. The weather would only benefit us, the rivers swelled beyond their limits with the excess water that had been dumped on us in the last twenty-four hours.

A hawk shifter darted through the air past me, landing on the ground before shaking off some of the excess water. "There's a spillway on the north side of the dam!"

"We start there," I said, and Micah nodded before we hurried along the dam wall to find the river full of rushing water.

"Gods," Micah groaned as we pressed on through the rain and wind, trees moaning as they swayed against one another in the dark around us. "I've never seen so much rain."

Neither had I, and I wasn't sure if this weather was a gift from the gods or a curse of The Fates to see us fail. There had to be a way to sabotage the dam, force it to fail in a way that looked natural. Surely, the humans wouldn't know whether the dam had simply failed due to poor stonework, or—

A loud crack cut through the air, and my eyes shot up. "Watch out!"

The tree crashed down on us, and Micah's arm wrapped around my waist as he dove forward, pulling me out of the way of the trunk as it plowed into the ground. We hit the muddied path and twisted around in time to watch as a dendron user trapped the tree with roots before it could roll over top of the other warriors at our back.

"Thank the fates," Micah breathed as he released me.

"Don't thank the old crones yet," I groaned as he helped me to my feet, and mud slicked down the front of my leathers. "Is anyone hurt?"

"All accounted for!" one of the warriors shouted back.

"Let's get this done!" I shouted, and we all hurried along the river toward what I hoped might be a way to bring a flood. We couldn't suffer any further delays; word would eventually get out of the damage in the city by an unsuspecting human wandering from a nearby town. Lucia and the others would only be able to intervene so much; someone might slip through the cracks, and we would be left with an even bigger mess to clean up.

"Did Lucia seem off to you?" Micah asked, his voice barely loud enough to be heard over the downpour, over the roaring winds and rushing waters.

"It's not as if we just lost countless of our kind," I said, giving him a look.

"You know what I mean."

I couldn't deny that he was right. Something was bothering her, that much was certain, and it was more than the battle. But what?

"She did," I admitted unsure what else to make of it.

She'd always been a little off, working in strange ways in the background. The look in her eyes, though, spoke of someone burdened with knowledge too great to bear.

The trees parted, and we found a small bridge where water crested the top of the hill before flowing down the mountainside and forming the river that eventually crossed through Johnstown. There was so much water, the river flowing with furious energy as it crashed over the river rocks and boulders, swallowing up downed trees and debris as it tore through the land along its edge.

"I'm sure it'll be all right. She's likely just exhausted from the battle," I said, praying my words were truth.

I scanned the bridge before my gaze landed to the water flowing under it, and I narrowed my eyes to see through the heavy rain. There appeared to be something stretched across the opening beneath the bridge, the woven ropes bulging against the heavy flow of water. "Is that a net?"

Micah tilted his head at the edge of the overflowing creek to look. "It would appear so."

The hawk shifter who had scouted ahead came to a stop at my side. "The lake is already threatening to spill over the dam."

"If we clog up that net, the water will have nowhere to escape..."

"And the dam fails," Micah said, finishing my trail of thought, and he turned to the warriors at our back.

"Hopefully. It could burst through here instead of the dam, and then we'll have to find another way," I said, praying I wasn't putting too much faith in this one solution. "Water and earth wielders! See if there is anything in the lake to clog this net."

Our warriors raced to the top of the hill, and I followed after them, the ground so saturated that our boots slipped and tore through grass and mud. I came to a stop at the top, looking out over the lake, waves surging in the storm like an angry creature eager to devour us all. The water wielders fell to their knees at the lake's edge, throwing their hands into the raging tides as the earth users planted their palms in the soil.

The only sound that filled my ears was the roaring of the wind. I turned my gaze to the top of the dam, where water already crashed against the top, already pushing at its limits. Micah came to a stop at my side, following my gaze.

I watched as they dove into their powers, moving sediment and stone, drawing any debris they could toward the net as I called out, "Let's not keep Lady Lucia waiting any longer!"

CHAPTER 34

BARRETT

For too long had Lucia held the minds of the humans in her command, bending them to her will so they might escape what was coming. It had taken longer than we had hoped to get every survivor out of the valley; over thirty thousand humans had lived in this city, and while Lucia was powerful, her reach only went so far. When the fatigue had begun to show on her face, Damien had tried to stop her from continuing, stressing that she had done enough. She wouldn't budge, though, refusing to quit until she had located nearly every surviving soul to evacuate before the flood devoured what remained of the city, of the destructive evidence of the darklings.

There was no way she had managed to get everyone, though. There were far too many, some likely trapped in the debris, unconscious and unreachable by her mind. I wouldn't voice it, refused for her to push herself any more than she already had.

I lifted my eyes to the cloudy sky, water soaking through my leathers, filling my boots. The rain helped a little, washing away some of the dirt and grime from the battle two nights prior, but it wasn't enough to wash away everything. I wanted to change, wanted to feel clean again, but we were far from finished—too many bodies still unaccounted for in the aftermath of the battle, too few hands to recover them in a timely manner. The torrential downpour didn't help, leaving the battle-scarred earth a pit of mud, swelling corpses, and stench of death.

And still, the rain continued.

"How is she holding up?" I asked as Zephyr sat down beside me, his tawny skin pale.

"She's exhausted," he muttered, looking to where Lucia stood, Damien at her back as he helped support her while she worked. Her eyes remained closed, as they had been the better part of a day and a half, focused on maintaining her connection with the humans gathering on the edges of the valley. How could one person manipulate the minds of so many?

I grimaced at the deep ache in my stomach where my wound still healed but thankfully remained sealed due to Lucia's healing abilities. No one could spare any blood. Too many were injured, so it would be some time before I could feed and properly heal. "Any word from Thalia and Micah?"

He shook his head. "Still waiting for them to check in. They should have made it there by now."

"What if this doesn't work?" I muttered, unease coiling in my gut. "What happens if we can't make it convincing to the humans?"

"Damien has connections to ensure the truth remains hidden if they fail," Zephyr said, and I arched a brow at him before he shook his head. "Need to know."

I glanced at Damien, wondering just what connections he might have. Was it with the humans? With the gods? I couldn't help but scoff at the idea. What would the gods do for us? They had remained silent on this side of the veil ever since our kind had been banished over six hundred years ago, Selene our only remaining connection to the Godsrealm.

Zephyr tensed for a moment, his brows furrowing in concentration. He shot to his feet. "They've done it! The water is already starting to spill over the top of the dam."

Something deep within me stirred as the words left his lips, the flames sparking to attention beneath my skin at the thought of Thalia and Micah at the dam. I should have been there with them, helping them, but I'd barely been able to make my way across the killing field to search for survivors with the wound in my gut, let alone keep up with crossing the mountains. I closed my eyes, praying The Fates would spare them from harm, that they would make it back to us safely.

She would be all right.

I turned to look down into the destroyed city nestled in the valley, avoiding thoughts of the female who had somehow claimed my thoughts. The river was already flowing fuller than I had ever seen as it carved a path through the valley. Dread crawled into the pit of my stomach at the thought of what we would witness when the flood came.

This town had been our home for centuries. I knew every street, every home and business. It was as if I was staring at the remains of Moonhaven again. Despite the destruction, we couldn't leave, not with the darklings still lingering somewhere nearby.

We wouldn't be free until they were destroyed.

Silence stretched on for hours as we waited for Thalia to return, for the destruction of the flood to come, and my mind only spiraled in the deafening quiet. The storm eased, but the sky remained just as dull as we all felt. Zephyr paced before me, passing nervous glances at Lucia, who had finally lowered to her knees but remained in deep concentration. With each passing moment, I worried more for her, for the babe growing in her womb, for Thalia and Micah. I was desperate to see their faces, to know they were all right, that nothing had gone wrong in the hours since they had departed.

"Thalia's team is back!" a voice rang out, and I shot to my feet, twisting around to look.

A small group of leather-clad warriors approached, and the sight of her drenched cornsilk hair in the distance nearly brought me to my knees.

I ran, my boots sloshing through mud with each step, my hand clutching my stomach as it protested, but I needed to see them, the flames within me reaching out to some intangible connection...

To her.

Relief washed over me to see them again as our gazes met, despite how pale her skin appeared, how dull and weary her eyes were. Her pace quickened, her face lighting up a fraction as she caught sight of me. Our steps slowed as we neared one another, and Micah came up to a stop beside her.

"You're all right? It worked?" I asked on shallow breaths, gaze sweeping between them.

Thalia nodded, offering me an exhausted smile. "No casualties."

Micah came to a stop at her side, his breathing labored. "Nicholas and the others stayed behind to ensure no humans interfere with the dam failing and that everything goes according to plan. He just confirmed about twenty minutes ago that the dam collapsed, and the flooding is making its way down the Conemaugh."

Gods, they were filthy, mud in every nook and crevice of their leather armor, their weapons. I pulled them both into a hug. Thalia melted against me, her body fitting so perfectly against mine, and Micah caged her between us, squeezing tightly as I took what felt like the first breath of relief after stepping into the hell we'd faced.

"It's coming!" Zephyr shouted, and I released Thalia and Micah as I twisted around to see the waters explode from the ravine north of the city, devouring the valley like a ravenous beast.

"Hold!" Lucia shouted, her closed eyes tightening, her teeth grounding together as her focus on maintaining control of the countless humans wavered the moment the shouts of agony and sorrow cut through the air, as warriors watched their homes fall to destruction.

"Everyone remain quiet!" Damien shouted, and my stomach twisted as distant screams pierced the air amidst the crashing waves and rushing water.

"No," Lucia whimpered under her breath.

"You saved enough," Damien said, holding her tightly. "You did enough."

"Gods," Micah breathed from the other side of Thalia, watching as the wave rushed over the houses, the buildings, what few humans had awoken after Lucia had completed the evacuation barely visible as they ran for higher ground, only to be swept up into the wave of water as it came for all that remained.

And within minutes, everything was gone, swallowed whole by the water, debris and remnants of homes floating on the waves, fires still clutching whatever wood they could before the water snuffed their lives out as well.

Thalia's hand clasped over her mouth as a cry broke from her lips, tears welling in her eyes as we watched our home fall once again. Micah and I leaned into her, our arms coming around one another as we held her, offering her any comfort we could.

Because we were all that was left.

CHAPTER 35

BARRETT

Three months had passed since that dreadful night, every day a new horror as we faced the task of searching through the destruction for any survivors, for those who were still missing, their bodies likely washed away or buried under the silt, never to be found. Some had been found miles away along the riverside once the flood waters had receded, our search going on far longer for fear their bodies might be found by humans.

None of them had survived, though, and thousands remained missing.

The loss of life had taken a heavy toll on our people and the humans in the city, who believed everything they'd called home had been wiped out by a failed dam. We had lost every healer of House Latros, which greatly impacted our recovery efforts, and the remaining houses of power had lost so many of their bloodline that some now hovered on the brink of extinction.

"Figured you could use some coffee," Zephyr said, entering the makeshift study in one of the buildings left still standing after the flood with two mugs. The damp scent of the muddy waters still clung to the brick, and it had taken a long while to ignore the musty smell.

"We'll see if it's enough to give me a second wind," I groaned as he offered me one.

Zephyr took a seat at the opposite end of the table, looking over the paperwork strewn about. We'd taken up shifts, helping Damien with his work and recovery efforts, rotating out periodically to keep Lucia company.

What she had done in manipulating thousands of human minds the night of the battle was nothing short of amazing, but it had cost her dearly. Thank The Fates their babe was well, but Lucia had been bedridden ever since, her body weak and drained under the stress of the magic and the pregnancy. We all worried for her and what long-term effects the battle might have left her with.

My eyes drifted over the paperwork before me, the final tallies of survivors in each house finally collected after months of identifying bodies and performing funeral rites in Selene's temple. Thalia, Micah, Zephyr, and I had worked together on updating the census of every immortal, both civilian and warrior, recording the deaths each house of power had endured. We had lost so many of our own...too many. House Leukós, the wielders of light, were dwindling when they had already been as small in number as House Latros. The blood wielders of House Aíma had fared even worse.

We had gone into battle with four hundred and thirty-two warriors.

Only two hundred and twelve had made it to the other side.

Countless civilians had been killed in the attack on the city, and the loss of human life was just as severe. Over two thousand human lives had been snuffed out, and over four hundred immortal souls had returned to Elysium's embrace.

And that was just what we knew. There were still hundreds of our own unaccounted for; hundreds I feared would never receive the rites to deliver their souls across The River Styx to Elysium.

The Fall of Kingdoms. That was what they were calling it, what Salwa had labeled it as when she recorded it into the historical texts.

I took a drink before grimacing. "Fuck, this is nasty. Did you even add any sugar?"

He glanced at me sidelong as he took a sip of his. "Go make it yourself next time if you want sugar."

"Only you would like your coffee so bitter," I said as I set the mug down on the table.

"Damien and Lucia wanted you to stop by," Zephyr said without looking up from the piece of parchment laid out before him. "You've been up all night working, though. You think you'll have the energy?"

I blinked and looked at the clock. "Shit, I didn't realize what time it was. I can swing by on my way home."

"I'll take over and finish this up before Damien gets in," he said, gesturing to the door. "I'm sure she'll be glad for your company. You're good at lightening the mood."

"Is that a compliment?" I asked arching a brow.

"Don't let it go to your head," he deadpanned without looking up at me.

I huffed a laugh and rose from the table before leaving him to his work. I hoped she was in better spirits today, hoped she had more energy.

The sun pierced my eyes as I stepped outside, and I winced before they adjusted to the brightness. Dried mud and residual silt still covered the dusty roads as I continued through the city, which seemed to finally be clear of heavy flood debris. Surviving humans and immortals alike had come together to rebuild, though the humans still knew nothing of our existence. There was no telling what would've happened if Lucia hadn't altered their memories.

Would The Twelve have intervened if we had failed?

I didn't want to imagine what would have happened had they crossed over to mete out their judgment as they had with our goddess, Selene.

"Barrett!" a young voice called, and I looked up to find a boy with a mop of blond hair watching me from a nearby rooftop, an old worn hammer in his dirt-stained hand.

"So you're a roofer now, Vincent?" I shouted back as he rose to his feet.

"Everyone's chipping in. I didn't want to stay cooped up in the tent all day," he said as he climbed down the ladder and squeezed past workers who ruffled his hair as he passed, breaking out into laughter at the dirt smeared on his face.

Gods, he was getting tall, had just turned thirteen the previous month. My cousin, born on Mother's side, had become my shadow from the moment he was able to step outside. Thankfully, his mother's family was kinder, and he had been raised with love.

"How's your mother doing?" I asked, happy to see him in such high spirits after the battle with his father having been among the fallen.

His gaze wavered, a weak smile tugging at his lips. "She's distracting herself. It's been hard not having him around."

"It's been difficult for everyone," I said and placed my hand on his shoulder. "If you guys ever need anything, don't hesitate to come to me."

He nodded. "As soon as I go through my settling, I'm signing up to join The Order. Then, Mother won't have to work any longer and can relax."

I ruffled his hair. "Get through your settling, and then we'll talk."

"Vincent!" a male called from the roof he had been working on. "You quittin' on me already?"

"Coming!" Vincent shouted back before glancing at me. "Are you going to visit Lady Lucia?"

"I am."

"I hope she is doing better," he said and turned to return to work with a wave over his shoulder. "Tell her to rest up; we'll handle the rest!"

I tapped my knuckle against the open door to Damien and Lucia's room. "Knock, knock."

Damien and Lucia looked up, and Lucia's tired smile widened. She was still in bed, exactly where I had left her a couple of days before, her hand resting against her belly which had grown so much in the last few months.

"Thanks for stopping by," Damien said, gesturing to a chair beside him.

I cocked a brow and gave Lucia a teasing grin. "Couldn't let me get some work in, could you? I knew you missed my company."

She rolled her eyes and shook her head but couldn't keep from smiling. "Sit down, hothead."

My brows furrowed when Damien didn't get up from his seat. "You called me in to keep her company while you worked, right?"

"Yes, but there is another matter of great importance we must discuss," he said.

Lucia spoke up, drawing my attention to her. "I've decided to step down as *Strategos* of The Order."

"Step down?" My gaze swept back and forth between them.

She nodded, and for a moment, something like resignation passed across Damien's face before he offered her a soft smile and a gentle squeeze of her hand.

I rose from my chair, nearly sending it toppling to the floor. How could she just step down as the general of The Order? As Damien's right hand? "But...why would you do that?"

Her brows rose, and I couldn't understand why she would be surprised that I asked.

"The warriors need you," I said. "What are we gonna do without you?"

Her gaze wavered, and there it was; that damned look of guilt that had painted her face since the battle.

"It is time for me to step down," she said calmly, as if it was something that had been decided long before this moment. "Just as it was time for me to find you and help you clear your name, just as Thalia was intended to return to the Mortalrealm and meet you and Micah."

Intended to meet me? Something both bloomed and shriveled in my chest at her words, at the thought that she truly seemed to believe our meeting was something orchestrated by The Fates...that my meeting Thalia was fated. I shook the thought off, desperate to abandon any thoughts or possibilities that she was, in fact, my mate.

What was this really about?

"There is the matter of who will take my place," she said, and my heart stilled.

"Who's replacing you?" I asked.

The warmth returned to her silver eyes. "Zephyr is taking my place. He served as Strategos in my absence before, but I need someone to step up to fill his role."

Taxiarchos... Brigadier. My stomach flipped at the implication her words held.

"That's why we brought you here," Damien explained. "You've gone above and beyond in proving yourself since you joined The Order. The warriors trust in your judgment, and you showed great leadership and care during the battle with the darkling queen."

"No," I muttered under my breath, and they blinked.

Lucia's brows wrinkled, and she proceeded to fidget her fingers atop her blanket. "No?"

My pulse pounded in my ears. Third in command of The Order? Me? "Surely someone else is more qualified."

Lucia let out a soft chuckle, and I frowned. "Of course, you would feel you weren't enough."

Damien took her hand but leveled his gaze on me. "We originally offered Thalia the position, but she turned it down."

"Why? She would be a perfect fit."

Lucia's gaze wavered, and the weight of it sliced through me. "She couldn't bear the thought of being responsible for so many lives again."

She couldn't bear it because she felt she'd failed so many in The Pits.

We'd never spoken of it, but I knew enough from Lucia and Micah to put the pieces together, from witnessing the horrors when we'd dismantled what remained of it all those centuries ago.

I sat in silence for a moment, trying to wrap my head around the idea.

"You guys must be pretty desperate if you're promoting a dungeon rat to the rank of Taxiarchos," I said, trying to wrap my head around the idea.

Lucia shook her head. "There's no one I trust more to handle the position than you or Thalia."

"Micah?" I suggested.

"He is where he needs to be," Lucia said with a warm smile, as if she had everything planned out to the smallest detail.

I chewed my lip, shifting uncomfortably in my seat. Once Lucia made up her mind, there was no talking her out of it. It was as if every step she took, every decision she contemplated was orchestrated by The Fates.

What if I couldn't live up to their expectations?

"Can I think about it?"

Damien nodded. "I know it's a lot to process. Take a couple days to think on it."

Lucia seemed to almost tense at his words, but she eased almost immediately.

This wasn't right.

"I'll let you know in a few days," I said.

"Thank you," Damien said and leaned in to press a kiss to Lucia's forehead. "Do you mind keeping her company today? I figured I'd help Zephyr catch up on some work since I wasn't in yesterday."

I shrugged. "I didn't have any plans. As long as she's all right putting up with me."

Her lips curved into a knowing smile. "I guess I can deal with your antics for a bit."

"She's had some contractions off and on over the last twenty-four hours," Damien said. "The midwives don't think she's in active labor yet. Send for me if anything changes, though."

I nodded. "Zephyr told me yesterday."

"I'll try to get things done quickly. I should only be a few hours," he said and turned to Lucia. "See you this evening, *mea luna*."

"Don't work too hard, *mea sol*," she teased and tensed suddenly before a soft laugh slipped from her throat as her hand fell to her stomach. "Goodness, she's full of energy today."

I blinked. "She?"

Lucia's eyes lit up. "Yes. I've felt her energy for a while. We kept it a secret, but I guess it's time you knew."

My heart soared at the news, and I tried to imagine what she might look like, if she would have Lucia's dark hair. "Have you picked out a name?"

"Emilia," she said, resting a hand against her belly.

"It's perfect," I muttered, eager to see her through this, to see them together and happy. "I hope you know I plan to spoil her rotten."

She snickered. "Oh, I don't doubt that."

"I wonder what she'll be," Damien whispered, almost to himself. "If she'll have magic as you do."

Lucia looked down at her stomach knowingly. "I guess you'll have to wait and see."

Damien pressed a kiss to her knuckles once more. "I'll try not to be gone long."

He turned and headed for the door, and I glanced at Lucia. "I'll be right back."

I rose and followed him into the hallway, waiting until we were some distance from their room before grabbing his arm. "Damien, can I speak to you for a second?"

He stopped and turned to me, dark brows rising. "What is it?"

"What's all this really about?" I asked.

His brows furrowed, and for a moment I thought he was going to deny that something was off. He glanced past me before letting out a sigh. "She decided to step down a few weeks ago."

"Why, though?"

"I don't know," he said with such defeat, it halted my train of thought. "I don't think I'm the only one who has noticed how she's changed since the battle with the darkling queen."

"You're not."

He raked his fingers through his hair and let out a heavy sigh. "I don't know what else to do. She won't tell me what happened—even mentioning it seems to tear down her spirits—and I can't bring myself to ask her any further."

There had been many times when I had found her alone, staring off into nothing, as if her mind was somewhere else entirely. At times she would lose track of our conversations, and she seemed to be slowly closing herself off from the outside world. If it wasn't for the fact that she was on bed rest, I'd have taken her out to see the city, the relief efforts. The people missed her, asked about her constantly—prayed for her safety, an easy delivery, a healthy babe.

"She brushes it off like its nothing to be concerned about, but..." Damien lifted his eyes to me, and the concern in them broke me. "I'm worried about her."

"You all right?" Micah asked, and I blinked, realizing my quill had lingered in one place for too long, leaving droplets of ink on the parchment.

"Yeah," I said with a sigh. I set my quill aside before grabbing a fresh piece of parchment to begin again. The list of names was too short, far shorter than it should be.

Micah eyed me wearily, and I rolled my neck, feeling the tension release with each pop. "I'll be all right."

He hesitated a moment, his lips parting and closing before he finally said, "You turned Lucia and Damien down for the promotion."

"Heard about that did you?" I muttered, returning to the writing in the names, each weighing heavier on my soul. The list from our last census done a couple of years ago was laid out on the table for reference, notations and scribbles marked along it to modify our records.

Alive.
Deceased.
Missing.

As I scrolled through the seemingly endless list, my attention snagged on a particular name.

Marcus Blackwood. Deserter. April 13th, 1886

It had been a few years since his disappearance. The fallout had been disastrous—he'd been so lost in his sorrow after Vivienne's death. I still remembered how he'd looked when he'd walked out on Damien and Lucia. He'd been different, as if the friend we'd known for decades was no longer there.

"There's nothing wrong with turning down a position," Micah said, as if to reason with me, and I blinked, pulled from thoughts of Marcus. "I'm just surprised you did is all."

My shoulders sagged. The guilt had been eating at me since she'd asked. "You should have seen the look on her face, though."

Her eyes were distant, as if looking far beyond the garden outside her window as she whispered, so low I almost couldn't hear, "Not enough time."

I tilted my head to get a better look at her. "Lucia?"

She blinked, as if drawn from a dream, and then she looked back at me. "Apologies. I summoned you here."

"Don't apologize," I said, laying a hand atop hers. Her skin didn't feel warm enough, her hands clammy despite the summer's waning heat. "Are you all right? Should I call the midwives or a healer?"

She shook her head. "Just the usual exhaustion. I won't keep you, though, I know you're busy."

"My work isn't going anywhere. Whatever you need of me, all you have to do is ask."

"I want to you take Zephyr's place as Taxiarchos."

I froze, my skin turning icy and hot as my heart dropped into the pit of my stomach. "What?"

She bit her lip, the inner corners of her brows curving upward. "I don't mean to blindside you with it, but I have decided to step down as Strategos, and while Zephyr will be taking my place as Damien's second in command, I need someone to fill his ro—"

"I can't," I blurted, my heart racing as memories of all those who had died in The Pits under my watch flooded my mind in a destructive wave.

She hesitated, her eyes widening a fraction before lowering, and slowly, a soft smile curved her lips as her gaze fell to the floor. "I had hoped for a different outcome, but I should have known."

"I'm so sorry, I just..." She lifted her weary eyes to me, and I loathed myself so much in that moment. "I can't bear the thought of being responsible for so many lives. Never again."

Micah let out a sigh. "You've done enough."

"*She's* done enough," I retorted, unable to look up from the parchment, unable to swallow the guilt as I reconsidered my decision for what felt like the millionth time. I had hardly slept in the nights since she'd asked, haunted by her disappointment. "She's sacrificed so much more than any of us could even come close to."

"I can't believe she's stepping down," he said, all productivity halting as he ran his fingers through his hair. "Is it to be with the babe?"

I shrugged. "It didn't seem like that. Originally, she planned to take a year or two to spend with the baby after she was born, but this... This felt permanent. Something changed. She seems almost desperate for it, and it made me afraid to accept despite my feelings."

"I haven't seen her since she went on bed rest after the battle," he said, leaning back in his chair, the wood groaning. "What do you think happened?"

"I don't know, but I'm worried she's hiding something."

Micah took my hand and squeezed it in gentle reassurance. Our bond swelled between us, warmth filling my chest. "Everything will be all right."

I let out a sigh. "I hope she can find someone else to take the position, I just... I can't do it."

My eyes passed over the list of names once more, my heart twisting at each notation. "I can't be responsible for anyone else's death."

CHAPTER 37

BARRETT

"Your due date's right around the corner, isn't it?" I asked as I stepped through the doorway, looking around Lucia and Damien's chambers. They were decorated with a number of baby items, a bassinet tucked away in the corner, stuffed animals their servants had made, blankets, even some books, which looked suspiciously like some from the Archivallia. How had she convinced the Astral Sprites to allow them to leave the library?

Lucia was staring out the window, a sense of longing in her gaze, and her brows rose as she turned to me. "Oh! Yes. We'll see if I make it that far, though. She seems ready to get out. Just as impatient as her father."

"You've made it further than many have," I admitted, thinking of how many children had been orphaned in the battle, how many mothers, even those who had been with child, had been slaughtered when the darklings attacked the city. Thalia had aided in helping mothers find assistance in ensuring their young were fed, some struggling to do that on what little rations we could provide. Some mothers were going so far as to nurse not only their own babes, but orphaned infants just to help them survive.

"I heard you finally started building that house on the mountain," I said, hoping to get her mind elsewhere, anywhere but where she'd remained for too long in her restless thoughts. Perhaps I needed the distraction as much as she did when it came to the possibility of what was to come with her delivery.

"We did a few weeks ago—well, I guess Damien did. I haven't been able to visit the site to see it. It was beautiful when we first picked the land earlier this year," she said, her smile somber, as if she longed to go there. "It's not far from where the humans are discussing building a mountainside rail system to transport people from the valley to the top of the mountain in cases of emergency. The view is going to be incredible."

"Damien told me how excited you've been to design the house."

She nodded. "I wanted to plant some maple trees in the front yard for shade, maybe some beds of foxglove. They're my favorite." Her voice trailed off, as if envisioning it. "Have a nice big porch with one of those beautiful bay windows to sit and read in." A sigh slipped from her lips. "There are so many homes to rebuild, though, so it likely won't be finished until next year."

Her gaze wandered to the window again, and I watched her for a moment. The air should be full of excitement, of happiness for what was to come...so why did I smell sadness, like the scent of freshly fallen rain, in the air? Why was it faintly laced with fear?

"How long has it been since you left this house?" I asked as I approached her bedside, following her gaze to the outside gardens. "Been in your garden?"

Her silver eyes dulled. "I haven't had the strength to."

"Would you *like* to go outside?" I asked. "Get some fresh air?"

She perked up and hesitated a moment before looking back at me. "I'm supposed to be taking it easy and lying down."

"If I carry you, you're technically not walking," I said, offering her a smile.

She arched a brow at me, the corner of her lips kicking up into a half grin. "Barrett Stratos, are you suggesting I not listen to the midwives?"

"I never said anything of the sort. You'd still be *taking it easy and lying down*," I said, leaning onto the bed. "Come on. Let's break the rules one more time before you have to be a responsible mother and I'm left to get into trouble on my own. I'll carry you wherever you'd like so you aren't exerting yourself."

Her laughter bubbled up her throat, and it warmed my heart to see her smile again. "You're a terrible influence."

"Would you prefer me any other way?" I asked, cocking a brow.

She wiped a stray tear from her eye before shaking her head.

"Where to, *Your Majesty*?" I asked, opening my arms to her.

"The gardens would be nice, and there's a bench so you don't have to carry me the entire time," she said as she pulled the blanket away before I scooped her into my arms.

"Are you implying I'm too weak to carry you?" I asked, in an insulted tone as I cradled her.

"I'm *implying*," she clarified, stifling her laughter, "that I'm not exactly light right now. I feel like a sky whale."

I scoffed, flexing and lifting her higher in my arms. "Light as a feather, *Your Majesty*."

She snickered as I started for the doorway, but I froze the moment I stepped into the hallway as we found ourselves face to face with their head caretaker, Isla.

Fuck.

Isla blinked, her blue eyes widening as they flitted between Lucia and me.

I opened and closed my mouth, trying to find words. "Isla, I can—"

"Some fresh air will do ye some good," she said with a smile before glancing over her shoulder to the hall behind her. "But ye'll want tae go out the back entrance to avoid the other servants so they donnae make a fuss."

"Thank you, Isla," Lucia whispered, and I nodded before carefully hurrying in the opposite direction to slip out into the garden unnoticed.

"Zephyr and Damien told me you started feeling some contractions yesterday," I said.

"They've been here and there, but nothing too severe," she said as I nudged the rear door open. "I had one before you came back into the room."

"If it gets to be too much excitement, let me know, and I'll take you back to bed," I said, all joking aside.

"Oh, please," she groaned, letting her head fall against my chest in defeat. "Between Damien and Zephyr, I have enough males doting on me. I don't need you in on it too."

"Apologies for caring," I chided as we walked through the garden, taking in the pinks and blues painting both sides of the stony path.

"And here I thought you were a hardened criminal," she teased before drawing a deep breath of fresh air. "I guess I've finally rubbed off on you."

I rolled my eyes. "Don't let it go to your head."

Her gaze swept across the garden, beyond to the valley in the distance. While it had come a long way in the clean-up, the city looked nothing like it had before the battle, and I hated the darklings and their queen for the destruction they had left in their wake.

"How are the humans holding up?" Lucia asked as I eased her onto the stone bench amidst a bed of foxgloves under a large maple tree. "Damien tells me of the recovery efforts, but I'm always afraid I might've messed something up while controlling their minds and altering their memories."

"The mental manipulation is holding up," I assured her. "You wouldn't know any of them had witnessed such horrors."

"We weren't able to save them from the sorrow of loss, though," she said, her smile fading.

I couldn't deny her statement. "We've all lost something in this battle, but it doesn't mean we can't recover from it."

She didn't speak for a moment, her gaze lingering on the city in the distance. This was how she had been since the battle, losing herself to her thoughts, falling into silence and leaving us wondering what troubled her so deeply. We all had suffered the pain and nightmares left in the aftermath of the battle; the horrors of war were still freshly engraved in our minds. Some were handling it worse than others—Salwa was working overtime offering her services to those who needed of therapy.

Lucia had declined her assistance, though, claiming there were others who needed her help more.

"It seems like only yesterday I was pulling you out of that cell," she said, and a snicker bubbled up her throat. "You made it so hard to maintain any sort of composure with how you riled the guard."

I gave her a disapproving look. "And you were foolish enough to dismiss him and be left alone with a criminal who didn't care if he hurt you. Honestly, I don't understand why we leave you unattended. You're just begging to get into trouble."

"You didn't hurt me, though," she said, tilting her head to glance at me from the corner of her eye. "I handled you just fine."

"You were just lucky," I said, easing back against the back of the bench.

Her hand rosed to hover over her mouth as she laughed. "Keep telling yourself that, hothead."

The birds sang in the nearby trees, hopping from branch to branch as they danced with one another. A gentle breeze caressed our skin, and it was a nice reprieve from the hot August air.

"How are you, Thalia, and Micah getting along?" she asked.

I arched a brow. "If I didn't know any better, I'd think you were trying to set me up with them."

Her dark brows rose, and she blinked for a moment. I couldn't miss the way her lips twitched as she resisted the smile. "Is that what you want?"

I frowned. "Why would I want that?"

She shrugged. "You said it, not me."

I opened my mouth to retort, but she winced, her hands gripping the edge of the bench.

My heart lurched, and I shot to my feet, hands jolting to hover around her in case she fell.

She waved me off, offering me a pained smile as she let out a controlled breath. "It's just another contraction."

"Should I get Damien?" I asked, unsure of what to do. Fuck, maybe I shouldn't have taken her out of the house.

She shook her head. "I'll be fine. It was just one. They've been coming and going more today. It's all part of the process."

I eyed her wearily, and eventually, she eased, her fingers loosening from the stone before her shoulders relaxed and she let out a breath of relief. Minutes passed in silence as I allowed her the room to relax, her eyes closed, head resting against the stone as she seemed to gather herself.

"Those look rough," I said.

"They're not too bad; I've dealt with worse pain," she said with a smile as she rested her hand on her stomach.

"No need to act tough on my account," I said.

"Who knew you'd become such a gentleman?" she teased before wincing, lips parting as a gasp slipped from her lips and she grabbed onto the bench again. I offered her my hand, and she grabbed it, squeezing as she breathed through the pain. A few seconds passed before her shoulders sagged with a sigh. "Oh, that was a strong one."

"Perhaps we should get you back, contact the midwives," I said, and she nodded faintly with a weak smile as she took the hand I offered.

"That would probably be wise," she admitted.

"Come on, let's get you inside," I said, gently lifting her into my arms. "I'll send someone for Damien."

She nodded, and by the time we made it through the garden and into the house, another contraction hit. My heart twisted at the way she held onto me as she tried to breathe through it.

"Isla!" I called out as I carried Lucia down the hall toward her room.

She appeared in the doorway as I eased Lucia onto her bed. "What is it?"

"The contractions are getting closer," Lucia explained. "Still inconsistent, though."

"Ah'll send fer Lord Damien and the midwives," Isla said, turning and hurrying down the hall, calling out for one of the other servants.

"What can I get for you?" I asked Lucia. "How can I help?"

"Some water would be nice," she said before she exhaled a slow breath.

I nodded and hurried to retrieve a drink for her. By the time I returned, some of the servants were in the room tending to her, discussing plans to prepare her for labor and the arrival of the babe.

"Thank you," Lucia said as I offered her the drink. She took it, drinking deeply before I set it on her bedside table.

"They're on their way, deary," Isla said as she entered the room, tying her coppery hair into a low bun. "How far apart are they now?"

"Maybe five to ten minutes? They're still a little inconsistent," Lucia answered wearily as one of her attendants supported her, her skin already covered in a faint sheen of sweat.

"Lucia?" Damien said, his voice full of concern at my back. I twisted around to find him emerging from the converging shadows along the wall, Zephyr following close behind him.

"*Mea sol,*" she breathed, a smile of relief curving her lips as he rushed to her.

"I'm here," he whispered as he took her hand and pressed a kiss to her forehead.

Lucia leaned into him before her eyes shut tightly, a moan of pain slipping from her lips as she gripped the sheets on the edge of the bed.

"They're getting closer. Just try tae breathe through them," Isla muttered, and Lucia did so, breathing deeply through her nose before letting all the air expel from her lungs through her mouth.

Isla looked at Zephyr. "Ah think it's really happenin' this time."

Zephyr nodded before proceeding to discuss needs with the attendants. He slid past me, and I couldn't seem to do more than stand frozen.

"Would ye like tae rest in bed until the midwives arrive? Or try to get on your feet?" Isla said as she approached, and her tone softened, turning into something warm and encouraging. "Gravity always helps the baby move along."

Lucia nodded. "I think I might try standing."

"I'll retrieve the midwives. I can get them here faster," Damien said, and Lucia nodded before he ducked into the shadows.

Zephyr rushed into the room again, arms full of linens, towels, and a basin. "Here are the things you requested."

"Thank ye," Isla said, taking them from him.

I stepped closer to Lucia, offering her a reassuring hand in Damien's absence, and whispered, "You've got this."

She lifted her eyes to me, slumping as she braced herself against the edge of their bed in the wake of another contraction. Sweat beaded along her brow in the summer heat, and I grabbed a damp washcloth from a nearby basin of water.

"You're the strongest warrior I know," I said, dabbing the rag against her forehead as she let out a sigh of relief. "You're a goddess, a damned powerful one at that. You've faced more terrifying things than this."

For a moment, her eyes seemed to waver as she absorbed my words, but then her lips curved into a weak smile, and she nodded.

"Lady Lucia," a woman's voice called from a shadow doorway as three females in gray robes entered the room before Damien. They carried a number of bags in their arms, likely loaded down with various tools and instruments they might need to help deliver the babe.

"Let's get ye changed intae somethin' more comfortable," Isla said, approaching with a linen gown draped across her arms.

"I'll be right outside," I said, turning to Lucia once more. "You can do this."

"I can do this," Lucia echoed weakly, and I wasn't sure if it was for her own reassurance or mine. I offered her a smile before reluctantly stepping back to allow Damien to return to her side.

The room erupted into chaos, midwives and attendants going in different directions as they prepped the bed, lit candles, and brought Lucia a gown to change into. It was all happening so fast—too fast.

I stepped out of the room, closing the door to allow them privacy. Zephyr had pulled up a couple of chairs and was sitting across the hall, his chin resting atop his interlaced fingers.

Our uneasy gazes met, and I knew by how his green eyes wavered, he was just as fearful as I was.

I wasn't sure how long Zephyr and I paced the hall, unable to speak. How long would they be in there? How long would she suffer? The only sounds we had heard over the last few hours had been words of encouragement and moans of pain, some so intense that Zephyr and I had to resist the urge to open the door and make sure Lucia was all right.

Attendants stood outside the chambers, ready to enter if needed. They quietly whispered to each other, and I tried to avoid hearing them discuss the risks and complications Lucia faced.

Isla stepped out of the room, and Zephyr and I twisted around to face her. Her cheeks were flushed, sweat coating her skin, and she glanced at me before looking at Zephyr. "Can ye get me some fresh towels?" She then turned to me and held out an empty basin. "And could ye bring me some fresh water?"

"Is she all right?" Zephyr and I asked in unison.

She didn't respond at first, glancing back at the door nervously. "She's tired, but everything is going as hoped. It won't be long now."

A loud groan sounded from beyond the door, and Isla whipped around before glancing back at us. "Go, please," she begged. "I need to return to them."

We nodded and split off to do as she asked. I could faintly hear Zephyr muttering prayers under his breath as he hurried down the hall, begging The Fates to protect Lucia and the babe—to spare them the fate so many of our kind suffered in childbirth. When we returned to the door, Lucia cried out from the other side, and my heart twisted at the agony in her voice.

"You're doing amazing, *mea luna*. Hang in there. You're almost there," Damien coached, and we stood there, useless. Utterly fucking useless.

How could we just stand here? How could we not be able to help her? I'd always been at her side, fighting every battle with her, but now... Now, I was stuck outside, unable to help her face this.

"I'll take those," one of the attendants said, taking the linens from Zephyr.

As the attendant cracked the door enough to slip through, Damien's voice reached my ears as he urged Lucia to push, and she let out a cry of pain. Zephyr and I froze, unable to move, to pull ourselves away from the door as it closed once more, to do anything but lose ourselves in our terror of what might happen.

We waited in silence, narrowing in on every sound, every moan of pain, every word of encouragement, every order from the midwives, every cry of agony.

"She's beautiful," Damien said from the other side of the door, and for a moment, my heart soared, hope welling in my chest.

An attendant slipped out, her face grave. She wouldn't meet our gazes, and Zephyr and I exchanged looks of unease as she called to the attendants.

"What's wrong with her?" Damien demanded from within the room, and the strong scent of blood reached my nose. "*Mea luna*? Stay with me, stay awake."

The attendants rushed in, and I couldn't bring myself to move as I caught the faintest glimpse of Damien climbing onto the bed, cradling Lucia in his arms as he spoke to her. She was muttering something to him, too faint for me to hear. Gods, her skin was pale, her lips losing their color.

"They're taking care of her," Damien said, his voice full of terror. "Stay with me, Lucia. I need you to keep your eyes open for me."

"What's happening?" Zephyr demanded of the attendants as they rushed in and out of the room.

Isla emerged, soft cries reaching my ears from the tiny bundle wrapped tightly in her arms as she looked over her shoulder. This was wrong. *This can't be happening.*

"Isla," Zephyr said, and she twisted back to face him as he demanded an answer, each word clipped, "what is happening?"

Tears welled in her eyes, and my heart plummeted.

"No," I muttered, taking a step forward.

"She's bleedin' out; we don't know when it started," she said, her voice thick before she returned her attention to the bundle in her arms.

No. I shook my head, looking back just as Damien sliced his blade across his wrist.

"Can't we do anything for her?" Zephyr asked, panic marring every word.

"There are nae any healers left," Isla said, her voice breaking as she stepped past us.

Because they had all been killed in the battle, leaving no one with the healing ability of House Latros. Lucia possessed the magic, but its only disadvantage was the inability to heal oneself.

"Drink, Lucia, please!"

Our attention snapped to the room where Damien cradled Lucia, her eyes flickering, and the world went quiet as her blood-stained lips moved. Damien shook his head as he pulled her against him, begging her to stay with him.

She sagged in his arms, head falling against his chest, lashes lowering over those silver eyes that once held such love for everything around her.

And every bit of hope died within me.

Her smile flashed across my thoughts—the smile she had given me when we first met. I'd hated that smile at first, hated the pity... I'd hated that she had tried to work her way beyond the walls I had built up around myself. I'd pushed her away, said things she never deserved to hear.

I'd never deserved her kindness, never deserved her light...and yet, I wanted it, couldn't imagine a life without it, couldn't imagine a world where she didn't exist. I didn't *want* to imagine it.

What was I without her, the one person who had held faith in me when everyone else had left me to rot. The person who had pulled me from the dark depths and given me purpose—where would we go without her?

Isla's hand clasped over her mouth as a sob broke free, the babe in her arm quieting.

One of the midwives emerged from the room, the only sounds Damien's sobs. My vision blurred as the midwife gave us a sorrowful look and shook her head.

"No..." Zephyr muttered. "She was fine. She was doing good. You said so yourself."

"It all happened so fast," the midwife whispered.

Zephyr's pain and anger burned through the air, filling my nose like rain falling on a forest fire. I couldn't bring myself to form any words as I stared at my best friend lifeless on the bed, her mate holding onto her tightly as he cried for her to come back to him.

She couldn't be gone, not like this.

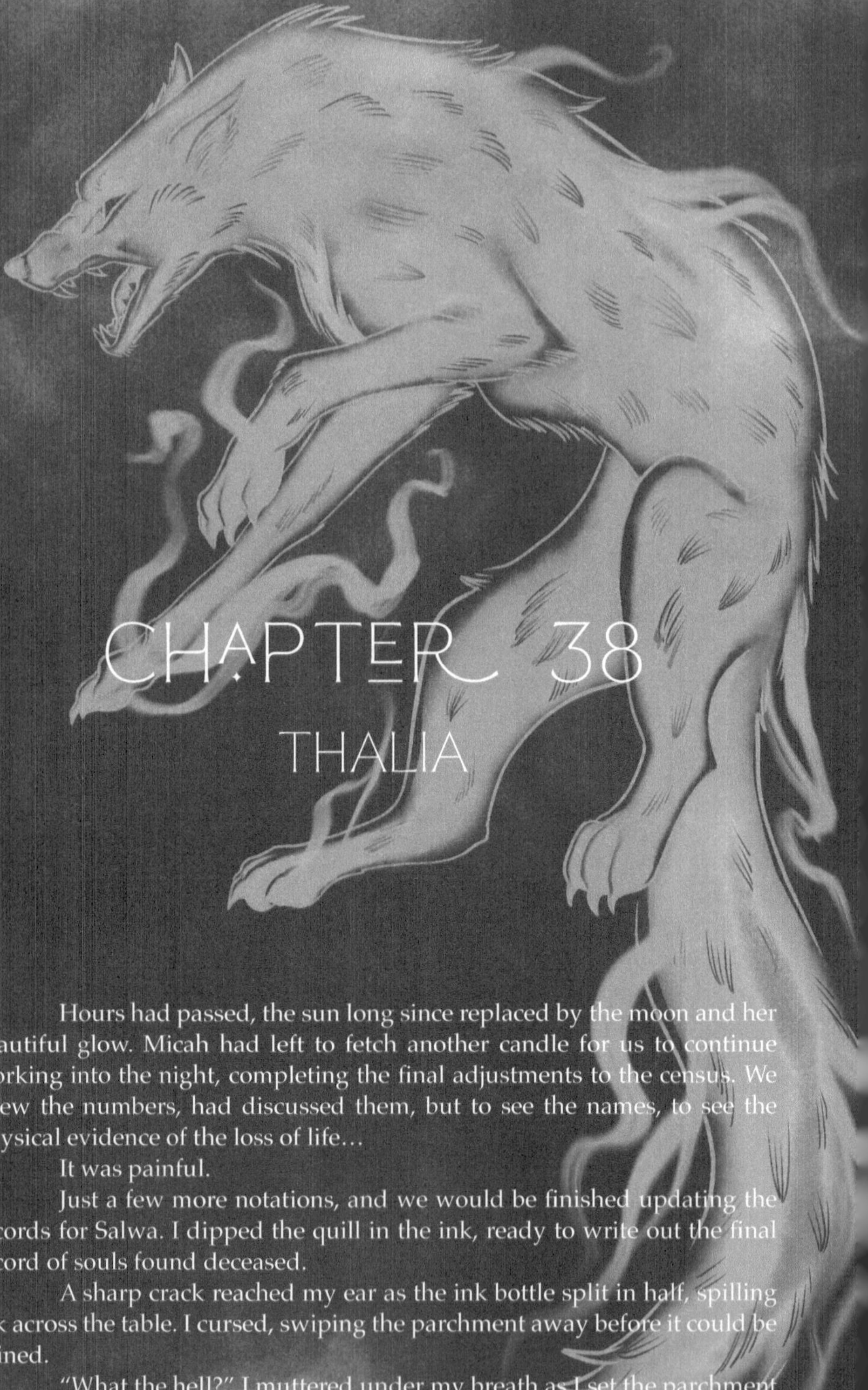

CHAPTER 38

THALIA

Hours had passed, the sun long since replaced by the moon and her beautiful glow. Micah had left to fetch another candle for us to continue working into the night, completing the final adjustments to the census. We knew the numbers, had discussed them, but to see the names, to see the physical evidence of the loss of life…

It was painful.

Just a few more notations, and we would be finished updating the records for Salwa. I dipped the quill in the ink, ready to write out the final record of souls found deceased.

A sharp crack reached my ear as the ink bottle split in half, spilling ink across the table. I cursed, swiping the parchment away before it could be ruined.

"What the hell?" I muttered under my breath as I set the parchment aside and looked at the broken bottle. I ran a hand over my face before turning to search for something to clean up the mess. Perhaps it was a sign I should quit for the night, get some sleep.

"She's in labor?" Micah's voice reached my ears from the hall, and I stilled.

"Damien retrieved the midwives a few hours ago," one of the servants said.

I rushed into the hall, my heart in my throat. "Have you heard anything since?"

The servant turned to me, her eyes wide as she shook her head. I glanced back at the broken bottle at my desk, my heart stilling before I shoved past her. Micah called after me, the sound of his boots barely audible over the roaring in my ears.

The hot night air rushed over me as I burst through the door. Darkness swallowed me as I gave into the shift, feathers overtaking my body before I took to the sky, desperate to see that Lucia was all right.

"Thalia, wait!" Micah called, but I didn't, *couldn't*.

How long had she been in labor? Was the baby already here? My mind raced, every terrifying thought rising to counteract any ounce of excitement I felt. I hadn't seen her since I'd turned down the promotion a week prior.

Pain ricocheted through my talons and into my legs as I hit the ground outside their home, shifting back into my immortal form. The house was silent as I rushed through the door, and my heart sank.

The scent of blood and freshly fallen rain hit my nose, and the air halted in my lungs. My hands shook as I hurried down the hall, my feet cemented in place when I found Barrett and Zephyr sitting in the hall, their faces in their hands.

Pressure built in my chest, making it more and more difficult to breathe with each second. Barrett lifted his head, his eyes red and swollen as he found me. He didn't speak, and I wanted so badly for him to tell me everything was all right, that *she* was all right.

Say it… Fucking tell me she's okay.

He drew a deep breath and shook his head.

No.

The room blurred.

My gaze snagged on the door nearby, and I stumbled toward it.

Barrett shot to his feet. "Thalia—"

I shoved the door open, halting in the entry as I found her laid out on the bed.

The room was quiet, candles lit on every surface, their soft glow dancing across her pale skin. Her black hair dusted the bed in a soft blanket beneath her, her hands folded neatly across her still-swollen stomach.

It was as if she was merely sleeping.

Barrett stopped at my side as I stood frozen next to the bed.

"She..." My voice broke.

"It happened so fast," he said in barely more than a whisper.

Tears rolled down my cheeks. "She can't be gone."

He pulled me into his arms, hugging me tightly, as if he could shelter me from this pain, this agony.

Zephyr appeared in the doorway, his cheeks stained with tears, his pale green eyes just as red and swollen as Barrett's. The sight of his tears, knowing he had now lost his sister twice...

"Damien," I said, looking around.

Barrett drew an uneven breath. "He's with Emilia."

"Is she all right?" I asked.

He nodded. "They're tending to her now."

My knees shook as I turned my gaze back to Lucia, and I stumbled toward her bedside, reaching out to touch her. My fingers trembled, fear rising within me that she might vanish before I could feel that she was real.

As my fingers met her cold hand, a sob tore from me so violently, I thought it might shatter me—break me into shards too tiny to piece back together.

I leaned over her, wishing I could see her smile one more time, hear her laughter, talk to her once more, even if only to tell her how much I loved her, how much she meant to me. Gods, she didn't deserve this, didn't deserve to have every chance at happiness torn from her.

Tears dripped onto Lucia's pale cheeks as I leaned over her, praying she might open her eyes, might offer me that reassuring smile she always shared. She always had a way to fix things, a way to get out of the worst.

I crumbled to the floor at her side, unable to let go, unable to accept that she was truly gone...

Unable to release her to whatever evil took her from us.

CHAPTER 39

BARRETT

I lingered in the hallway for a moment, listening to Damien sing a lullaby to Emilia on the other side of the door. His voice cracked more with each word.

"Damien?" I muttered, tapping my knuckle against the door frame.

He cleared his throat. "Come in."

I cracked the door open, leaning in, and my eyes fell on the babe, swaddled in a blanket of pure starlight. My heart squeezed at the sight of her, so tiny in his arms. It was the first time I'd seen her since Isla had whisked her out of the room, since Lucia had...

"It was Moira's when she was born," he said, running his finger over the blanket, the shimmering light shifting and flickering with each movement, as if distant stars had been trapped within the threads. "She was swaddled in it when we first met. I was only five."

A lump formed in my throat, and any words I might say stayed lodged within my throat.

"Selene gifted it to us when we learned she was pregnant. Lucia was so excited to see her swaddled in it." He blinked before sweeping a hand over his reddened eyes, wiping away stray tears. "Sorry, I, uh... I called you in here for a reason. I need to tend to Lucia's body, see that she's brought to Selene's temple in preparation for the funeral."

I stepped closer to him, my attention lingering on the babe, her tiny head covered in a mess of soft black waves just as dark as Lucia's, her silver eyes moving around but never latching onto anything.

"How can I help?"

"Can you stay with her while Zephyr and I see it done?" he asked. "I don't want to risk taking her out of the house, and the servants are all busy with other matters after... well..."

"Is Isla around?" I knew what to do yet was unsure at the same time. I hadn't held a baby since Calliope had been born.

"She's helping clean up and seeing to preparations if you need anything or are unsure of what to do," he said, and he looked down at Emilia as he swayed back and forth. "She just ate, so she should be good for an hour or two. I'll be back before then."

I nodded. "All right. Yeah, I can keep her company."

"I know she would have wanted you to hold her," he said, a sorrowful smile curving his lips, his eyes welling with tears.

He shifted Emilia in his arms, holding her out for me to take, and I cautiously accepted her, holding her to my chest. Gods, she was beautiful, so tiny, yet I could feel the magic welling inside her, could feel and see every bit of Lucia within her tiny face.

"She's been very calm, but if she gets to be too much just call, and Isla will come to help calm her down," Damien said, running his hand over her head.

"She's so tiny." My eyes remained fixated on her, every part of me in awe of this tiny being. "I remember when my sister was born. She was just as small."

Damien's eyes flitted to me briefly before falling to Emilia once more. "You be good for Uncle Barrett," he whispered, and leaned in to press a kiss to her forehead. She squirmed in response before she yawned, her eyes squeezing shut tightly for a moment before looking around once more.

"Selene is already aware, so this shouldn't take long," he said, hovering a moment, his hand lingering on the blanket.

"I'll protect her," I said, lifting my eyes to him. "I'll make sure she's all right. You take care of Lucia."

"Thank you," Damien muttered, placing his hand on my shoulder. He leaned his forehead to mine, and we lingered there, letting the weight of our grief anchor us.

"I'd better not hold things up anymore," he said, the dread of the reality of Lucia's passing clear as day on his face.

I offered him a half smile. "I promise not to teach her any bad habits just yet."

His lips twitched, and he rolled his eyes before heading for the door.

My eyes fell to her curled up in her blanket, the galaxies and constellations seeming alive in the fibers. She startled, her face tightening, her hand shooting out as she whimpered.

"Shhhh." I swayed as Damien had and ran my finger over her tiny palm. Her fingers wrapped around mine, so tiny in comparison. She settled, and I allowed her to keep hold of my finger as I paced toward the window.

The candle's glow flickered across the room, moonlight leaking in through the window, and I stopped to look up at it.

"See? Everything's all right," I said, looking down at her, shifting my weight back and forth as I rocked her. "Nothing will happen to you while I'm here."

Her eyes lingered on me, never latching onto a detail though, and I smiled down at her. She continued to hold my finger, and I could feel the hum of her magic where our skin touched.

"You're going to be powerful, just like your mother," I said, blinking back tears. "She loved you so much. She should be the one holding you, not me."

Tears dripped onto the swaddle, the galaxies and stars swirling as the droplets turned to stardust amidst the constellations, and I rubbed them away before smiling down at her.

"Would you like to hear a story?" I whispered before looking out the window, my heart twisting as my gaze landed on the empty bench beneath the maple tree in the moonlight. I could almost see Lucia sitting there, smiling as she always did.

"Centuries ago, there was a kingdom," I said, smiling down at her, "inhabited by beings with powers that rivaled the gods."

Her lashes lowered, and that she found comfort in my arms flooded my chest with warmth.

"Within the kingdom lived a princess." My voice quivered as Lucia's smile flashed across my memories. "And she was treasured by her people, gifted to them by the gods, blessed with more power than any of them could bear." Her grip loosened on my finger, and I gently eased her hand onto her chest. "The ruler of the kingdom fell in love with the princess."

Something fractured deep within my soul, but I wouldn't let the sorrow capture me, not while I held Emilia. I would share everything with her, help her know the mother who never got to hold her.

"When the princess returned his affection, they united, forming a bond more powerful than the foundations of their realm." I held her close, feeling her tiny body relax as she slipped into sleep.

I eased into the chair beside the window, unable to take my eyes off her. "It will be a while, but she'll return to us, I promise. She always does..."

PART 3

1976

(87 YEARS LATER)

CHAPTER 40

BARRETT

Sun leaked onto me through the trees in warm rays. The forest was filled with life, birds singing in the trees, the sound of water rushing over the stony bed of the creek reaching my ears, twilight flowers littering the grass around me, dusting the green grass in a blanket of blues and purples. My eyes fell to my small hands, my poorly woven flower crown resting within my grasp.

I wanted to give it to someone, someone special, someone I barely knew but wanted to learn all I could about her.

Laughter reached my ears, clear and bright, and my heart warmed at how Calliope's smile could lift my spirits, no matter how down I felt. I turned to where she was, and a strange sadness swelled in my chest that I couldn't understand when I found her kneeling at another girl's back, weaving a flower crown into her hair. I couldn't quite make out the girl's features, only that her hair was pale, like the silk from the cornstalks harvested in the fields my friend's family tended.

Something tugged deep, as if a thread had wound itself so tightly around my soul, drawn tight in her direction.

"Barrett!" Calliope called out, her voice radiant as she glanced back at me, her sage eyes catching the sunlight. "Did you finish your crown?"

A loud smack jolted me awake, and I shot up to find a thick, unfamiliar manila folder lying atop the mess of paperwork I'd been working on most of the night, dust scattering in the air like a flock of birds. I looked up to find Damien pacing toward the window, where morning light was leaking through the barely parted curtains.

"Long night?" he asked, pulling the fabric back to reveal the burning sunshine.

"You're just as bad as Lucia was," I groaned and clamped my mouth shut, immediately regretting mentioning her name, regretted stirring up the pain of her loss despite how many decades had passed.

"What can I say?" he started, his voice dipping slightly, shadows darkening his eyes. "She rubbed off on me."

"What's this?" I asked, grabbing the folder from the mess of papers littering my desk as I rubbed my hand over my face. I could barely remember what the table looked like beneath it all with how busy he kept me.

"Something I want you to look into," he said as he stopped pacing. Dark circles lingered under his eyes, but exhaustion wasn't anything new for him. He'd been a mess ever since Lucia and Emilia died nearly ninety years ago. He had grown worse when Lucia hadn't been reborn, and each year, he seemed to slip further into his own darkened mind.

I'd been told the reincarnation cycle was typically tripped fifteen to twenty-five years after she died, but she hadn't returned. While many of our kind worried about what that meant for us in the war against the darklings, for those of us who knew her personally, it only brought pain, a wound left festering, doomed never to heal.

"What? Did a recruit spike the water system with ambrosia liquor again? It was some harmless fun. No humans got into it." I huffed a laugh as I opened the folder. "And you can't deny we had a damned good time that..." My eyes fell over the first few pictures clipped to the first stack of papers, and the words fell short on my tongue as my heart dipped. "...night."

It was a body, a human female. She had been discarded in an alley, her body mangled, limbs broken and twisted, skin marred with cuts and what appeared to be cigarette burns, her wrists bruised.

"What happened?" I asked as I lifted it to reveal another stack of papers. Another female, her body just as broken.

"That's what I want you to find out," he said, gripping the edge of the desk.

"Since when do we get involved in human murders?" I asked, checking the separately clipped papers beneath it to find another female, and another... and another. "Are the police no longer doing an adequate job? It's not enough we protect them from the darklings.? Now we have to protect them from each other?"

"Take a closer look at their necks," he said, nodding to the folder. "Twelve cases in the last six months, all with the same patterns."

I let out a sigh and grabbed the photo from the first pile to inspect it closer. It was faint, but two healed puncture wounds marked her throat. A human might have written it off as a blemish, but to us, there was no mistaking it.

"One of our kind did this?" I muttered, eyes narrowing as I took in more detail. Her wrists weren't simply bruised as if someone had held her down—they were chafed, blistered. I'd seen wounds like this before, and something twisted in my gut. They'd been left by shackles, and as I looked over the cuts, the bruises...I began to see the very patterns he spoke of.

"These are markings similar to those inflicted during interrogations done by The Order," Damien said, his eyes narrowing with disgust as they fell to the photograph.

"Do you think a deserter did this?" I asked. There hadn't been many in the years following The Fall of Kingdoms, when we had suffered such a blow to our ranks.

Damien paced around my desk. "How long has it been since you've worked for Atlas?"

I frowned at the change of subject. Atlas was the leader of The Underworld, a criminal organization within immortal society that remained outside of Damien's control—or so they thought. "I helped him with that job last month, when he smuggled a shipment of Brierleaf from the Godsrealm."

Through that job, I'd finally uncovered the location of the unregistered propylaea he had bargained for with Damien in exchange for his help in fighting the darklings during The Fall of Kingdoms—the very one that allowed The Underworld to traverse across the veil to the Godsrealm. It had taken me decades to gain Atlas' trust enough for him to share such information, and I'd begun to give up hope of ever truly getting close enough to gain any real knowledge of worth to their connections to the Godsrealm—or whether any gods favored them.

It was dangerous for them to have access to a propylaea, I'd argued with Damien when he'd considered the offer, but their presence had been the only thing that helped us hold up against the darklings until Lucia had brought down the darkling queen. Damien had instructed me to merely keep tabs on it. It didn't allow them access to Selene's temple, instead providing a direct route to Belimus, Zeus's domain—the seat of power within Elythias, where The Twelve resided, each commanding their own territories. The only issue was that Propylaeas' path could be altered with a God's blessing.

And the favor they had received was from The God Of The Dead, Hades, who had altered its path to his kingdom of Aidonia.

"I want you to see if he has any involvement in this."

I turned my attention back to the pictures. "I know he's not fond of humans, but this seems a bit extreme, even for him."

"You never know. It might be one of his men working on their own," Damien said with a sigh. "Either way, I want answers, and he might have some."

I flipped through the details of the cases, reading out their names. They were all between eighteen and twenty-five, with brown hair and hazel eyes, just over five feet in height.

"You think it's a coincidence they're all close to the age of *settling*?" I asked.

Damien frowned and blinked before leaning over the table. "They are?"

I nodded, and he took the papers, flipping through them, his expression growing more grave.

The *settling* was a monumental time for our kind, a transition of sorts. It was when we came into our magic, stopped aging. Every cell in our body was remade, rebuilt to be more powerful. With the magic and strength came the need to consume blood, the toll on our bodies too much to subsist on regular food alone. It was never guaranteed when we would undergo the *settling*, but it typically happened between the ages of eighteen and twenty-three.

"Surely it's just a coincidence," Damien said, running his fingers through the dusting of hair lining his jaw. "Humans don't go through anything like a settling. The killer probably just has a taste for women around that age."

It wasn't unheard of. There had been cases in the past of rogue immortals targeting humans, and sometimes, there were patterns, favored traits in their blood type or physical appearance. Either way, we always got to the bottom of it and swiftly dealt with the threat. This was a new level of obsession, though; I'd never seen such a definitive pattern.

"I have other matters to attend to," Damien said as he headed for the door. He stopped short as he grabbed the doorknob and glanced back at me. "Get to the bottom of this."

I let out a sigh—as if I didn't have enough to deal with—but as my eyes roamed over the mess of case files, my gaze snagged on a photo of one of the victim's forearms, on the words carved into her flesh.

'*Imposter*'.

CHAPTER 41

THALIA

Music pounded through the black brick walls of Stokers as I stepped through the door, knowing damned well this was the only place they could be hiding out.

Vincent rounded the bar with a glass of ambrosia liquor in each hand, freezing the moment he caught sight of me, his eyes immediately darting to the assholes I was searching for. I stalked toward him, grabbing one of the glasses he held. "This for Micah?"

He cracked a guilty smile, relinquishing the drink to me without hesitation. "Skipped training, didn't he?"

I knocked back the glass, the amber liquid burning its way down my throat before I set it on the bar. "They both did."

They had left me to train alone with ten new recruits, not only avoiding the responsibility but slacking off and shirking their own training all afternoon to do gods knew what.

"Don't let me stop you," he said, stepping back and out of my way.

"And here I thought you'd at least have Barrett's back," I crooned, glancing at him.

"I'm not getting my head bitten off by the wolf," he said with a laugh as he turned to find somewhere else to be.

I couldn't help but reminisce on how much he had grown from the little boy I'd met so long ago to the warrior before me now. He'd been Barrett's shadow everywhere he went, had gotten into all sorts of trouble at his side, but he'd grown into a male his mother could be proud of.

The beast within me swelled with satisfaction as I turned toward Barrett and Micah, who had yet to notice my presence. The bastards were lucky to be hiding out in Semele and Eiko's bar, or my first greeting would have been to tackle them to the ground, teeth bared. I couldn't bring myself to cause any damage to the females' space, though, no matter how ticked off I was with the duo who had left me high and dry to deal with the new blood.

I stalked toward them, bar patrons parting ways to allow me through, as if they could sense what lurked beneath the surface of my skin, ready to bite.

"I wonder how long it'll be before she shows up," Micah whispered as I neared, and my lips curved at his statement.

"Better get your drinks in fast. She's probably already on her way over," Barrett responded, tipping his glass back and grimacing as he drank the liquor down.

"Yeah, I'd say that was your last one. Hope you enjoyed it," I said, arms crossed as I stopped at their backs.

Micah choked on his drink, coughing and sputtering as he set his glass down. "Thalia, my love."

"Don't even," I said as I glared down at him.

"It was one afternoon," Micah said with a guilty smile, and I ignored the part of me that softened at the look in his sky-blue eyes. "Barrett pulled an all-nighter last night working on paperwork, and I was tired from patrol."

My eyes narrowed. "We train to keep our bodies in shape, to remain prepared to fight *them*."

"One missed day of training isn't going to kill us," Barrett said, turning to face me as he leaned back against the bar, strong arms draped over the dark wood. I avoided letting my eyes roam over every inch of carved muscle filling his shirt as he cocked his head to the side.

"I could make it up to you," Micah said, running his tongue over his lower lip, and my heart fell into a heavy rhythm at the way his soft blue eyes darkened.

"You can make it up to me by taking my training shift tomorrow," I said, arching a brow with a coy grin.

Micah cursed under his breath as his head fell back, but he then smiled and threw his hands up in defeat. "Fine, I'll take over tomorrow's shift for you."

Barrett huffed a laugh as he lifted his glass to take another swig.

"You can join him," I growled, my gaze shifting to him.

Barrett's steel eyes lifted to me, the glass hovering at his lips, a hint of challenge gleaming within his metallic stare. "Last I checked, I outrank you."

"And last I checked," I said, meeting his gaze with a challenge of my own as the beast relished how he stood against me, how he rarely cowered or backed down, "if I told Damien you were shirking your duties, he'd tear you a new one."

He took a drink, his throat bobbing as he swallowed, and I tried not to focus on it. "More important things required my attention."

I arched a brow. "Drinking is more important than training?"

The smile faded from his lips, and his eyes dipped. "I can assure you, I wasn't drinking."

I frowned and my lips parted, but I halted at the faint presence of someone at my back.

"Barrett."

The air around Barrett changed, heated with a dull anger, just enough to allow an inkling of his magic to permeate the air like the molten breath of a wyvern, and I turned to find Aiden standing at my back. The fully tattooed male looked to have acquired more ink since I'd seen him last, the black markings peeking from beneath the collar of his shirt where they crawled up his neck.

"Atlas is ready to see you," Aiden said, his face unreadable save for the cold flame that lingered in his gray eyes.

"Hey to you too, Aiden," I said bitterly, allowing the annoyance to coat my tongue. "How kind of you to grace us with your presence."

The male was a notorious asshole in The Order, constantly picking fights with others in his unit. I'd gone toe-to-toe with him a time or two, and while I'd won out in the end, I'd spat blood to do it.

"He expects you in two hours," Aiden said without acknowledging me. The beast within me bristled at the disrespect, and, for a moment, I nearly considered paying Semele more than the cost of repairs to slam the bastard into her bartop.

Without another glance, Aiden turned and stalked back through the crowd.

"Nice talking to you too," I said sarcastically before turning to Barrett, whose eyes were cold and distant as they followed Aiden's path.

"Atlas?" I asked. Where had I heard that name before?

"As in," Micah's voice dipped, "The Underworld Atlas?"

Barrett downed the last of his liquor before saying lowly, "No one for you to worry about."

"What are you getting involved in?" I asked. "Is there some way we can help?"

A muscle ticked in Barrett's jaw. "Forget about what you heard. That's an order."

I ground my teeth, stifling the urge to call him out on his heroic bullshit and the way he shut me out every time I tried to help. The fucker sure loved to pull rank when it benefitted him.

He let out a sigh, set his glass and a handful of cash on the counter, and rose from his stool. His irritation painted each short, tension-laden movement, like he was a cord wound too tight, ready to snap. Micah and I exchanged hesitant glances before looking back at Barrett, who was pulling on his coat.

"I'll try to show up to tomorrow's training to make it up to you for missing today," he said, his eyes slipping from mine, and despite the annoyance coating his words, something else lingered in his eyes when they briefly flitted to mine once more. Guilt?

"Don't be late," I said wearily, watching as he slipped through the crowds. "You know what's going on?" I asked without looking at Micah once Barrett was out of earshot.

Micah shrugged, looking just as confused as I was. "Damien's got him working on some sort of case; that's all I know. He's got it tight under wraps."

Whatever it was, it seemed to bother him. I hadn't seen that look in his eyes for years, and something about the sight of it left me unsure of what to feel. Worry? Concern? I resisted the urge to follow him, to demand he let us help him.

It wasn't like it was for any reason other than our friendship. At least... I thought we were friends.

There had been a shift in the atmosphere the last several years, and while I wanted to pretend I couldn't place it, I knew. Despite my continued dance around the fire, narrowly avoiding its burning touch, just as I had for centuries, ignoring how badly I would burn if I got too close, I continued to pretend it wasn't there...

Because if I acknowledged it, it would be real.

Micah's fingers interlaced with mine, drawing me back, and I looked down at my bonded, chest swelling at the look of endearment in his eyes. "Damien gave me something when I went looking for Barrett at The Complex."

"Oh?"

"A box. With your name on it," he said, and I frowned.

"What's in it?" I asked, my mind wandering to all the possibilities.

"He doesn't know. They found it in one of the chambers beneath the Archivallia. It's small, and your name..." His gaze wavered. "It's written in Lucia's handwriting."

My heart fractured at her name.

He gave me a sympathetic smile. "It's waiting for you at home."

After so many decades had passed since her death, I was almost nervous to see what it contained. If it was from Lucia, it must be important.

"I am sorry for skipping out on you today," he said, running his thumb over my hand in tender strokes. "I tried to call The Outpost, but no one answered."

I let out a sigh. "I guess I can't get your calls if I'm not inside."

"Does that mean I'm forgiven?" he said with a sheepish grin.

"That depends... You said something about making it up to me," I said, arching a brow, the corner of my lip curving into a flirtatious half-smile as I stepped between his legs and leaned against him. I ran my fingers through his shaggy brown hair, and his head tilted back as he stared up at me. "Make it worth my time, and not only will I forgive you, but maybe I'll help you with training tomorrow."

The soft sounds of Micah's easy breathing left my chest filled with warmth as I watched him sleep later that night. His soft, shaggy waves dusted cheekbones, and I brushed them away from his closed eyes, resisting the urge to lean down and kiss him—to drag him from his restful sleep and pick up where we had left off just an hour prior.

My skin tingled in the wake of his touch, a deep hunger still heating my blood.

Carefully, I slipped from beneath the blanket and rose from the bed, freezing when he stirred before settling back into a restful slumber. My eyes landed on the box atop the dresser, the one Micah had spoken of. There was no mistaking it. The box was ancient looking, the fabric edges worn and raw, as if it had been tossed and jostled around while in the Astral Sprites' care.

I lifted it, fearing it might crumble under my touch with how fragile and worn it appeared. My name was written in black ink across the top; and despite the decades since her death, I could still recognize her handwriting. Other scribbles and inscriptions in the old language littered the box with dates that spanned the last five hundred years, with paw print signatures of the astral sprites next to each date.

Five hundred years. My mind raced through the centuries, retracing the dates. That would have been around the time they had freed me from The Pits. My heart fell into a frenzy, my chest swelling with anxious anticipation, and I carefully lifted the lid. Nestled within the box was a bed of silken fabric and a single envelope with my name written in neat letters.

My pulse thrummed in my ears, my heart galloping as I lifted the envelope from the bedding of delicate linen. I pulled a small piece of parchment from the envelope's protection that still faintly smelled like her, a hint of jasmine and the citrus soap she loved so much, despite the musty scent of time that stained the paper just as the ink did. Her soft scent still somehow managed to calm me after all these decades.

Tears welled in my eyes as I began to read.

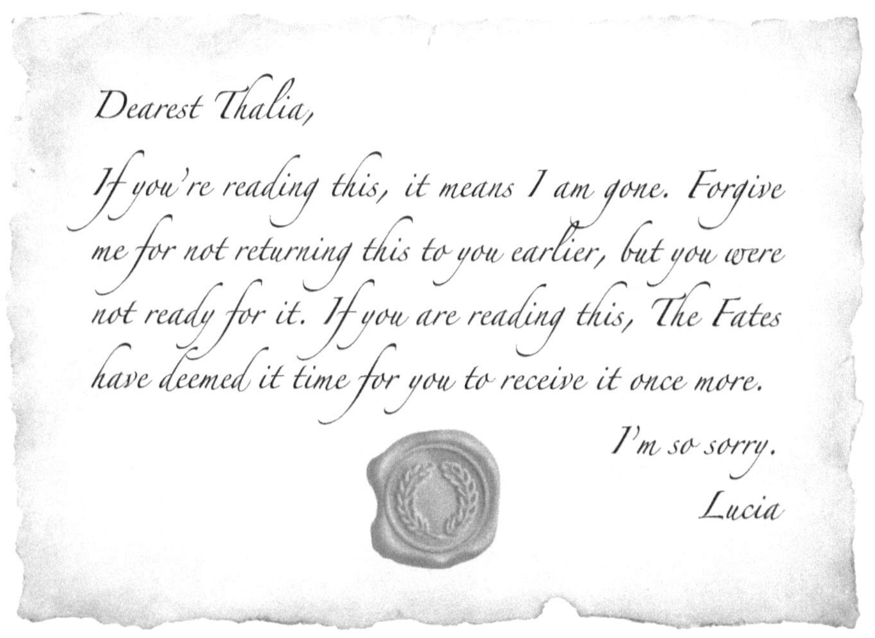

I frowned, my fingers trembling as I read the letter over and over again, picking each word apart like the puzzle it was. What did any of it mean? How could she have known she would be gone when we found this?

My eyes fell to the linen in the box, my pulse roaring in my ears, drowning out my surroundings. I set the letter aside before reaching in to lift it away and my heart plummeted at the familiar gray scrap of tattered fabric. It was what remained of the coat the boy had gifted me all those centuries ago. I'd thought it had been lost in The Pits, that I'd never see it again. Its very existence had slipped from my mind in the centuries of its absence.

I wondered if the boy still lived, or if he had been lost during The Fall of Kingdoms...perhaps even before that. My hands moved of their own accord, muscle memory bringing the fabric to my nose to breathe in the familiar scent I had almost forgotten, one that had brought me comfort in many nights of despair—

I froze as the scent of smoky oak filled my nose, as the familiar scent brought images of Barrett to my mind. His steel eyes had felt so achingly familiar for so many centuries, burning into me like a brand, like a distant

memory rippling beyond recognition on the surface of the pool of my childhood.

I'd written it off as nothing, but they had always been in my memories, had been there since the beginning.

The hardened steel eyes faded to the softened steel of a boy. Not a boy, but *the* boy of my childhood, the one who had cared for me, gifted me his coat to keep me warm...

It was him.

CHAPTER 42

BARRETT

The stench of the damned tunnels under the city filled my nose—a combination of waste, rot, and gods knew what else. I hated it, hated how there was no other way in or out if you wanted to reach The Underworld. The tunnels were intricate, a maze meant to leave anyone—human or immortal—lost and confused. Atlas had ensured that anyone who found their way here without invitation wound up as fodder to his pets that wandered these tunnels, searching for lost souls.

I'd never seen the creatures personally, had only heard horror stories of the monsters he'd smuggled across The Veil, made of pure terror—their kind only found in the Shadow Steppes, where the very soil was leeched of life from the battles wrought by the gods and titans so many millennia ago.

They didn't belong in this realm but in all honesty...did any of us?

Aiden stalked in front of me, his hands tucked into the pockets of his ripped black jacket as he watched the darkness around us. He had been working to infiltrate their ranks over the last twenty years as well, working in other ways to monitor the organization. The Underworld had been sizeable during Lucia's time, and their numbers had only grown since The Fall of Kingdoms. The losses we'd endured during the battle had proven too great to maintain morale for many of those who once served with us. There was no telling just how many had defected in the end, how many secretly worked with Atlas while maintaining their service to The Order.

"Any new entertainment down here?" I asked casually, a question I often asked to gauge the state of The Underworld without raising suspicion if anyone was listening.

"Should've seen the human females they brought in last night," he said with a huffed laugh, and I could hear the smug grin curving his lips. "Put on a pretty nice show before offering themselves to us."

Disgust filled my stomach, and I couldn't tell if he actually enjoyed treating the humans the way he did when he joined in to keep his cover intact. He was fucked up, had his own demons haunting him. Despite that, though, he always pulled through. We'd managed to covertly extract some humans who didn't wish to serve Atlas and his underlings—humans who had been coerced and left trapped in their clutches. trafficked until they were broken or eventually wound-up dead and discarded.

We came to a stop at a large, circular steel door cutting off the tunnel, where a single massive male stood. He wasn't quite as tall as I was, but the fucker was built like a godsdamned tank, his arms crossed over his chest decked out in tattoos.

"Zeus wants his blowup sex swan back," Aiden said flatly.

I resisted the urge to laugh at the phrase used to gain access to The Underworld. It changed every few months, and I wondered if Zeus had done something recently to piss Atlas off.

The brute eyed Aiden before sliding his gaze to me. His narrowed eyes crinkled the black tattoos inking the skin along the side of his face. Shit looked incomplete, the linework sloppy and obviously done in a back alley somewhere with shaky hands. I almost felt sorry for the guy.

Almost.

I nodded my chin to him. "Got something to say, coloring book?"

He rolled his eyes and muttered under his breath, but he stepped aside. The steel door groaned as it rolled, the ground rumbling beneath our feet as it cleared the way for our passage.

I patted him on the shoulder as I passed. "You should try smiling more. I bet you're pretty when you smile. Might even make those shitty tattoos look better."

He bared his teeth, fangs elongating, and jerked his shoulder from my touch.

I twisted around as I continued forward, flashing him a haughty grin. "See? You're not so ugly after all. I bet your mom might even kiss you now. Maybe if you just stay on your best behavior, she'll get you some crayons to complete your look."

I barely made it through the entrance before the steel door slammed shut in my face. "Poor sap can't take a joke."

Aiden huffed a laugh without looking over his shoulder. "He can't stand you."

"But he's such a ray of sunshine. I thought we were connecting."

Aiden shook his head. "Don't look to me to bail you out when you get jumped."

"I'd love to see him try," I said, stepping past him and through the bustling underground city. Countless immortals lined the intersecting market streets filled with string lights, neon signs, and old stolen streetlamps. The pathways were illuminated in various shades of greens, oranges, and blues, lights powered by a combination of hardwiring into the local power grid and smuggled energy crystals from the Godsrealm. Music pumped through the streets, though it was nothing like the music the humans listened to topside. This was rough, as violent as the occupants of the underground city—most likely something from the Godsrealm, where they had achieved more advanced lifestyles and different tastes in well...everything.

From the corner of my eye, I caught sight of the countless thugs grouped up alongside our path, some playing a game of Aphrodite's Throw—tossing dice onto a small table. They weren't normal dice; they were made of bone, the only acceptable dice to play the game. A few females, both immortal and human, leaned against an open doorway, and I caught sight of one in the alley next to the pleasure house. Her back was pressed against the brick wall, her legs wrapped around the waist of a male whose pants sagged at his hips as he pounded into her, her head falling back as she moaned.

Shouts dragged my attention away as I continued through the streets, to an open gap between the buildings. I spotted a male and female were fighting, bloodied fists swinging through the air as they dodged each other with gritty determination. Onlookers shouted from the sidelines, laying bets and arguing amongst themselves; they swore in unison as the male landed a crippling hit to the female's jaw before she crashed to the dirty ground, only to be dragged out for the next fighter to step in.

Every person here, be them immortal or human, operated under Atlas' command, participating in any and all activity. Whether illegal by human standards or immortal, it didn't matter. Smuggling, trafficking, theft, blackmail, drugs—this was the command center for all of it, the veritable belly of the beast.

"Atlas is in his usual place," Aiden said, pulling up his hood before nodding to the building at the far end of the main street.

I nodded as he split off, stopping at a nearby stall to look at some nasty-looking knives and daggers. By the look of their inscriptions, they were enchanted. They were likely another commodity they'd smuggled across the veil, for the only blades on this side with that level of magic were owned by The Order.

"Brierleaf?" a raspy voice muttered nearby, nearly catching me off-guard. I schooled my expression into indifference and tucked my hands into my jacket pockets before pressing on.

The immortal followed close on my heels, and as I glanced over my shoulder, I caught his eyes darting around, unable to lock on me for more than a few seconds. "If Brierleaf isn't strong enough, I've got Crystal Shisha, Bacchus Tears, Murk Root..."

"I've got a source," I growled, turning my gaze forward.

The bastard didn't let up, stumbling forward and nearly blocking my path. "I bet I've got better quality than your source. Just try it; and you'll—"

I grabbed the front of his ratty shirt before slamming him up against the alley wall. "What part of *I've got a source* did you not fuckin' get?"

He lifted his shaking hands, and an anxious smile curved his lips as he stumbled over his words, none of it discernable.

"I think he got the message," a male voice said from the neon lit street nearby and I turned to find a face I hadn't seen in quite some time. He turned his green eyes to the male currently cowering against me, his brown hair shabby compared to what I knew his glamour hid. "You did get the message, right? Or do I have to sit here and watch him burn it into your skin?"

"N-no need for that," he stuttered as he nodded his head eagerly, letting out a nervous laugh. "Loud and clear. You got a source."

I loosened my hold, and he slipped free before running into the darkness of the alley.

"Slippery bastard," the male said, eyes following the dealer as he escaped.

"It's been a while, Santor," I said, eyeing the fae male who had glamoured himself to look like one of our kind.

"You know Hades keeps me busy," he said with a shrug before he jerked his chin in a quiet gesture for me to follow. I fell into step beside him. "It's never-ending when it comes to serving The Twelve."

"You can count me out of that shit," I grumbled. A lantern of blue fae light caught my eye as we passed another market table filled to the brim with containers of trapped creatures and forest wisps for sale.

"You might not get a choice in that," he said, tucking his hands into his pockets.

I arched a brow at him.

"I'm not here on vacation." He glanced sidelong at me. "I'm here for business."

I didn't let the interest show in my expression; instead, I sighed, rolling my eyes. "Joy."

The noise of the streets quieted as we entered Atlas' headquarters. As Santor strode through the space, his glamour fell away, revealing his short, curved horns adorning his forehead, a long, thin tail with a tuft of brown fur at the tip swaying with each step he took. The rooms were filled with thick smoke, rich with the combined sweet and addictive scents of Brierleaf and Murk Root. Santor's green eyes passed over the individuals strewn out on the various surfaces, their eyes in drug-induced hallucinations. I stepped through the mess of bodies quickly, passing into the hallway before the Murk Root had a chance to leave me seeing shit.

Santor took the lead, opening the door, and a painful combination of grunts and gasps put me on high alert as we stepped inside. A male sat slouched in a wooden chair in the center of the room, arms wrapped around his abdomen as one of Atlas' larger guards righted himself after laying a massive punch to the gut. The male coughed, blood dripping on the ground in front of him from the busted nose and lip he'd just been dealt.

"You think you can steal from me and get away with it?" Atlas asked, his voice full of cold, calm death as he stepped from the shadows of a nearby corner, twirling a thin knife in his hand, his boots echoing his powerful presence with each step. The sleeves of his black button-down shirt were rolled up, the leather holsters strapped over his chest holding more of the same blades. The gold inked into his skin caught the green fae light as he crossed the room, and a scar stretched diagonally from his jaw to his forehead before carving a path through his hair. It made him look just as much the monster he was beneath the surface, hidden by clever words and strategically shared smiles.

"No! I swear, Atlas! I'm good for it. I'll get you the money," the male blubbered.

Atlas stepped closer, his eyes meeting Santor's as he crossed the room and leaned against the wall before Atlas' gaze found me. He turned his attention back on the male, who looked as if his heart was about to give out, his eyes wild with fear as he sucked in panicked breaths.

Atlas leaned down, leveling his gaze with the male as he shrank back in his seat, lips quivering. Atlas tilted the knife toward the male, the tip of the blade hovering before one of his wide eyes. His voice dropped low as he said, "The next time I catch wind of you dealing in my streets without paying your cut, I'll peel the payment from your hide."

"U-understood," the male said, nodding his head.

Atlas rose to his full height, combing his fingers through his short brown hair to tame it, and nodded to his guards as he straightened his shirt. "Get him out of my sight."

They grabbed the male by his arms and yanked him up from his chair before dragging him out of the room, his boots squeaking along the old wood floor.

"Barrett," Atlas crooned, holding his arms wide as he approached me. "You've been topside for far too long."

He wrapped his arms around me, and I returned the gesture. "It's hard work keeping up appearances."

"I'm sure Damien's working you like a dog," he said as he released me, gesturing to the glasses on his desk at the head of the room. "Help yourself."

I took a seat at the table littered with papers, gold, and crystals.

"No rest for the wicked, right?" I said, glancing sidelong at the four figures occupying chairs, noting each and every one of them.

"Fates spare us," Atlas said, rubbing his hand over his eyes before grabbing his glass and settling back in his swivel chair.

Laid back on a chaise was Sonya, his ethereal Mistress of Pleasures who oversaw the entertainment in The Underworld. Occupying a small table, cracking small crystals, were the twins; Holland, who oversaw all trade and commerce, and Lupis, in charge of gambling. Their eyes lit up with a rippling greenish glow as they inhaled the essence that rose from the fissures in the crystals in their fingers. The fourth watched from the shadows where she sat—the head of security and enforcer of his rules, Driska—a female who even I would reconsider going toe to toe with.

"Sadly, I have no more rest for you down here. You wanted to see me, which was perfect timing, as I was planning on calling you down here anyway."

I settled back against the chair, draping an arm over the velvet-cushioned back, and glanced at Santor. "So I hear."

"I need you to look into something for me," he said, his voice hardening, smile fading from his lips as he lifted his glass to take a swig, only to pause and look at me over the rim. "And I'm curious to see if our issues align."

I frowned.

"Word has made its way to me of several murders above," he said. He knocked back his drink before grimacing and reaching for one of the crystals on his desk.

I held my response, not wanting to give him too much, but if he knew of it, was asking me to look into it...

"The human females who have been murdered by one of our kind," he clarified, gray eyes sliding back to me briefly.

"It wasn't one of yours?" I asked, my voice level, as if the murders didn't bother me.

"It better not fucking be. That shit's drawing too much attention," he said as he settled back in his chair. He held the crystal up to the light, inspecting the subtle green glow of the essence within it. "I turn a blind eye to a death here and there, but that many in a short amount of time is too much trouble—too much attention. I've got enough on my plate with Hades asking for my help."

My eyes shifted briefly to Santor as he settled into a chair, helping himself to some of Atlas' ambrosia liquor.

"Hades is asking you for help?" I scoffed before taking a drink. "Since when do The Twelve ask for assistance from immortals?"

"Something was stolen from him," he said, dropping the crystal onto the desk, the rock clinking as it rolled to a stop amidst the others. "A magical artifact from his collection."

"And how would we be able to help him with that?" I asked.

"Because he no longer feels its presence within the Godsrealm."

I paused, absorbing that bit of information.

"It was taken across The Veil," I muttered, acknowledging the quiet part, and Atlas nodded.

It would make sense as to why he would reach out to the immortals for assistance, then. He likely hadn't told the other members of The Twelve, the knowledge of it more of an embarrassment than anything.

But why did he go to Atlas and not Damien?

"What sort of object is it?" I asked, curious as to whether he'd actually tell me.

"An object once in Charon's possession before he fell."

I halted the glass at my lips, and my brows furrowed. "The ferryman?"

He nodded. "His necklace said to possess the ability to siphon souls from their true forms."

That was a powerful object, a dangerous one. Its presence in the Mortalrealm could be disastrous.

"You need help with that as well?" I asked, hoping he might let me in.

Atlas eyed me wearily. "Take care of the murderer, and we'll talk."

CHAPTER 43

MICAH

Of three things, I was certain.

1.   Barrett was Thalia's mate.
2.   Thalia and Barrett—no matter how much they tried to hide it from the world, tried to ignore it—had harbored feelings for one another for centuries.
3.   I would do everything in my power to ensure they had the chance to be together, and I would be more than willing to share if it meant I could give Thalia everything she could ever want.

Some males might have felt jealousy, but there wasn't a scrap of it festering within me. There was only the sadness and utter adoration I felt for her, knowing she would choose me over her mate, her fated—the one her soul was created for by Celestia.

That she *had* chosen me.

I loved Barrett dearly, had grown close to him in the centuries since we'd met, and there wasn't anyone in all the realms I would love more to bring into our relationship than him.

Barrett halted at the edge of The Outpost's training yard, his skin slick with sweat from the hard run he'd just put the new recruits through. The way they slumped the moment he halted, their heaved breaths rattling their bodies, made it clear they were completely unprepared for how hard the training had been. That, or he had gone particularly hard on them, for he'd been in a foul mood all morning.

Thalia glanced over her shoulder at him, her eyes immediately averting before their gazes could meet as she focused all efforts on throwing her own recruit to the ground. I grimaced at the way he hit the dirt. It was a bit harder than she probably needed to, but Barrett hadn't been the only one in a foul mood. She blinked when it took a moment for the recruit to rise, pain plastered across his features, and she seemed to realize how hard she'd thrown him in her desperation for a distraction.

Gods, could they be more obvious?

I approached them, offering Thalia's recruit a hand to pull him up. "You've gotta stay aware of your opponent's movements. You didn't even try to avoid that, let alone counter it."

"I didn't expect her to throw me," he rasped as he rose to his unsteady feet before brushing the dirt from his training gear.

Thalia cleared her throat and crossed her arms. "Do you expect the darklings to go easy on you?"

"No, ma'am," he said stiffly as he tried to straighten his posture, like a rickety house threatening to collapse. I had to give the male props for toughing it out; I might not have been so quick to get up after being thrown like that.

"You've got them terrified of you," I whispered with a laugh as he slipped away for a much-deserved drink of water.

"Do you expect me to coddle them?" she asked, sighing as she checked her hand wraps.

"No, but they're new. You could give them a break every so often."

She gave me a sidelong glance and shook her head before moving to the next recruit. Her steps faltered as Barrett approached, and the dark bags lingering under his eyes left me wondering if he had suffered as little sleep last night as Thalia had.

Before he could get any closer, she turned, brushing past me. "Can you take over this group? I need to see to something."

I opened my mouth to speak, but she was gone before I could get the chance, and Barrett frowned when I turned to him.

"She all right?" he asked, his eyes tracking her hasty retreat, and I shrugged.

"Your guess is as good as mine," I lied, thankful he didn't harbor *Nous* abilities to see through it.

She wasn't all right, not by a long shot. Guilt twisted my gut as I remembered how I'd remained quiet the night before as she opened the box Lucia had left for her, disguising that I'd awoken. The scent of her emotions had flooded the room with such panicked intensity, it would have awoken me either way. I wasn't sure what exactly was in the box nor what the note had said, but it had shaken her.

Barrett let out a huff and stalked off to get a drink of water alongside the recruits he'd just drilled into the dirt. Whatever task Damien had dumped in his lap, it was taking a toll on him. I took the chance to slip away, eager to see where Thalia had wandered off to.

What could Lucia have left for her that could have her so messed up?

My steps slowed, suddenly innately aware of the way Thalia had been avoiding Barrett all morning. Did it have something to do with him? If so, what? My mind reeled as I continued in search of her, rounding the corner of the building, only to halt and dip back out of sight when I found her leaned back against a tree, head tilted back as she seemed to try and compose herself. Her eyes then fell on a small scrap of fabric in her palm. She closed her fingers around it, and her head fell back against the trunk of the tree once more as she let out a heavy sigh.

The breeze danced through the trees, catching her hair and dragging her scent toward me. My heart twisted at the look in her eyes, so torn by whatever Lucia had dropped in her lap so long after her death. I stilled as another scent reached my nose, so faint, I almost couldn't smell it. I'd know it anywhere, had become so used to it that it had become something of a sense of home I'd found in my best friend.

The subtle scent of smoky oak. Barrett. I frowned as her eyes fell back to the scrap of fabric, and I stilled at the familiarity.

A part of me doubted she remembered I was the one who had pulled her from the hell of The Pits. We never really talked about it, not in a way that truly mattered, and I honestly didn't care whether she ever knew. I didn't need to hear any sort of thank you for what I'd done; I'd do it again in a heartbeat. I couldn't have left her behind even if I'd tried.

I had nearly written off the scrap of fabric, though, all but forgotten its existence.

I grabbed the female's arm, her skin slick with sweat and blood, the sight of the scars painting every inch leaving me craving blood in a way I never had. She whipped around to look back at me, her stormy eyes wild, promising a swift, painful death to any who challenged her. I lifted my gaze to the tunnel walls as they trembled, dirt and rocks falling loose and hitting the ground around us. "It's gonna cave in. We have to get out!"

"No!" she cried out, turning back to look at her friend who had slowed to a near stop further behind us, her back turned. What was she thinking? Why had she turned back? I stilled as a group of fae warriors drew closer, the sound of their boots

pounding barely audible over the rumbling of The Pit. I glanced back at Lucia leading the group further up the cave, leaving us behind. She pulled against my hold, her strength waning, arms trembling from the exhaustion that held us all in its clutches. Even my magic was depleted, too weak to call forth so much as a single bloom in this desolate place.

Her friend turned back to us, her hand resting against the wall of the tunnel. A pained smile crept across her face, and my heart stilled. The female pulled harder against my hold to get to her, her pleas turning into screams, but I couldn't bring myself to release her, could do little but stand there, frozen. Why couldn't I fucking move?

"Kish! Stop!" she cried out.

I sucked in air as the walls rippled beneath her touch, earth magic winding its way through rock and stone like an earth wyrm, commanding the tunnel to collapse on her and the men pursuing us.

She was gone. In a matter of seconds, she was gone, and she had not only halted our enemy's pursuit but had taken them out with her.

An agonized scream tore its way from the female I still clung to, echoing through the tunnel as her knees met stone, her eyes latched wholly on the wall of rocks that had devoured her friends. The damp scent of freshly fallen rain poured into my lungs as she cried, the saltiness of her tears overpowering the scent of earth and damp rock, melding with her sorrow so potently, I couldn't find the words to try and comfort her. I lowered myself beside her, my lips parting to offer her any comfort I could muster, but I stilled as I watched the tattoo inked into her skin start to fade, the inscriptions receding like a creature retreating from a destructive flame.

She tore from my hold and ran for the cave-in, crashing against it with every shred of remaining strength she harbored—as if she might force the stones to unearth her friend, reverse the destruction she'd brought down on herself and the males tailing us. Her sobs filled the tunnel as she sank to her knees, her body wracked with tremors as she cried out, crying for her fallen friend over and over again in a way that I feared might haunt my memories.

"Micah!" Marcus called out. "Come on! This tunnel could come down any minute!"

I nodded to him and shoved to my feet to rush to her side, scooping her into my arms and hurrying after them as the ground quaked beneath my feet, the ceiling collapsing around us until I feared we might not make it out either.

"See she's taken care of," I ordered one of the healers as I approached a tent outside of The Pits, the female clutched tightly in my arms.

"At once, sir," she said, dipping her head.

It took everything in me to release her into the healer's care, her body still wracked with sobs, quivering as the mountain had. Some strange part of me wanted to tend to her myself, but I forced myself to ease her onto her feet and give her space.

The healer nodded to me, brushing the dust from her white robes as she rose to guide the female to a nearby bed. The female didn't respond, didn't say anything didn't even acknowledge me as she stepped numbly toward the bed.

I turned to look for Lucia, but I froze as something slipped from the female's pocket, a tattered scrap of fabric that looked as if it had been through Tartarus and back. It landed on the ground, and I frowned as I ducked to pick it up. Her clothes didn't seem to be falling apart.

"I'll take that," Lucia said at my back, startling me, and I sucked in a breath.

"Fates spare me, Lucia. Why do you always sneak up on me like that?" I said, hand pressed to my chest as if to prevent my racing heart from punching out of it.

She snickered and held out her hand. "I'll see she gets it back."

CHAPTER 44

MICAH

Fall's chill permeated my Elythian leather armor as Thalia and I patrolled the south sector of Johnstown later that night. Darkling sightings had been few and far between, thank The Fates, and that pattern had continued into our patrol for the night.

I slid a glance at Thalia as she shifted back into her immortal form, the black dust dissipating into the crisp air. Our conversations had been unusual, to say the least, Thalia's thoughts seeming to linger elsewhere. I wanted to ask, wanted to bring up the box Lucia had left for her, and yet, I couldn't find the right words, couldn't find where to begin.

"Spit it out," Thalia said, and my gaze snapped to her. "I know you've been dying to ask."

"I'm that obvious, huh?" I asked.

"As you've always been," she said, sliding me a knowing smile.

"Was the box from Lucia?"

"It was." The smile slid from her lips, and she seemed to steady herself as she drew a deep breath.

"She left me a note," Thalia finally said, the words chipping away some fractured part of me that had pieced itself back together in the decades following Lucia's death. "It didn't make sense, though. It was as if she knew she would be gone when I found it."

How could she have known that?

"It also contained a keepsake—a memento from when I was held as a prisoner of The Pits, one I had completely forgotten."

Her stormy eyes fell to the cracked pavement as we continued down the dark alley. "It was the only thing I had left from before I was taken."

She had never spoken of before The Pits, as if the time before that terrible place had simply ceased to exist in her memories.

"I don't remember much of my childhood," she said, and my heart twisted at the truth I knew, the truth I wished I could reverse. "Only that my parents were killed when the darklings attacked Moonhaven, and when I found myself lost in the woods—hiding from the terrible monsters who had chased me from my home—I met a boy and his sister."

Each word felt like a confession, like something she had held so close to her heart that she couldn't bring herself to share, like a prized possession that could be stolen from her.

A weak smile tugged at the corners of her lips, the sight of it pulling at my heart in a way that made me want to take her in my arms, to hold her and tell her it was okay to share this knowledge with me—that it would be safe, that their memory would be safe.

And that what I knew to be true would do nothing to the feelings I harbored for her.

"They were kind to me. Fed me, lifted my spirits when I had felt broken and lost. The girl, Cali, showed me how to make flower crowns." Her eyes went distant. "The boy... He gifted me his coat so I could stay warm that night, promised to bring a blanket the following day."

I could almost see the unspoken words lingering on the tip of her tongue, and I wanted so badly to tell her I knew it was Barrett. No matter how much I wanted to, though, I couldn't bring myself to force that truth from her, not before she was ready.

"I had hoped to see them again, to thank them for their kindness, but that was the night Rhyas took me across the veil."

The leather of her gloves groaned as her hands tightened into fists. "I lost so much that night: the tiny trinket my father had gifted me, my name, my freedom, everything. The coat the boy gifted me was all I had left—all that survived the countless decades I spent fighting in The Pits."

She lifted her gaze to me, and her steps came to a halt. My heart launched into my throat at the consideration in her gaze. Her lips parted, as if to speak some truth she had been afraid to share.

Tell me. Please.

A gasped cry and a scuffle of shoes against the ground dragged my attention from her, and we turned to find a young woman stumbling from a nearby alley. Her clothes were dirty, sweater ripped, her braided chestnut hair was disheveled, stray curls breaking free in her panic.

"Someone—" She gasped for air. "Someone, please!"

Her wild, hazel eyes found us, and we stiffened. I had never encountered a human on patrol, and for a moment, I hesitated. As she twisted to look over her shoulder, though, I realized this was no normal encounter. This human was being chased.

Thalia immediately rushed toward her, hands held out, and my hand flew to my sheathed dagger, my eyes darting to the shadows at her back in search of darklings.

"Are you all right? What happened?" Thalia asked.

The girl fell into Thalia's arms, grabbing onto her as if she feared she might be torn away. She sobbed, tears streaking her dirt-stained cheeks. "Please, don't let him take me!"

The scent of blood reached my nose, and as I drew closer, I could see the traces of cuts and scrapes peeking from beneath the tears and rips of her sweater and jeans. Gods, what happened to her? A fine sheen of sweat painted her skin despite the cold air, and I could almost hear her heart racing to the beat of her terror.

"Who? Who's chasing you?" Thalia asked as she steadied her.

The human's head whipped around, her terrified eyes darting to where she'd come as I came to a stop at Thalia's side. I followed her gaze before catching a glimpse of a figure watching us from the shadows of a nearby alley.

"Hey!" I called out as the figure turned and ran.

"Stay here," I demanded before taking off after him, my boots pounding into the pavement, echoing off the brick walls and dying out in the night.

As I rounded the corner, my pace quickening, I could barely make out the hint of blond hair, a male figure clothed in black as he raced toward the downtown district. This couldn't have been a darkling. It was too deep in the night for a darkling to take human form, but his pace left me barely able to keep up...

An immortal?

I quickened my steps, hand gripping my dagger as I drew closer, prepared for him to turn and strike. He grabbed trash cans as he ran, yanking them down to bar my path, and I leaped over them. Each obstacle slowed my advance, and I growled in frustration each time I managed to clear the debris. I rounded a corner and slid to a stop at the darkness that welcomed me, eyes scanning the hollow expanse before me.

Each step sent my heart into a frenzy, anticipation winding my organs tighter and tighter with the possibility of an attack from a nearby corner. The dark street opened to numerous paths, creating a number of chances for him to take me by surprise. My grip on my dagger tightened as I cautiously stepped forward, searching.

His laughter echoed through the streets, somehow never from one location, and I whipped around to the street at my back before pacing in a circle, searching.

"Pretty light on your feet," he said, his voice rough. "You think you can catch me, though?"

I continued forward, listening for even the slightest sound. "Show yourself.

"Where's the fun in that?" he crooned. "The chase is the best part, but you've gotta be faster than that to catch me."

Boots echoed off the lid of a metal trashcan, and I leaped into a run toward it, catching a glimpse of him disappearing onto a rooftop. I followed, launching myself onto the trashcan before climbing. I grunted as I pushed myself to my feet, the asphalt of the shingles scraping into the tips of my fingers, and I scanned the expanse of rooftops until I found him, leaping from roof to roof in a chaotic pattern toward downtown Johnstown.

I gulped air and took off after him, leaping from roof to roof, my boots slamming into the brick and asphalt, stumbling when my feet met soft spots that threatened to collapse beneath my weight.

"Too slow!" He dropped off the roof before me, back into the alleys.

I made it to the edge and dropped to the darkened street below, gaze sweeping back and forth before I found him sailing toward the light of downtown. With a muttered curse, I followed, the distance between us growing wider.

He burst from the mouth of the alley into a busy street near Central Park where humans gathered. I hesitated, unsure if I should risk stepping out of the shadows in my leathers, armed with my weapons.

"Fuck," I muttered and shoved past the hesitation, leaping from the shadows. Humans stumbled out of our way, murmuring amongst themselves, some shouting as they fell onto the sidewalk.

The male tapped the shoulder of a passing human female then slapped the chest of a male and continued to lay his hand on another and another before me. Their eyes hazed over, and they stumbled to a stop before turning their attention to me. They paced drunkenly toward me, gathering, bodies colliding with one another to block my path as they grabbed ahold of my arms and legs.

"Please let me thro—" I froze at the drunken gazes latching onto me, their mouths moving in a blur as they muttered words of the old language, a language none of them should know even existed, and yet, they spoke it so fluently. A chorus of questions overlapped one another, too jumbled to discern, and I stumbled back.

A female human stood approached, and they parted ways for her, holding me in place as she stalked closer. Her hands rose to cut my face as she gazed into my eyes. A whisper slipped from her lips, a near hiss painted with poison. "Do you know the blood that stains your master's hands?"

I froze, chest heaving as I resisted every urge to throw them off me, to cut them down. They were humans; how could they—

My gaze snapped to where the immortal had disappeared. A *Nous* user. They were bewitched, charmed, minds bent to his will.

The human female forced my gaze back to hers, her nails biting into my skin. "How many more of your kind will you send to slaughter?"

"What the hell happened?" Thalia asked as I stumbled back onto the street where I had left her, sweat coating my skin, my hands shaking. "Gods, your face. What did this to you?"

I couldn't speak, didn't know where to start. I had been left with no choice but to knock the humans out, leaving them unconscious on the sidewalk. There had been no time to wipe their memories for risk of more onlookers crossing our path, and I only prayed the *Nous* user's influence had rendered them unaware.

"Micah," Thalia pressed as she brushed her thumb along the cuts left by the human's nails. My eyes fell to the unconscious human girl propped up against the brick wall at her feet

"It was an immortal," I finally said, my gaze latched onto the girl. "A fucking powerful one. I've never seen one with the ability to bend the minds of so many people beyond Lucia."

"A *Nous* user?" Thalia confirmed.

"Dragged the chase into the fucking open streets," I said, my hands clenching into fists. "He bent the minds of several people to his will at once before making his escape northward."

"Did you see his face?" she asked. "Anything to identify him?"

"No," I said, drawing a deep breath. My gaze landed back on the girl, her chestnut lashes resting against her cheeks as she slept. Her chest rose and fell in a quiet, calm rhythm. "Only that he had blond hair and was probably just shy of six feet."

Thalia ran her hand over her face. "I managed to get a bit more out of her before I knocked her out. She didn't know much, just that she met the guy at the bar and he had followed her down the street, kept asking her weird questions. Then he got angry when she couldn't answer them." Thalia looked down at the girl. "She thought he was going to kill her."

"He probably intended to," I said.

My mind dredged up the words the humans had spoken to me in the old language, and I couldn't shake the dread it had stirred.

How many more of your kind will you send to slaughter?

CHAPTER 45

THALIA

"What the hell happened?" Barrett asked, his wide eyes falling on the unconscious human women in my arms as I brushed past him down the halls of The Complex. Warriors parted ways, clearing a path as I rushed through the doors to the stairwell, Micah close behind as we descended quickly.

"She was being hunted by an immortal," I said without sparing him a glance, ignoring the rush as my heart quickened when his footsteps followed us. Micah held the double doors to Dr. Johnson's medical bay open, clearing my path as I quickly carried her in.

"What can I do for—" Dr. Johnson's eyes fell to the human. "What happened?"

"An immortal?" Barrett asked, pace picking up to come into my line of sight.

My steps halted, and I turned to him, irrational irritation swelling in my chest.

"Were you not listening?" I bit out, immediately regretting the tone. I cleared my throat as I turned to carry her toward a bed. Dr. Johnson followed close behind me, immediately checking over her wounds.

I backed away, giving him room to assess her. "We don't know how much she saw. If she saw too much, wiping her memories will be beyond our abilities."

Dr. Johnson nodded and gestured to a nearby nurse. "Nicholas is a Nous user; he will be able to help."

"Where did you find her?" Barrett asked, brows furrowing as he stepped closer to her bedside.

Micah frowned, and we exchanged confused looks before he answered. "Near Central Park."

Since when had Barrett taken an interest in humans?

The nurse, Nicholas, approached, dipping his head to us as he stopped at the head of her bed. "I'll make quick work so Dr. Johnson can care for her. Then, we can take her back into town before she wakes up."

"Do you know her?" I asked, my question nearly overlapping Nicholas' words as Barrett continued to stare at her. Dr. Johnson stepped back, giving him room as his eyes passed over her hair, her wounds. Then, he leaned over her and forced one of her eyes open to look at it.

Nicholas turned his attention to the girl, but Barrett's hand shot out, grabbing his forearm to stop him from wiping the human's mind. I frowned, glancing at Micah, who looked just as puzzled.

"No," Barrett said, ignoring my question, and my gaze snapped to him.

"No?" Nicholas asked.

"No?" I echoed under my breath.

"I want her bewitched. There're questions I need her to answer," Barrett explained, releasing him.

"Does it have something to do with that assignment Damien gave you?" Micah asked, and Barrett stiffened but didn't look his way, didn't answer.

"Wake her up," Barrett ordered.

Nicholas nodded. "Right away, sir."

His hands rose to hover near her temples, and he closed his eyes. Barrett took a step back, and I remained silent, biting back the urge to press, to demand answers.

The woman's eyes fluttered opened, the hazel of her irises dulled and drunken as she sat up.

"What's your name?" Nicholas asked.

"Erika," she said without hesitation, her words a near slur.

Nicholas glanced at Barrett and nodded.

"Do you know the man who attacked you?" Barrett asked.

"No," she said, her voice flat.

Barrett let out a sigh. "Tell me what you know about him."

"I met him at the bar," she said, her eyes almost unseeing as she stared forward.

"Did you get a good look at him?" Barrett pressed.

"He wore a hood. His face..." Her lips started to quiver, the words cutting short, but there was no fear in her voice, her expression. It was as if the knowledge she'd been tasked to relinquish simply ceased to exist.

"What about his face?" Barrett demanded, brows pinching together.

"I have no memory of it," she said, blinking. "Blurred. Darkened."

Barrett let out a groan of frustration. "Tell me what happened."

"He asked me how old I was," she said. "Then, he wouldn't leave me alone, asked me if I had any strange dreams lately. When I told him I wasn't interested in talking anymore, he got agitated and stormed off."

My heart plummeted in anticipation of what I knew was to come, what I feared had happened given the state we'd found her in.

"I hadn't realized he'd followed me from the bar. He cornered me, started asking me strange questions. None of it made sen—"

"What questions?" Barrett demanded.

"He wanted to..." Once again the words fell short, and she blinked, a pained look slipping through the drunken mask. "I can't..."

"Barrett," I warned, watching the numb look on her face fracture, her brows furrowing as her mind began to buckle under some invisible weight.

"Think. You must remember," Barrett growled, planting his hands on the bed on either side of her.

I grabbed his shoulder. "Barrett!"

He whipped around to look back at me, his eyes furious, but he didn't speak. The girl's eyes fluttered before she slumped back onto the bed, Nicholas catching her before her head hit the mattress.

Nicholas panted, a sheen of sweat coating his brow. "Apologies."

A muscle ticked in Barrett's jaw as he stared down at me. Never had he looked so angry at me, his steel eyes burning with a sort of resentment that mirrored my own. It hurt to look at, hurt to feel that gaze sear into me.

"Search her memories," Barrett said without looking away from me. "See if you can find anything."

"Right away, sir," Nicholas said, arranging the girl into a more comfortable position.

Barrett shoved past me, and I twisted to watch him storm out of the medical bay. The beast bristled within me, its affection for Barrett not enough to take his temper as I followed him through the double doors.

"What the hell is your problem?" I demanded, grabbing his shoulder and forcing him to turn back to me.

His lips parted but then shut as he seemed to struggle to form words. He pulled his gaze from me, his hands balling into fists. "You're interfering with my work."

"Your work?" I balked. "I was only trying to help you!"

"Thalia," Micah said in warning as he approached me from behind, his hand coming to rest on my shoulder.

"No, this is bullshit," I shouted, glancing back at him before leveling my gaze on Barrett whose eyes briefly flitted to Micah's hand. "What's going on with you? You're always in a foul mood, skipping out on training, irritable whenever we hang out. Then, you push that poor girl past her mental limit when it's clear the fucking Nous user altered her memories. You could have hurt her!"

He tilted his head and arched a brow, his voice bitter as he spat his words at me. "Oh, you care so much for these humans now, do you?"

"I do when they are unjustly harmed!" I shouted. "Unlike you, I have a conscious. Unlike you, I've seen the cruelty those without power suffer at the hands of those with it."

His chest heaved as he took a step back, a muscle ticking in his jaw despite the flicker of guilt in his eyes.

"Have you spent so much time with those foul creatures of The Underworld that you now share their taste for human disdain?"

He stiffened, gaze briefly shifting to the curious eyes around us, and I sucked in a breath. That was confidential knowledge, something no one was to know; technically, not even I should know about his ties to The Underworld. Barrett didn't respond, his silence too loud, and the quiet murmurs of the onlooking warriors in the hall of The Complex began to fill my ears.

Barrett leaned down just a fraction, meeting my gaze. "Don't fucking get involved."

"I'm worried about you," I admitted in a near whisper.

Something flickered across his steel eyes, a molten softness that immediately hardened once more, tempering into something that could cut me down.

"Your worry is a burden I'd rather not suffer."

CHAPTER 46

BARRETT

Hurt flashed across Micah's face as I glanced at him. I averted my gaze, unable to hold his, unable to take the pain I'd dished out to my best friend—to my fucking mate. Could I even call him my best friend for how I had treated him the last several years, the unintentional avoidance, the bitterness I'd let slip through as I watched their happiness after too many decades pretending Thalia wasn't my mate? The judgment of the surrounding warriors radiated off them like a feverish cloud as I stormed out of The Complex and into the dark.

"Fuck!" I shouted, my voice cutting through the silent night air as I smashed my fist into a nearby brick wall.

Was I so miserable that I had to take out my frustrations on her? On Micah?

The look on her face was seared into my mind, burning me far worse than any flame ever could. If only I could set the pain in my chest ablaze, burn it until nothing remained of our bond but ashes. It was the only reason I couldn't stomach being around them, couldn't stomach how she smiled at him, how she kissed him.

I almost wished Micah had slugged me, knocked my ass out on the floor for everyone to see.

Wind whipped around me as I stalked down Short Street, and I shoved my hand into my pocket to pull out a pack of rolled Brierleaf, desperate for the hit. A few cars blurred past me intermittently, kicking up the cool air as I stopped at my Honda CB750 parked along the sidewalk, the racing bike too powerful to be street-legal, but fast enough to give me the rush I always needed. My mind dredged up all the ways Micah would comfort her, how his hand had come to rest on her shoulder to prevent her from following me. The flames writhed beneath my skin, a torrent of pent-up anger and possession, like a beast whose treasure had been stolen, only...

She had never been mine.

Leaning against my bike, I put the rolled Brierleaf to my lips, sparking the flame to life atop my fingertip and holding it to the end, taking a hit the moment the paper lit. The smoke filled my lungs, the numbing effect slipping into my bloodstream, though it was too weak to combat the torrential emotions flooding my system. I needed a drink, plus a face to smash in if that wasn't enough to dull this overwhelming feeling. I threw my leg over my bike, kicking the engine to life before taking off down the road.

Stoker's bar was packed in the late-night hours, music blaring throughout the room as I stepped through the old door. Vincent caught my gaze from where he sat with Anna, dressed in her scrubs and likely fresh off her shift at Dr. Johnson's clinic.

"Barrett!" he called, holding up a glass.

I beelined for him, the amber liquid like a siren to the hulking, scaled beast burrowing further into my bloodstream, boiling my blood to the point of lava.

Vincent grimaced when he got a better look at me. "Rough night?"

"Try shoving your foot in your mouth to your mate and then tell me how you feel," I muttered and immediately stiffened as I glanced at Anna. She was lost in a conversation with Eiko, the half-human, half-immortal bar owner, and hadn't seemed to hear.

"Ouch," Vincent said, sliding a glass in front of me. "You can have mine; you clearly need it more than I do."

I downed it without hesitation, relishing in the burn snaking down my throat as I set the glass on the bar top. "Semele!"

"On it, hothead!" she said, immediately getting to work on another drink for me.

I let out a sigh as the name dredged up memories of Lucia. Semele had never forgotten our first meeting, still held a bar fight I had no memory of over my head. She and Lucia had continued to tease me, and the nickname stuck with her as well.

"What happened?" he asked.

"They're getting too close," I grumbled, setting my elbows atop the bar.

"Close?" he echoed, cocking an eyebrow.

I dropped my voice. "I'm working a murder case—some immortal has been killing women left and right—and I'm getting pulled back into

Underworld work. They keep prying, and it'll only result in them gaining a target on their back."

"Good thing I'm bulletproof," Vincent mused with a smirk before taking a drink.

"I shouldn't have even told you," I grumbled. "Just being seen with me could put you in danger if I ever fucked up."

"Sadly, I'm too stupid, and you're stuck with me," he said, lifting his glass briefly in a mock toast. "Just don't fuck up."

I rolled my eyes.

Vincent leaned back against the bar, draping his arms over the edge. "Why do you keep talking to them if it hurts this much?"

"Every time I try, I just...can't." Perhaps I was a glutton for misery. Perhaps I was punishing myself for all my shortcomings, all my failures.

Semele slid a glass toward me, and I swiped it up before downing the contents. I flashed her two fingers, and she nodded, getting to work on more drinks for me.

"It's self-destructive," Vincent said, tilting his head.

"No shit." I grimaced as I set the empty tumbler.

Glass shattered somewhere in the bar behind us.

"Hey! Knock it off!" Semele shouted, and I followed her gaze to a group of males getting a bit too rough.

"Come put your hands on me and make me!" one of them shouted with a taunting laugh before turning his back to her. "Annoying cunt."

I rose from my stool.

"Barrett," Vincent warned.

I stalked through the crowd, some quickly scattering from my path, some stumbling out of my way as I shoved past them. The fuckers stood in a group, their backs turned to me as they focused on their game of pool, completely unaware of the blistering destruction they had just riled up. I laid a hand on the shoulder of the largest male, the flames within me swelling with a savage desire to taste blood.

The male turned toward me. "Fuck of—"

My fingers dug into his shoulder, and I slammed my forehead into his face, busting his nose and sending him crashing to the ground. Blood dotted my skin as the bar fell silent, voices falling away like a receding tide.

The others launched themselves at me.

Laughter echoed through the hazy meadow, and the faint ripple of rushing creek water reached my ears. I lifted my eyes from the poorly constructed floral crown in my hands, the flowers falling out, leaving only scraggly vines and grass.

Calliope sang the rhymes our nursemaid recited to us about a foolish god who had fallen in love with a mortal only to be separated by the veil, lest they destroy both realms to be together. The girl with cornsilk hair dancing with her didn't join in on her sing-song, but the hoarse laughter she managed to get past her sore throat was like fractured sunshine.

Barrett.

I lifted my eyes to her, but she wasn't looking at me. "What, Cali?"

Barrett.

I frowned as her voice filled my ears, but her mouth didn't move as they continued to dance in the meadow along the creek. The laughter—Cali's singing— fell silent, a rush of wind cutting through it all like a creature devouring our joy as the sky darkened.

Barrett!

My heart sank, and I dropped the crown as I jumped to my feet. I rushed for them, grabbing Calliope's hand, but before I could reach the girl, blackened clouds swept in around us, tree branches bending in the wind as the sun was swallowed whole by the torrential storm.

"Barrett!"

My eyes shot open, pain echoing in the back of my eyes, an even sharper pain throbbing in the back of my skull. Damien stood over me, arms crossed, brow arched. Vincent knelt on my other side, looking down at me with a relieved grin.

"Fuck," I groaned.

"Almost got them all before one pulled a bat on you," Vincent said.

"Where the fuck is he?" I growled, pushing myself up.

"Already taken care of," Damien said. "All of them have been."

I took in the sight of Vincent's black eye, and guilt dragged my heart into my stomach. "Couldn't let them get you while you were down."

"I swear, the both of you are going to be the death of me," Anna said, dragging my attention to where she was crouched behind me.

She leaned in with a small flashlight and checked my eyes. "Good thing you've got a hard head, or that bat might have done you in."

"It's my finest quality." I grimaced, flinching away from the bright light.

"Is he all right?" Semele called, her boots smacking against the pavement as she jogged over to me from the entrance of the bar.

"I think he'll live to torment us another day," Damien said.

"Oh, thank The Fates," Semele said with a sigh of relief.

Something brushed against the edges of my consciousness, a familiar presence.

Barrett?

I held up a hand to the others, silencing them, and Damien's brows furrowed.

Yeah, Atlas?

Vincent, Anna, and Semele exchanged confused looks. Damien nodded his chin to the bar in a quiet gesture for them to leave us, and they dipped their heads before returning to the bar. Atlas's voice slipped through my mind again, clear as if he stood next to me.

You got an update for me up there?

I chewed my lip, irritation swelling in my chest. I hadn't seemed to get any closer to finding the slippery bastard responsible for the murders beyond the fact he was a Nous user.

Not enough to name him, but I'm getting closer. All I know is he's blond and a Nous user. Attacked a human girl tonight and had a run-in with two warriors on patrol around eleven, twelve o'clock.

Damien crouched beside me, remaining silent so as to avoid any chance Atlas might pick up that he was aware of our conversation.

I'll check my men's whereabouts during those times, see if we can pinpoint anyone who fits that description. Fin and Clo came upon a pair of humans left in the tunnel.

I stiffened, sucking in a breath. Fin and Clo were the nightmarish creatures that stalked the tunnels around The Underworld. My mind dredged up the horror those souls suffered in their final moments.

Both matched the description of the others you spoke of.

I cursed under my breath.

So it is someone associated with The Underworld.

Yep, and I want them found and their throat slit. A dog who can't be controlled isn't one I want in my company.

I ran my hands over my face. While it gave me something of a lead, The Underworld was so innately intertwined with The Order in ways neither I nor Damien could fully comprehend. No matter how much favor I gained with Atlas, he still had his pawns, still had his connections he disclosed to no one, not even to his right hand.

You still interested in joining me for a visit with Hades?

I sucked in a breath, and Damien tilted his head. My eyes slid to him, but I remained silent.

Yeah, when you leaving?

Be at the Propylaea in twelve hours.

Fuck. That left little room to prepare, but that was how he did his dealings. Movement on short notice was more difficult to track, more difficult to anticipate if we wanted to intercept them and continue to chip away at their operation without blowing my cover.

I'll be there.

CHAPTER 47

MICAH

Metal clanged across the training yard of The Outpost, the sound mixed with Thalia's grunts as she blocked the downward stroke of a trainee's training dagger, catching the wooden blade with her own. She hadn't spoken a word of what had occurred last night, and I wondered if she planned to simply pretend it never happened.

Barrett hadn't shown up to training.

And while the two of them seemed to avoid addressing it, I lingered on the edge of the urge to smash my fist into his face the next time I saw him for how he'd thrown Thalia's feelings back in her face. Sadly, though, that was classic Barrett. Even after hundreds of years of friendship, he still couldn't bring himself to fully let us in. He'd lost his sister, and just as he had started to let his walls down, he lost Lucia. Despite neither being his fault, he still seemed to bear the weight of their passing, shouldering the blame and guilt of his helplessness.

Thalia had never liked Barrett's involvement with The Underworld, though she'd never voiced it to Damien. Regardless of how she felt, I didn't want her to get involved in the dealings of that wretched place. Barrett was right to keep her away from that mess, safe from any backlash he may face if he was ever exposed.

Thalia was strong enough to hold her own, though, and he was so hellbent on protecting her that he couldn't seem to see it.

How could I get him to see past his own bullshit?

"Micah."

My head shot up at the sound of Barrett's voice from the nearby forest. I twisted to find him hidden amidst the trees before glancing back to see if Thalia had seen him. Her back was turned, her focus locked on the recruit she was currently fighting. I grimaced when she hooked his ankle with her foot and yanked it out from under him, sending him onto his back.

These recruits couldn't seem to get a break from her wrath. If she and Barrett didn't get past this, we might not have any recruits survive to their vows.

I rose and quickly slipped away into the trees.

"Where the fuck have you been?" I hissed, grabbing him by the collar of his shirt as I slammed him up against a tree, resisting the urge to do what I'd been contemplating all morning.

He grunted as his back met bark, but he didn't resist. "I don't have time."

"I don't give a fuck if you've got time or not," I growled as I leaned into him, teeth bared. "You need to apologize to her."

"I will, but I've got important shit to see to first," he said, a silent plea lighting his eyes before they slipped to where Thalia was training.

I frowned.

"I'm leaving for the Godsrealm," he said, and my grip slackened. His shoulders slumped as he sagged against the tree, and he pulled a pack of rolled Brierleaf from his pocket, the sweet scent immediately hitting my nose.

"When?"

He glanced nervously in Thalia's direction as he put one of the rolls to his lips and lit it. "In less than an hour, but I had to see you first."

"It better involve an explanation of what the fuck happened last night," I said, stepping back to give him room as I crossed my arms over my chest.

He drew a heavy hit before letting the smoke slip free of his lips. "Damien has me investigating a string of murders, and now Atlas wants the murderer found as well. The shit's gotten so out of hand now that I'm under Atlas' command and watch, and I've been working overtime trying to get any answers I can."

Memories resurfaced of the night before, the look of terror on the human's face, the blond Nous user and the bewitched humans who had spoken the old language like it was their own.

"You think the Nous user is responsible for all of them?"

He nodded. "The girl fit the description."

"Description?"

"All of the victims are female humans with brown hair and hazel eyes between the ages of eighteen and twenty-three, every one of them."

"How many are we talking?"

"Known? Seventeen. Last night's victim would have been number eighteen."

"Gods," I breathed.

"Be cautious around Hades," Thalia said, her tone icy.

Barrett sucked in a breath and choked on the smoke, falling into a fit of coughs. I turned to find she had snuck up on us, leaning against a nearby tree, arms crossed. Her stormy eyes remained fixated on Barrett, brimming with a silent power that bordered on catastrophic.

Barrett cleared his throat, drawing a deep breath of fresh air.

She pushed off the trunk, her eyes dismissive, nearly cold as she turned to leave us. "He may be more docile now that Persephone's in the picture, but I remember the times I saw him in The Pits. He's not to be trusted."

CHAPTER 48

BARRETT

"You ever been to Aidonia?" Atlas asked as the shadows receded, revealing the lush flower-covered slopes of a valley cast in shades of pinks, purples, and blues around us. A river cut down the middle of the valley, snaking through flowery fields, pebbled with small boulders and rocks.

"No," I said, unable to pull my eyes from the view.

"The Valleys of the Stryass," Atlas explained. "They were once desolate; nothing could grow here, and the river was poisonous."

I had heard stories of Hades' domain, once solely ruled by him until he met Persephone, who brought life back to his lands. The sight of the valley made it nearly impossible to imagine it to be nothing but death and waste.

No matter how many times I'd been to the Godsrealm, no matter which domain I visited, every time was like a punch to the senses. Despite the sunrise casting its warm light across the steep mountain's ridges, the two massive moons could still faintly be seen amidst the clouds, where a pod of sky whales played. They dipped and danced, their melody like a sad song as they sang to each other, the sound echoing through the air, the very sound sinking into my bones in a way I would never forget.

"Magnificent aren't they?" Atlas asked, watching them from my side, the sunlight illuminating the gold-inked tattoos that decorated his face and neck. "They're said to bring good luck to those traveling by airship."

"Perhaps they will bestow their favor on us as well," I said, turning away from the sight to lift my eyes to the towering mountain at our backs.

Atlas slid me a smile. "We can only hope."

Earth rumbled from the mountain as the face of it seemed to crack, revealing massive gates, separating to make way for an approaching airship. The airships of the Godsrealm were nothing like the airplanes of the Mortalrealm. They were just as much ships in the air as were their sister ships in the sea; wooden and metal vessels, fitted with sails and wings of all different shapes, sizes, and colors. Some were small, private vessels made to carry a family while some were massive, carrying fae to other domains or cargo for trade.

"Wait till you see what it looks like inside," he said, nodding to where his two personal guards had taken the lead. We started the trek toward the main gate at the base of the mountainside where the river split and flowed underground, connecting to the River Styx.

A small village stood around the entrance to the capital city, Aidonia. Fae folk of every domain came and went along our path, casting weary glances at us as they moved. A goblin-like creature peddling wares from his rickety, wooden cart came to a stop in front of us, blocking our path as he wiped the sweat from his wrinkly, gray-green forehead. When we made to step around him, he sneered at us, grumbling insults in the old language before hoisting the handles of his two-wheeled cart up to continue rolling it forward.

"*Katàratos,*" he muttered, voice rough, before disappearing into the crowd—the word falling from his lips like a spit on my boots.

I narrowed my eyes on the creature, and Atlas laid a hand on my shoulder.

"Ignore him," Atlas said and turned his gaze forward as we drew closer to the main gate.

"*Kńrysoi vôu volúntae,*" a satyr in black armor said, demanding to know our intentions as he tapped the butt of his ornate, Elythian steel spear to the stone ground. Sparks kicked up from where the enchanted metal cracked against rock. It had been some time since I'd spoken the Elythian language, and it still felt strangely like home to hear it.

"My name is Atlas Sideris, and these are my companions," he said in Elythian as he held his hand out to us. "We are here at Hades' behest. He should be expecting us."

"Follow me," the other guard said, a fae with small, ram-like horns protruding from her helmet, her tail swishing as she turned to place a palm to an etched circle on the wall next to the entrance. She leaned in, as if talking to someone within the stone. "Atlas is here to see Hades."

She glanced over her shoulder as the gates opened and jerked her chin toward it. "I will escort you to your chambers."

Atlas' two guards took the lead, and we followed after them, stepping into the mouth of what was the most monstrous mountain I had ever seen.

"Gods," I breathed, eyes rising to the countless sky ships flying in all directions beneath the ceiling towering thousands of feet above us, charmed to look like glass. The sky filtered through it, illuminating the interior walls of the hollow mountain city in rich daylight. Houses and shops were built or carved into the walls of the mountain, pathways and steps winding in all directions. Some were cozy little cottages, some grand villas with balconies overseeing the capital with what must have been the most spectacular view. The city was bustling, fae of every shape and size buying and selling, enjoying the market and restaurants, their voices melding into a distant hum of a thriving metropolis.

"Hades has done well for himself in the recent decades. He has expanded trade with the completion of the second largest airship hanger in all of Elythias," Atlas said as I passed through the main portion of the city, where countless shops and market stalls stood. Creeping vines clung to the walls of the stone buildings, and lush gardens lined every nook and cranny along the sidewalks and roads. Through the windows of the shops, I found all sorts of wares—small book merchants, potion masters, clothiers, tea shops.

"When I thought about visiting the ruler of the underworld, I did not expect it to be so colorful," I said, lifting my eyes to what I assumed was Hades' palace. It was monumental structure carved into the wall of the mountain in such fine detail, I knew it had to have been raised with magic and not built by hand.

We drew the attention of the fae who called the capital home, some halting conversations to cast curious looks our way.

"Many of them have probably never seen an immortal before," Atlas said, inclining his head with a smile that dripped hidden poison to a passing fae with long, rabbit-like ears—a Kunilas.

Her eyes were filled with a knowing distrust as he smiled at her, and she turned her gaze forward, head held high as she walked past us with long, delicate strides. She towered over me, body built with lean power down to her lower legs, which were more like that of a jack rabbit; the pads of her feet were small and delicate, yet powerful enough to likely put someone down with a single kick. She was dressed in finery, her hair braided with delicate chains and crystals. White freckles dusted her dark skin, and a pearlescent ink decorated her cheeks in horizontal stripes, along with another that streaked down the center of her lower lip.

"I'm amazed they can feel such comfort dwelling this close to where souls find judgment," I said as I met the curious gaze of a pair of passing feather folk. Their gray and cerulean skin caught the sun in hues of green and blue, and their long, feather-tipped ears were adorned with delicate gold chains and pendants dusting the tops of their feathered shoulders. Their clothes, unlike the simple garments the village dwellers donned, were a sheer, decadent material that seemed as light as the air that swirled around their sky Islands in Pelagonia.

"I've not seen feather folk in these parts in a long time," Atlas whispered as we continued onward. "Hades has been working hard in the recent centuries, extending his reach across Elythias."

I arched a brow. "Since when is Hades so friendly?"

"I'm sure Persephone had a hand in it, especially when offering refuge to those fearful of Zeus' ongoing conflict with Hesperian's reach."

The flames within me rippled at the sound of the familiar name, calling to something deep within the lingering, distant memories of a form they once took.

"Zeus is picking a fight with the Wyverns?" I asked.

"You know how he is—always searching for threats in the wrong places, turning a blind eye to where they truly lie."

The guard escorting us glanced over her shoulder as we reached the base of the steps to Hades' Palace, eyes briefly narrowed, her tail swaying with each step, her staff tapping against stone to a steady beat.

We ascended, and with each step my mind wandered to the possibilities of what we would see, of what Hades might be like.

"These shall be your quarters for the duration of your stay," she said as she guided us into a large sitting room, turning to face us. Her face remained unreadable, just as it had from the beginning, giving no notion of her thoughts or emotions. I wondered if she realized, like others, what we were, if she harbored the same judgment the goblin had.

Katàratos.

Cursed.

There were some who remembered what befell our kingdom, Lunoscia, and I wondered if the old goblin was truly that old, or if he was one of many who shared the stories of the kingdom that fell to darkness.

I took it all in—the fine furniture dressed in silk and velvet in the richest colors, the windows adorned with thick curtains, fae lights captured in glass sconces along the walls, and just as the city was, the room was filled with all sorts of plant life: flowering vines creeping along the walls, moss clinging to the legs and edges of tables.

"Each of you have a room through those doorways," she said, pointing toward each of the doors. "Food, wine, and entertainment will be brought to you, and if there is anything else you require, you need only ask the servants."

I frowned as she stepped past us and through the door, taking hold of the knob.

"You are to remain here until he summons you."

Two days, we had sat in these rooms.

I sat on the window ledge of our quarters, looking out on the city cloaked under the blanket of night, the lights of the city glittering in the darkness. A half-smoked roll of Brierleaf hung between my fingers, the hazing effects blurring the edges of my vision—leaving my skin warm and near tingling. I had wanted so badly to explore in my boredom while we waited to see Hades, to do anything but sit in this godsforsaken suite with nothing to keep my mind off Thalia.

Music filled room, a lulling melody chiming from the harp a wood nymph played on a nearby chaise, the sweet sound accompanied by the angelic voices of the Fae dancers, dressed in sheer chiffon that left little to the imagination. The gold chains adorning their garments jingled with each sway of their hips, each thrust of their breasts as they twisted and twirled to the music.

One of Atlas' guards gestured to the male dancer, an intrigued smile curving his lips as the fae male grazed the top of his thigh with his fingertips before sliding onto his lap.

"You should join us," Atlas said as he plopped down onto the window ledge next to me.

"Tempting," I said with a dry voice as I lifted a glass of godswine to my lips, the rich, red liquid fruity and strong.

"He'll call for us soon," Atlas assured me, turning his attention back to the dancers.

I didn't answer, my gaze returned to the city.

"Missing someone?" Atlas asked, and I stifled the urge to react to his words, to let on that I had anyone "special".

"Everything that happens here, stays here," he said, giving me a knowing smile.

It wasn't as if Thalia was mine, wasn't as if I owed her my loyalties in bed. Perhaps it wasn't just actions that could stay here. Perhaps *I* could stay here, get away from the pain of seeing her every day, knowing that that was all I would ever get to do.

She wasn't mine, and she never would be.

I turned my gaze from the window as the dancers approached us. A water nymph settled her glittering, sapphire eyes on me as her pearlescent blue lips curved into a sultry smile. The fae lights danced across her glistening turquoise skin with each dip of her hips as she sauntered toward us to the music alongside another dancer—an elf, one equally as beautiful and tantalizing.

"What's the phrase humans use? When in Rome?" he whispered before rising to meet the elvish dancer, his hands sweeping out to scoop her up until her legs were wrapped around his waist. Flirtatious laughter slipped from her lips as he buried his face in her neck, peppering her tawny skin with slow, heated kisses.

The water nymph stepped closer, her sultry eyes dusted with powdered pearls, her body adorned with gemstones. She settled between my legs, the swell of her full hips brushing the inside of my thighs as her delicate fingers trailed up my legs, continuing up until they rested against my chest.

The sight of her didn't stir anything, didn't spark the flame within my chest to an inferno.

But did it have to?

I lifted my hand to hook my finger under her chin, guiding her gaze to mine. Tilting my head, I took in every detail of her: the way her lips parted, the way her full breasts rose and fell, her nipples taut and visible through the chiffon fabric of her dancing garments.

"When in Rome," I muttered and leaned in to capture her lips.

CHAPTER 49

BARRETT

A knock rang at my door, and I groaned as I rolled over. Sunlight leaked from between the curtains near my bed, dappling the room in streaks of gold from the rising sun.

"Get dressed. Hades is ready to see us," Atlas said from the other side of the door.

"About fucking time," I muttered. It had been four days since we'd arrived, only to be barred in these rooms, unable to explore his city until our meeting. While he provided us with plenty of things to eat, drink, smoke, and fuck, something within me had grown anxious, the flames within my soul as restless as a scaled beast pacing within the confines of a cage.

A soft sigh dragged my attention to the sleeping female beside me, her rose-colored skin a stark contrast to the white sheets, the long, delicate tip of one of her ears peaking from her hair. The sheets ruffled enough to expose the dip and rise of her waist, sloping into the curve of her ass.

The last couple of days had been a haze, my mind constantly returning to Thalia and Micah. Every night, Hades had sent dancers for entertainment, and while they were skilled in the art of dancing and seduction, no matter how many females I fucked, I was left feeling empty, unsatisfied, needing more. My thoughts remained elsewhere despite Atlas' antics, and our conversations I could barely remember. I couldn't keep from wondering how Micah and Thalia were; wondering if Thalia would ever look at me the same after the way I had treated her.

Maybe I could find a place to lose myself in the Godsrealm, never set foot in the Mortalrealm again, leave Micah and Thalia to their happiness and avoid hurting her ever again. The possibility had plagued me over the last few days, and I'd warred with myself on the matter for too long.

I pushed myself out of bed and headed for the armoire, where the servants had provided us with clothes to wear during our stay.

Regardless of what I decided, I would have to return to the Mortalrealm once more to fill Damien in on everything I'd learned, tie up loose ends before I found somewhere to occupy my time. Would Hades have use of an immortal in his capital? He seemed to have use of Atlas from across the veil; perhaps he could find a purpose for me within his court.

A dull ringing filled my ears, and for a moment, the room around me shifted, blurring, and from the corner of my eye, I could have sworn I saw a figure sitting on the bed. As I blinked it vanished, the ringing fading, and I shook my head before pulling a shirt over my head.

Dressed in the fine attire befitting the noble houses of Hades' domain, I stalked toward the door, not caring to wake or acknowledge the slumbering female in my bed who, for all I knew, had no name.

I didn't care to know it.

"Apologies for the wait," a deep voice echoed through the chamber as we entered through the arched doorway, the guards' attentive eyes tracking our every movement as we passed them.

I wasn't sure if this was intended to be a museum or trophy room for all the objects on display around us. Pedestals lined the walls, illuminated in a blue glow, all except one where the male who had spoken stood.

He was tall, a dark metal crown adorning his short black hair, which dusted the top of his ears in subtle waves. His onyx eyes drifted from me to Atlas, an ancient energy lighting them. At his side was the fae male I'd met countless times—Hades' emissary, Santor. Santor was dressed in fine clothes, nothing like what I had ever seen him in on the other side of the Veil, his short horns polished to a near glow, his tail swaying back and forth.

"It's been a while," Atlas said as he drew closer and threw his arms around Hades, who welcomed him with an equally warm embrace.

"You've been a stranger lately," Hades said as they released each other.

"I've been busy keeping things in line on the other side. The riff-raff can't be left unattended, lest they ruin everything I've worked hard for," Atlas said with a huffed laugh, and the sounds of their conversation faded, the ringing returning to my ears, a weight filling my bones as I looked around the room.

Giggles echoed through the hall, and I caught a glimpse of a girl with cornsilk hair disappearing through a doorway. I frowned, the room twisting and writhing like a dream.

"Hades, this is Barrett."

I blinked as Atlas' voice cut through the ringing, and I looked back at them.

"Ah, we finally meet," Hades said, brows rising. "Atlas has spoken highly of you. He tells me you're the man to get jobs done, no matter how dirty."

I shrugged as I slipped my hands into the pockets of my velvet coat, eyes slipping to where the girl had disappeared. "I guess you could say that."

"I may have use of your services in the future," Hades mused.

"You got quite the collection here," Atlas said as he looked around the room. "How have I never seen this room before?"

"Well, that would be due to the fact that, to many, this room doesn't exist," Hades said, his gaze sweeping across the room. "I've spent many centuries gathering magical artifacts under the orders of The Twelve, whether they still possess the powers or curses inlaid in the fabric of their creation or drained of every ounce of it. This is where they are safeguarded."

So he was the keeper of dangerous magical artifacts, it seemed.

"They've proven of use to me from time to time," he added, releasing the clasp of a long, ornate pipe from his belt. "But none of The Twelve need know of such ventures."

He struck a match before lighting whatever herbs were held in the bowl of the pipe and drawing in a deep drag on it before letting the smoke slip from his lips in a cloud of purplish gray. "I don't know how anyone learned of its whereabouts, let alone made it past my security." His gaze slid back to the empty pedestal. "And this was the only thing taken, which tells me they knew exactly what they were looking for."

"I hear this particular object is quite dangerous in the wrong hands," I said, tilting my head.

"Charon's siphon," he said, black eyes hardening before he drew in a few puffs from his pipe. His anger heated the air, the blue flame sconces on the walls growing in unstable strength. "One gifted to him by Celestia's fallen mate." Hades' voice dropped an octave, as if muttering to himself, the smoke billowing from his lips as he spoke in short puffs. "Should his name remain sealed with him."

"Do you know who might've stolen it?" Atlas asked. "Who might have wanted it?"

Santor folded his arms behind his back and held his head high. "The guards who were on watch that night have no memory of what transpired, as if someone had taken an hour of their lives and wiped it from existence."

I let out a sigh as I turned my attention to the empty pedestal. "So no one knows what the person looks like, where they might have come from, or where they might have gone?"

"The only thing I can tell you is that I felt their presence within my chamber the moment they entered," Hades said. "And I would know it again in a heartbeat if I ever crossed paths with them. It was tainted, manipulative, and touched with moonlight, which left me wondering if it might be an immortal."

Atlas and I exchanged glances as Hades lifted the pipe to his lips once more to take another hit.

"It remained within the Godsrealm for some time until it suddenly vanished a little over 20 years ago." Hades paced through the room, and we fell into step at his side. "I sent servants to every region, every continent across the Godsrealm beyond Elythias, but no matter where they searched there was no sign of it."

"Which is why you think it's in the Mortalrealm," I said.

He nodded. "I would send my servants to find whoever took it, but the laws of The Twelve prevent me from setting foot in the Mortalrealm, let alone interfering in their world by sending fae to conduct a retrieval."

My eyes slid to Santor as he stopped to look at a nearby pedestal displaying a golden orb, the plate etched with an inscription in the old language.

'Lover's Sacrifice. Crafted by the witch Medea.'

I remained wary of the fae male, had aways felt unsure of him, of his loyalties—whether they remained with Hades, Atlas, or perhaps even only himself. Perhaps that was any of the fae or the gods, though. They dealt in trickery and deceit, only doing whatever benefitted them most.

"You still not getting along with Damien?" Hades asked.

Atlas scoffed. "He's too closed off to the possibilities of what we could be if we stopped catering to the humans..."

Their voices quieted once more, the dull ringing filling my ears and, for a moment I could have sworn I heard Thalia's voice whispering into my ear, her presence pressing into my back as if she stood behind me.

I'm worried about you.

I turned as the room darkened, melting like paint around me, save for her figure standing before a pedestal several feet away. She glanced over her shoulder, her eyes full of the hurt I'd seen that night.

"You good, Barrett?" Atlas asked, brows furrowed.

I blinked and she was gone, the ringing vanishing once more, and I turned to find Atlas looking at me with a frown.

"Yeah," I said with a nod. "Thought I heard something."

"Some of these items are prone to stirring up trouble despite the warding," Hades said with a laugh.

"How could you have an audience without me?" a melodic female voice echoed from the entrance of the hall, and I turned to find a female floating toward us with the same grace as Selene. Her cheeks were dusted with a rich blush, her copper hair glittering with gold chains, the waves pulled back in complex braids that caged the remaining locks left to cascade down her back. The fabric of her soft green gown floated and swayed around her feet as she approached us.

"Apologies, my dearest," Hades said, and I realized it was the goddess Persephone.

"Atlas. Staying out of trouble, I hope," she said, giving him a knowing smile.

Atlas bowed before her and placed a kiss on the back of her hand. "Never."

"I apologize if my mate kept you waiting long," she said, looping her arm through his. "We've been attending to some delicate matters in the south. I hope he has been a better host. The fact an object of such power was stolen under his watch has him very stressed."

I glanced around the room, paranoia leaving me restless, wondering when another hallucination might surface. Was I still feeling the lingering effects of whatever I'd done the night before? The hallucinations didn't return, and air filled my lungs as I tried to regain my composure and focus on the conversation.

"The Twelve remain unaware of its theft, and I would like it to remain that way. My brother is paranoid enough. I don't need him poking his nose in my domain," Hades warned. "The retrieval of this object is of the utmost importance. In the wrong hands, not only could The Siphon steal the soul of a god, but it could also allow the wielder to manipulate the soul, possibly even bend it to their will if the soul was weak enough."

What use could someone have for an object of that power in the Mortalrealm?

Hades' eyes shifted to Atlas. "I implore you to do everything in your power to find me that Siphon."

CHAPTER 50
BARRETT

I may have use of your services in the future.

Hades' words lingered in the back of my mind as I sat at Semele's bar. Hades had insisted we stay a few more days to indulge in the hospitalities of his palace and city after our meeting. I barely remembered half the festivities for how messed up I'd been. We'd partied endlessly, lost ourselves in the revelry until we'd passed out.

At some point, it had become difficult to even look at a female, let alone touch them, no matter how beautiful and tempting. All I could see was her the moment our clothes came off—the look of hurt on her face, or the look of cold resentment she'd given me when I'd last seen her... So, I drank until I couldn't see straight, smoked until I couldn't feel every inch of my body—of the agonizing desire for something I couldn't have welling in my chest. Perhaps a part of me wanted to stay, wanted to return to it, the endless numbness where I couldn't think of Thalia or Micah.

I wasn't sure how the fuck we were going to find this stolen object, but I couldn't find the energy to focus on it. I'd only been in the Mortalrealm for a few hours and had so far avoided seeing Damien, eager to drown out the thoughts that intensified the moment I'd stepped across the veil. The mating bond had grown demanding for Thalia's presence, for her attention...for her forgiveness.

It took everything in me not to throw myself at her feet.

Something tugged deep in my chest as I glanced over my shoulder at the mass of bodies moving in time to the pumping music, the beat pounding its way into my system. The bodies blurred together as they swayed and ground against one another.

My chest ached, the longing for Thalia near unbearable from the days I'd been away to the point where it was driving me insane. I couldn't think straight, couldn't focus on the conversations Vincent tried to hold. He'd been trying to cut me off for the last hour, going on about how much of a mess I looked.

I couldn't help it, couldn't stop myself from knocking back another glass.

"Sorry?" I muttered, glancing at him when he waved his hand in front of my face.

He let out a sigh. "You've gotta get a hold of yourself, get this self-loathing and punishment under control. How bad are you gonna get before you start taking better care of yourself?"

I dragged a heavy hit from my rolled Brierleaf, the high already swimming through my system like a siren's song, lulling me into a haze I never wanted to be free of. I never wanted to rise above the surface and...*feel*.

From the corner of my eye, I caught sight of Micah as Thalia where they danced amidst the crowd. Her head was tilted back against Micah's shoulder as she ground her ass against him, her hips swaying to the beat of the music as his fingers dug into them.

She looked equally as drunk as I felt, her cheeks flushed. Micah brushed his lips to her neck as they moved together, and Gods, I couldn't take my eyes off them. His eyes lifted to mine, and for a moment, I wondered if I was hallucinating when he nodded to me to come.

I hesitated, Vincent's voice melting into the sea of noises around me. "Barrett?"

"I'll be right back," I said, setting the glass on the edge of the bar top and tamping out the embers on my roll. He lurched forward to catch it before it tipped over.

Each step felt too fast and yet too slow, my body not moving fast enough to bring me closer to her, and yet at the same time, I wasn't ready to face her, wasn't ready to face the possibility of rejection if she decided to cast me to the side. I deserved as much.

My surroundings blurred into nothing as I drew closer to them, everything else around us falling away until we were all that remained, all that mattered. Thalia's eyes found me, and the stormy gray dulled with a sort of sadness that demanded every fiber of my being do anything and everything to right the wrong.

I stood there frozen, and the words spilled from my lips. "I'm so sorry..."

She blinked as if her mind couldn't wholly latch onto the words I said.

My heart hammered in my chest, pushing the alcohol through my system harder, the haze coaxing anything and everything from my lips. I wanted to tell her everything, tell her how I felt, tell her my wishes.

Tell her what she was to me. "I..."

Her hand rose, her fingers pressing to my lips. "We both...said things we shouldn't have."

Thalia's hand tentatively reached out to mine but halted before she could take hold of me. Something fractured deep within me, the flames dousing at the fear of her rejection, of her once again ignoring what I hoped she felt.

What the fuck was I doing?

Micah brushed his lips along the shell of her ear, his eyes sliding to me as she drew her hand back to her chest. She twisted around to look at him, and he lifted his hand to cup her cheek before pressing a tender kiss to her lips. She looked between us and, for a moment, I wondered if I was imagining at the look of longing in her eyes. Micah reached out to grab my wrist, pulling me closer until Thalia was sandwiched between us, her back to my chest, ass pressed firmly against me. I resisted the urge to slide my hands up her thighs, but then Micah took my hands and placed them on her hips, and my heart threatened to sputter out. The air rushed from Thalia's lungs, her lips parting as Micah pressed her tighter between us, her body fitting so perfectly against ours.

The flames swayed beneath my skin like a beast relishing in affection—relishing in the feel of her skin against mine. Thalia turned her head as we moved in sync, and she lifted her hand to brush her fingertips against my neck before pulling me closer to her. Micah dragged drunken kisses along her neck, guiding her hips to the beat of the music as we danced, our bodies molding together in perfect, sinful harmony.

The flames swelled, desiring more, to feel her skin, taste her lips, feel her naked body move against mine...

Micah met my heated gaze, his eyes drunk with desire before they slid back to Thalia, whose eyes were closed as she lost herself between us. He took her hand and nodded to me as he started through the crowd to the exit.

I drew a deep breath, her scent of black spruce, of wildwoods that could never be tamed, too much to resist. I wanted to drown myself in her scent, cover myself in it until no other could deny that she was mine and I was hers.

The thought made me hesitate as I found Micah, and he seemed to catch wind of it. A corner of his lip kicked up in a half smile, and he nodded before Thalia met my gaze as well, her hand reaching out to take mine.

And I caved as she dragged me out into the night air.

The walk from Stokers to Micah and Thalia's house was a blur of stolen kisses and touches: Thalia pressing Micah against the wall as she kissed him while I pressed against her back, lips burning trails of kisses along her shoulder, her neck; Micah's hands roaming up the back of her shirt as he bit down on her throat while she moaned, head tilting back as her eyes locked with mine, fingers digging into my arms as she pulled me closer.

Fuck, the sight of her bending for him was delicious.

The door creaked open as we entered Micah and Thalia's home, the darkness welcoming us. Micah kicked the door shut impatiently as Thalia and I stumbled to a stop, one of her hands locked with Micah's, the other entwined with mine. He crashed into her, his lips capturing hers as he pulled her tighter against him, and he backed her up to me, her ass pressing against the swell of my hard cock. She arched her back, pressing herself tighter against me, silently begging me to touch her more, and I obliged. I couldn't resist her demands if I wanted to. My hands snaked around her waist, fingers dipping beneath the hem of her shirt as I brushed my lips against her neck, dragging drunken kisses up along her skin before nipping at the shell of her ear.

Her body tensed, thighs pressing tighter together, and I slid my knee between them, forcing them apart as Micah's hand slipped lower. She whimpered as Micah ran his finger back and forth along her center, his knuckle running against the top of my thigh, and I spread her legs further, encouraging him, wanting to feel her shiver and quake as he drew forth her pleasure. Her scent flooded the room, the sweetness of her arousal filling my nose, and my mouth watered at the thought of how wet she was, how she soaked her lace underwear. He trailed kisses down her opposite collarbone and pulled his hand away from her just as she began to pant and moan. She slumped against me, chest heaving, heated breaths bursting from her swollen, parted lips.

Micah's hands worked in tandem with mine to lift her shirt, revealing her creamy skin, her black lace bra. I wanted to see more of her, wanted to lose myself in exploring and marveling at every inch of her body, inside and out.

She twisted around to me before pressing tender, hesitant kisses to my lips. Gods, she tasted heavenly. Micah trailed kisses from the back of her neck down her spine, and her lips parted against mine on a silent moan, lower and lower until he reached around and began undoing her jeans to work them down her hips.

I cupped her cheeks, pulling her back to me as Micah worked her jeans off, and she broke our kiss to turn to him, her hands reaching for the button of his shirt as she pulled him in for a kiss. He growled against her lips as she undid his shirt and slid her hands up against his exposed chest, dragging her fingers up to his shoulders to ultimately push it off his shoulders, and he let it slide to the floor.

The flames writhed and slammed against the confinement of my body, hungry to taste her skin, to burn away every scrap of clothing separating us. Her hands slid from Micah's chest, and I nudged her to the side, guiding her to the wall as Micah and I came together, shoulders brushing as we cornered her. Her attention split between us, one hand ensnaring in Micah's hair to pull him in to kiss her while her other hand slid up my t-shirt, pushing it up. I helped her in lifting it over my head, giving her all the access to my body she wanted.

I'd let her touch and taste every inch she desired, give in to whatever she wished of me, drag out her pleasure and leave her wanting more. And Gods, I'd give her more if it was what she wanted.

Micah kissed her with a hunger I'd never seen in him, and it sparked something within me, a hunger I had been ignoring for centuries. Thalia's pale lashes lifted a fraction, her stormy eyes drifting to me, and Micah released her lips, dropping his face to the crook of her neck to bite down on her throat. A moan broke free of her, and her fingers tangled in my hair as she pulled me in for a kiss. I devoured her, her taste everything I ever wanted, everything I needed.

The hunger and desire swelled to an undeniable need that demanded I bend to its will, that I give in and savor her for what she was.

My mate.

Mine.

Chapter 51

Thalia

Glass shattered, momentarily clearing the drunken haze as Micah pushed me up onto the island countertop, knocking glasses onto the floor. But as he slid between my thighs and bit down on my throat, drawing me into him, I fell into the deep end once more, drowning in a murky abyss I wanted to lose myself in until I never saw the light of day again.

He released my throat and placed his palm against the binding tattoo between my breasts to push me down until my back was pressed against the cool stone. Barrett stalked around to the other side like a beast assessing his prey, waiting for the moment when he could take me for his own, and my heart thrummed at the sight—of his muscles taut and wound so tightly, he looked ready to combust.

I wanted to taste that flame, let it consume me.

Barrett came to a stop at my head, now resting at the edge of the countertop. His distressed jeans sagged around his hips, the deep V carving a path along his lower stomach before disappearing beneath his boxers. Micah's hand slid up to my neck, his thumb brushing over the tingling bite mark he'd left before he dragged his bloodied thumb over my lip, smearing blood across my skin. A rush of need pooled between my thighs, and his sky-blue eyes darkened with desire as I held his hungered gaze. He lowered himself, trailing kisses between my breasts, down my sternum, along my stomach, and I panted as each kiss dragged me into a torrent of need.

Barrett's steel eyes fell on me, lips parted as his eyes roamed to watch Micah taste and nip at my skin. I let out a shaky breath as Barrett traced his finger up my arm, over my collarbone, the roughness of his thumb combined with Micah's lips making me shiver. Barrett slid his hand up my throat before he tilted my chin, forcing my gaze to him as he grazed his thumb over my lower lip. I drew his thumb into my mouth, rolling my tongue over it before sucking as I tasted my blood on him. His chest expanded as he drew in a sharp breath, and his skin warmed, the room heating as his steel eyes turned molten.

Micah's fingers slid beneath the top of my lace underwear as he lowered himself between my legs, and I drew in a breath as Barrett took hold of my wrists, anchoring them to the counter. Their eyes met, and my heart roared in my chest as Micah worked my underwear down my legs inch by torturous inch. Barrett pulled my hands above my head, fastening them together in one hand before reaching with his free hand for my bra. He pushed the lace down, exposing one of my breasts before rolling his thumb over my tender nipple. My back arched, my lips parting as I moaned.

A deep hum of satisfaction rumbled from Barrett's throat, his hooded eyes tracking my every movement, every twitch as he rolled my nipple between his fingers, every whimper as Micah dragged his teeth and lips up the inside of one of my thighs. My mind swam in ecstasy, my skin tingling at the feel of them dragging me toward the edge of a cliffside I'd desperately wanted to leap from, had fought and resisted for too long.

My eyes dropped to Micah between my thighs, watching me with hungry eyes as he hovered inches from where I wanted to feel him. He looped his arms around my thighs, spreading me wider for him before he ran his tongue up my center, flicking my clit with the tip of his tongue. I gasped, and Barrett lowered himself, giving me no time to gain control of myself as he rolled his tongue around the taut peak of my breast before bringing it between his teeth.

I moaned, my head falling to the side as my body writhed. Micah anchored my thighs, Barrett anchored my wrists as they tasted me, giving me no room to shy away from the pleasure they demanded.

"Gods, you look so perfect between us," Micah whispered against my heated flesh, his eyes wholly locked on me and Barrett as Barrett continued to nip and suck at my breast.

My stomach tightened, body winding like a cord about to snap as he worked his tongue against my clit in heavy strokes, building me higher and higher until I cried out, my release rolling through me. Barrett rose, his eyes burning into me as I writhed beneath him and Micah.

"Fuck, you're beautiful when you come," Barrett growled as he watched me collapse, in a shaking mess on the countertop. "So fucking beautiful."

Barrett released my wrists as Micah rose and slid his hands under my back to pull me off the counter. I wrapped my legs around his waist as he carried me toward our bedroom. Barrett stalked after us, like a hungry beast eager to devour me body and soul. I wanted nothing more than that, to be devoured by them both until nothing remained.

My hold on Micah tightened as I imagined them both, the haze lifting for a moment to leave me rational enough to face the reality of what his presence meant. It didn't matter, whether this was right or wrong. I was theirs, had always been. Every fiber of my being was lost to both Micah and Barrett, no matter how much I had tried to deny it, no matter how much I fought it. That intangible presence in my chest swelled, pulling me to Barrett, while the binding tattoo between my breasts pulled me to Micah, my heart divided between the two.

Maybe it didn't have to be one or the other. Just as I was theirs, perhaps they could be...mine.

Micah captured my lips with his, his tongue sweeping in to taste me, and I moaned against his mouth as Barrett came up behind me, his hands molding against the skin of my hips as he nipped at my shoulder.

Barrett stepped to the side before Micah eased me onto the bed. He reached around to undo the clasps of my bra while I fumbled with the zipper of his jeans. I held our kiss, giving him no chance to break away, our tongues dancing.

I shoved his jeans and boxers down, his hard cock popping free, and I took him into my hands, feeling every ridge and ripple of the thick veins along his shaft, the thick, proud head. He grabbed my wrists, halting me before releasing his hold to grasp my hips and push me further onto the bed. The sound of a zipper followed by the whisper of Barrett's jeans hitting the floor drew my attention to where he watched from the other side of the bed.

My eyes fell to his cock, full and hard for me, and I swallowed, heart skipping a beat as I imagined what he would feel like, what his skin would feel like against mine, what he tasted like. Micah hooked my chin, pulling me back to him before his hand slid down to my hip to tug me onto my side to face him, the sheets brushing against our naked skin. His eyes shifted to Barrett, and he nodded. My heart threatened to explode when the bed dipped as Barrett climbed in behind me. Barrett's hands roamed up my back, fingers brushing against the nape of my neck before ensnaring in my hair to tilt my head back.

"You want both of us right, my love?" Micah asked, his eyes burning into mine as he gripped my chin, his thumb brushing over my lower lip.

I hesitated, the truth lingering on my tongue, but before I could think better of it, I whispered, "Yes."

Micah dragged his hand down my side, sweeping over my ass before descending further to hook his hand under my knee and drag it over his hip. He guided his cock between us as I grabbed his arm, feeling his biceps bulge beneath my touch as he slid himself along my center, coating himself in my wetness.

The sound of a bottle top being popped reached my ears before Barrett leaned in to whisper in my ear. "Relax for me, *kelisa*."

My heart jolted at the word. Most beautiful. Surely, he hadn't meant to say that. He kissed my neck, drawing my mind back into the haze, and my eyes fell closed as a breath escaped my lungs. His fingers slid to my ass, and before I could think too deeply, Micah plunged himself inside me. My head fell back, a moan bursting from my lips as he filled me.

"You think you can take us both?" Micah asked, his voice low and raw as he slid out of me, drawing himself to the tip before thrusting deeper, seating himself inside me.

"I think she can," Barrett whispered as his lips brushed against the shell of my ear.

Their hands slid over my sides, my waist, my hips, before I felt Barrett's hand slide down to guide himself inside. I tensed at the intrusion as he worked himself into me in gentle, shallow thrusts as Micah filled me and receded. Micah kissed me tenderly, his hand cupping my cheek as Barrett worked himself into me, and when he filled me fully, he bit down on my throat.

"Barrett!" I cried out, my back arching, and as he withdrew, nearly pulling out, Micah plunged himself deep, dragging another moan from my lips. "Gods, Micah."

"Fuck, you feel amazing," Barrett growled against my neck.

Micah smiled against my lips before releasing me. "And she's all ours."

This couldn't be real; this had to be a dream.

They worked in tandem, Barrett's thrusts in opposition to Micah's, a fight for ground as they worked themselves into me in deep thrusts. They filled me with such pleasure, I couldn't think of how I'd lived without it all these years. I wanted more of it, all of it, wanted to feel them against me always. Something wound itself around a deeper part of me, winding tighter and tighter, drawing me closer to Barrett as his fingers dug into my hips, his moving against my ass as he pounded into me, losing himself as he drew closer to his finish.

I twisted, my hand rising to tangle my fingers in his blond hair as I pulled him closer, capturing his lips with mine, tasting him, tasting me. He growled against my lips, his thrusts growing more demanding as Micah kissed my collarbone, moaning my name as he drove himself into me as well.

And together, we launched ourselves over the edge.

CHAPTER 52

BARRETT

A dull ache lingered in the back of my head when I opened my eyes, the room swaying and blurring as I blinked. I lifted my hand to rub my eyes as I rolled over and grimaced at the faint streaks of light leaking from the nearby curtains.

I frowned, and my eyes clenched shut as I shifted to the edge of the bed. My head fell in my hands as I sat there a moment, trying to get my bearings amidst the hazy confusion of where I was, how I'd gotten here, and what had happened.

The softest sigh dragged my attention to the sleeping figure in the bed at my back. So I'd wound up leaving the bar with someone last night, it seemed, but then another groan of sleepiness caught my attention, the voice familiar, and my heart halted in my chest. I twisted around and froze at the sight of Thalia and Micah passed out amidst the sheets of their bed. My eyes flew around the room, taking in all the details as I sobered and realized where the fuck I was.

This couldn't be happening...

Moments resurfaced amidst the haze of the drug and alcohol-induced night—the feel of Thalia's skin against mine, her lips, the feel of her body pressed tightly between us as we took her, and...fuck, it had been amazing, everything I had ever wanted.

Only we had been drunk, and now I'd tasted something that I wasn't meant to have, something I never should have partaken in. I pushed off the bed, my pulse roaring in my ears as I silently cursed myself.

What the fuck was I thinking?

You weren't fucking thinking.

I searched the mess of clothes before ducking to grab my jeans on the floor next to the dresser. As I rose, I froze at the faint familiar scent of jasmine and citrus, and I caught sight of the open box atop the dresser, a note laid out beside it in Lucia's handwriting. My eyes latched on to the scrap of fabric lying nestled amidst the pale linen.

Before I could think better of it, I took the scrap of damaged fabric in my hand, the edges frayed, rips and tears dotting it from years of rough handling.

Cali's laughter echoed in the back of my mind as I looked closer, something scratching the back of my head as I lifted it. When the faint hint of my scent hit my nose I stopped breathing.

A girl, lost and frightened. I'd gifted her my coat. I'd forgotten her, forgotten she'd even existed so many years after her disappearance, and I...

I dropped the fabric as realization crashed into me, and I looked over my shoulder to where Thalia slept. It was her, the one from all those centuries ago. Her stormy eyes had haunted me...and why wouldn't they? They were my future, my torment, my heartbreak. They were everything I wanted and everything I would never have because she wasn't fucking mine.

How could The Fates have dangled her in front of me, only to rip her out of my life, to torment us both, only to throw us back together after she'd already bound herself to another?

My chest heaved as everything came crashing around me, as the memories of us playing with Calliope in the meadow filled my mind. The dreams—they had all fucking been her. She was who I'd been searching for all these centuries, whether I knew it or not. Every set of eyes I'd met, I'd found myself searching them for something, searching for her, for the storms in her eyes that might temper the raging inferno spiraling out of control within me.

How fucking cruel of The Fates to sentence me to be fated to a female who'd already chosen, who'd already fallen in love with someone else before I'd even had the chance. Was this my punishment? After everything I'd done in my life, every person I'd failed, was this what The Fates would punish me with, to watch as my mate and love of my life lived out her life with someone else?

I yanked my jeans on, desperate to get out of here.

"Barrett?" Thalia groaned, and I stiffened, unable to turn to her, unable to look her in the eyes.

Did she remember the night before? Did she choose this? I didn't dare ask, couldn't face the possibility of her regret as I zipped up my jeans and pulled my shirt on.

Her pale brows pinched together as she sat up, her cornsilk hair spilling over her shoulder as she shifted toward the edge of the bed. "What are you—"

I stormed toward the door, swiping my socks off the ground as I went. I froze as my hand halted at the doorknob. "This was a mistake."

CHAPTER 53

THALIA

I flinched as Barrett slammed the door, and I stood frozen at the foot of my bed, my hands trembling, vision blurring as tears welled in my eyes. What had I done?

Most of the night before was lost to a drunken dream, only bits and pieces of it flitting across my memory. How could I have been so foolish to think everything would be all right after last night? How could I have given in so easily to my desires?

Micah let out a sigh, and I turned to find his face in his hands.

"What have we done?" I muttered, my heart fracturing more with each passing second in the echoing silence of Barrett's departure.

"Thalia," Micah started, pushing himself to the edge of the bed as I hurried to grab my clothes.

"I have to go after him," I said, pulling my underwear on in a panic, not knowing what I would even say. Would he ever look at me again? Would he ever talk to me? Or had I just fucked everything up?

This was a mistake.

What had he meant by that? Was it a mistake because we'd pushed things too far too fast—before we were ready? Or was it a mistake because...

"Thalia," Micah said, as I pulled a shirt over my head, not bothering to put a bra on. He grabbed my hands, halting me from doing anything else.

"I need to talk to him," I said, tears rolling down my cheeks.

"I know," he said, pulling me into his arms. "Give him some time to process his feelings."

I froze and pulled away to look up at him, brows furrowing.

"I know," he said, his eyes soft despite the knowing light there.

"You know?" I echoed, my breath catching. My heart plummeted.

"I know he's your mate," he finally said, cupping my cheeks before pressing his forehead against mine. "I've known for years."

I blinked, mouth opening and closing as panic tore through me. What did he think? What would he do? If he knew what I'd suspected for a long time, how could he pull Barrett into our bed?

"Why would you do this, then, if you knew?" I demanded, pulling away from him. Sadness touched at his features as he drew a deep breath, but I didn't give him the chance. "What if he never talks to us again? What if he—" I drew short shaky breaths. "Dammit, Micah."

"I wanted to see if he'd give into his feelings. I had to know if he would ever acknowledge it." He let out a sigh and ran his hand over his face. "Yes, it was stupid of me, but I've been trying to get you two to see the possibilities for a while."

I blinked, trying to make sense of what he was saying. "What are you talking about?"

He tentatively reached out to take my hand, and I let him, unable to pull away, too afraid to lose them both in this mess. "If you could have him, would you want him?"

"I..." What was he asking of me? "But we're—"

Micah pulled me closer and leaned his forehead against mine, his eyes lighting up with such intensity that I couldn't pull away. "No matter what you say, it will never change the way I feel for you. It won't change us."

My gaze swept between his eyes, trying to read whatever thoughts lingered behind them. "I don't understand."

He huffed a weak laugh, and one corner of his lips kicked up into a half smile. "There is no reality in which I would deny you the chance to be with your mate."

"But you... I—" I shook my head. "I love you. I don't want—"

"And nothing would ever change the fact that I love you, that I am yours. I will still be yours, just as he could be."

I blinked, my mind latching onto his words. "Both of you?"

He nodded. "We would not be the first relationship formed of more than two souls."

My eyes drifted to the door where Barrett had disappeared through.

Micah hooked my chin and drew my attention back to him. "If this is what you want, I will do everything in my power to make it so."

My lips parted, the hope swelling in my chest, the fear dragging it back down into my gut like an anchor of dread. What if Barrett rejected it all? What if Barrett rejected me? What if I'd lost him for good this time?

Micah kissed me tenderly and pulled me into a hug. "He's patrolling tonight. I'll take over the shift and talk to him, see where his head is at. I'll fix this, I swear."

CHAPTER 54

BARRETT

My glass clinked against the table as I set it down before grabbing the bottle of ambrosia liquor and pouring more. The last remnants of sunlight leaking from the nearby window illuminated the amber liquid as I lifted it to my lips, pausing before I could take a drink as I rested my head against my hand. The feather-light touch of the glass against my lips dredged up thoughts of Thalia, the sight of her reaching for me, fingers skimming my lips, her drunken eyes silently begging me to touch her, her lips parting as she moaned, how she melted between Micah and me.

I cursed before downing the glass, desperate to douse the raging inferno inside me, and I dropped it on the table amidst the strewn files and images of murdered women littering my desk. The glass tipped over and nearly rolled off the table, and yet, I couldn't bring myself to care if it fell, if it shattered into a million pieces.

Had she truly wanted me? Or had she merely been drunk? I dropped my face into my hands, my mind too full to try and think straight.

Something deep within my chest burned, leaving me jittery and breathless, demanding more of her attention, more of her blood, her body.

How could I have been so foolish? How could I just go back to pretending there was nothing between us after having a taste of her?

I couldn't.

There was no way I could go on pretending I was all right, that I wasn't fucking head over heels in love with her, that she wasn't my mate. *My fucking mate.*

My eyes passed over the paperwork on my table, halting on my letter of resignation I'd finished writing a few hours ago. There was no way I could continue as if last night hadn't happened, no way I could look at Thalia and not want to hold her, to taste her, to tell her all the things I had been bottling up for centuries.

"Sorry, Lucia. Looks like I'll be letting you down again," I muttered under my breath.

Regardless of what had happened, I couldn't leave Damien to deal with the serial killer, if only for Lucia. I'd see it handled and figure out what the hell I was going to do about Atlas. As soon as I put this murderer down, I would tell Damien and petition Hades for work in the Godsrealm. Perhaps if I lost myself in the revelries of the fae, I could find some drunken peace, some way to forget her face. Perhaps I was delusional to think I could ever find peace without her, but I sure as hell wouldn't find it here, with this endless torment of longing and heartache.

I lifted my eyes to the clock, the fading light signifying the approaching patrol, and my chance to take some of this anger out on darklings. Gods, I prayed I encountered some tonight. I fully intended to bathe in their black blood if given the chance.

I rose from my desk and grabbed my holstered dagger from the desk before securing it to my hip as I stalked out of my office.

"There's been a change in shifts," Zephyr said as I stepped down the hall of The Complex, checking that my knives were secured to the holster strapped across my chest.

I halted and arched a brow. "What do you mean?"

"Micah's taking over for Zach."

What. The. Fuck?

I turned to Zephyr. "I don't—"

The main door swung open, and Micah peered inside, already donning his Elythian leathers. "You ready?"

"Fates watch over your patrol," Zephyr said, patting my shoulder before he left us in the entry before I could protest.

I made to follow him, but Micah's hand landed on my shoulder, and whatever I was about to say to Zephyr scattered from my thoughts.

"Let's fucking get this over with," I muttered as I jerked out of his hold, pulled my hood up, and stalked out into the chilly night air.

Micah followed. "Barrett—"

"Don't start," I growled as we made our way down Short Street. I didn't bother to look at him as we headed for the east side of the city, where we would begin our patrol of the central sector. "I don't want to talk about what happened last night."

He let out a sigh, but thankfully he didn't speak further, and something twisted in my chest at the look of defeat in his eyes as his gaze drifted away from me.

Hours passed, our patrol a misery of silence that offered me no comfort, only the endless echoing thoughts of the night before, of the fears and doubts tearing away at my mind. My impatience had swelled to a boiling point in the absence of darklings, my dagger unused in my grip.

Of course, the one night I wanted to take out a darkling, there would be none in sight.

"Can we talk?" Micah said, glancing back at me as thunder rolled in the clouds above us, and I drew a slow breath. "Please."

"There's nothing to talk about," I said, fingers tightening around the hilt of my dagger. "We were drunk. It was a mistake. I know she's yours."

"Barrett, it wasn't—"

I halted as his words were cut short, and I glanced in his direction to find him stopped, his brows furrowed as he scanned the street ahead of us. The scent of blood hit me then, and I stepped closer to him.

"Human blood," he said, glancing at me, and I nodded before we hurried down the street, our boots echoing before the sound was drowned out by the distant rumble of thunder.

Maybe I'd be lucky enough to encounter a darkling tonight after all.

Rain dotted my face, and I lifted my eyes to the sky as more fell in quick succession, casting us in a downpour. The icy water soaked through my armor quickly, and lightning streaked across the sky. I froze as we rounded the corner to find a human girl on the ground, her lifeless body flat against the pavement. Her blood pooled beneath her, the rainwater drawing it away from her into a crimson stream. She couldn't have been older than her early twenties, her brown hair matted and bloodied, skin marred with cuts and bruises, her throat twisted at an odd angle. I didn't have to look to know her eyes would be hazel.

The rain flooded the street in a hazy curtain of water, leaving me to wonder if I was hallucinating when I saw a dark figure standing over her body. Lightning flashed, and for a moment, I wanted to believe I *was* hallucinating at the bloodied face staring back at me, at the blond hair and cold pewter eyes.

"Marcus?"

CHAPTER 55

BARRETT

"Long time no see," Marcus crooned, his words sliding out like poison.

It felt as if I was staring at a ghost, dark circles shadowing his pewter eyes, his skin paler than I remembered. He didn't look like the friend I remembered, more a shell of a man lost.

"Tell me you aren't the one who did this," I said, taking a step toward him. It had been decades since I'd last seen him—only a few years before Lucia's passing when we'd lost Vivienne to the darkling nest.

He swayed, stumbling to the side as if drunk, and lifted his crimson-stained hand to his lips before dragging his tongue up his palm, coating his tongue in the girl's blood. His head fell back, eyes falling closed as he let out a sigh that turned into a groan of frustration.

"It's not her," he muttered under his breath as he stared up at the sky, head tilted as if looking up at someone who wasn't there.

My brows furrowed, and I followed his gaze to the storm clouds churning above us, rain stinging my eyes before I looked back at him. He had turned his gaze downward to the woman's lifeless body, and he shifted his weight, tilting his head to get a better look as he hooked her chin with the edge of his boot.

"Such a shame," he muttered, wiping the bloodied blade of his knife on his jeans to clean it. I'd hoped you'd be the one."

"What the fuck are you doing, Marcus?" I demanded, taking another step toward him.

He stiffened, his murderous gaze snapping to me, and I stilled, my heart plummeting at the unrelenting fury raging within his eyes.

"Don't fucking come any closer," he growled, teeth bared as he pointed the blade of his knife at us.

"It's been you this whole time?" I demanded, his face flashing across my thoughts, the soul I'd once called brother.

His hateful eyes fluttered as if he was close to passing out, and he blinked as he shook his head. His lips curved into a cruel smile. "It's always been me. Every one of them. And I'm nowhere near finished."

"Why would you do this?" Micah asked. "We thought you were dead."

He huffed a laugh and ran his bloodied fingers through his hair, painting it in streaks of crimson, shoving it back out of his face as the soaked strands clung to his skin. "Not dead...never dead. I can't rest."

He began muttering to himself, words jumbled and slurred until it shifted in a near tune, as if he was singing to himself. "...no rest for the wicked."

My mind raced, every face of every woman he'd murdered flashing across my thoughts.

"You still serving that murderous cunt of a goddess?" Marcus crooned, his eyes drifting between the two of us, cold and unrecognizable from who I once knew.

"Watch your mouth," Micah snapped.

Marcus laughed. "Ah, Micah. Always loyal until the end. What a good soldier."

"No more games, Marcus," I growled, flames coming to life in my palm. Micah's eyes shifted to me, but I held my gaze forward, watching Marcus' every move. A Nous user would be difficult to take down, and Marcus was especially gifted.

"Nah, ah, ah," Marcus said with a shake of his finger and I stilled, my eyes falling to my hand as the flames doused.

I tried to recall them, tried to spark whatever fire I could back to life, but they wouldn't heed my command. "Fuck."

"This is how we're gonna do things," Marcus said, twirling his knife as he paced to the side. "I'm gonna take my leave, and you're going to go about your night."

"Like hell we are," Micah growled.

Marcus let out a sigh, his shoulders sagging as he rubbed the bridge of his nose with his thumb and forefinger. "I don't have time for this. I've got shit to do."

Micah ran forward, and I sucked in a breath before taking off after him. "Micah!"

Marcus stiffened, his eyes going wild as he stumbled back.

But then, he smiled. "Let's see if you can catch me this time, flower boy!"

Marcus ducked into a nearby alley, and we followed, the distance too much for us to do anything, especially with my magic locked away.

The rain pelted us like chips of ice, stinging my eyes, cutting into my skin in its relenting waves, and the chill tore through my leathers. I stumbled to a stop, grabbing Micah's arm as my breath left my lips in a puff of white mist, the air freezing around us.

Micah's eyes met mine, realization flashing across his face before we scanned the darkness around us. The roar of the rain blinded our senses, filling our ears in its rush, dulling our vision with its veiled droplets, snuffing our sense of smell.

Marcus' laughter echoed through the alleys, his trail lost to us, and I took a step back as faint clicks reached my ears over the rain. The direction from which it came was unclear. Micah and I took a step back.

Micah grunted as he hit the ground beside me, and I twisted around to find him being dragged back, a claw-tipped hand wrapped around his ankle.

"Fuck!" he shouted as he twisted around and threw his hands out, as if to summon his magic, but no vines came to ensnare the darkling.

I launched myself toward him, and the wind rushed from my lungs as a body crashed into me, knocking me to the side. My head smacked against the pavement, and the world swam around me. I groaned, trying to push myself up.

Micah's panicked shouts reached my ears, and I rolled to the side, finding him pinned beneath a darkling.

"Get the fuck off me!" he shouted, pressing his forearm to the darkling's throat as it snapped its torn jaws.

I groaned, saliva flooding my mouth as I tried to regain myself, tried to think past the shattering pain echoing in the back of my head.

"Hang on!" I shouted, my words a near slur as I pushed myself up. Two darklings charged for me from the darkness, their jaws stretched wide, claws reaching as they launched themselves at me. I drew my dagger as they pinned me to the wall, and it was knocked from my hand, sliding across the pavement. I grasped the shoulder of one of the darklings, and the neck of the other, grinding my teeth as I fought to keep them off me.

Micah cried out, and I turned my gaze to find him struggling beneath the weight of the darkling as it snapped and clawed at him.

"Don't you fucking give up!" I shouted as I tried to summon the flames Marcus had silenced.

He reached down with his free hand, ripping his dagger out before plunging it into the darkling's chest. It shrieked before collapsing on him, body crumbling into dust.

The darklings snapped at me as I held them at bay, unable to grab my dagger, unable to get to Micah. I reached for the flames, beckoning them, begging them to answer my call. Sparks flashed at my fingertips but doused instantly.

"Come on," I growled as they sparked and doused once more. "Come on, come on, come on!"

Micah cried out, and I cursed as darklings swarmed him, grabbing his arms, his legs, dragging him further away, fighting with one another to claim him.

"No!" I shouted as the scent of his blood reached my nose. "Fucking fight them, Micah!"

The flames flickered at my fingertips before flaring to life, and I roared as I unleashed them, incinerating the darklings holding me down in a pyre. Their shrieks echoed through the street long after their bodies collapsed into dust, and I turned, throwing my hands out to send a wave of fire crashing into the hoard of darklings pinning Micah down.

They disintegrated before they could hit the ground, their ashes melding with the rain. I ran for Micah, dropping to my knees as I slid to his side.

"No," I muttered, my eyes darting over his body, his leather armor torn and shredded, his blood pooling on the ground around him, mixing with the ashes of the darklings.

His chest heaved as he panted and coughed, his eyes clamping shut as he lay on the ground, unable to move. I slid my arm under him, trying to pick him up, to rush him to Johnson's clinic.

"Stop," he gasped, clutching onto my shirt.

I pulled him against me. "I need to get you help."

He shook his head and let it fall back, eyes rising to the sky before they fluttered shut. "Too late…"

My heart stalled, and I searched him once more.

"Three." He gasped for air before coughing up blood. "They got me at least three times. I've—"

He cried out, head falling back as he clutched at his stomach where they'd torn through his armor, blood oozing from the wound. Black veins crawled up his throat, darkness swirling in his eyes at such an alarming rate, I froze. "I've probably got…a few minutes…at best."

"Gods," I breathed, mind racing as I leaned over him, ready to do whatever it took to stop this. "I'm gonna fix this. Just hang on."

"Don't you even—" he rasped, grabbing my shirt and preventing me from coming any closer, from sucking the darkness out of his system. He grimaced as the veins worked their way under his skin. "Don't even fucking think about it... She can't... She can't lose both of us."

"Don't—" My voice broke as I grabbed his hand. "Don't do this, Micah."

"Sorry," he said, blood rolling from his lips down his chin as he grabbed my free hand and placed his dagger in my palm. "This wasn't supposed to happen."

His skin grew cold against mine, blood gushing from his wound too fast. His eyes fluttered closed before he grimaced, his fangs elongating as he cried out. "Fuck. Don't let me change."

"Don't do this," I begged him, my vision blurring as I held him. "Don't make me put you down."

He sagged, chest heaving, and he lifted his eyes to me. "She..."

I watched him, mind latching onto that single word as his voice fell short. "What?"

Air slipped from his lungs, and the dark veins faded as his body sagged in my arms, his grip on my hand where he'd forced his dagger loosening.

"Micah?"

He didn't respond.

"No..." I whispered, my hands shaking, tears flooding my vision as I looked between his eyes, but they didn't meet mine, didn't look back.

"Micah," I begged. "Say something."

He didn't, didn't speak, didn't look my way. He just continued to stare up at the storm clouds above us. I cried out, holding his lifeless body against me as I cursed The Fates, cursed the gods, cursed anyone and everyone at the chance I might finally bring ruin to the one who had cursed me to suffer as I had, to lose everyone I loved.

Time passed, and I wasn't sure when I'd finally lost the ability to cry, when I finally scooped him into my arms. My body had grown numb to the icy chill that had once held me in its clutches, the rain continuing its onslaught, rolling down my cheeks as if the sky itself was mourning at my side, replacing the tears I couldn't bring myself to cry any longer.

I held him as I walked aimlessly, each step kicking up fragments of memories, moments we'd shared. His smile replaced the lifeless expression staring up at me, a smile that would forever haunt me, just as Calliope haunted me... Just as Lucia haunted me.

Distant shouts reached my ears, their words muddled by the rain, but his roaring silence held me captive. Lights pierced the darkness from the alleys ahead of me, movement bleeding together as the world slowed, but I didn't stop walking, couldn't stop walking. I had to get him to safety, had to ensure his remains were safeguarded until he could be sent to Elysium. I'd long ago lost faith that any sort of paradise awaited us when we departed this hell, but Thalia... She did. She would want that—to see him laid to rest, soul sent off as every warrior had before him.

Zephyr appeared before me, his mouth moving, but no sound reached my ears. His movements were a blur as he grasped my arms, wide eyes falling to Micah's body. "Damien! They're here!"

Bodies cloaked in black swarmed the street around us, booted steps lost to the roar of the rain. Damien rushed to us, stopping short when his eyes found Micah. He cursed and whipped around, arms flying out. "Marcus is still out there! I want him found. Now!"

"Barrett," Zephyr muttered, his hand coming to rest on my shoulder. "I'll take him."

"No," I whispered, clutching him tighter to my chest as I brushed past him.

Warriors rushed past me in every direction as Zephyr and Damien shouted orders. Lupai yipped and barked as they ran through the streets, darkness nipping at their heels as they hunted.

And I continued walking.

LUNA LAURIER

CHAPTER 56

THALIA

A knock echoed through the house, dragging me from sleep, and I groaned as I pushed myself up. My feet dragged as I trudged into the kitchen toward the front door, the room swaying, and I frowned at the strange numbness swelling in my chest.

"I'm coming, I'm coming," I muttered as another knock came, my words slurring as I pulled Micah's shirt back over my shoulder from where it had sagged.

Another knock hammered against the door, impatient and demanding, and my hand halted as I reached for the doorknob. Clarity flooded my mind, replacing the sleepy haze, and I frowned. My hand rose to my chest, fingers pressing to the fabric covering my binding tattoo, where I felt...nothing.

I unlocked the door hastily and swung it open, the icy wind flooding the entry as my heart fell into a terrifying rush.

Barrett stood before me, his black leather armor soaked through, water-slicked blond hair clinging to his skin. Blood was smeared along his cheek, his neck, down the front of his armor.

Air thickened in my lungs as I stepped toward him. "Barrett? What..."

His steel eyes couldn't seem to hold my gaze, and his breaths turned shaky as his lips parted. "Micah. He..."

I looked around, searching for him, dread clawing its way into my heart. "Where is he, Barrett?"

"Thalia," he said, taking a step toward me. Suddenly the world was caving in around me as Micah's faint scent reached my nose, nearly drowned out by darkling blood, by the damp scent of the rain.

I turned, searching for him. "This isn't funny."

"Thalia," Barrett said, reaching for me. "He..."

I smacked his hand away, stepping back as his presence turned suffocating. "Don't—" I tried to breathe, tried to steady myself. "Don't touch me. Just...tell me—"

My voice cracked, tears welling in my eyes at the pain painting his face.

"No..." I muttered, my hand flying to cup my mouth as a sob threatened to spill out. "No, you're lying."

"We encountered darklings on our hunt..."

"No..." I cried, crumbling against the wall, my vision blurring as he drew closer.

"I tried..."

"He wasn't supposed to go on a hunt tonight!" I cried out as he wrapped his arms around me, pulling me against his chest. I slammed my hands against his chest, shaking my head as I hit him again and again. "He wasn't supposed—"

"I'm so sorry," he muttered.

"He went because of you!" I cried out, shoving him away from me, guilt churning in my chest.

Barrett stiffened.

I ran my hands over my face as I stumbled back. He went because of me, because Barrett was my mate, because he wanted to bring us together. If Barrett hadn't been my mate, if Micah hadn't gone with him tonight...he would still be here.

"Don't touch me!" I cried out as Barrett's hand brushed my shoulder. He recoiled, hurt flashing across his face, along with something else I didn't want to see. I turned, bare feet smacking against the sidewalk as I walked, unsure of where I was going. "Where is he? I need to see him."

"You don't need to see that—"

"Don't fucking tell me what I do and don't need to see!" I bit back, turning to shove him away as he followed.

"I can't let you do that right now, Thalia. They need to clean him up."

"I don't need your coddling!" I shouted, shoving his hand away when he reached for me as every bit of Micah's absence came crashing down around me. "I need..." I fell to my knees, sobs tearing from my throat, tears spilling down my cheeks as I folded into myself, clutching at a binding mark that had long since faded in the wake of his death.

His death.

Micah was gone.

I'd never get to see him smile again, never get to kiss him, hold him, watch him sleep, comb my fingers through his hair, tease him. I'd never get to tell him how much I loved him, never get to tell him just how much he meant to me. I wanted to hear his voice again, wanted to hear him call me his love, wanted so much more.

Barrett knelt beside me as I broke, as I shattered into millions of pieces. I pushed him away, the guilt too much, his face now a painful reminder. "Leave!"

He stumbled back, brows furrowing.

"I wish I never met you," I muttered, pushing to my feet as Micah's smile faded away in my mind, swept away in the dark clutches of the darklings who'd taken him from me. "It's because of you he took the shift tonight!"

Hurt filled Barrett's eyes.

"I can't look at you right now. He wouldn't have done it if he hadn't realized..." My voice broke.

If he hadn't realized Barrett was my mate...

Tears rolled down my cheeks, my hands hanging limp at my side as a hollow cold filled me. "Why did it have to be you?"

His hands balled into fists, his eyes darting around, as if searching for what he might say before he stormed closer. "You wish it had been me instead of him? That he was here telling you I was dead?"

I shrank back, his words burning me in more ways than I could have imagined. My lips parted to tell him that wasn't what I had meant, but he continued.

"You think I don't wish I was the one who'd fallen?" he said, his voice laced with furious agony. "You wish I'd died? Well, so do I! You hate me for what I am? So do I! I wish so badly I could go back in time and take his place because trust me, Thalia, I'd do it in a fucking heartbeat!"

He stormed closer, his presence too much for me to bear. "Don't worry, you won't have to see my fucking face anymore."

I opened my mouth, brows furrowing. "What—"

"You're off patrol, effective tonight," he said, his voice a powerful command.

"You can't do tha—"

"I outrank you," he said, his voice bitter. "You turned Lucia down for that position, remember?"

"Fuck you!" I shouted as I shoved him back, tears welling in my eyes as anger swelled in my chest, the beast baring its teeth.

"Yeah, fuck me!" he shouted, slamming his still-bloodied fist against his chest. "Hate me, I fucking deserve every bit of it."

I pushed off the wall and ducked through the front door, slamming it in his face before falling back against it, my chest expanding as I tried and failed to breathe before caving to the agony.

CHAPTER 57

BARRETT

The sound of her slammed door echoed endlessly across the vast hollowness of my mind, the salt of her tears, the scent of her sorrow, overwhelming my senses.

Why did it have to be you?

I clutched at my chest, the flames deep within me sputtering as they tried to reignite, biting at the fuel of her words. The rain had stopped long ago, but the sound of its roar still lingered in my mind, the smell of Micah's blood still clinging to me in a way that left me wondering if I'd ever truly be able to wash my skin of it.

Why did it have to be me?

My boots scuffed against the pavement as I stumbled from her door, my heart racing. I balled my hands into fists as the flames roared to life, catching on the hurt left in her wake and exploding around me as I fell to my knees. I cried out to the heavens, to Celestia, to whoever might listen. The fire vanished just as quickly as it erupted, leaving the pavement around me hot and soft, any water from the rain turning to steam in the air. I slumped on my knees, head hanging forward in defeat.

I lifted my gaze to her door as I imagined her on the other side, imagined tears spilling down her cheeks, her hand clutching at her faded binding tattoo. I knew she hadn't meant what she said, and yet, I'd fed into it, bit back at her when she was wounded.

The heat of her anger was far sweeter than the salty bitterness of her tears. If anger was what got her through this, if anger was all I got to taste of her from this moment onward, then I would be the spark to ignite the flame.

EPILOGUE

MARCUS

I stumbled to a stop in the alley, the pavement lurching beneath my feet as the world spun, shifted, and heaved like a wild creature as tormented as I was. My eyes clamped shut, a sharp pain stabbing behind them as my mind buckled under the darkness clawing at it. Always clawing, clawing, clawing....

The rough brick bit into my forearm as I braced myself, my bloodied hand rising to my head as I panted, the once-warm liquid now cold against my skin, and my eyes fell to the crimson-painted knife clutched in my other hand. My hand slid down, smearing remnants of the woman's blood across my face. Laughter bubbled up my throat as the image of Barrett and Micah's fear-filled eyes flashed through my mind, and I slumped against the wall as it continued to pour from me, echoing off the walls.

I lifted my gaze skyward, the rain blurring my vision as I soaked in its misery and heaved a sigh. Something fought against the darkness deep within my mind like a caged animal.

Pounding, pounding, and...

Their terror is delicious.

I shook my head, the voices dancing through my thoughts as images flashed across my mind. Barrett cursing as he held me...us off, our teeth snapping within inches of his face, desperate to taste his blood, to fill his veins with the delicious darkness coursing through ours.

Don't you fucking give up!

Something pounded against a cage in the back of my mind as Barrett's desperate plea flitted across my thoughts, and I flinched, eyes falling shut.

They deserve it. She would still be here if it wasn't for their goddess.

"I know!" I growled, chest heaving as the dark voice slithered in, coiling around me until I thought I might suffocate. I threw the knife as I cried out in an attempt to expel the overwhelming sound of voices, the blade ricocheting off the brick wall opposite me, the dull ringing leaving my vision fizzling before flashing back to reality. My eyes darted around, ghosts of faces long gone slipping into view, bloodied hands reaching for me. "It's their own fault."

The ringing faded, the faces falling into darkness, and the roar of the rain returned. A smile stretched across my face at the distant sound of Barrett's shouts, and I pushed myself to my feet, closing my eyes as I reached out, further and further, to a familiar mind.

He stiffened in the distant quiet, feeling my consciousness brush against his.

Who is this?

Damien's voice was hardened, tired, even, as if he were already on the cusp of breaking under the weight of his fallen mate's memory.

That hurts, Damien. You don't even recognize your best friend's voice?

His mind flooded with emotions, words buzzing to a tune that made me flinch. The ringing returned, the faces and ghastly cries of those I'd murdered filling my ears as I shook my head, stumbling to a stop, panting. A figure fizzled into existence, peering at me from around the nearby corner with sad eyes, her curly golden hair curtaining her face untouched by the downpour. I blinked, and she vanished.

Marcus?

I turned, attention drawn from the ghost at the sound of his voice, so full of sorrowful disbelief that I laughed.

Don't pretend you care that I'm still alive.

His hesitation and confusion slipped through our connection.

What are you —

If you hurry, you might be able to save them.

He didn't respond, and I shared a glimpse of what I'd last seen of Barrett and Micah as the darklings attacked them during my retreat.

I mean, you could be too late already. Better be quick.

His panic flooded my mind.

Marc—

I severed the connection and let out a heavy breath, my mind heavy—too heavy.

Darkness stretched from the shadows around me, the walls and sky melting until they were swallowed up into the gloom, and I lifted my face as the lights winked out.

"Hello, Eris," I muttered.

She emerged from the shadows, her onyx eyes gliding over me. "Have you found her yet?"

I let out a sigh and shook my head. "It wasn't her."

She clicked her tongue, her frustration crawling over me like hot waves tearing at my mind. "She will turn up. Keep searching."

I rolled my eyes. "What makes you think it'll do what you want?"

"It takes time. This is powerful magic we are dealing with," she said, turning as she waved her hand through the air. A necklace appeared from the misty shadows around us. The pendant howled with the voices of the dead, lost souls trapped inside, waiting to be put to use.

"Perhaps it would help if you carried it," she said, lifting it in front of her eyes. "Allow it to guide you to her soul, to whichever human it reawakens in."

I stiffened as she drew closer, the necklace floating through the air as she guided it toward me. It fell into my hands, the metal icy to the touch, swarming with energy.

"Why does it matter?" I muttered.

"She *must* be human," she hissed. "It will only work if she's human."

The voices grew louder the longer I held the necklace. I'd hated the sound from the first moment I'd stolen it from Hade's domain, had been desperate to discard it.

She turned from me, sweeping her hand across the darkness as Damien's face appeared, stricken with fear as he rushed to the aid of those he loved. A part of me relished in the despair lighting his eyes, but another part of me, something deep down, pounded against a wall, a cage.

Pounding. Pounding. Pounding.

Eris tilted her head as she watched him. "He is so close to breaking, and when he finds himself facing the possibility of losing her again—" She slashed her fingers through his image, dark claws tearing at his face until the darkness claimed the vision— "he will fall at my feet."

My eyes fell back to the necklace, the metal humming with the demand to be used, to claim souls and bend them to its will.

"Change your approach," she said as the darkness climbed up her body, the shadows receding. "You are drawing too much attention to yourself. Hades has caught wind of the necklace's presence in the Mortalrealm. Continue as you are and you'll expose us both."

The darkness slithered away from me, sinking back to the shadows as the distant lights of the city returned. I stood alone in the street, clutching the cursed necklace as Eris' presence pressed against my consciousness once more.

"Find her, Marcus. I want Moira's reincarnation."

To be continued...

Luna Laurier's Taste of Darkness

Can't get enough of the Shadow and Moonlight Universe and it's characters? Join the Patreon to gain access to bonus scenes and content not in the books, bonus spicy scenes between characters (both canon and non-canon *eyes the spicy scene between Cassie, Damien, and Marcus*), NSFW artwork, ARC Team access, discounts on merch and signed books, and more!

---

www.patreon.com/lunalaurier

SHOP THE OFFICIAL MERCH STORE

LUNALAURIER.COM

GLOSSARY

Aethersbane - A plant native to the Godsrealm, the toxin is harvested and used as a poison to render fae and other magical beings of Elythias powerless. It is a rare plant, but someone has managed to cultivate it to sell illegally.

Aleirene touen/tauen enlisnó en solos - A phrase spoken to honor the fallen meaning "peace embrace his/her soul".

Ambrosia Liquor - A potent drink that is distilled and bottled in the Godsrealm. Due to the high metabolism of immortals and other beings of the Godsrealm, alcohols of the mortalrealm have little to no effect. Humans should never drink as a single sip could cause sever alcohol poisoning and possibly even death.

Archivallia (ark-i-vahl-E-uh) - The massive library housing every record of the immortal race.

Aristocracy - A group of pure-blooded immortals.

Astral Sprites (Librarians) - Sprites created by Selene to tend to the Archivallia and the rest of the temple. They are small standing about two feet tall, their bodies are made up of night sky and starlight and have little tails. Majority of them reside in the Archivallia, assisting Salwa and caring for the books. They do not speak, but they do chitter to each other, communication with feelings and intentions rather than words.

Bacchus Tears (b-ah-kus)– Hallucinogenic potion

Belariôs Retala (bel-ar-ee-Os-ree-tah-la) -A ceremony every warrior of The Order undergoes to exchange their vows with Selene and received her blessing. In exchange for their vow to her they are imbued with a mark that enhances their magical abilities.

Brierleaf (br-eye-er-leaf) - a potent herb that when smoked can give psychoactive affects similar to that of marijuana.

Celestia (Seh-les-t-ee-uh) - The single deity worshipped by the Elythians and many of the residents of the Godsrealm.

Coronis (cor-O-nis) - A swarm of crow-like birds summoned by House Skiá from the Godsrealm. In the Godsrealm their forms are more like large crows, but when summoned by House Skiá, they take on a form of black mist and shadow and are often used to swarm enemies. They were turned against the immortals by Melantha during The Fall of Kingdoms. Anyone who falls prey to them suffer a slow and agonizing death.

Crystal Shisha – A crystal that has been infused with a potent essence that brings on a sense of euphoria that is extremely addictive

Dimós trees (deem-yOs) - A tree of the Godsrealm, with velvety smooth bark that is pale and glows. These trees have no leaves and are ageless, living for millennia. They are believed to have sprouted from the tears of Celestia, the one deity the Elythian's worship, when she cast her mate from the heavens.

Elythia (el-i-thia) - One of 26 countries in the Godsrealm. It is divided into 12 kingdoms/domains which are governed by 12 Elythian's. There are many races that inhabit Elythia: elythians, elves, fae, wyverns, and many other creatures of myth and legend.

Elythians - A race of ancient beings who were worshipped in Ancient Greece when they wandered across the veil and met humans. They among one of the most ancient races, descendants of the first created by Celestia. Elythian's inhabit the continent of Elythia within the Godsrealm.

Feather folk – feathered fat that reside in the sky islands of Pelagonia

Featherclaw - cat-like beasts with feather tipped fur.

Godsrealm - A realm, parallel to the Mortalrealm, where magic exists, everything creature of myth and legends resides within this realm. The myths and legends within the Mortalrealm are formed when creatures of the Godsrealm wander through "ripples" in the veil that separates the Godsrealm from the Mortalrealm. The greek gods exist within the realm which are an ancient race known as Elythians. There are many continents housing many other ancient races much like the Elythians, which have each had their own impact on certain places in the Mortalrealm.

Houses of Power - A number of guilds within the immortal race where immortals are sorted or aligned based on which magical affinity they have.

House of Skiá (skee-uh) - Users skilled in shadowmancy

House of Nous (noos) - Users skilled in mindbending

House of Stoicheion (st-eye-chyon) - Users skilled in element magic

House of Thiríon (ther-E-on) – Users skilled in beast shifting

House of Psukhế (tsu-kay) – Users skilled in telekinesis

House of Dendron – Users skilled in plant magic

House of Leukos (loo-k-O-s) - Users skilled in lightmancy

House of Aíma (eye-ma) – Users skilled in blood manipulation

House of Latros (lat-r-O-s) – Users skilled in healing magic

Kalruk - coyote-like creatures that hunt in packs.

Kobalos – Goblin-like creatures

Kunilas – Rabbit-like fae

Kyrios (k-ear-E-O-s) - Leaders of the Houses of Power.

Lunassia Flower - A pale flower from the Godsrealm that only blooms on the Astral Mountains once a year during the lunar solstice.

Lupai (loo-p-eye) - Wolves summoned by House Skiá from the Godsrealm, in the Godsrealm their forms are more like large wolves, but when summoned by House Skiá, they take on a form of black mist and shadow.

Mikros (mee-kr-O-s) - A term of endearment referring to children meaning "little one", or from parent to offspring.

Moira's Rest - The tomb of immortals that resides within Selene's Temple

Moonhaven - A village built by the immortals to be a new home after they moved to the Mortalrealm to hunt the darklings.

Murk Root – hallucinogenic root, can be taken in various forms that affect its potency

Nymphs - Type of fae that are closely linked with the elements (water, earth, air, fire, forest, etc)

Oneiroi (O-near-ee) - A nous user with unique amplified abilities that only a rare few are born with. The few immortals with this ability were trained during the Godswar as spies and assassins, infiltrating enemy domains to "tether" themselves to their target and use their unique dreamwalking ability to gain information or assassinate their target.

Pantheon - Refers to the individual groups those who descended from the origin race within the Godsrealm. The Elythians are one of the groups. Different pantheons rule over their own continents and domains.

Strategos (str-ah-tee-gOs) - A rank of command in The Order. Second in command under the king of the immortals; equivalent to a General.

Tabularius (Tah-boo-LAR-ee-oos) - The historian of the immortal race. The title is only given to one immortal, only passed on from teacher to student when the title's holder dies.

Taxiarchos (tax-ee-ah-r-hOs) - A rank of command in The Order. Third in command, second to Strategos; equivalent to a Brigadier.

Telos Pyrai (teh-l-O-s-Pear-eye) - An ability used by the flame Stoicheion that builds up the flame magic and unleashes it all at one like a bomb. It is not often that the user survives the use of this ability and it is often used as a last resort. If the user survives they are left vulnerable and depleted.

The Fall of Kingdoms (1889) - the battle between the immortals and the darkling queen. Thousands of humans and immortals were killed in the battle.

The Order - A group of warriors serving under Selene that are tasked with fighting the darklings.

The Pits - a criminal organization that steals children and raises them as fighters.

The Twelve - A group that govern the continent of Elythia, each of the twelve rule within their own domain.

The Underworld - A criminal organization within the immortal society ran by an immortal named Atlas, unlike Damien, they believe humans are beneath them and should serve the immortal society in exchange for their protection.

Trogs – lizard like cave dwellers who frequent The Pits and are considered part of the unseelie faction that hate humans.

Silvash - An ancient beast that resembles a monstrously tall stag who guards a forest within Erebus' domain.

Wyverns - An ancient race of highly intelligent and powerful winged beasts that reside within the mountain kingdom of Hesperian's Reach near Zeus' kingdom, Belimus.

ELYTHIAN TRANSLATIONS

adôs (odd-Os) - brother

afin (ah-fin) - let, allow

Aleirene (al-ir-ee-n) - Peace, peaceful

apeirïsï (ah-pie-ree-see) - Infinity, infinitely, without end or limit

asidia (ah-s-id-ya) - shield

atresei (at-res-eye) - As, like

belariôs (bel-ar-ee-Os) - Warrior

charisti (cah-ree-stee) - to give thanks

dorai (door-eye) - gift, to gift

Dýnamis (dee-nah-mee-s) - strength

ekein (eh-keen) - those

Elysium (ee-l-i-see-um) - a place in the afterlife where warriors and virtuous souls are sent

emei (em-ee) - We, us, our

emôs (em-yo-s) - Mine

èn (connective word) - in, on, of

enlisnô (en-lis-nO) - Embrace, to hold

esti (es-tee) - so

èstin (es-tin) - is, has

etai (e-t-eye) - from

etu (e-too) - to

ge (zsh-ay) - for

gravôsia (gra-v-O-shia) - to carry, pregnant

hallôs (hal-Os) - Heart, love

kalôsa (k-al-O-sa) - welcome

katàratos (kah-tah-rah-tOs) cursed (used as an insult)

kelisa (k-el-ee-sa) - Most beautiful

kērysoi (k-air-ee-see) - to state, declare, inform, preech

lamprei (lamp-r-eye) - bright, shining

leukôs / leukô (l-ewk-Os) - Light

llispsais (ill-ip-s-eye) - missed you, miss you

luna (l-oo-na) - Moon

manya (m-ah-n-ya) - cloak, cloaked, to cloak

Mávrôsia (mav-ro-shya) - black, blackened

mea (may-a) - My, my own

Metai (met-eye) - Mother

Metavia (meh-tah-via) Grandmother

miño (m-een-yo) - no

mouèn (m-O-en) - I, me

nalas (n-ah-las) - will

nemos (n-Ay-m-O-s) - life

nôlôs (no-l-O-s) - will not

ntropo (n-tr-O-p-O) - disgraced, to disgrace

ntrosi (n-tro-see) - disgrace, shame

nychtôs (n-ee-k-tos) - night

odigei (O-d-ee-g-eye) - lead, guide, take

Oneiroi (O-near-ee) - dream walker

paiôs (pie-Os) - Child

Pètai (pet-eye) - Father

prin - before

règis (re-zsh-ee) - Guide, guiding

Retala (ree-tah-la) - Rite, rite of passage, ceremony

rēvinia (re-v-een-ya) - Rest

saliestas (sal-yes-tas) - Hello, greetings

sei (say) - Shows ownership

skiasei / skia (sk-ee-ah-see) - the shadow, a shadow

solos (s-O-l-Os) - soul, spirit

stellarôs (stel-ar-Os) - Star

styllaris (stil-ar-is) - Afterlife

tauēn (t-ow-en) - she, her

telôs (tel-O-s) - end, completion

Telôs pyrai (Tel-O-s Peer-eye) - flames end

tenes (ten-es) - to hold, hold

tôuèn (toe-en) - he, him, his

vai (v-eye) - yes

varyó (var-yO) - Hunter, to hunt

volúntae (vol-oon-tay) - intentions, plans, what you intent to do.

vôu (voe) - you, your

y (ee) (connective word) - and

zestia (zes-t-ee-ah) - Warm